Guilty Innocence

MAGGIE JAMES

First published in paperback 2013 by CreateSpace.

ACKNOWLEDGEMENTS

Thanks to Gary Powell and Mary Moss for all their help and feedback.

This novel is dedicated to Karen Harris, a wonderful friend who has been an invaluable source of support in my writing journey.

Visit Maggie James's website! You can find it at www.maggiejamesfiction.com.

Follow Maggie James on Facebook: Maggie James Fiction.

And on Twitter: @mjamesfiction.

1

THE LETTER

Natalie Richards's first reaction to the letter in her hands is one of suspicion. A response fuelled by her misgivings, the ones prompting her to search through her boyfriend's possessions, like an addict seeking a fix. Who the hell is Joshua Barker, and why does Mark have a letter addressed to him?

She first discovers it at the bottom of his bedside cabinet, when she's almost given up on finding anything. From the outside, the letter holds no clue as to the explosive nature of its contents. She almost misses it; it's tucked away at the very bottom of the last drawer, under a pile of bank statements. Natalie flips through them quickly; what she's seeking isn't likely to be concealed amongst cash withdrawals and direct debits. She goes to replace the bank statements and close the drawer, when she notices the envelope. It's lying face down, almost as if it's hiding. In the interests of being thorough in her search, she pulls it out.

She reads the letter, the name of Joshua Barker nagging at her as she does so, its vague familiarity teasing her. As the contents sink into her mind, the realisation of who Joshua Barker is claws its way to the surface in her brain, exploding through her skull in a myriad of disbelief and denial.

Natalie hurls the letter from her grasp as though the paper has burned her. Which, in a way, it has. It lands near the door, the momentum causing it to slide partly underneath, as if to crawl away from her. A low moan escapes her as she sinks to the floor, her stomach clenching in rebuttal of what's hammering through her brain. She stares at the cheap melamine bedside cabinet as though it has betrayed her by offering sanctuary to Joshua Barker's letter. Would to God she'd never decided to search through Mark's things. She's been expecting to find shit, but not something that stinks this bad. Nobody could have anticipated the contents of the letter taunting her from the other side of the room. *You screwed up again, Natalie. Drawn to bad boys, aren't you? Well, they don't come much worse than this one.*

She huddles against Mark's bed, which is neatly made, of course. Everything with Mark is always tidy, regimented, in its place. The almost antiseptic neatness of his cramped flat reveals little about the man she's been dating, on and off, for the last four months. The on part is mostly down to her; she doesn't let herself wonder if Mark ever contemplates pressing the off button.

Natalie's come here today because she suspects her boyfriend may be seeing another woman. Given her track record with men, it's the obvious conclusion when Mark seems distant, evasive, oblivious to her hints about taking their relationship further. Getting their own place. Perhaps a baby in due course. So far Natalie has only given the vaguest of suggestions on the baby issue; Mark's abrupt withdrawal when she does so silences her immediately.

Finding a man who wants what she does - commitment, togetherness, stability - doesn't come easily to Natalie. She knows men like that exist. Take her cousin Janine, for instance. Married for five years now, with a two-year-old daughter and another baby on the way, her husband Gavin the archetypal faithful adoring partner. Janine, though, has the shining example of her parents, happily married for thirty years. Not so with Natalie. Before the divorce, her father seems determined to bed every available woman in Bristol. Eventually he walks out on his wife and eleven-year-old daughter and doesn't come back. His contact with Natalie is reduced to sporadic Christmas and birthday cards that eventually peter out. Callie Richards, angry and embittered, is left to bring up her daughter alone.

No wonder Natalie has a track record of always going for the bad boys. A psychologist might say she's on a mission to find and reform her errant father. The finding's not been a problem; it's the reforming that's proved a fruitless quest so far with the men she dates.

Mark, though - well, he's always seemed different. At first, anyway. Even now, at times she gets the impression he likes her more than he lets on. Gradually, though, his evasiveness, the apparent lack of any desire to move things between them off casual status, erodes Natalie's hopes. Another woman is the obvious conclusion she reaches. Someone prettier, funnier, more interesting. Someone carrying twenty kilos less in weight.

She's off work this week, taking time out from the demands of her job as a television production assistant. Mark will be at the builder's yard, ordering concrete, checking purchase orders, doing whatever he does there. His absence means she has the opportunity to search his flat, seeing as the spare key nestles so temptingly under the potted plant in the hallway outside. A key that invites her to take it, turn it in the lock and go inside, to see if she can find evidence to confirm her worst fears. That Mark is seeing another woman.

More specifically, a woman with the initials A.J.

Oh, yes. It's not just Natalie's genetically programmed-in homing device for bad boys that's brought her here today. She has firmer foundations on which to base her suspicions. A few days ago, angry and hurt after Mark has ignored her hints about their relationship once again, she grabs his mobile whilst he's taking a piss. Her fingers flick through the contents. Nothing incriminating in the messages, either sent or received; he's only kept the last few and they're all to or from her. Mark's calendar is what gives her cause for concern. Marked down every few weeks is the entry 'A.J. Here, 6pm.'

When he comes back, still zipping himself up, she confronts him.

'Who's A.J.?' she demands, her self-righteousness sweeping away the need for preamble. Alarm creeps into his eyes, before he tells her she shouldn't snoop through his phone. Well, duh, she knows that already, doesn't she? His reaction convinces her A.J. is female and, of course, not carrying the rolls of surplus flesh Natalie does. All Mark will say is that no, he's not seeing anyone else, and yes, he wants to be with her, she mustn't think he doesn't. How A.J. is an old school friend, and male, not female. Except that the alarm she's already clocked in his face, together with her radar for detecting lies, a skill born out of having a philandering father, warn her he's not telling the truth. Hence why she's here today, on a quest to find out who this bitch A.J. is and how long she's been sleeping with Mark.

Now, crumpled on the floor beside his bed after reading the letter, she remembers the old saying about eavesdroppers hearing no good about themselves. Does the same hold true for snoopers, she wonders. Because what she's found is utter shit; right now all she wants to do is press the eject button in her head and thrust the name of Joshua Barker into the far reaches of outer space. The envelope still taunts her from its vantage point on the floor, the portion that's visible under the doorjamb mocking her.

The letter. The one Natalie almost doesn't read, addressed as it is to someone called Joshua Barker. Initials J.B., not A.J., and male to boot. A letter with seemingly no connection to Mark and her misgivings about him, of no interest to her. When she finds it, she goes to replace it, unread, in the drawer. Then her suspicions flare up along with her curiosity. Of course the letter is connected to Mark; it's in his flat, isn't it?

She turns it over in her hands, checking it out. The envelope is plain white, the paper good quality. Expensive stuff, the kind favoured by an older generation. No return address on the back. The writing is neat, regular, its black ballpoint easy to read. A soft slope from left to right, the loops and swirls announcing the addressee as Joshua Barker. Address: Vinney Green Secure Unit, Emersons Green, Bristol.

Vinney Green. A name vaguely familiar to Natalie, although she can't quite place it at first. Ah, yes. The detention centre for juvenile offenders on the outskirts of Bristol. Whoever Joshua Barker is, he's been a bad boy, it seems. The stamp appears old fashioned and, peering closer, she can just about discern the postmark: Exeter, November 15, nearly fourteen years ago. Mark would have been eleven back then.

The envelope has been neatly slit open along the top, inviting Natalie to draw out the contents. One sheet only, in matching thick, heavy paper. Her fingers stroke the surface, caressing its coolness. A slight hint of mustiness reaches her nostrils. No date or address at the top. Just the words. She perches on the edge of the bed and starts to read.

My dear Joshua,

I am writing this letter to tell you something that will hurt you, although that is the last thing either your grandfather or I would want. There's no easy way to put this. Joshua, my love, your mother has decided to move away from Exeter and change her name, and it is her intention to begin a new life, a life without you. You must have wondered why she has not visited you and from what she tells me she has not written or called either. Try to understand, Joshua. She has found life very difficult since your detention. This is her way of dealing with what happened.

Both your grandfather and I have tried to persuade her not to break off contact with you but she is adamant on this point. I realise this must be hard for you, my love. You know how your mother can be at times. Rest assured we will continue to write and I can only hope that will be of some comfort.

Your loving grandmother,
Linda Curtis

Natalie's first thoughts centre on how harsh, how unforgiving, a woman must be to abandon her child. And for what reason? Whoever Joshua Barker and his mother may be, Natalie thinks, one thing's for sure; they've never had a normal parent and child relationship. Impossible to experience pregnancy and birth, bond with a child and then desert him, surely? This woman, so adamant about starting a new life without her son, has probably always denied him maternal love. Natalie briefly wonders where Joshua's father is, hoping he's forged from different metal to the boy's steely mother. A man more in tune with Linda Curtis, with any luck.

Joshua Barker. Impossible to tell how old he is when he receives the letter. She wonders what offence he's committed. What has been bad enough to get him sent to Vinney Green? A crime so terrible his own mother rejects him? So awful she doesn't even tell him herself she's moving away, changing her name?

Then Natalie remembers. The vague stirrings of memory when she reads Joshua Barker's name on the envelope coalesce into a sharp, stabbing thrust in her mind, one causing her to recoil in denial, shock, revulsion. A possible reason as to why her boyfriend has this letter forces its way into her consciousness. It all comes together in a millisecond in her horrified brain, causing her to fling the letter across the room and sink to the floor, hugging her knees. Her stomach churns and she wonders if she's going to puke, eject the vileness of her thoughts in one long stinking stream of vomit. If only it were that easy, she thinks.

Joshua Barker. Another name bursts forth from Natalie's memories to join it. Adam Campbell. Pictures connect with the names in her head. Two photos, first seen fourteen years ago on television and whenever they've merited news time since then. Both of boys with dark hair, although one wears it longer and more unkempt. That particular boy is unsmiling and sullen, clearly unwilling to pose for the camera. The other looks nervous, a rabbit before a wolf, his expression uncertain. Natalie can't be sure which is Joshua Barker and which is Adam Campbell, although she thinks Unkempt and Sullen might be Adam. Which means Rabbit Boy is Joshua Barker. The boy so summarily rejected by his mother. Did Adam Campbell's mother react the same way, Natalie wonders. Was he similarly dismissed from his parents' lives, abandoned to a secure detention unit, like Joshua? Rejected because, together, at the age of eleven, still children themselves, they committed a crime so shocking and sickening it hardly seemed possible. Not for two eleven-year-olds, anyway; an older man, perhaps, some twisted loner from a tortured background, but not two young boys. Not children brought up in stable home environments, with no known abuse.

Kids of eleven don't lure a two-year-old child, blonde and pretty Abby Morgan, from her home and first batter then stab her to death.

Except, fourteen years ago, in the case of Adam Campbell and Joshua Barker, that's exactly what they did.

Nausea wrenches at Natalie's stomach again.

Her memories zoom back to Rabbit Boy, all wide-eyed and worried, and then shoot forward to Mark Slater. She pictures his hair, his eyes, so similar to Rabbit Boy's, and desperately hopes she's mistaken. That the two aren't the same, and that a perfectly innocent explanation exists as to why Mark has Joshua Barker's letter in his possession. Other than the obvious, hideous, too painful to be contemplated reason.

That Mark Slater is Joshua Barker, fourteen years older. And that she's been dating a child killer, who's protected by a new identity.

Natalie hauls herself to her feet. She can't bear to be in the same room as the letter a minute longer. Her nausea forgotten, she resorts to food, the way she always does when upset. She walks through into the kitchenette, pulling the fridge open, seeking rich soothing carbohydrates, shelving all concerns about her excess kilos. She takes out whatever comes to hand, slapping butter thickly onto bread before pressing several slices of ham on top. She yanks a stool out from the breakfast bar, ploughing into the sandwich, her jaws chewing furiously, the taste of the food unimportant. A packet of chocolate biscuits catches her eye and she grabs them. She'll need every ounce of carbohydrate comfort the sandwich and biscuits can offer if she's to confront Mark. Will she, though? Natalie squashes down an inner voice, the alarmist one, telling her how someone who can batter and stab a two-year-old to death may not take kindly to having the lid ripped off his new identity, his fresh start. Especially by a girlfriend who's resorted to snooping through his possessions.

She glances around as she crams the food in her mouth. The kitchenette is as neat and orderly as everything else in Mark's flat is. No plates left to drain in the rack, no dirty coffee mugs on the table, no overflowing pedal bins. The scent of lemons drifts over to her from the sink. So clean, so organised, unlike Natalie's own kitchen, where the fridge is a place for food to die and the tea towels are always grubby. She's frequently teased Mark about his penchant for tidiness. He always shrugs, telling her that's just the way he prefers things.

Now she considers his sterile surroundings symbolic of how little she knows about the man she's been dating. Mark's never been one to talk much about his past. From what he's told her, his mother and father are dead and he has no other family. How, as a child, he had an ordinary upbringing here in Bristol. If he's really Joshua Barker, then that's a lie. Natalie remembers both of Abby Morgan's killers come from Exeter. Same as the letter. As for his parents being dead, well, his mother certainly intends to be exactly that where her son's concerned. Natalie's not sure any longer whether she blames the woman for deserting him.

The letter. Natalie recalls how worn the creases are, how often it must have been read over the years. What emotions does it evoke in Mark each time he unfolds it? Those stark words, revealing a mother's rejection of her son. Small wonder, she thinks, Mark has always been reluctant to discuss anything that hints at them having a future together. He's been concealing the capacity to murder a child, a defenceless two-year-old, and she's been considering having kids with him. Such a man has no business being a father. *You've got to admit it, Natalie*, the voice within her berates. *You've picked some turkeys in the past when it comes to men, but this one beats them all. A child killer? Really?*

Some small part of her protests, however. She remembers moments of tenderness, rare and thus precious, from Mark. Sometimes he seems like he's holding his emotions on a leash before temporarily setting them free, his smile soft and warm as he bends to kiss her. Moments like these have kept her going every time he's shied away from her hints about seeing each other more often, perhaps getting a place together. They're now insisting she allow Mark a chance to explain. Either give her some credible explanation as to why he has Linda Curtis's letter to her grandson in his bedside cabinet, if he's not Joshua Barker. Or, if he is, explain Abby Morgan's death to her. How he was just a child at the time; how he never intended anything so dreadful to happen.

Natalie looks at her watch. Four o'clock. Mark won't be home until six. Decision made. She'll wait, and confront him when he walks through the door.

She'll have to skip any more comfort food, though. She recalls again how she's hoped this man will father a baby with her, and with that, the image of a bloodied and battered Abby Morgan forces its way into her brain. Her stomach clenches and heaves and she only just makes it to the bathroom in time. A vile mess of bread, ham and biscuits surges up from Natalie's guts as she retches over the toilet bowl, one thought hammering through her brain. *Dear God, let it be a mistake. Don't let him be Joshua Barker. Please.*

2

SEVEN, EIGHT, LAY THEM STRAIGHT

'We need more sacks of bonding compound, the twenty-five kilo ones. Ditto for six-mil gravel. Sort it before you leave, would you? Twenty of each should do us for the Wilson order.'

'On it, boss.' Where the hell is his order pad? Anxiety rises in Mark Slater, flooding him the way it always does when he's mislaid something, the order in his cubbyhole office mirroring the neatness in his flat. As does the lack of dust, the scent of lemon air freshener. Natalie, ever the untidy one, likes to tease him about being a neat freak, as she calls him. He can hear her in his head now, the laughter in her voice as she speaks. 'A place for everything and everything in its place,' she mocks. 'Just like me. Or not, as you'll have realised now you've been to my flat. Did you get this from your parents?'

Mark's at a loss when Natalie asks questions about his life before her. Often his only refuge is a lie. 'Yes,' he replies, not caring to be more specific, changing the subject, understanding Natalie is only teasing and doesn't expect anything more than a joking response. She'll never know his answer isn't true. OK, his mother always demanded tidiness from him, but the urge for greater regularity comes later for Mark, after her flinty brand of maternal care no longer features in his life. For him, methodology represents a desperate attempt to impose control on a world that so far has proved unpredictable.

He finds the missing pad under some invoices in his filing tray and breathes out the tension he's been holding. All is well in his world again. He glances at the clock. Nearly five; just enough time to order the gravel, file the day's paperwork and then head for home.

Once he's finished on the phone, he tears off the completed purchase slip and places it on top of the others he's done that day, squaring the edges up so they align perfectly. *Seven, eight, lay them straight,* he chants to himself in his head. He batches them in groups of ten, a nice, round comforting number he likes, and lines them up in his hole punch as close to the exact middle as possible. He squeezes hard, and then slides out the purchase slips, sticking reinforcements over the holes before filing everything away in date sequence. Order has been imposed once more on his office, meaning Mark can breathe more easily.

'You got anything planned for tonight, mate?' It's his boss, Steve Taylor, again. A good guy, someone prepared to take a gamble on him four years ago. Something for which Mark's always been grateful. Steve hasn't a clue who his assistant manager really is, beyond knowing he's an ex-offender, but the man has grown to trust him. As have his colleagues. The official story is that Mark has served time for burglary and nobody's ever enquired too deeply. Not the most exciting of jobs, working at Steve's building supplies firm, but Mark, at twenty-five, has had enough excitement in his life, and he's quietly proud of the way he's transformed himself from raw ex-offender to assistant manager in four years.

'Going for a run, as per usual.' He doesn't mention his plans with Natalie. Mark's never told Steve about her. If his boss wonders why his employee never mentions dating women, thinks perhaps he might be gay, he never says anything, never poses awkward questions. Truth is, Mark's had a slew of women since his release from prison four years ago, his body eager to catch up with the fantasies he's had to make do with throughout the long years of incarceration. He doesn't allow his innate shyness to hold him back when he's first let out; although not classically good-looking, he's got that certain something that reels women in, and they're not shy about coming forward about it. They drool over his cropped mahogany-hued hair and his matching eyes. They like his height, all six feet of it. They're partial to the tuft of dark hair peeking over his T-shirt, promising a manly, hairy chest. Mark gives the impression he knows how to deliver a good fuck, even though he's clueless when first released. With practice, though, his level of expertise rapidly rises.

He never allows himself to get too close to any particular woman, though. Too risky. He's bound under the terms of his release to inform Tony Jackson, the police officer who monitors him, if he gets into any relationship that goes beyond a few quick shags. Mark realises that if he does, Jackson will grill him relentlessly about the woman concerned. Why? Because preserving his anonymity is crucial.

His new identity. He's only been Mark Slater for the past four years, ever since his release from the adult prison he's transferred to after Vinney Green. Joshua Barker vanishes that day, replaced by Mark Slater, the name effectively erasing all traces of his old life. A transformation contingent on him severing all ties with the past, including his family, although of course everyone involved in creating his new identity is aware his father is dead and his mother long gone. Only his grandparents, Roy and Linda Curtis, remain, assuming they're still alive. As a result, Mark's always been as tight-lipped as a clam about his past. The threat of vigilante action hangs over him like a malevolent cloud, along with the need to avoid even more taxpayers' money being used to forge a second fresh identity.

As for personal relationships, any woman he dates has to be someone who won't go running straight to the press if she ever finds out the truth. Mark's not allowed to tell her, of course. He's supposed to mention he's on the Violent and Sex Offenders Register, at which point most women will run in the opposite direction. Prospective partners need to deal with the fact that, although Mark's unable to give specifics, he's either a violent offender, a sexual predator, or both. Not many women are prepared to accept a skeleton as big, ugly and undefined as that in someone's past. Tony Jackson has always stressed this point. So every month when they meet, Mark gets asked whether he's dating anyone on a regular basis. He always assures Jackson he's playing the field, long and hard, an answer that satisfies the other man. Another box on his list ticked.

It's been true up to recently. Four months ago, he met Natalie Richards, though, and since that day, everything's changed.

He should really tell Tony Jackson about her. She's definitely more than a convenient fuck buddy; he realises he's in deep emotionally with this one. Besides, she's made it plain she wants more from him.

More than he's able to give, though.

Mark sighs, and heads off for a piss before the walk home. He chooses a stall rather than one of the urinals, simply so he can sit for a minute and clear the crap of his working day out of his brain. That way, he'll be fresh for his daily seven-mile run. Head in his hands, breathing in the lingering whiff of urine in the air, he thinks more about Natalie.

He's seeing her tonight. Nothing fancy, just Mark going to her flat after his run. They'll order in Chinese, watch a DVD and later they'll fuck. He hopes like hell she won't press him about moving things between them forward, not that she's ever overly pushy about it. No strident demands, thank God. Not Natalie's style. Merely the odd hint now and again, about seeing each other more often, getting a place together someday. As well as mentioning how much she loves babies. Mark's pained by the hurt in her face when he abruptly turns the conversation once the pin's been pulled from that particular grenade. He's clocked her insecurities long ago, along with the comfort eating. Might explain why he's taken to her so much. They're alike, he and Natalie, he reckons, both as messed-up and fragile inside their heads as each other. She's pretty, of course, which obviously helps, even though she doesn't believe in her own attractiveness. Natalie views the extra kilos she carries as ugly; Mark sees them as soft and squishy flesh, resulting in her large boobs and the gentle curve of her belly. Flesh that's delicious to squeeze, to stroke, to savour. Far sexier than some woman who may have a medically acceptable body mass index but whose stomach doesn't provide the comforting cushion Natalie's does. He tells her, in the warm afterglow of sex, what a lovely shade of brunette her hair is, shiny as a ripe conker; how he has a thing for chocolate eyes like hers. She always looks embarrassed, but pleased, when he talks that way, and Mark knows he should say more of that sort of thing.

It's hard, though. Can he ever permit himself to get closer to Natalie? No. She'll want more, eventually, than he's able to give. Marriage, babies, a future. Things, if he's honest with himself, he also yearns for but can't allow himself. Like Natalie, he's not exactly overloaded with self-belief. Something practically guaranteed with a mother like Joanna Barker. His lack of self-confidence translates into an absence of ambition for his life beyond wanting it to be safe, normal. Mark goes to work each day and whereas the dullness of his job would piss many guys off, he revels in the sheer normality of it, the regularity, the monthly pay cheque confirming he's a bona fide member of society. He'd happily work at S.T. Building Supplies until retirement, and if he could throw in a wife, a couple of kids and a mortgage, he would.

But he can't, of course. *Unclean, unclean*; Mark is as disfigured by his past as any leper. He's been rejected by his mother for what he and Adam Campbell did and he's sure if any woman ever discovers the truth about his past she'll reject him as decisively as Joanna Barker has done. He's hardly great husband material, after all. Even if by some miracle Natalie or anyone else agrees to marry him, how can he ever allow himself to become a parent? Let alone father a daughter. Because then he'll have a living, breathing Abby Morgan forever before him, a permanent reminder of that day fourteen years ago.

Natalie's becoming a fixture in his life now, though, and he can't deny he'd like to explore what they have together, see if it holds the potential for more. Her lack of self-esteem, however, is obviously warning her he's not bothered about commitment, maybe even that he sees other women. Hell, he knows for sure she thinks that, even though it's not true. Take the endless questions about A.J. after she snoops through his phone. Not the other woman she so clearly fears, but Anthony Jackson, Tony or A.J. to those who know him well. His supervising officer from the police, with whom he meets every month to prove he's being a good boy and complying with the terms of his release.

Which he is, of course. Mostly. A.J. doesn't know about the visit Mark made, four years ago, to Dartmoor, back to where it all happened. Staying away from Moretonhampstead and the scene of the crime is just one of the many conditions laid down in order for him to be released, and Mark isn't going to admit to breaking it anytime soon. It's easy enough to deceive Tony Jackson anyway, should he wish to. After four years of Mark giving every appearance of abiding by the rules, their monthly meeting is down to a mere half-hour now, confined to routine questions about whether Mark is still employed, how he's spending his time and whether he's dating.

Impossible, of course, to tell Natalie who A.J. really is. Or why the appointment is in his phone calendar. She'll simply have to stay jealous. He's well aware she doesn't believe his story about A.J. being an old school friend, but what else can he say?

Mark sits back on the toilet pan, letting out a long breath. He's had fourteen years of living a lie and nothing's going to change; he'll simply have to deal with it as he's always done.

The situation isn't fair, though, however much the thought sounds like a childish whine. Because he may have been tried and convicted on an equal basis with Adam Campbell, but only Adam and he know how far their sentencing was from reflecting what really happened, fourteen years ago in an abandoned farm building close to Dartmoor.

Mark Slater, formerly Joshua Barker, is no child killer, but Adam Campbell won't be telling the truth anytime soon concerning Abby Morgan's brutal murder.

'You gone to sleep in there? I need to lock up.' Steve's voice punctures the balloon of Mark's thoughts.

'Coming.' His brain veers away from Adam Campbell, anticipating the sweaty exhilaration of his blood pounding through his veins as he does his daily seven-mile run around the track in his local park. He'll force his mother, A.J. and prison life out of his mind, working up an appetite for the Chinese meal with Natalie. Sweet and sour pork balls, he thinks, or maybe beef in black bean sauce. Egg fried rice. Spring rolls as well.

He says goodbye to Steve, who's busy checking everything is locked up, and heads out of the industrial estate in Bristol where he works, towards home. His cramped yet orderly flat, a mere twenty minutes away by foot; deliberately chosen by Mark because it's not near any primary schools or children's playgrounds. Family houses line the nearby streets, but any children who live in them tend to play in the back gardens, not the front, so Mark feels safe. He forces his mind away from the vision of Abby Morgan that arises in his head. So blonde, so pretty. Only two years old. Playing with her dolls' house in the side garden of her home fourteen years ago.

Not tonight, he tells himself. Don't think of her tonight. Focus on Natalie, Chinese food, what DVD you'll watch later, but not her. Not Abby Morgan.

Zero chance of that. As Mark looks up, he sees Abby, not fifty feet from him, clutching her mother's hand. He draws his breath in sharply, stopping, staring.

It's not her, of course. Abby Morgan died of multiple stab wounds. She'll never hold anyone's hand ever again, but plenty of pretty blonde toddlers live in Bristol; Mark has been haunted by them ever since his release from prison. Every time he sees one, he yearns to be back inside, where small female children can't torment him. Remind him how Abby Morgan will never grow up, never get old, and all because of him. Every time a blonde toddler crosses his path, the awfulness of it all floods back to him. Especially if she's wearing pink, as so many little girls do. The colour of Abby's entire ensemble the day Adam Campbell lured her from the garden of her parents' house.

The child ahead of him has a cerise-coloured jacket on. A blonde female toddler in pink. A sure-fire trigger for Mark's counting rituals.

One, Two, Buckle My Shoe.

He wrenches his gaze away from Abby's doppelganger, forcing his mind onto the old children's nursery rhyme. Verses seared onto his memory by the events of fourteen years ago. Anxiety grips him tightly, its fingers clutching hard until he begins counting. It's an important part of his ritual to start at the beginning, even though he doesn't want to, eager as he is to get to the higher numbers, seven and beyond. *One, two, buckle my shoe*, he chants in his head. He glances up, sees the child being led by her mother towards one of the side roads. He wonders if she's wearing pink trainers; he can't tell from where he is. His throat seems to be closing over, the width of a straw, no more, and he fights for breath.

He walks on, exactly seven paces, and then stops.

Three, four, knock at the door. The police have come for you, Mark. Or Joshua, as you were back then. The child is almost out of view. Soon she'll have vanished from his sight but his anxiety will remain until he finishes the ritual, so familiar now.

Another seven paces forward, another halt. Deep breaths in.

Five, six, pick up sticks. Sticks. Adam Campbell's expression, his exultation at the thought of the injuries he'll inflict with the rake in his hand, flashes across Mark's brain, and he hurries forward another seven paces.

Seven, eight, lay them straight. That's better. Higher numbers always are. Seven, lucky number seven. Once he reaches it, he's past the blood, the screaming, evoked by shoes, knocks on doors, sticks.

The child has disappeared now, but Mark is compelled, as always, to complete the counting and the pacing. He doesn't care if anyone notices he's behaving oddly. He paces and counts, paces and counts, until he reaches the end. *Nineteen, twenty, my plate's empty.* A relieved exhalation releases the pressure in his chest; he can breathe more easily now. Ten more minutes and he'll reach the sanctuary of his flat, where everything is as neat and orderly as his office at work and blonde two-year-old girls never venture.

The neatness. The counting. Mark knows his behaviour has a name. Obsessive-compulsive disorder, not that he's ever been formally diagnosed. He's right up there with the hoarders, hand washers and lock checkers, but for Mark his vice is counting. For him, safety does indeed lie in numbers, as well as in his compulsion for neatness. At Vinney Green, his tidy streak is often commented on but not thought worthy of investigation. Natalie often tells him he's getting as bad as Patrick Bergin's character in *Sleeping With The Enemy*.

'Martin Burney's got nothing on you,' she says, laughing. He smiles back at her, not wanting to make an issue of it, and anyway she's familiar only with Mark's neatness obsession. Nobody has any idea about the counting or the pacing. Those rituals start once he's released from prison and he sees, for the first time in ten years, a pretty blonde toddler, and yes, she's wearing pink, of course. He stares at the child, frantically and for too long, until her mother notices and pulls her daughter quickly away, clearly rattled by Mark's fixed gaze. Afterwards, he can't breathe. He thinks his throat is going to close completely over; he's back there, in Moretonhampstead, with Abby Morgan, hearing the childish nursery rhyme tinkle from her Fisher-Price CD player.

One, Two, Buckle My Shoe.

He doesn't quite understand the psychology behind his obsession, but after seeing the first Abby lookalike, he begins to count, slowly, along with the nursery rhyme and it helps, especially when he gets into the higher numbers. By *eleven, twelve, dig and delve*, he's starting to breathe more easily. By *nineteen, twenty, my plate's empty* and a bit more of the walk seven paces, stop for a count of seven, he's more or less back to normal.

Until the next time. Too many blonde female toddlers exist for his compulsion ever to go away, and Mark never knows when he'll see Abby Morgan again. Small wonder his neatness obsession has grown steadily worse. Food cupboards worthy of Martin Burney, DVDs in alphabetical order, books arranged by size and colour. It's his way of imposing order on an essentially chaotic world. He doesn't seek help for it, because it's his safety valve, his magic pill. A sure-fire method of obtaining relief from the guilt swamping him every time he sees another incarnation of Abby Morgan.

It's not just guilt plaguing him. Mark suffers a constant, overwhelming need to atone for her death, not that he has any idea how to achieve the impossible. Not when the whole world believes him every bit as culpable as Adam Campbell for her murder.

3

UNMASKED

Natalie's stomach is less queasy now, but she's certain she won't be having Chinese food later. And definitely not with Mark. He's supposed to come round to her flat at eight, and she's very sure she'll be there alone by then, berating herself for her poor taste in men. Then she'll remember her father, and the psychology will be all too obvious.

Where the hell is Mark? He should be here by now. Chances are her suspicions are right; besides being a child killer, he's probably stopping off for a quickie with a woman with the initials A.J. Rage pounds through Natalie and if Mark were to walk through the door within the next minute, she might well slap him one.

She fights hard to regain control, push the anger down inside, shove it out of range, so she can confront him calmly. Such a contradiction in terms. The word confrontation itself is loaded, laced with connotations of aggression. Besides, she knows anger won't do any good if she wants to get the truth out of Mark. Although on one level she doesn't know him at all, on another she recognises any sign of fury from her will drive him away, and all she'll get will be evasiveness.

Words from long ago drift back to her. An eleven-year-old Natalie, her pubescent self convinced she has the answer to her mother Callie's puffy eyes, reddened after discovering her husband has been playing away from home yet again.

'Why do you put up with it? Why not tell him what a jerk he's being?'

She's enraged by the passivity of Callie's response.

'I can't, love. I don't want to antagonise him, drive him away for good.' At the time, Natalie can't grasp how her mother can be, as she thinks to herself later on, such a fucking wimp. Sure, her parents argue about her father's infidelities, but Callie always responds with tears rather than anger. More wrath might have grown her a pair of much-needed lady balls. Especially given how her husband moves out amid talk of divorce a few weeks later.

The irony is, Natalie reckons, she's turned out every bit as bad when it comes to screwing up relationships. Even now, with what seems like incontrovertible evidence, part of her still believes Mark incapable of committing such an atrocity. Some other explanation has to exist as to why he possesses such a letter. What, she wonders. Nothing credible comes to mind, other than the obvious: Mark Slater and Joshua Barker inhabit the same body. He's a child killer. And even if Mark provides some convincing explanation, can their fragile relationship withstand Natalie striking it such a blow? An accusation of being a notorious murderer isn't one that can be shrugged off, cast aside like a lesser charge, such as infidelity with A.J.

As she looks at her watch, concerned now about his lateness, she hears the main door to the building being opened. Footsteps echo in the hallway. A pause, the rustle of letters being rifled through. Mark will be checking the post on the communal table, seeing if anyone's sent him mail. He won't find anything;

Natalie's got there before him. The only important letter is the one she holds clenched in her hand.

He crosses the hallway, puts his key in the latch; Natalie imagines his concern when he finds it unlocked. The door inches open and then Mark is framed in the doorway, surprise registering on his face as he takes in the sight of Natalie, standing there pale and unwelcoming. One hand clutches Mark's sofa; the other is held behind her back.

He doesn't speak at first, but she watches his eyes glance from her to the empty plate and biscuit packet on the table. He's well aware of her comfort eating and the evidence is there before him, along with her silent, accusatory stare.

'Nat,' he says, his voice uncertain and a note or three above his normal pitch. 'What...what are you doing here?' It sounds as though his throat is as closed over as Natalie's is. When she doesn't reply, he tries again.

'Has something happened? Are you all right?'

For answer, she brings her hand out from behind her back. In it, she holds the letter, now replaced in the envelope.

She thrusts it towards Mark's face. Confusion floods his expression in the seconds before he recognises what she's holding. Then all she sees is a weary acceptance, and hope for a plausible explanation of its existence fades within her. Natalie interprets his expression as one of guilt mixed with shame. He doesn't speak, merely switches his gaze between her face and the letter. Behind Natalie, the kitchen clock ticks the time away, the sound magnified by the tension choking the room. She drags air into her lungs, eventually getting her tongue to work.

'Why…' She wets her lips, despite there being precious little saliva in her mouth. 'This letter…why do you have it?'

Until he speaks, she tells herself, the chance exists he can explain this, rip away the dread in her gut at the suspicion she's been sleeping with a child killer.

The clock continues to tick away behind her, measuring the seconds until he opens his mouth. He doesn't, though, and Natalie tries again, forcing a calmness she doesn't feel into her voice.

'Are you Joshua Barker?' she asks.

No reply. Mark won't even look at her.

'Answer me, for fuck's sake.'

Anger mixed with fear bites hard at her as Mark turns away. He leans his palms on the kitchen table, pressing his weight forward onto them, increasing the distance between himself and Natalie as though he's carrying some deadly contagion. She hears him sigh.

'You've been going through my things again.' No trace of annoyance in his voice, just a sad resignation.

She ignores his words. 'I'll ask you again. Why the fuck do you have a letter addressed to Joshua Barker? The child killer?'

Mark shakes his head. 'Oh, Nat. Don't do this. Please.'

'Do what? Check whether the man I've been sleeping with is who he says he is? As opposed to a murderer?' She tosses the letter aside, attempting to shove his arms off the table. Anything to get him to meet her eyes. 'Don't you think I've a right to do that?'

He does return her gaze then, weariness in his expression. 'Yeah. I guess.'

'Then answer me. Are you Joshua Barker?'

Sadness creeps over his face as the silence thickens between them.

'For God's sake, tell me. Yes or no?'

Eventually he nods, extinguishing all hope within her. 'Yes.'

'You killed that little girl. Abby Morgan.' The accusation bursts out of Natalie now he's confirmed his guilt. She sees him flinch on hearing the child's name. Her fists fly at him, rage and revulsion in every blow; the man before her becomes symbolic of all those who have ever hurt her. A list that includes *him*. The one who abused her, so many years ago. Oh, the horror of it. Don't go there, she warns herself, as she continues to punch Mark, her resolve not to get angry now forgotten. He doesn't stop her and she pounds away before dropping down on the sofa, her throat full of tears, despair choking her voice. 'You bastard. You fucking bastard.'

Mark stands in front of her, silent. She can't look at him. 'How the hell...' She gasps in air. 'How could you do something so awful? You and that other boy. You killed a child. A defenceless two-year-old.'

'Nat.' His voice reaches her, cutting through her misery. 'I can explain.'

'Like hell you can. You were convicted, you and that Adam Campbell.'

Natalie stands up, thrusting the letter into his face, the force of her fingers crumpling the envelope. 'Your own mother. She rejected you.'

He turns his head away before she's able to gauge his reaction. She presses on, driven by her overwhelming need to grasp whatever it is she's dealing with here.

'She didn't even bother to tell you herself.' He tilts his face towards her then, and she sees him flinch again as her words whip against him. His reply is so quiet she has to ask him to repeat it.

'I said, yes, she rejected me.'

'You're surprised?'

'No. Are you going to do the same?'

'Do you blame me?'

He shakes his head sadly. This defeatist attitude isn't what Natalie expected at all. Where is the anger at her snooping through his things, where are the passionate denials that he's anyone other than Mark Slater, where is the explanation for having the letter? She can deal with shouting, blatant lies, anything other than this weary resignation at whatever she throws at him.

'I'm sorry, Nat. I'm not what you need me to be.'

'You can say that again.' She spits the words out as though they're poison.

'I never have been.'

'You fucking bastard.'

'I can explain. If you'll let me.'

'How?' Natalie is struggling to understand. She's always yearned for kids of her own and can't comprehend how anyone can hurt them. What explanation exists for how a child ends up murdered? Battered with a rake and then knifed to death? By two eleven-year-olds, for Christ's sake. Mark has once had the capacity to harm and kill a child and Natalie's not so naïve as to believe ten years of detention in a secure unit and then prison will have knocked that out of him.

'I didn't do it, Nat.' His eyes plead with her to accept his words.

'Of course you did.' Fury pounds through her at his glib denial. 'You were convicted, weren't you?'

'Yes, but listen - '

'You and the other boy. I don't remember much about the crime, but I do recall there being substantial evidence, enough to incriminate the pair of you. Bastards. Vile, twisted killers. Sick and evil, even at the age of eleven.' Anguish sweeps away the fury. 'How could you do something so awful? That little girl...'

'Nat.' He prises the letter from her grasp and places it on the coffee table, before trying to take her hands.

She wrenches them away. 'Don't touch me, you bastard.'

'That's not how it was, Nat. I didn't kill Abby Morgan. I swear I didn't. Like I say, I can explain. If you'll let me.'

She pushes past him, making for the door, but he stops her, not forcefully or in an intimidating way, simply an attempt at detaining her so he can deliver his explanation. His words bounce around in her skull. *I didn't do it, Nat.* Her desperation for all this crap not to be the way it appears leads her to sit back down on the sofa. She waits for Mark's explanation.

He takes his time before he says anything. When he does, Natalie almost gets up to leave, so disappointed is she with the weakness of his words.

'I didn't want to,' he says. 'Adam - the other boy - made me go along with it.' She stares at him in disbelief.

'That's it? That's your great explanation?' She can't believe she's hearing such crap. 'What little kids say when they're caught doing something they shouldn't? How someone else is to blame, never them?' She stands up. It's dark outside now and she yearns to be back in her flat, away from the disappointment the man before her represents. 'Do you know how pathetic you sound?'

'It's true, Nat, I swear.' She steels herself against the plea in his voice.

'Yeah, right. So how come you got convicted? You were found guilty. Same as Adam Campbell. Given an identical sentence.'

He doesn't reply. His silence grates on her. Surely he can find the words to speak in his defence when the charge against him is so serious?

'I don't remember anyone ever saying you were less guilty, not as involved in what happened to that child, than Adam Campbell.'

'It's like I told you, Nat. He forced me into it. Made me go along with the whole thing. I didn't realise what he had planned until it was all too late.'

Lies, complete bollocks, Natalie tells herself. If he's so innocent, why didn't that come out during the police questioning or at the trial? Equal sentences were handed down and for Natalie that means matching guilt. A detail from back then floats down the years towards her. *Detained at Her Majesty's Pleasure...a recommended minimum term of ten years in custody.* Abby Morgan's mother led an unsuccessful campaign to get the sentence increased, Natalie recalls, remembering her own mother remarking on the inadequacy of ten years when a child's life has been taken, despite the youth of her murderers.

Her next question is a direct challenge. 'So how come you got an equal sentence with the other boy?'

He answers obliquely, merely repeating what he's said before. 'I didn't want to hurt her, Nat, I swear.'

Why the hell won't he give her a direct answer? Because he's a bastard, that's why. Worse; he's a child killer, for God's sake, and the sanctuary of her flat calls to her again, along with the bar of Dairy Milk she'll buy on the way home. Except the idea of chocolate sends her stomach heaving again and she pushes Mark aside, running to the bathroom to bring up more of the sandwich and biscuits when she'd thought she had nothing left to vomit.

She's aware of him standing behind her as the sour stench of puke rises from the toilet bowl into her face. The faint lemony tang of his aftershave causes her to retch once more. She stands up shakily, rinsing the acid from her mouth with cool water from the sink.

'Are you OK?' Now it's her turn to flinch at the concern in his voice. It doesn't gel with her new image of him as a heartless child killer; she can't marry the two up and the divergence makes her angry and confused.

'No, I'm fucking well not OK.' She pushes past him, intent on leaving. He grabs her arm as she does so. Part of her, a rapidly shrinking one, still needs to believe he's not an evil child killer; she doesn't pull away.

'I'm sorry, Nat,' he says. 'Sorry you found out this crap. I couldn't tell you any of it, of course.'

She stands there mutely. Yes, she gets that. How do you tell your girlfriend you're a child killer?

'I wanted to.' His voice is plaintive. 'Didn't think you'd understand. Besides, it seemed too soon. We've not been together long, after all. Had no idea how you'd react. Anyway, under the terms of my release, I'm supposed to tell my supervising officer if I get serious with anyone.'

Natalie doesn't understand. He's supposed to obtain permission to date her?

'So whoever it is can be warned, you see. Told I'm on the Violent and Sex Offenders Register, although I'm not allowed to say why.' He sighs. 'You think I don't care about you. Not true, Nat. Always liked you, more than I've let on. I want to get closer but -' He shrugs. 'Not easy, when I've got something so awful hanging over my head. The police don't give out information about my past, of course. All part of keeping my new identity intact. No idea what I'd have told you if things had gone further between us. Probably not the whole truth.'

Certain phrases leap out at Natalie. *Always liked you. Want to get closer.*

She forces words past dry lips. 'I thought you were sleeping with someone else. Decided that must be why you didn't want to see more of me. It's the reason I came here today.'

'A.J.'

'Yes; who -'

'Tony Jackson, my supervising officer. I meet with him once a month. The guy in the police force who makes sure I'm complying with the terms of my release.'

'Like a parole officer?'

'Yes. Has to be a cop, though, not anyone from the Probation Service, not for someone like me. Jackson's one of the few people aware of my true identity.'

The words of the letter come back to Natalie. 'Did you have to break off contact with everyone you knew?'

He shrugs again. 'More or less already done, Nat.' He pushes past her to pick up the letter from Linda Curtis. 'You've already gathered how my mother reacted to my arrest and conviction.'

'You've not seen her since? She really did move away, change her name?'

He nods.

'What about your father? Is he dead, like you told me?'

'He died when I was nine. His parents were long gone, too. Had to end all communication with my grandparents on my mother's side once released, although whilst I was locked up they wrote to me, sent cards for birthdays and Christmas. Good people, both of them, but they didn't visit me in Vinney Green. Too disturbing for them.'

He waves the letter at her. 'Can't tell you how bad it was, getting this. Never let myself get close to anyone afterwards. Didn't seem any point. Not as if I have much to offer a woman. I can't be honest about my past, that's for sure.'

'Did you think about a future? With me?' She hardly dares ask.

'Yes. Wanted to get closer, Nat, I really did, but it seemed impossible. Catch 22, you see. I can't trust a woman enough to reveal I'm on the Register if I don't get close to her, and I can't do that whilst lying about my past. Or without discussing it with Tony Jackson.'

Natalie is silent. Part of her understands how difficult it's been for him; what he said about his father dying when he was still so young tugs at her emotions. Did his death play some role in shaping the nine-year-old Joshua into a killer two years later? Especially when coupled with a mother who seems the archetypal cold, hard bitch. She's no armchair psychologist but both those factors have to have exerted some influence. Something she recalls her mother saying about the Morgan murder comes back to her. *I blame the parenting*, Callie Richards pronounces decisively, and Natalie's inclined to do the same.

There hasn't been another woman. He wants to get close to her. Can she overlook what happened to Abby Morgan, though?

Mark's always seemed the non-aggressive type. Natalie finds it difficult to reconcile the man before her with the stereotype of a brutal child killer. She wants to accept he's telling the truth about the girl's death. The problem of her messy history with relationships concerns her, though. Can she trust her instincts around men?

Without warning, a male voice sounds in her head. 'Frigging fat bitch.'

Natalie thrusts the memory away. No thoughts about *him*, not here, not now. She forces her mind instead onto Darren, her first boyfriend, who ends up stealing money from her. After him comes Rob, who screws half the female population of Bristol behind her back, echoing her father. After those two, Natalie vows she'll do better in future when it comes to men. And Mark's not a thief or a womaniser. He's been convicted of murder, though, a far bigger and uglier can of worms. One she can't bring herself to open.

She accepts then it's not just Abby Morgan Mark's killed. He's murdered another child, the one they'll never have together, not now. The desperate need for a partner who doesn't steal, cheat or kill children but one who's simply *normal* overwhelms her, crushing her hopes for a future with this man. She shoves Mark's hand from her arm, squashing down the lingering desire to understand, instead forcing the anger of before back into her mind.

She stands up. 'I'm leaving.' The need to inflict hurt on him, the way she's hurting, burns through her. 'We're finished. I never want to see you again.' Her jacket goes on with a few furious shrugs. 'I'm not surprised your mother rejected you. Nobody will ever want you. Not after what you did.'

'Natalie, I repeat, I didn't hurt Abby Morgan. The whole thing was Adam Campbell's doing.'

Her fingers yank up the jacket's zip. She can't allow herself to listen. Denial's the safe option, ensuring she won't get hurt any further. Of course, it also guarantees loneliness, but Natalie doesn't permit herself to dwell on that. Instead, she wonders how much weight she'll pile on through the inevitable comfort eating. Darren ended up adding two extra kilos to her body, Rob four, none of which she's subsequently shifted. She reckons Mark might add as many as ten.

'I'd rather it had been another woman.' Natalie yanks open the door, striding into the hallway to walk out of Mark - no, Joshua's - life.

4

REJECTION

Eight o'clock, later the same evening. The time Mark should have been arriving at Natalie's for Chinese and some God-awful rom-com. Instead, he's pounding around the running track at Bristol's Eastville Park. A light drizzle is in the air, the temperature consistent with a cool March dusk. *One, two, one, two*; Mark's feet thud over the ground, but he's not paying attention to his hammering heart or the ache in his calves.

Twice now he's been rejected by a woman for the events of fourteen years ago. *Nobody will ever want you again, not after what you did,* he recalls Natalie flinging at him as she walks out. Her words sting, but maybe he's always been unlovable. Perhaps since birth.

Mark Slater, now a nine-year-old Joshua Barker in his head, remembers the moment he realises his mother doesn't love him. Never has.

A damp Saturday morning, three months after the shock of his father's fatal car crash. Joshua and his mother have just finished breakfast. Joanna Barker's mood seems benign, which isn't the norm, not at all. He decides to risk the question he's never dared ask before.

'Why did you and Daddy wait so long before having me?'

The answer comes as a shock even though he tells himself subsequently: *you should have realised.*

A frown of irritation clouds his mother's face.

'We never decided to have you. You were an accident.'

An accident. Like spilt milk, not worth crying over. Or like his father, bloody and mangled behind the wheel of his wrecked car. He's cried over that all right. His grief's reserved for when he's in bed at night, a haven where his mother can't witness his sorrow for the father who isn't coming back.

An accident. Unplanned, unwanted. At nine, he's picked up enough from playground gossip to know what she means. Some failure has occurred; perhaps her little round pills haven't worked, a condom's been defective, she's miscalculated her dates. He doesn't know which one it is and it doesn't matter. The result has been the same; sperm has met egg when the two should have been kept firmly apart, their cells destined never to splice and turn into him, Joshua Barker.

Only they do, and he, an accident, is the result.

His mother is speaking again.

'I couldn't believe it when I found out. I'd been so careful...' Her voice holds disbelief. 'Your father was pleased, though, and he went on and on about having a son. Didn't think about me, forced to carry a baby for nine months, getting more like a whale every day. So selfish, only considering what *he* wanted.'

At least his father never thought of him as an accident, Joshua consoles himself. One of his parents has wanted him, even if it's not his mother. What quirk has led him to long for the love of a woman who seems incapable of the emotion, rather than the father who, until his death, is always there for him? Does her affection, so out of reach, seem more desirable because getting it represents such a challenge, whereas his father gave his unconditionally?

Andrew Barker, Mark thinks as he pounds along the running track, was what's now known as an enabler.

A good man, a loving father, but essentially weak when it came to standing up to his wife. When still alive, he colludes with Joanna Barker's whims and moods. 'Anything for a quiet life,' he tells Joshua with a wink, although his son notices that the smile accompanying his words is often strained. He understands why his father acts this way, though. Joanna Barker, like Adam Campbell, isn't someone who tolerates opposition in any form. It's her way or the highway. With hindsight, Mark sees that his father's docility is probably the very reason his mother married him. She's an alpha female and as such, she needs a subservient husband. One who poses no competition.

His mother's irritation at having produced Joshua is nothing, of course, compared to what she later experiences in being the parent of a child killer. It's not until he's been tried, convicted and receives his grandmother's letter that he has time and space to process her reaction. Why, he asks himself during his detention at Vinney Green, do Adam Campbell's parents stand by him when his own mother doesn't? Even now, at the age of twenty-five, her rejection of him seems incomprehensible.

In his head, now aged eleven, he's back at his childhood home. Joanna Barker responds to a knock on her front door to find police officers with questions that need answers. The murder of Abby Morgan has been broken in the media a couple of days before, the coverage intense. Joshua hasn't been able to watch; since he witnessed her life draining away in that abandoned farm building, he's been unable to hold food down, repeatedly vomiting up the vile memory. Joanna Barker is annoyed at being forced into the role of nurse and at having to clean up after him, the sickness being worse when Joshua overhears the news on the television downstairs. In his mind, he's as guilty as Adam

Campbell is, by virtue of weakness of character if nothing else. Why the hell didn't he stop Adam when he had the chance? He should have realised what would happen, find a way to circumvent Abby Morgan's death somehow, but he failed. Weak, weak, he tells himself, an echo of the way his mother has always described her dead husband. Like father, like son, he later decides whilst in the detention unit. Andrew Barker never stood up to his wife and his feebleness is mirrored in his son's failure to confront Adam Campbell.

By the time the police arrive, Joshua's not been sick for a few hours and he's relieved he's been caught. Later, he finds out how a witness reported seeing two boys leading a blonde-haired toddler dressed in pink towards the murder scene. The child was seen clutching a soft toy, a green hippopotamus. Vicky Campbell later finds such an item, stained with blood and unfamiliar to her, in her son's bedroom. Adam, by the age of eleven, already has a record of what's euphemistically called challenging behaviour, but to believe he's capable of something so awful is a stretch for his parents. They question him; he screams and lashes out with his fists, and his father takes the bloodied hippo to the police, although Vicky begs him not to. The result is the two officers now standing in Joanna Barker's living room.

Joshua sees in his mother's eyes that he's already been judged guilty.

Still experiencing the after-effects of the sickness, terrified at the seemingly endless questions fired at him by unsympathetic police officers, dread clutching tight at his gut, telling the truth seems impossible. Adam has threatened to kill him if he ever reveals what really happened. He pictures the two of them being sentenced to the same custodial unit, where Adam will have any number of opportunities to carry out his threat. Joshua ends up lying, saying he swapped turns with Adam to use the rake and the knife. He's remanded in a temporary detention centre in Exeter before sentencing. At the trial, he sees the other boy's parents, emphasising the absence of his own. The injustice of it slams into him as he becomes aware Mr and Mrs Campbell intend to stick by their son, whereas Joanna Barker has deserted him. She refuses to attend the trial, apart from when compelled to do so by the court, and doesn't respond to her son's letters. Joshua's confused, hurt, bewildered, until the day he receives the letter from his grandmother.

He remembers the day it arrives. Such a moment is a pivotal one in his life, after all. He's already been at Vinney Green for a couple of months. Once a week he writes to Joanna Barker, not daring to make it more often, but so far all he's received in return has been silence. His grandmother's handwriting, instantly recognisable, disappoints Joshua at first, simply because it's not that of his mother. He opens it, expecting nothing different from Linda Curtis's usual chatty, grandmotherly letters.

His brain can't assimilate the words at first and he reads the letter three times before he really starts to get it. The contents burn him, much as they do Natalie fourteen years later, some parts doubly caustic. *Very difficult since your detention…she is adamant on this point.* One sentence in particular stings: *it is her intention to begin a new life, a life without you.* Joshua begins to doubt he's ever had a mother in the true sense; maternity, after all, involves more than a woman opening her legs for the conception and birth.

Shock at the finality the letter brings, and the cruelty of it, slam through him, even though he's not seen his mother for weeks and on one level he already understands she wants nothing more to do with him. After the shock, bitterness arrives. He pictures Adam's parents at the trial, attending every day without fail. The other boys at the unit also anger him. Take Danny Carpenter, for example. A serial arsonist who kills his uncle in a blaze of burning petrol at his home. His parents visit him once a week, never missing a Friday, despite the fact their son is responsible for the death of his father's brother. Or there's Matt Wainwright, aged thirteen, who stabs his grandmother to death when she refuses to buy him new trainers. No lack of family visits there either. It's unfair, thinks Joshua, self-pity overwhelming him. Reverting to the maturity level of a five-year-old, he tells himself: *I didn't do nothing wrong.*

He's angry, pissed off he allowed Adam Campbell's threats to stop him telling how it really happened with Abby Morgan, because they've ended up being detained in separate juvenile units, rendering Adam's intimidation hollow. It's too late now, of course, to backtrack and tell the truth, so he has no option but to resign himself to detention as a child killer.

The unfairness of his situation, the whole fucking misery of it all, infuriates Joshua so much he destroys his bedroom at Vinney Green. He overturns furniture, throwing everything he can get his hands on to the floor, kicking, smashing, trampling, all the while screaming his rage and frustration, until the door opens and he's restrained. His fury doesn't end there; in the coming weeks, he lashes out at other boys in the unit, reserving the brunt of his anger for Danny Carpenter and Matt Wainwright. He's particularly proud of the cracking punch he lands on the arsonist's nose, breaking it, and after that he gets a reputation for being a hard nut.

The fights get worse after he tries writing to his mother again. The tone of his letter is pleading, how he's not guilty, how she has to believe him. How Adam forced him into going along with what happened, how he's sorry he's caused her so much trouble. Even as he writes, he can hear her voice, condemning him as weak. She's already branded him a loser like his father. No wonder she wants nothing more to do with him. He decides to send the letter anyway, folding it neatly in three before sealing it up. Pen poised, he starts to write her name and address on the envelope before remembering. He doesn't know either any longer.

Your mother has decided to move away from Exeter and change her name...

Joshua considers his options. Someone on the staff must have her new details, surely. He'll give them the letter and ask them to post it to her. Then his grandmother's words flood over him, how his mother is starting a new life without him, brought about by the embarrassment he's caused her, and he abandons the idea of sending the letter. It contains nothing she'll want to hear. He tears it into shreds, then slams his fist into the wall, repeatedly, until again the door opens and he's prevented from doing himself further harm.

Joshua subsequently develops two personalities. The aggressive one, which makes the arsonist and the granny stabber think twice about having anything to do with him, contrasting with his withdrawn side. When he's not taking out his anger on the other boys, Joshua turns in on himself, closing down his emotions, shuttering them away. If he doesn't feel, he can't get hurt, he reasons, leading years later to Mark Slater's inability to let his guard down with Natalie Richards. He's a complicated, emotional mess, although that's hardly unusual for the residents at Vinney Green. Sessions are booked for him with the unit's child psychiatrist, tortured blocks of time when he refuses to co-operate in any way. Impossible to do so. This woman has a university degree. A home, a life outside the unit. He doubts she's ever done anything besides follow society's rules; how can she get even a tiny grasp on what it's like to be Joshua Barker? She's been briefed, of course, about him not getting maternal visits, about the death of his father, and she tries, she really does, to be empathetic and delve under his skin, failing abjectly. Joshua reads, upside down from across the table, phrases in her notes about abandonment, unresolved grief, and he recognises she's doing her best but he still has nothing to say to her.

The neatness obsession creeps up on him gradually, an antidote to the aggression fuelling the fights. Joshua has to channel his churned-up emotions somehow and so the fixation with regularity, symmetry and order kicks in. It works, too. Tidiness imposes a sense of consistency on his world and the sessions with the psychiatrist get shorter and fewer until they stop. By the time he's transferred to adult prison, aged eighteen, Joshua is a model detainee, the fist fights long gone, replaced by the rigidity of his obsessions.

Oh, yes. Obsessions in the plural, not singular. Whilst at Vinney Green, another compulsion besides tidiness tugs at his brain, refusing to let go. Abruzzo. A surname, one he remembers because it's Italian and therefore unusual in his limited experience. 'Abruzzo,' he often says aloud, letting his tongue rasp against the cheese-grater quality of the -zo. He first encounters the name during a lazy afternoon spent messing around in Adam Campbell's bedroom. It's written in a diary, along with the owner's address. Copthorne Close; its alliterative sound pleases him and like Abruzzo, it's filed away in the eleven-year-old Joshua's brain. Later, when he's in bed after another day at the detention centre, unable to sleep, the name and address worry away at him. He can't get the thought, dark and hideous as it is, out of his mind; that Adam Campbell has hurt another child besides Abby Morgan.

Back in the present moment, his seven laps of the running track completed, Mark thrusts Joshua Barker out of his head. He jogs back through the drizzle to his flat. Once home, he throws his damp, sweaty clothes into the washing machine, changing into fresh ones. A faint hint of Natalie's perfume lingers in the air and he breathes in the musky scent, the pain of her rejection stabbing him again. Really, though, he's not surprised she's dumped him. It's as she said; Abby Morgan's death has branded him unlovable. Some crimes simply aren't forgivable.

He switches his laptop on. A quick flick through the Internet before bed, mainly to check the football fixtures for the weekend. He clicks on the BBC's news website, skimming down the football section. Bristol Rovers will be playing away; he lacks the cash to attend every fixture, though, and given their current form it's probably not worth the effort. Shame; a diversion from the pain consuming him over Natalie's rejection would have been welcome.

He clicks over to the news. As usual, doom and gloom dominate. More problems in the Middle East, the usual wrangling in the House of Commons, concerns over terrorist threats in London. A prostitute found murdered in Southampton. Stabbed, bloodily and brutally, to death. He remembers something similar a few months ago, a different city, he can't recall where. Somewhere on the South Coast. Of course, street girls being killed by rogue punters is nothing new. In Mark's current frame of mind, though, reading about the savage murder of a female hits too close to home. For fuck's sake, he thinks. Does everything in his life have to lead back to Abby Morgan's death?

5

KNOWLEDGE IS POWER

As she drives home after the break-up with Mark, Natalie's consumed, almost destroyed, by the revelation he's a child killer. It's as though her brain's been hijacked by the need to understand, fit the pieces together in her head, get to grips with the fact she's been so badly wrong about him. Will she ever comprehend the sonar in her head, the tracking device that leads her, unerringly, to life's bad boys? This is way beyond the realms of petty theft and screwing around, though. Child murder tops a different league and Natalie's at a loss to fathom how her internal radar has betrayed her yet again.

The strident blast of a car horn cuts through her thoughts. Oh God. Whilst she's been whipping herself for her innate ability to pick losers, her car's drifted into the path of the oncoming traffic. Time to pull over; Natalie's barely able to see for the tears of self-recrimination burning the backs of her eyeballs. She parks up and switches off the engine, allowing the persistent March drizzle to obscure the windscreen.

Crushed, she crosses her arms on the steering wheel, pillowing her forehead on top. Her tears take with them her hopes for something solid and lasting with Mark Slater. She remembers, with a shiver of revulsion, the last time they made love, the memory of his body now repugnant. Hands have caressed her that are responsible for the brutal murder of a tiny child;

Natalie's been soiled by their touch and she's not sure she'll ever feel clean again.

Eventually she restarts the engine. This time she's more careful, more aware, as she drives. Back in her flat, she makes straight for the biscuit tin, a pure reflex action, before the memory of her earlier vomiting stops her. For once, she doesn't seek refuge in comfort eating, her stomach sending a silent message of protest against food. The urge to dig deeper into the enigma of Mark Slater claws at her. She's gone from hopeful girlfriend to destroyed ex in the space of an evening, so she needs answers. Now. Mark's so-called explanation is inadequate, insultingly thin, and as she'll never see him again, she's unable to unearth the truth of this – whatever this is – through him.

Something else is required to sort the mess in her head.

Natalie digs deep into her memory, trying to force out facts about the murder of Abby Morgan, but few emerge. The killing that shocked the whole of Britain took place too long ago, when Natalie was the same age as Mark, or Joshua, or whatever his name is. Eleven years old. Holy shit. The reality of it rushes over her. Whilst she's struggling to cope with the breakdown of her parents' marriage, he's battering a child to death. At the same time as menstruation becomes an unwelcome factor in her life, a toddler's blood is soaking into the ground somewhere close by. Where, exactly? Dartmoor, Dorset, Devon? She can't remember, but the likely proximity of the murder site to Bristol adds fuel to the revulsion gathering force in her brain.

Despite not being able to recall many details about the crime, Natalie's familiar with the basics. Hell, everyone in Britain knows about the murder of Abby Morgan. It's one of those legendary crimes, like the Moors Murders, never forgotten. Two eleven-year-old boys deliberately luring a toddler from her garden with the intent of killing her? Following through by forcing her into an abandoned farm building? Battering her with a rake handle and then stabbing her to death? No, thinks Natalie, crimes like that don't fade from the collective consciousness. They remain and fester, torturing the conscience of Mr and Mrs Joe and Joanna Public with the obvious question. How the hell can something so terrible happen in a so-called civilised society?

She vaguely remembers hearing her mother discussing the case at the time with their next-door neighbour, who's come round for coffee.

'I blame the parenting,' Callie says, nodding with satisfaction at having been astute enough to pinpoint the raison d'être behind the killing. 'You can't tell me those two grew up being taught right from wrong. More than likely you'll find neglect, or abuse, or worse, has been going on behind closed doors.'

'Not just with those boys, either.' Natalie recalls the grim line of the neighbour's mouth. 'How come they were able to take the child so easily? Why wasn't someone keeping an eye on her?'

'Well, you can't be watching them all the time, I suppose…'

Natalie's memories swing forward to a television broadcast, four years ago or thereabouts. She's twenty-one, still living at home. Callie Richards and her daughter have just finished a fish and chip supper and are watching the early evening news. Joshua Barker and Adam Campbell are again hitting the headlines, this time because they're being released under special licence. Complete with new identities, different names and faked backgrounds. A move necessary to prevent them from vigilante action from a public that's never forgiven or forgotten the murder of two-year-old Abby Morgan.

'Should have locked them up and thrown away the key,' Callie Richards remarks.

More or less what Abby's mother says when she's interviewed for the broadcast. Michelle Morgan speaks movingly about how Joshua Barker and Adam Campbell have been let off far too lightly for her daughter's murder. How they've received a comfortable life, including an education, at the taxpayer's expense, and now they've been released after serving a mere ten years. She dismisses suggestions that they were only children themselves at the time of the murder, too young to realise what they were doing. 'They knew all right,' she says, venom flicking from her voice as she spits the words out. 'They planned it. Came prepared, with a knife. They killed my child because they're sick and twisted, both of them, right the way through, and they should pay in full for her death. She lost her life through them and it's only fair they should spend the rest of theirs in prison in return.' The broadcast cuts back to the newscaster.

'What gets me is the waste of public money,' Callie Richards says. 'You can't tell me it'll come cheap, giving those two new names, and who'll foot the bill? The taxpayer, that's who.'

Natalie's inability to remember more than the barest of details frustrates her. She's battling the flicker of hope in her gut, the one repeating his words to her. *I didn't kill Abby Morgan, Nat.* She's desperate to believe him on one level and yet, on another, it's easier to brand him a child killer. Safety lies in spurning Mark Slater, in retreating to lick her wounds via singleton status. If she's alone, she reasons, no man can hurt her the way her father did her mother with his frequent infidelities.

Knowledge is power, so she's heard, and right now, she's lacking in power. Time to set that straight. She switches on her computer and does a search on

'Abby Morgan murder.' Over three hundred and fifty thousand hits come up. Wikipedia's top of the list, but she doesn't click the link. Too dull, the articles always too long, too annotated, to suit Natalie's tastes. A YouTube link beneath it entitled 'Yearly Vigil' catches her attention, and, intrigued, she clicks on it. Seems Michelle Morgan holds a vigil each year at the site of the murder, at the time when her daughter died. This is news to Natalie; she doesn't remember seeing or hearing anything of this. The blurb gives her the bare facts, with the video link connecting to the latest vigil, the one held last year. Natalie skims through the comments. Most are of the 'lock them up and throw away the key' variety.

Her fingers shaking, she clicks on the video link.

Natalie can't tear her eyes from the screen. Michelle Morgan stands in front of a microphone. The setting's a field, the weather damp and drizzly. Abby's mother appears older than her age, more mid-fifties rather than the late forties she must be. She's of average height, carrying at least ten kilos of excess fat strapped to her belly and thighs. Reddish-hued hair, pulled back in an unkempt ponytail, wisps of which escape around her neck. No make-up. Unlike her face, her clothes are younger than her years, a little too tight, a tad too bright. Green trousers a size too small, a shiny butter-coloured top that strains across her breasts. She's flanked on her left by a young woman who looks barely out of her teens as well as a man who's possibly in his late twenties. After having read the blurb accompanying the video, Natalie realises who they are. Rachel and Shaun Morgan, Abby's older sister and brother. Rachel's stance is awkward, her shoulders hunched, her hands thrust deep into her jacket pockets. She's clearly unnerved by the television camera pointed her way. Low self-esteem lurks in her poor posture and frequent glances at her brother, who seems altogether more stoical. He stands tall, immobile, with no discernible expression on his face.

'It angers me that the two individuals responsible for depriving my family of a cherished daughter are now at liberty, protected by new identities, living their lives in freedom, when my child has been deprived of her own life. Robbed of it in a most brutal and callous fashion.' Michelle Morgan's voice is forged from steel, her posture straight and strong, unlike Rachel's. 'Where is the justice for the victim? Why did the two boys who murdered my child get food, clothing and education, all at the taxpayer's expense, when my daughter was denied her right to these things? A culture has emerged in this country of prioritising the criminal over the victim and it has to stop.'

'You think they were released too early?'

Michelle Morgan snorts her contempt into the reporter's microphone.

'Of course they were. Ten years for the murder of a defenceless toddler? The sentence was an insult to my dead daughter.' The camera pans away from Michelle, showing the trees, the field behind her, with the explanation that the wooden farm building where Abby Morgan died has long since been destroyed. A few more platitudes from the reporter and then the link ends.

Natalie wonders about Rachel's father, conspicuous by his absence in the video. She braves the Wikipedia link, but it yields no explanation as to why Matthew Morgan – his name is now added to her scant knowledge about the family – doesn't appear with his wife and children. No mention of his death or emigration.

Unable to help herself even though she's aware she's indulging in a form of self-flagellation, Natalie clicks on the links to footage from earlier years. Michelle Morgan is always there, along with Rachel and

Shaun; Matthew Morgan never is. Little difference exists between the links; Michelle says much the same things, her anger unabated, and Rachel looks downtrodden and unhappy, her arms folded to ward off the television cameras. Shaun always stands alongside his mother, Natalie notes, with Rachel on the other side of her brother. Never beside Michelle Morgan. Natalie watches, fascinated, as Abby's sister morphs from awkward adolescence through to womanhood, her copper hair long at first, then migrating up around her ears in an unflattering pixie cut before settling into the long straight style of recent years.

She switches her focus to Shaun Morgan, Michelle's oldest child. He's a looker, the gangly teenager of the earlier video links changing into a solid, easy on the eye man. Each year, he stands, rock-like, beside his mother and sister. Like Rachel, he never speaks, allowing Michelle her starring role in her own personal tragic play.

Natalie's seen enough of the Morgan family. She does a fresh search on Joshua Barker, and close to three hundred and fifty thousand results ping back at her. Numerous newspaper articles quoting Michelle Morgan's views on the subject of his release. Another one claims to be an interview with a social worker in regular contact with Joshua Barker during his detention at Vinney Green. The picture she paints doesn't tally in any way with the man Natalie's been dating. For one thing, Mark has never displayed any hint of aggression, which is why his conviction for child murder confuses the hell out of her. Yet here is this woman claiming multiple incidents of violence from Joshua Barker. How he beat up other inmates, frequently trashed his room, how the staff confided in her that they feared him.

'Being with him always sent a chill down my spine,' the woman tells her interviewer, in deliberately theatrical tones. Her clichéd phrasing betrays her secret enjoyment of her fifteen minutes of fame. 'He's already shown what he's capable of. I often thought – what if I ended up being his next victim?'

Natalie's brain imagines an eleven-year-old boy, capable of murder, then morphs him down through the years as he breaks furniture and punches noses in the cinema of her mind. She watches this boy as he terrorises inmates and staff but somehow the movie in her head stops short of fusing the image with Mark Slater. The two simply don't tally up and nothing Natalie does will get them to splice together. The dichotomy confuses her no end. If she's unable to believe Mark Slater emerged from the chrysalis of Joshua Barker, how the hell can she believe him guilty of murdering a two-year-old child?

'I didn't do it, Nat.' His words come back to her, and she remembers how young he was when Abby Morgan died. Is it really beyond her to accept it might have happened the way he says it did? That he was forced into going along with events by the more dominant Adam Campbell?

The answer is yes. She can't, she won't, allow herself the luxury of such a belief, even though part of her remains desperate to do so.

No, she's made the right decision in cutting Mark adrift. Natalie doesn't intend to waste any more of her life on him. *He's a vicious killer*, she reminds herself. *Forget him.* Her resolution sorted, her stomach more settled, she heads for the biscuit tin. As she crams the sweet chocolaty comfort into her mouth, Natalie clamps down hard on the nagging voice inside her brain. The one telling her she's misjudged Mark.

6

INSANITY, OF COURSE

'Women,' Tony Jackson says.

Mark's guts tense.

'Been seeing anyone in particular?'

Mark shakes his head. If Natalie Richards has been off limits before in his conversations with Jackson, he's certainly not going to mention their relationship now she's dumped him.

He shrugs. 'No. Not my style, as you know.'

Jackson gazes at Mark, causing the knot in his belly to tighten, pulling it tauter, the constriction surging upwards to compress his lungs.

'You're aware you need to come clean if you're getting in deep with anyone. We've been over this a thousand times.'

'There's nobody.' Mark's tone is emphatic. Besides, it's true.

Tension squeezes the air between them. Jackson's no fool; three decades in the police force have imbued him with a stellar internal radar for bullshit. Thing is, though, he's screwed if Mark's unwilling to divulge details of who he's been shagging. Besides, other things matter more, such as Mark's ability to hold down a job and keep out of trouble. Tony Jackson shrugs, evidently willing to let it go, and turns back to his notes.

It's the day after Natalie walks out on Mark. The two men are at his flat, where their monthly meetings always take place after Mark finishes work. As usual, Jackson wears civilian clothes to hide his role as Mark's monitoring officer. He's somewhere in his early fifties, carrying too many pints of beer around his middle, and prone to large sweat patches under his armpits. A tad florid and more than slightly bald. Mark likes the man; Tony Jackson has always behaved professionally. Whatever emotions he might have about Abby Morgan's murder are kept shelved. Never once has he fired barbed comments about kiddie killers Mark's way, unlike plenty of other law officers have done. Moreover, he has a granddaughter who's now the same age as Abby Morgan was when she died. Making Jackson's professional detachment all the more remarkable.

An impartiality that will definitely end should Mark reveal not only has he been dating a woman regularly, but also that she's unmasked Joshua Barker. Something of which he's well aware Jackson needs to be appraised. Right here. Right now.

Mark stays silent, however. The meeting, never very long these days, ends; Jackson gets ready to leave, all boxes on his list satisfactorily checked.

'See you next month,' he says. 'Keep your nose clean and your arse out of trouble.'

Later on, after his usual seven-mile run, Mark slides into the hot water of his bath, willing the heat to relax his muscles after the punishing workout. He switches his mind back to Natalie. Impossible to blame her for sneaking into his flat and discovering the letter. Not if he accepts responsibility for his own behaviour. How his reluctance to move their relationship beyond the casual has obviously inflamed every one of her insecurities.

In a way, he's glad the pretence of being Mark Slater, regular guy, is over and she knows the truth. Even if he's been rejected because of it. The constant need for subterfuge where Natalie's concerned has weighed heavily on him. Is it really finished between them, though? Is it so impossible that he can be loved despite having witnessed the murder of Abby Morgan, having seen the rake batter her delicate flesh, the knife slide in between her ribs? Women are, after all, notorious for this kind of thing, maintaining correspondence for years with serial killers in jail, marrying prisoners on Death Row in America, seemingly drawn to the psychopathic side of human nature. Perhaps Natalie will be of the same ilk. Maybe she'll reconsider, once she's had time to get over the initial shock. He realises she yearns for love, for security and permanence; the chance exists she might regret dumping him as her anger recedes.

But then, he reflects, he doesn't want a woman who's with him because he's a convicted child killer but one who'll love him because he's worthy of the emotion, and at that point he abandons his self-pretence. Because he's not lovable, not at all, as his mother has demonstrated so decisively.

Natalie and her penchant for snooping. He sighs. Tony Jackson will go ballistic if he ever finds out Mark didn't inform him immediately of the breach of his identity. One that might unleash vigilante action against him if the public find out one of Abby Morgan's killers is sheltering amongst them. Thugs who like nothing better than an excuse to release their ever-ready aggression are as common as skid marks in a crapper.

Thing is, Mark doesn't believe Natalie will reveal to anyone what she's discovered. Admit she's been dating a convicted child killer? Nope. Not going to happen. Besides, Natalie's from a solid lower middle-class background. Odds are she has no connections to the kind of thug who'd like nothing better than to dispense him a dose of his own medicine.

Anyway, the part of Mark that yearns for stability, routine, shies fiercely away from what admitting the breach will entail. A fresh identity, a new life, the idea of which holds little attraction. Hell, he's taken four years to establish what he has now: a stable job, the respect of his boss and colleagues, his home, shabby and cramped though his flat is. The notion of starting again, with a different workplace, a new controlling officer, holds the same appeal as a shit sandwich for Mark.

No. Better by far to accept he's blown it with Natalie Richards, and pray he's right in his assumption she'll keep quiet about him being Joshua Barker.

He reaches across to let out some of the now tepid water, turning on the hot tap full blast to top it up and adding another slug of lemon bath gel. Once it's replenished, he slides back into the soothing heat, inhaling the sharp citrus scent.

Something's been nagging in his head since he got back to his flat. Now, with the tension starting to drain away, it comes back to him. The date. Today is March 12, which means the fourteenth anniversary of Abby Morgan's murder is a mere nine days away. A fact that's been chewing Mark up in recent weeks, the date always raw and painful for him. What with all the drama yesterday with the letter, it slipped temporarily into his subconscious and has now resurfaced, ugly and mocking, to taunt him. Somehow, with Natalie's rejection still smarting, it seems worse this time around. So many years have passed and yet the horror remains as keen, as fresh, in his mind as ever.

Mark's mind travels back to Abby Morgan's murder. More specifically, March 21, the date when she died. Whilst he's serving his detention, he's unaware of the annual vigil that takes place at the scene of her murder. Then he's released at the age of twenty-one, with a raft of restrictions governing his life and behaviour. When March 21 next rolls around, Mark's antsy all day, his memories making him uncharacteristically restless. He's in his flat after work, the small television in one corner his connection to world events. He turns it on and settles down to watch the news, his mind elsewhere. His hands shovel his pie and chips from the local takeaway into his mouth. Mark's busy savouring the meaty filling, the greasy pastry, the tang of the salt and vinegar. Then his fork stalls and clatters back onto the plate, scattering ketchup and chips across the table.

Abby Morgan's name is the catalyst. On the television, Michelle Morgan spouts forth her tirade against her daughter's killers, and Mark becomes aware for the first time of the annual vigil. Michelle's fiery rhetoric tortures him. Forbidden though it is, Mark's drawn by a desperate need to revisit the small market town on the edge of Dartmoor where Abby Morgan died.

Once the idea takes hold, he finds achieving it straightforward. His meetings with Tony Jackson are currently weekly, due to his recent discharge from prison, but so far Mark's been compliant enough not to arouse any suspicion in the man. He's holding down a steady job, he's not got into any trouble, and the police can't monitor him twenty-four hours a day.

Moretonhampstead is an easy drive from Bristol, motorway most of the journey. Mark's there shortly before lunchtime, having taken a day's leave from work. It's a weekday, with the March weather being chilly and unpredictable, meaning few tourists have chosen to visit. Certainly nobody who'll notice or care about him. He's nervous, though. The obsessive rituals begin the minute he gets out of his car. *One, two, buckle my shoe.* Mark walks through the town, counting all the way, turning his head away as his route takes him past Abby Morgan's house. An unavoidable hurdle; Abby's murder takes place on farmland on the outskirts of Moretonhampstead, and the public right of way he and Adam Campbell use the day she dies lies immediately past her childhood home. *Three, four, knock at the door.* Michelle Morgan might still live there and even though he doubts she'd recognise Joshua Barker in the face of Mark Slater, the notion of encountering the woman is unendurable.

Mark winds his way down the narrow path, up through the field at the bottom, before turning right towards the scene of Abby's death. Disappointment floods him at the sense of nothingness he experiences. He's not sure what he hoped to gain from coming here, but with the farm building demolished, it's just an ordinary field, the trees on its edge simply trees, the hedges commonplace, the grass unremarkable. Silence surrounds Mark apart from the occasional crow squawk; the cold March wind whips up his hair as he surveys the spot where the old wooden building once stood. *Nineteen, twenty, my plate's empty.* No hint of the blood, terror or screams of Abby Morgan lingers in the air and Mark leaves after a mere quarter of an hour.

Throughout the ensuing years, the urge to return never repeats itself. Whatever he's looking for, he won't find it in Moretonhampstead.

Ever since Abby Morgan's death, Mark's been searching for answers. Atonement, to be precise. The word best describing what he's been striving for all this time. Hell, not surprising really. A child died because he was too weak to protect her. Sure, he's already spent ten years in the lock-up, but Michelle Morgan's right. A decade's insufficient punishment for a child's death. Mark has no idea how to achieve atonement, though, despite the familiarity he's gained with the YouTube videos of the vigil. How can he give Michelle the justice she's been denied? Wipe the unhappiness from Rachel's expression? Find out what emotions Shaun experiences behind his impassive façade? Discover why Abby's father is always absent from the vigil?

Now March 21 is a mere nine days away, and Mark acknowledges his urge for atonement will only intensify during the countdown, particularly if he encounters any more incarnations of Abby. He's exhausted by trying to sort his complex emotions into some kind of order; from now on, a different approach seems required.

Mark abruptly realises what's needed.

This year, he'll attend the vigil.

An insane idea, of course. Completely forbidden; he'll be breaking two of his parole rules. He shouldn't even contemplate going to where Abby Morgan died, let alone risk locking eyes with Michelle Morgan. Mark's growing ever more desperate in his quest to secure release from his guilt, though. His usual practice of watching the vigil at home then making a donation to a local children's charity hasn't provided the relief he seeks. A need to delve deeper into the Morgan family tortures him. The insane idea that's grasping him tight has to be worth a shot. Perhaps he'll understand more if he's back in that field in person, hearing Michelle Morgan's wrath first-hand, instead of experiencing the vigil via his television.

It'll be easy enough to attend, like when he visited Moretonhampstead before. He'll either take the day off, or bunk off sick, and memories of Adam and him skipping school, the way they frequently did, wash over him with bittersweet irony. The vigil will start at four o'clock, the time of Abby's death; Mark reckons he can leave straight after lunch and be back by mid-evening. He has the advantage, of course, that nobody will recognise him as the eleven-year-old complicit in the murder. At the time, photographs of the two boys were widely published and their names openly broadcast, hence the need for new identities on their release. The public has no idea, though, of how Joshua Barker has morphed into the adult Mark Slater, swapping the childish features of the boy for the fully-formed ones of the man. He can lock eyes with Michelle Morgan without her ever knowing one of the objects of her tirade is anywhere near her. He'll stand well back from any television cameras, pretend to be an interested onlooker and blend in. As for clothing, he'll wear something nondescript, a jacket with a hood he can pull over his face. Once the vigil starts, he'll do his best to get a grasp of how he's shattered this family's lives and perhaps he'll understand how to atone for his misdeeds. If that's even possible.

Back in the present moment, Mark pulls the plug from his bath, draining out water that's now cold, and then stands up. He has nine days in which to change his mind. He won't, though. Some resolution has to occur, otherwise in ten, fifteen, twenty years' time Michelle Morgan will still be spouting forth how he's not been punished enough. Besides, now he's got the idea, the compulsion is too strong to resist.

Mark dries himself off, pulls on fresh clothes and goes into the kitchenette to make coffee. Decision made. The tension of the day recedes a little, although it returns when Natalie comes to mind. He can't picture a satisfactory conclusion where she's concerned; she'll be happier without him. *Like your mother, I never want to see you again. I'm not surprised she rejected you.* Her words burn like acid.

7

GIVE ME A CALL

Nearly three o'clock on the afternoon of March 21. Mark's sitting in a coffee shop in Moretonhampstead, downing an espresso to calm his nerves; he'll set off towards the scene of the vigil in about half an hour. Plenty of time yet. As usual, he's arrived early, punctuality being another one of his compulsions. He sips the thick brew, savouring its taste, desperate for the caffeine jolt it delivers. The weak March sunshine filters in through the window, highlighting dust motes floating through the air as Mark stares through the glass.

Thankfully, no blonde female toddlers pass by. A man, probably mid-twenties, crosses the road in front of the coffee shop and Mark studies him. Something familiar about the guy, the self-assurance of his gait bordering on a swagger, triggers a distant memory, although Mark can't place where he might have seen him before. Ah, he's got it. The man's confident stride reminds him how Adam Campbell used to strut around as though he owned the world, oozing supreme self-confidence with every step. Mark can do without the reminder on today of all days, thank you very much, and he forces his gaze away, back to his now empty coffee cup, purging the memory of the other boy from his mind. Today is about Abby Morgan, not Adam Campbell.

He leaves the coffee shop and steps out into the pale March sunshine, heading towards the edge of town, not far from the A382. It doesn't take long for him to reach the scene of the vigil; the route is burned onto his memory. To do so necessitates walking past Abby Morgan's house again; Mark averts his gaze and picks up his pace, but it's not enough to stop his heart from squeezing his lungs so he can't breathe. He stops, head down, gasping, at the top of the lane leading to the field where the vigil will take place. As always, Mark takes comfort in numbers, counting slowly upwards in his head, allowing the soothing digits to melt the iron fist constricting his breath. *One, two.* Eventually he's able to carry on, continuing down the lane and across the field to reach the site of the vigil.

It's ten minutes to four now, and from what he can see, very few people are attending this year. Most appear to be general onlookers, along with a press photographer and a television crew. Mark has deliberately dressed down, in nondescript clothing, with a hood over his head; he doesn't think anyone will notice him, though, despite the lack of attendees. Just another curious bystander.

He positions himself behind the camera crew. To his right, the man he spotted from the cafe window is standing near the press photographer, stamping from one leg to the other, seemingly impatient. Like all of them here, they're waiting for the Morgan family to arrive. Mark wonders if Matthew Morgan will attend this year, assuming he's still alive, or whether it'll be the usual trio of Michelle, Shaun and Rachel.

It's a cold March day, despite the sunshine, and Mark shuffles from side to side, hands in his pockets, in an attempt to generate heat. He promises himself a pint and a pub meal on the way back to warm up, regretting not choosing a thicker sweatshirt under his jacket. He doesn't have to wait long, however. After a few minutes, he's aware of more noise, and people talking, and dragging his gaze from the ground, he watches as Michelle, Shaun and Rachel arrive.

It's one hell of a shock for Mark to see them in person, and panic washes over him again. His chest constricts as the familiar counting starts in his head. *Breathe*, he tells himself. *One, two.* Having Abby Morgan's family in front of him is ten times more intimidating than viewing them on screen from the safety of his sofa. He's seen Michelle Morgan in the flesh before, of course; she appears in the courtroom every day of his trial. He remembers the way she stares at Jon Campbell, Adam's father, a gaze some might interpret as accusatory. A challenge to the man whose son killed her daughter, demanding what kind of a parent he thinks he is. Difficult for her to do the same with Joanna Barker, given how his mother attends the trial only when compelled to give evidence.

Mark forces his gaze back to the scenario in front of him. Michelle takes up her usual position behind the microphone, Shaun to her left, with Rachel next to him, nearest to Mark. He uses the opportunity to get a better look at Abby's sister. She's petite, slim, almost doll-like, an image strengthened by her very fair skin and long red hair. Pretty, he thinks, although redheads aren't to his taste. Glancing across to Michelle's coppery hair, he can see from where Rachel's inherited her colouring. She keeps tugging the sleeves of her jacket down, the gesture nervous, slightly panicky. As usual, her expression is tense, unhappy. She's not someone, Mark decides, who anyone would ever look at and pronounce: *she's got a lot of confidence.*

He switches his attention to Shaun Morgan. A tall guy, probably a tad over six feet, athletic in build. He hasn't inherited the family tendency to reddish hair, his being light brown in shade, and cropped short. Probably late twenties. Overall, he appears a more relaxed, confident individual than Rachel. Mark watches as Shaun turns to his sister, putting an arm around her to give her a quick squeeze. She looks up at him, her smile fleeting, before glancing away again.

Something about the dynamics of the Morgan family strikes Mark forcefully, a nuance he's never noticed when watching them on television. Now, here in this field, with the three of them in front of him, he realises they always stand the same way. First Michelle, then Shaun on her left, with Rachel next to him.

Not once has Rachel ever stood next to her mother.

Now he thinks about it, Mark can't remember the two of them even looking at each other, much less speaking.

Michelle Morgan begins her speech. She's piled on weight over the years, Mark thinks, but still squeezes herself into tight clothes; perhaps she's a comfort eater like Natalie. The crow's feet at the sides of her eyes gouge deeply into her face, as do the lines carved between her nose and mouth. Mark catches a glimpse of yellowing teeth. Probably a heavy smoker. Some of her premature ageing will be down to the cigarettes, he reckons, but he wonders with a guilty stab of conscience how much is down to her unresolved anger at him and Adam Campbell.

'We are here today, as we have been every year since her death, to remember and mark the appalling murder of my daughter, Abigail Louise Morgan,' Michelle says, the same as Mark remembers her doing in previous years. He can predict what will come next; her speech never changes much. After all, what can she say that's new?

'Fourteen years ago, my child was lured away from the garden of my house by her murderers, Joshua Barker and Adam Campbell. Two eleven-year-olds, young in years, but both imbued with an evil beyond their age,' she says. 'They took her to this spot and brutally murdered her for their own gratification. A senseless and inexplicable act.' She recites the facts of the murder with steel shot through her expression; it's not just her crow's feet that are deepening, Mark thinks, but her hatred of her daughter's killers as well.

'They knew exactly what they were doing.' Michelle Morgan's voice hardens. Rachel shuffles her feet, and Shaun gives her shoulder another quick squeeze. 'They served just ten years for the death of my daughter. Nothing will convince me that's a fair punishment for what they did. They robbed Abigail of her life and they should have paid with spending the rest of theirs in jail. Imprisonment without hope of parole would have been a fitting retribution, not the leniency with which they have been treated.'

Heads nod in the crowd around Mark, amid mutterings of assent. The effect on him of seeing Michelle Morgan in the flesh is powerful, compelling, and the guilt he's always carried twists within him into agreement. At least where Adam Campbell is concerned. In his own case, he doesn't consider himself able to judge, but he's inclined to think Abby's mother has a point. He's guilty by association and by weakness of character, and both crimes deserve punishment beyond ten years' detention and the loss of his mother.

As Mark shifts his gaze away from Michelle, he spots the man he saw crossing the street earlier, staring at him. Their eyes lock into place for a few seconds, with Mark processing what he sees. The man is much taller than Mark, six feet four at least, stockier too; he's similarly dressed in a dark-coloured jacket with the hood pulled around his face, giving no hint of the colour of his hair. Without warning, the iron hand squeezes Mark's lungs again.

He might have got it wrong, of course, and the man isn't Adam Campbell; it's a big stretch from an eleven-year-old boy to a twenty-five-year-old man. Puberty wreaks havoc on childhood looks, after all. Intuition and the familiar arrogance behind the other man's gaze tell him he's right, though. No need to see his hair to know that it's dark, almost black, although the stubble on the man's face gives that fact away anyway. The knowledge is imparted through the flash of recognition Mark gets, like a jolt from a cattle prod, as the two men study each other.

The other man grins at Mark. A grin saying: *It's been fourteen years.*

Adam Campbell. How the fuck did he not recognise him before? Shit, hot and holy shit. He never thought it would happen, but he's sharing air space with the murderer of Abby Morgan.

In doing so, Mark breaks another of the terms of his release. The last thing on his mind right now, though, is sticking to the letter of the law. He forces his gaze away from the other man, annoyed at himself for breaking eye contact first yet relieved at avoiding the laser beam of Adam's scrutiny. *Breathe*, he reminds himself, determined to regain control over his lungs. Fourteen years haven't changed anything; he's affected by Adam Campbell as strongly today as when he was eleven.

No way can Mark risk walking over to speak to him; he's not sure he's got the balls for that anyway. They'll be overheard, or at the very least noticed, and Mark doesn't dare doing anything to draw attention to either one of them. Something inside him needs to make contact, though, however forbidden and dangerous it is. He's bound to this man for life through what happened. Now they've seen each other again, Mark's desperate to find out what's brought Adam here today, whether it's the same desire to atone, to offer retribution to the Morgan family. Has the leopard changed its spots? Does Adam Campbell still harbour the same dark, aggressive urges, or has time sanded off his rough edges?

Mark doesn't have many options for making contact. Sure, he can wait until after the vigil finishes, strike up a conversation with Adam when fewer people are around, but he's too rattled to deal effectively with a one-on-one meeting. Not yet, anyway, not when he's still jittery from the collective effect of the Morgans. Something more low-key is required. He fishes in the inside pocket of his jacket, finding a pen and the till receipt from the petrol he bought on the way here. After scribbling his mobile number on the back of the receipt, he moves towards Adam, whose attention is now with Michelle Morgan, until he's behind him. In one swift movement, he slips the receipt into Adam's jacket pocket.

His breath coming more easily now, Mark strides back to his original vantage point. From the corner of his eye, he sees Adam withdraw the petrol receipt from his pocket.

Michelle Morgan finishes her speech. Adam nods briefly in Mark's direction, causing a jolt of – what, exactly? Fear, definitely. Possibly anticipation, too. Then Adam moves away from the crowd to head off towards Moretonhampstead. Mark stays where he is, relief flooding him at his nemesis's departure. Michelle Morgan steps back from the microphone. Each year, she lights a candle in memory of her daughter, kneeling in silent contemplation on the spot where her child's bloodied body was discovered. She busies herself with the lighter, shielding it from the March breeze, whilst Shaun holds a small glass lantern ready to house the candle. Rachel stands, hesitant and unsure, behind her mother's turned back. Then she tugs up the zipper on her jacket. With a few words to Shaun, none to Michelle, she peels away, heading towards the town; she won't be joining her mother and brother this year for the candlelit session, it seems.

Around Mark, the sounds of people leaving filter through to him. Time for him to leave too. He follows Rachel, not intentionally, but because his car's parked back in Moretonhampstead. Thank God Adam's had enough of a head start to put him well in front of them; he's nowhere in sight. For someone with short legs, Rachel Morgan walks fast, as though eager to place distance between her and the scene of her sister's murder. Or between her and her mother.

She's now about a hundred yards ahead of Mark. She's so small, he thinks, liking the way her red hair swings in its ponytail as she moves. Swish, swish, from side to side, the only thing about her so far that seems in any way decisive. Unease seeps through Mark as he follows her. The terms of his release hammer through his head; he shouldn't be this near to her, although what's actually forbidden is any contact between them. What they're doing here isn't technically contact, though. It's not as if he has any intention of approaching her or striking up a conversation. She hasn't even seen him but Mark still doesn't think Tony Jackson would take too well to him being so close to Abby Morgan's sister.

Fuck it. He's already way over the line by even being here today. Not to mention slipping his phone number into Adam Campbell's pocket.

Mark keeps Rachel in view whilst questioning the likely result of what he's done. Is Adam going to call or text him? His palms ooze sweat at the thought. Mark prays life has mellowed the other man. He doesn't care to contemplate how Adam will be if juvenile detention followed by prison has hardened rather than softened him. The eleven-year-old version in his memory is scary enough. Mark tells himself if things get hairy, if Adam's as hard a nut as ever, he'll simply get a new mobile number. *Relax*, he reminds himself. *He doesn't know where you live.*

Mark's jolted out of his thoughts by the vibration of his mobile in his inside pocket. The anxiety floods back without warning, his heart racing as he pulls out his phone. An unknown number, but it'll be Adam, of course, making illicit contact, although Mark hasn't the balls to deal with the other man right now. He thrusts the phone back in his pocket, waiting for the call to go to voicemail. Once the ping comes through telling him he's got a message, he retrieves his mobile, pressing it against his ear, his gaze still fixed on Rachel's coppery ponytail.

It's a shock to hear Adam's voice, deepened now into a rich baritone. It's as strong, as commanding, in tone now that it's broken as it ever was in the pubescent boy. Still capable of sending Mark several steps down the pecking order.

'Hi.' A pause. 'Knew it was you as soon as I saw you. Long time no see, mate. Give me a call.' Brief, non-committal, not what Mark has been expecting, although the last four words sound more like an order rather than a request. No tangible aggression, though, nothing sufficient to cause the sweat currently dampening Mark's body. He saves Adam's number into his contacts list. A simple 'A', not Adam, a superstitious worry about their interaction being discovered preventing Mark from entering the full name. Such a measure will be futile if Tony Jackson ever gets wind of all this.

The number safely stored, Mark doesn't fool himself he'll resist the urge to call the other man back. It's a case of when, not if, he contacts Adam, even though Mark's fully aware of the incredible stupidity of his behaviour. Contact with Adam Campbell has always delivered trouble by the truckload to his door, but it's as though they're both eleven again and he's back to being Joshua Barker, helpless to stand his ground against the more dominant boy. He remembers the note of command in Adam's tone: *Give me a call.* Mark will comply, of course. Maybe not today or tomorrow, but eventually.

8

DIRTY LAUNDRY

Rachel's fast pace has pulled her almost out of Mark's sight. They're now back in Moretonhampstead, not far from where he's parked. He speeds up, unsure why it's so important he doesn't lose her. Perhaps, he thinks, it's because Rachel's his last link to the reasons he's here, in a day that's been pretty weird all round. As well as that, part of him is reluctant to reach his car and drive back to Bristol, alone with his guilt for another year until the next vigil.

She stops to peruse a jeweller's display, giving Mark a chance to catch up. He hesitates, pretending to browse the advertising cards in a nearby newsagent's window, all the while watching Rachel Morgan from his peripheral vision. He's unsure what to do, although he's well aware the smartest thing is to walk straight back to his car. The problem is, he's drawn to this petite, red-haired woman, who appears more of a girl, what with her being so fragile-looking; he's not sure why exactly. What might her reaction be, he wonders, if she finds out one of the individuals convicted of killing her sister is a mere twenty yards from her?

She remains absorbed with the jewellery in the shop window, her gaze focused ahead. Mark realises now why he's followed her, why he's considering talking to her. It's because he's returned here today for answers, but the vigil has thrown up more questions than it has resolved. Mark still knows nothing about the elusive Matthew Morgan. Or what lies behind Shaun's deadpan expression. And Rachel intrigues him. Her obvious unease during the vigil, for one thing, more than Mark can attribute to the occasion itself. He senses this elfin girl-woman might supply the answers he needs, if he'll only allow himself to reach out to her.

He makes a deal with himself, his superstitious side taking over. Fate will decide. If she turns her head and sees him before he can count to the number seven, he'll approach her and find something - anything - to say. If she doesn't, Mark will cross the road, go to his car and drive away, towards the pub meal he's promised himself. It's as good a way to choose as any, he thinks. He starts to count, slowly and steadily, in his head.

One.

Her only movement is to tug her sleeves down over her hands, in the same gesture he saw at the vigil. Her gaze remains fixed on the jeweller's window.

Two.

A slight shuffle of her feet, but nothing more. Mark's chest begins its familiar dance with tightness. He breathes in slowly, easing the tension off a little.

Three.

Then she turns her head and it's towards him. For the first time ever, Rachel Morgan's eyes rest on one of the two individuals convicted of her sister's death. They linger no more than a second but it's enough. Mark's been given his sign. He turns away from the newsagent's window and walks towards her, breathing slowly and deeply, completing the count up to seven in his head as he approaches. It'll be the third time this day he's broken the terms of his release; he might as well cram in as many sins as he can.

What the hell, he tells himself. As Adam Campbell would say, it's time for Mark to stop being such a fucking wuss.

'Excuse me; can you tell me where the nearest cash machine is?' It's the first thing Mark can think of. As good as any, he supposes.

She gestures behind him with her arm, swiftly tugging the sleeve of her jacket back into place. 'There's a Lloyds down that street.'

'Thanks.' She's turned her face back to the window and he's desperate to get her attention again. 'I saw you at the vigil just now. I can't imagine how difficult it must be for you and your family.'

As he speaks, the hypocrisy in his words bites at him. Shame floods him for having pestered her in this way; whatever was he thinking? Better to walk away now, leaving her in peace, than continue with this charade. But it's too late. She turns to face him, her expression reeking with hostility.

'Are you from the press?' Her tone is as brusque as her bearing. 'Because if you are, leave me the hell alone. I've nothing to say to you.'

'I'm not a reporter. I don't work for the papers or television.' He pulls open his jacket on both sides. 'See? No camera, no recording device. It's only in films you see them strapped to someone's body, you know.' Hopefully his attempt at humour will reassure her. He inserts his hands in both pockets and brings out nothing except his wallet and car keys. 'Not even a notebook.'

It works. Her body relaxes.

'I'm sorry.' She really is pretty, he thinks, especially with that repentant smile. 'It's just that we get loads of reporters round about this time of year, me and my family, and you wouldn't believe how intrusive they can be. Persistent, too. Usually they target my mum, but

Shaun - that's my brother - and I, we get our fair share of hassle too.'

Her fingers reach out to tug her sleeves down again. Close up, Mark notices her eyes are a pale shade of grape; as for her complexion, he doesn't think he's ever seen skin so fair before. She has the typical redhead's dusting of freckles, a scattering of oatmeal flakes across her nose, and he finds them oddly attractive. The sunshine picks up the sheen on her long, straight hair, highlighting its soft coppery shade, reminding him of his grandmother's stove-top kettle. It's as though she's been washed out, rinsed and wrung dry of any strong colours, although the flash of temper she showed earlier warns him her character may not be as pale as her exterior.

'I'm sorry if you thought I was hassling you. I really do need to get cash, and what with having seen you and your family at the vigil...' He shrugs, giving her a small smile. 'It seemed rude not to mention it, extend my sympathies, that kind of thing.'

She returns the smile, even white teeth winking at him behind her lip-gloss. 'Thank you. How come you were at the vigil? I don't recognise you.'

'I'm down from Bristol on a day trip. Took some time off work, decided I'd head out this way, check out the town. Doesn't take long to get here, once you're on the motorway.' Her eye contact with him is steady; he gets the impression she's buying his cover story, thank God. 'I was walking back there when people started arriving and setting up television cameras.'

'You must have wondered what on earth was going on.'

'Yes, especially when more people turned up. I asked one of the TV crew what was happening and he told me about the little girl who died, your sister, and the way your family remembers her each year.' Disgust at his deceptive words smacks Mark in the face but he's gone too far to stop now. Even though the next sentence is particularly repugnant. 'I thought I should stay and pay my respects.'

Her reply twists a knife in his gut. 'That was a kind thing to do. Thank you.'

Time to steer the conversation into safer waters. He's come here today with questions and here's Rachel Morgan standing in front of him, a gift horse, and he's going to take full advantage, however manipulative his behaviour might be. 'Do you live locally?'

She nods. 'Yes. Well, not far. My flat's in Exeter. Shaun, he lives there too, not with me, but close enough. Mum - ' She shrugs, her expression shuttering. 'She's never left our old family home. The one Abby was snatched from, here in Moretonhampstead. We passed it a while back.'

Mark senses he's been right about Rachel and Michelle Morgan, about what shouts at him during the vigil from their body language. Mother and daughter don't rub along together too well and he wonders what that stems from. He's surprised, reasoning that the loss of one daughter should have rendered the other doubly precious to Michelle Morgan, but it obviously hasn't worked that way. Strange, he thinks, how the woman's mothering seems focused on the dead rather than the living.

'She's never been able to bring herself to leave. She visits the spot where it happened every day.' Sadness creeps into Rachel's voice.

Christ, Mark thinks. Only a matter of luck and timing probably prevented him from meeting Michelle Morgan when he visited Moretonhampstead before.

'What about -' *Breathe,* he reminds himself. 'What about your father?'

'My dad?' The sadness extends into Rachel's expression. 'He's down in Taunton now. He didn't deal well with what happened, you see.'

'He had a breakdown?'

'Not exactly.' She tugs at her sleeves again.

Mark's unsure how hard or how far to push this. 'I'm sorry. I shouldn't be prying.'

She shrugs. 'It's OK. Not your fault I come from a dysfunctional family.'

Oh, the irony. Joanna Barker pushes her way into Mark's mind. 'Aren't most families a bit screwed-up?'

'Yeah, I guess.'

'You don't see much of your dad?'

'No. Booze is all he cares about these days.'

'He's an alcoholic?'

'Pretty much a full-blown one. He's always been a drinker, but it escalated after Abby was murdered.' She sighs. 'Like I said, he's in Taunton now. I go now and again with Shaun to visit. Years ago, Dad frequently swore he was going to get sober but it never happened. Nowadays, he's usually so drunk neither of us can talk to him and when we do, he denies having a problem. Like all alcoholics, I suppose.'

'I'm sorry.' Such utterly inadequate words. 'When did all that happen?'

'Mum kicked him out a couple of years after Abby was murdered.'

'How old were you?'

'Ten when she died, twelve when he left.'

'His drinking got worse after your sister's death, you said?'

'Yes. Mum and Dad had endless rows about it and eventually she packed his bags, threw them on the doorstep and changed the locks. He wouldn't stop yelling outside the house, calling her every vile name you could think of.' She sounds ashamed at washing such filthy family laundry in public. 'In the end, she phoned the police. I didn't see him for several years afterwards.'

No wonder she seems so fragile, this washed-out waif of a woman whose ten-year-old self, still damaged from the loss of her sister, peeks out from her expression. He should leave, he realises, get back to his car so Rachel can be free of him.

She tugs at her sleeves again. Mark senses she's withdrawing from him, probably embarrassed. She smiles. 'Listen to me, rambling on about my weird family. I'll walk with you to the cash machine. It's on the way to my car anyway.' She gestures across the road, and Mark realises they must have chosen the same car park. So the opportunity to walk away is thwarted, at least for now. They head towards the cashpoint.

As he takes out the money, Rachel stands beside him, seemingly unwilling to say a polite goodbye. A shred of suspicion grows in Mark about whether she fancies him. He's not long on confidence when it comes to women, but he's always found it easy enough in the past, during his years of casual fucks, to get laid. If Rachel thinks he's game for any of that, though, she's very much mistaken. Out of the question, given who she is. Besides, milk and apricot redheads have never appealed to him; neither do slim women. He prefers girls to have plenty of meat on their bones, favouring Natalie's plump curves over Rachel's doll-like body, her conker-coloured hair over Rachel's shade of copper. Besides not being attracted to Rachel, getting involved with her would be insanity, a relationship without a future. Worse than that, an abomination. It's bad enough he's even talking with her, but fucking her? Bedding the older sister of the girl for whose death he's partially responsible? Unthinkable, a body blow this fragile and damaged woman doesn't need. He'll not have a shred of self-respect left if he fucks her.

Not going to happen, he tells himself.

'What's your name?' she asks. 'You already know mine, I presume.'

'Mark. Mark Slater.' Like his lies, his new name peels easily off his tongue. He takes out his wallet, inserting the notes inside.

They turn and head towards the car park. She finds her keys, pressing off the central locking on her car, and the lights flash on a red Fiat Punto near to his Peugeot. Mark notices the sticker for City of Exeter Hash House Harriers in the Fiat's rear window.

'You run?' he asks.

'Every Sunday. Never miss a week, not if I can help it. Started when I moved to Exeter, didn't really know anyone, wanted to get out more. So I joined the Hashers. Now I'm hooked.' She laughs. 'Do you run as well?'

Mark nods. 'Most nights I go to the local park, do seven miles. It helps me chill out.' He's a little dismayed he asked her; finding things they have in common isn't going to help if he's right and she's reading something flirtatious into their conversation.

She pulls a face. 'Wow, seven miles every night? I'm humbled. I thought I was doing well, what with five miles every Sunday.'

'What can I say? Guess I need a lot of chilling out time.'

She laughs. 'Any fun runs, that sort of thing?'

'Whenever they come around. Mostly for children's charities.'

'Me too. Usually the N.S.P.C.C. What with losing Abby the way we did.'

'Makes sense.'

'Got a five-kilometre fun run coming up in a few weeks,' she mentions. Too casually, revealing the buried hint. Mark warns himself: care is needed here. The last thing he wants is for her to suffer more hurt, or, God forbid, discover his former identity. Then she's asking if he's interested in entering, and his need to get answers from her spurs him on, and the words *yes, why not* fall from his mouth. A huge smile brightens her face as she rattles on about how the entry deadline is looming, where the run will be taking place, which pub they'll be going to afterwards. Mark grows increasingly uncomfortable. He's using her for his own ends, and he hates himself for it.

Thing is, though, he wants to be normal, to be able to see little girls in the street without panicking, for the endless repetitions of *One, Two, Buckle My Shoe* to fade from his life. Many would say that after what he and Adam did, he doesn't have a right to wish for those things, and if Michelle Morgan had her way he wouldn't even have the freedom to piss in peace, but he's driven to crave them anyway. Rachel might be the key. The result? He'll see where this leads him, being mindful to keep her at arm's length, and to break it off between them as soon as possible, so she doesn't get hurt.

'What's the best way of staying in touch? You on Facebook?' she asks. Mark isn't, not having any friends other than Natalie, so he's never joined. She encourages him to check it out, saying something about how a Facebook page has been set up for the run.

'Look me up on there and add me in as a friend. My avatar's one of my old dolls from when I was a child. You'll find me easily enough. Listen, I must get back.' She tugs open the driver's door of the Fiat. Her expression turns shy, girlish. 'It was good talking to you, Mark. Sorry about before. I really did think you were some lowlife of a reporter.'

'Not a problem.'

'See you on Facebook,' she says.

Mark draws out his car keys, the comfort of steak and chips and a pint in a warm pub luring him on now it's clear their encounter is over. He watches her pull away.

Insane, stupid, ridiculous, one side of his mind tells the other.

An opportunity not to be missed, is the reply.

His mobile vibrates in his inside pocket, startling him. Shit. Adam Campbell again; it has to be. Mark decides to forget his previous crap about needing to find out why the other man was at the vigil. Screw that. He'll erase the messages from his phone the minute he gets back to Bristol. Today has been a mad, mad day; he doesn't intend to make it worse by contacting Adam Campbell. He'll delete his number and get on with his life.

Later on, mid-evening, Mark's back at his flat. He's about to make himself a coffee when his mobile rings again. The letter A pops up as the caller. Fuck. Adam Campbell. Looks like he's dead set on re-establishing contact. For Mark, it's weird knowing Adam is on the other end, trying to access him, as though he's stretching out to exert control over him again. Mark lets the call go to voicemail, unsure why he's not yet deleted Adam's number, telling himself it's because his mind's been tangled up with Rachel. Nothing to do with the fact he's still wondering whether Adam attended the vigil for the same reason he did. Time for coffee. Then he'll check out what Adam has to say.

Mug in hand, he listens to the voicemail message Adam's left for him.

'Not heard from you yet, mate. Give me a call. Be good to catch up after so long.' Nothing intimidating, nothing overtly pressurised. None of the terrifying aggression of fourteen years ago. Mark relaxes a little. Maybe he'll call Adam back in a day or so; any shit from the guy and he'll get a new mobile. He taps in a brief text.

'Got your message. Been busy. Will be in contact.' He presses send, breathing out a sigh of relief. Adam Campbell has been dealt with, at least for now.

Meanwhile, he needs to concentrate on Rachel and the issue of the fun run. *Not a good idea*, is the message being sent, loud and clear, from his subconscious. She might expect him to go and train with her, despite the event only being five kilometres in length. He'll need to give the situation more thought. On with his running shoes. A fast seven-miler will give him the answers, allow him to suss out what to do over the thorny question of staying in touch with Rachel Morgan.

Returning to his flat an hour later, sweaty and panting, he has the solution. He'll meet Rachel again, just the once, probably for lunch. It's risky, but he promises himself it'll be a one-off. He figures this way they can chat, and if he doesn't get the answers he wants, he'll stop using her so shamelessly. One more meeting, easy enough to do; he can be there and back without anyone, including Tony Jackson, realising he's gone. He reflects on how he'll be lunching with Abby Morgan's sister and how that's wrong on all kinds of levels, but he's driven by his need for answers. He'll run it by her when he joins Facebook.

Sorted, he tells himself.

9

FRIGGING FAT BITCH

Midnight. Nearly two weeks after breaking up with Mark, Natalie's in bed, unable to sleep. The nagging voice in her head, telling her she's been too hasty in dumping him, won't ease up on her. Not unusual, this; post-split doubts always plague her as to whether she's done the right thing. Each time, she tortures herself with not having given the ex in question one more chance. Convinces herself that, if she tries hard enough, he'll come good in the end. Ah, the redemptive power of love; a seductive idea for Natalie, despite the contradictory evidence offered by her parents' now defunct relationship.

Natalie's body as well as her mind is missing Mark. Her revulsion at the thought of his hands touching her is ebbing away. She's not had many men pass through her bed and so far, Mark's been the only one to hit her sweet spot, so to speak. Before him, sex holds little appeal for Natalie. She's on the large side, with plenty of hang-ups about her wobbly thighs, her jelly belly, her stretch-marked breasts. Inhibitions that haven't exactly turned her into a confident sexual partner. Revealing her body doesn't come easily. Nor does letting a man explore it. To compensate, she often projects a false confidence by taking the lead in bed, but it's more through shyness than sexual prowess, despite the apparent contradiction. When she's giving a man pleasure, he's focused on his body, not hers. So what if she's often left high and dry orgasm-wise? Better than enduring critical eyes comparing her body to slimmer, prettier, fitter women. She waits until her partner's asleep and then her hands slip south to bring herself off. Natalie's mastered the art of the silent orgasm, enjoying her release as the man of the moment snores beside her.

None of that crap applies to Mark. From the start, he refuses to allow her to turn off the lights, insisting on undressing her, apparently savouring all the parts of her body she loathes.

'Always loved women with curves.' His words caress her every bit as much as his hands and more often than not when they make love, she sees herself as he does. Every time they're in bed, Mark tells her she's sexy, desirable, beautiful. He strokes her as if it's a privilege; he closes his eyes as his tongue slides over her skin, her flesh a ripe peach for him to savour.

Their sex life isn't without issues, however. Natalie's hang-ups run too deep for her to accept unquestioningly Mark's appreciation of her body. For her, something more sinister than loathing of her flaws has drained her sexual confidence.

A familiar voice sounds in her head.

'Frigging fat bitch.'

Words Natalie would give pretty much anything she owns to scrub from her brain, but nothing will ever erase a scar burned so deeply into her psyche. Before she first sleeps with Mark, she consoles herself by remembering her shame's a private thing, known only to her. She prays her secret humiliation won't intrude into their sex life, but with hindsight, she realises she's been naïve in that respect.

She casts her mind back to when she's in bed with Mark for the first time. They've just made love, and since then the afterglow has pretty much reduced them to a comfortable stupor. Natalie's curled against Mark's chest, boneless with relaxation, savouring her surprise at how good her new boyfriend is at sex. At last, a man who arouses her brain before her body, a stark contrast to all who have gone, and come, previously in her bed. No worries about stretch marks or wobbly bits; Natalie's now viewing herself through Mark's eyes. For once, she's a beautiful, sexy woman, with a ripe, fleshy, luxuriant body.

Her illusion lasts until Mark attempts to initiate sex for a second time. Lust steals over his face as he gazes down at her. She's not thinking about the voice in her head, biding its time before snaking out to ruin what they're creating between them. All she's conscious of is how her desire rises to match his, how she needs them to fuck again, now, quickly, urgently. His hands slide over her. Before she realises what he's doing, he turns her onto her stomach. Then he presses against her buttocks, seeking to enter her from behind. Her sexual hunger deflates like a prick in an ice bucket.

To be replaced by the voice in her head.

'Frigging fat bitch.'

Along with the memory of other hands, another body. The pain of those words cuts deep, despite the fact it's been so many years since they first carved their way into her.

Mark's unaware of all this, of course. She's never told anyone, not ever.

Natalie twists round, pushing him away with all the force she's able to muster. Shock registers in Mark's expression on seeing the rejection in her face, the way her mouth is set as tight as a clam.

'What's wrong, Nat?' She clocks the mixture of hurt and surprise in his tone but she's too intent on shoving the memory down deep, where it can't soil the moment anymore. She shakes her head, unable to speak.

'I didn't mean...' Mark's clearly unsure how he's managed to fuck things up. 'Doggy-style's not to everyone's taste, I suppose. Or did you think I wanted...' He gropes for the right words, ones to placate rather than provoke. 'Well, you know.' His face flushes a faint pink. 'Anal sex. Wasn't going for that, I swear, Nat. Not that I don't enjoy it, because I do. Hell, listen to me rambling.'

Natalie can practically smell his embarrassment.

'Didn't think that,' she manages to say.

'Just thought it would be fun to do it from behind.'

She doesn't reply. The voice in her head taunts her again.

'Some women think doggy-style's degrading, of course. Didn't mean to upset you, Natalie.' He strokes her face warily, gauging her expression. 'You don't enjoy doing it that way?'

'Never done it.' Revulsion at the idea bites at her.

'Then how...'

'For fuck's sake, drop it, will you?' Shock floods his face. Natalie rarely swears and Mark's never heard even a mild profanity from her before. Contrition washes over her. Hell, not long ago her orgasm was wrenching gasps from her throat and sweat from her body, and now she's all snappy and moody. All because of the voice in her head, and Mark deserves better. She reaches out to pull him close, hugging the apology for which she lacks the words.

'Someone's hurt you,' he says.

Natalie stays silent, forcing back the vile memory, trying to drag the hot tears away from the backs of her eyelids. Without success. A wet trickle works its way down her cheek. Maybe Mark will attribute her outburst to some crazy premenstrual dip in her happy hormones if she doesn't reply. Safety lies in silence, so they say.

'You can tell me, you know.' His lips nuzzle her hair.

She squirms uncomfortably, unsure how to handle the unfamiliar male concern. Natalie's more used to being ignored than comforted by the men in her life. She doesn't respond and Mark gets the message, simply holding her.

The next time they're in bed, though, Natalie senses a barrier between them. Mark seems hesitant, unsure, as though expecting her to push him away again. The sex is clumsy and unsatisfying, a sad sequel to the hot hunger they shared during their first fuck. Natalie panics. Mark's kind and caring, if a little reserved; besides which, he's a looker. A guy to hang onto. She doesn't want to screw this relationship up and if she's not careful, he'll think she's both a moody mare and a lousy lay.

'Frigging fat bitch.' In her head, rough hands push her to the ground. Hot breath fans her ear. The odour of stale cigarette smoke assaults her nostrils.

Natalie's always forced the memory down deep, burying it under layers of denial. It erupts out of her now like steam from a pressure cooker, hot and searing.

She clings to Mark, hiding her face against the mat of hair on his chest.

'You were right,' she says.

He's quick; she'll give him that. Once the hot wetness of her tears soaks into his skin, he grasps her meaning immediately. His arms tighten around her.

'Somebody's hurt you,' he says.

She nods.

Against her cheek, Mark's chest stops, mid-inhalation. He breathes out, slowly, rhythmically, before answering. 'You were raped?'

'No.' She shakes her head in emphasis. 'Thank God, not that. But...'

'Tell me.' His arms squeeze her body again. Soothingly, reassuringly. He rocks her back and forth as she sobs against his chest. His mouth touches her hair and to Natalie's amazement, the memory of hot, mocking breath against her ear recedes.

Mark's silent, allowing her the space she needs, waiting for her to cry out all the tears. Natalie's surprised at herself. She's known this man only a few weeks, and yet she's about to expose the scar on her soul she's never even let her mother glimpse. Mark's different, though. Her intuition's already twigged he's damaged goods, despite the fact he's never divulged any details. Odds are he'll grasp how badly she's also been hurt. If he's as fucked up as she is, his understanding is a certainty, not a hope.

'He pushed me to the ground, you see. From behind.'

'You didn't know him?'

'No. I never saw his face. I remember he smelled...' She wrinkles her nose. 'Bad.'

'You never told anyone?'

'No.'

'Not even your mum?'

'No.'

'How old were you, Nat?'

'Eleven.'

'Christ.' Anger infuses his voice, along with something she can't quite identify. It's as though her words have confirmed something he's already guessed and she wonders whether she carries with her a whiff of low self-esteem, a scent he's picked up.

'Guess it's not the sort of thing a young girl tells her father, either,' Mark says. 'Your parents weren't divorced then, were they?'

'No.'

'So you bottled it all up. What happened, Nat?'

Natalie tenses, her fingers pleating the duvet cover. When she speaks, her voice is thin, fragile, in danger of breaking. 'He shoved me onto my stomach. Got on top of me, held me down. Can't really talk about the details.' She sniffs.

'You don't have to.'

'He hurt me, though. That's why...' She snorts snot back up her nose, forcing the tears into retreat. 'Why I can't do it that way. Doggy-style, I mean. Face down.'

'Brings it all back to you.' His hand glides over her hair.

'It shouldn't have happened.'

'Damn right it shouldn't.'

'No, you don't understand. It was my fault.'

Mark pulls back to catch her eyes briefly, before her shame forces her to clamp her eyelids tight, shutting out his incredulous expression. 'How the hell were you to blame, Nat?'

'I should have fought back. Struggled, pushed him off. But I didn't.'

'He was stronger than you. Bigger. Nothing you could have done.' Mark's words are flat; it's as though he's giving a running commentary on a scene he's witnessing in his head. His empathy is comforting, although Natalie needs him to understand the guilt she's always carried.

'I don't understand why I didn't even try,' she says. 'I just let him do it. I knew I should put up a fight, but I didn't. He scared me too badly, you see. That's why I've always felt so ashamed.'

'Because you believe you could have done something to stop it, but you didn't. So you feel guilty for not acting.'

Jeez, how does he *know*?

'Yes,' she replies.

Mark's arms squeeze around her again. 'Believe me, I understand exactly how that feels,' he says. Somehow, although she doesn't ask how, she's aware he really does get it, right through every cell in him. Her pain is his pain, her terror his terror.

'You want to know what my worst fear is?' she asks.

'Tell me.'

'Him finding me again one day.' She shudders. 'I know it's illogical. He never saw my face; there's zero chance he'd ever recognise me again. But I can't help it. I think about him, still being here in Bristol, having got worse, more aggressive, in the meantime. Scares the shit out of me.'

'I get that.'

'He's always with me. In my head, I mean. If anyone male comes up behind me in the street, I panic. I'm terrified it's him.'

Mark kisses her hair again.

'I should have told someone. But I didn't.'

'You were eleven years old. Kids of that age don't always do what they should.' His arms slacken their grip as he pulls away. As though his words have triggered a memory for him. 'Don't beat yourself up over it, Nat.'

'Can't help it.' Natalie's unconvinced. She should have done something. Anything.

'Want to talk some more about it?'

She shakes her head.

'That's OK,' Mark says, and they slip into silence, words no longer necessary. She's incapable of telling him more anyway. Safe beside him, her mind retreats through the years, until she's eleven years old again, transported back to the park near her childhood home in Bristol.

She's taken this route so many times before, down the slope under the trees, prior to walking up the other side towards where she lives. On this day, a Saturday, she's been to the shops to buy chocolate and is heading back for lunch. Eventually, but not yet. The rows between her parents have been escalating in recent months, and a bar of Dairy Milk provides Natalie with a welcome form of self-medication. She's been resorting to its sweet comfort more and more, along with sneaking biscuits from the kitchen into her bedroom to soothe herself when the raised voices downstairs grow unbearable. Here, alone with her thoughts in the park, she's safe, insulated from the nagging worry that her father will leave them. His vice, Natalie's gleaned from what she's overheard, is younger women. Aged eleven, she's already sceptical about the male capacity for fidelity.

A small copse lies ahead on the left of the park, where the trees are thick and it's dark and secluded. Natalie's often detoured through it, loving the way the branches swallow her up, shielding her from anyone on the main path. It's overgrown, and hard to penetrate, but a tiny clearing hides in the middle. A place to which Natalie frequently retreats with her sweet pleasures to shut out the rest of the world, leaning against a tree as she eats. Her bag slung over her shoulder, she's headed there now, anticipating the satisfying crack of the chocolate snapping under her teeth, the first gratifying release of its sugary delights.

Absorbed in her thoughts, she never hears her attacker approaching from behind.

An arm presses against her windpipe, cutting off her air, pulling her head backwards. She catches a whiff of stale breath as the arm hoists her upwards, so that her toes are the only part of her still in contact with the path.

That's when he says the words.

'Frigging fat bitch, ain't you? Been stuffing too many pies into yourself.' His contempt sears shame through her. She's incapable of any response, her throat crushed by the force of his arm, although an inarticulate moan escapes her. She's pushed forward, into the copse, shoved through the brambles and undergrowth, the thorns snagging her jacket, gouging scratches into any exposed flesh they encounter.

They reach the clearing, his arm still tight against her neck. Then she's forced to the ground, her right cheek slamming down against the earth, the peaty smell of which fills her nostrils. Her bag crashes off her shoulder, scattering its contents. No noise, not anywhere; it's as though only two people in the world exist, her and him. He's on top of her now, his weight oppressive as he pins her down into the dirt, his breath hot against her left ear.

'You're going to let me do what I want.' Total self-assurance in his words.

She nods, her head bobbing up and down as far as her restricted position allows. Surrender is her only option. He's too big, too heavy, too terrifying, for anything else.

'I'll hurt you, bitch. If you scream or do anything stupid.'

He will, too. Something about him, his tone, his strength, his words, are beyond menacing. She's rendered mute, passive, incapable of any response other than submitting to whatever foul thing he wants. She prays it's not *that*.

It's not, thank God, although what he does do is vile. Painful, invasive. He holds her with his left arm, whilst his right goes exploring. Her body bucks as his hand rakes underneath her, popping the button on her jeans, dragging them over her arse cheeks. Her panties get pulled down along with the jeans, leaving her buttocks exposed to the cold December air. His thighs press hard against hers, his chest against her spine, as he slides his hand around her right hip. Pain stabs through her as his fingers force their way inside, invading her, violating her, but he's anticipated this, and his left hand has already moved to seal her mouth. Her strangled moans find no way to escape. His fingers continue to twist and probe, stretching her, and a sudden wetness, warm and sticky, seeps onto her thighs. Later on, as she disposes of her stained knickers where her mother will never find them, she discovers it's blood.

He gets off on her fear, she realises. What excites him is not so much having his fingers inside her but the invasion they represent. Total control over her is the aim of the game. If she gives it to him, maybe he'll keep his promise and not hurt her even worse.

So Natalie lies there, crushed to the ground as her assailant takes his time, revelling in her discomfort, her submission, her helplessness. An odour enters her nose, acrid and foul, and shifting her head, she sees the half-dried dog turd a foot or so away. The pain in her lower body meshes with the shit in front of her and Natalie swears to herself she'll never reveal the horror of today to anyone, not ever.

She's not sure how much time passes, but eventually he gets bored with the game and pulls out his fingers, wiping them on the grass nearby. His chest peels away from her spine, his thighs shifting to straddle her. Natalie doesn't move, not a muscle, not an inch. She's aware of him stretching to pick something up. The crackle of packaging against his fingers reaches her; then she hears cloth rustle as he puts her Dairy Milk in his pocket.

'I'll take this,' he says. 'You shouldn't be eating chocolate. Not a porker like you.' His laugh is mocking as he eases his weight off her. Still she doesn't dare move or look round. Then the sounds of him striding through the brambles to the main path float back to her.

Natalie's grateful for the seclusion the copse offers, unaware of how long passes before the ability to peel herself off the ground comes to her. She's sore, and bleeding, and pain stabs her between the legs as she stands up, shaky and uncertain. She grabs her bag, shoving the scattered contents in hastily, before pushing her way blindly back to the main path.

Her mother shouts at her for being late for lunch, but Natalie barges past her, pleading sickness, desperate for the sanctuary of her bedroom. Later on, when Callie goes out, she raids the biscuit tin, stuffing chocolate chip comfort into her mouth to dull the pain saturating her body and her mind. So what if she doesn't need the extra calories? Food's become Natalie's solace, even if she is, as her assailant puts it, a porker and a frigging fat bitch. Heat floods her face as she recalls his words.

Within a month, her father walks out on her mother for good, his dick lured away by a twenty-year-old aerobics instructor. A week later, Natalie's beset by the onset of her first menstrual cramps, for which she seeks relief in extra chips and chocolate. Her body thickens and expands even more, her fat layers protection against the male of the species.

Once she moves into her middle teens, however, Natalie's sex drive rears its head. She's straight, so she has either to get to grips with fucking men or resign herself to perpetual virginity. Natalie chooses the former. Sex doesn't come easily to her, though. She can manage being astride a guy or having him on top, but getting fucked from behind – no way. Her first boyfriend tries it and as soon as Natalie's chest presses into the bed with his body against her, panic rises in her and she bucks upwards and backwards, pushing him off her. Gradually she eases into her routine of taking the initiative in bed, concentrating on pleasing her man, relegating her own pleasure to the side-lines, ensuring she's too busy with her mouth and fingers for them to contemplate fucking her doggy-style.

Shit. She's one screwed-up bitch, that's for sure.

'You've ended up afraid of men. Not just him, but all of us,' Mark says, his words bringing her back to the present.

'Yes.'

'I won't hurt you, Nat.' He pulls his head back, tilting up her chin so their eyes engage. 'You know that, don't you?'

10

HIS SIDEKICK

The call from Adam Campbell thrusts Mark's mind back through the years as he tries to sleep later on that night. He's Joshua Barker again, aged eleven. His first day at secondary school, Exeter Grammar, and he knows nobody, not really. His former classmates have either moved away, gone to different schools or else he never interacted much with them anyway. He spots a couple of them in the queue at the lunch counter, envying the ease with which they seem to be integrating into this unfamiliar social fabric. He finds it hard, anxiety oozing from him whenever he attempts to initiate contact, his awkwardness stemming from his mother's dislike of him having friends. Starting secondary school initially seems like a way to break through his social deprivation, but now, standing alone in the dining hall, not daring to join any of the tables, he's not so sure it'll work. The other boys ebb and flow around him, carrying trays, their apparent self-assurance mocking his own uncertainty. Various smells assault his nostrils: frying chips bubbling in oil, pastry warming in the serving dishes, orange Fanta. His isolation becomes unbearable and he escapes to the sanctuary of the toilets, locking himself in a cubicle, where he wills himself to get a grip on his spiralling emotions. If only Dad were still alive, he thinks.

Joshua's been grieving for his father for two

years now; he misses the man who played football with him, listened to him, spent time with him. His mother has long ago made it clear her dead husband isn't a topic for conversation. She provides her son's meals and pays his school fees but little else. Joshua's starving emotionally; his visits to his maternal grandparents are rare and the affection he gets from them isn't enough to plug the hole in his psyche. So he sits in his smelly toilet cubicle, willing the tears back from his eyes, stern reprimands to himself echoing in his brain. *Get a grip. You shouldn't be crying, not at your age. Grow up, for God's sake.*

It's partially successful, because when Joshua unlatches the door and walks out to wash his hands his eyes are only slightly reddened. The toilet block is silent, empty apart from him, a whiff of drains joining the usual piss and shit odours. Joshua rests his forearms on the rim of the sink, grabbing an extra shred of respite before returning to the dining hall.

Then Adam Campbell strides through the door.

A pivotal moment in both their lives.

Adam commands Joshua's attention. Impossible to ignore him. The boy is taller than the rest of Joshua's peers, puberty beckoning him already; his neck is thick, his shoulders chunky. The rest of his body is equally hefty, sending out unmistakable overtones of *don't mess with me*. All swagger and attitude. Dark hair, unwashed, flops over his eyes. As he checks out Joshua's pink-rimmed ones, a grin quirks his mouth.

Something about the other boy's piercing perusal roots Joshua to where he's standing. Without being able to voice it in words, on some deep subconscious level he acknowledges the other boy as far higher up the pecking order than he is, along with the fact Adam will lead the way in whatever future relationship they forge. Later on, he thinks the other boy also recognises Joshua's lower rung on the dominance ladder, zeroing in on him as posing no challenge. Adam singles him out as someone he can control, because Joshua's inherently weak, unable to stand up for himself. Back then, they fulfil a need in each other, slotting together for all the wrong reasons, the sum being greater than the parts. Between them, they create the monster responsible for a child's death.

At the time, though, Joshua needs someone to take him in hand. Right then, Adam Campbell seems the best thing to happen to him in a long while.

They don't say anything to each other, not at first. Joshua finishes drying his hands. Adam pisses noisily into a urinal. Then he speaks.

'Usually hang around in the park after last period,' he says. 'You can join me. Meet me by the gates when we finish.' Then he's gone. Joshua realises he doesn't even know the other boy's name.

He learns the only reason they've not encountered each other before is Adam's decision to skip morning classes. In the afternoon maths period, Joshua's keenly aware of Adam sitting a few desks in front of him. His body sprawls out of his seat, his thick legs spread wide, claiming his territory. He makes occasional wise-arse comments to the boy beside him. Joshua experiences a sudden rush of jealousy; he wants to be seated next to the mouthy Adam, who seems to have the world around him sussed out pretty well. It's a good thing, he thinks, the maths teacher is six feet four and built like a rugby player, because Adam Campbell appears to recognise he's met his match, not daring to cheek the man. Joshua subsequently witnesses in other classes what Adam will do to the teachers if he senses even a hint of weakness, and it's not pretty.

He goes to meet him after school and they mooch through the local park. Adam pulls a pack of cigarettes from his bag, offering one to Joshua, laughing when he refuses.

'What a wuss,' he jeers. Joshua flushes, embarrassed by his lack of savoir-faire.

'Take it,' Adam commands, thrusting the cigarette his way. Joshua is helpless, unable to decline, as refusal will make him seem even weaker. Besides, he's known Adam Campbell less than a day, but he's keenly aware he's not a boy to say no to. He takes the cigarette, unsure what to do, resulting in more contempt.

'Here. Put it in your mouth; drag on it whilst I light it. Jeez, what a nerd. Been smoking myself since I turned ten and nicked one of my dad's Marlboros.'

Joshua obeys, the first burning hit of smoke smacking the back of his throat, causing him to splutter, tears spilling from his eyes. The cigarette tastes foul. He tries again, without success, and Adam snatches it from him.

'Give it here. Don't want to waste a good ciggie.' He inhales deeply, no coughing, no spluttering, clearly an old hand at the game. 'We'll bunk off tomorrow, go down town, have a laugh.'

Again, certainty that Joshua will comply is inherent in Adam's tone.

The following afternoon, they wander through Exeter's Princesshay shopping centre, Joshua tailing Adam; it's late enough that they can tell anyone who challenges them they have a free period. Nobody does, though. The other boy oozes intimidation, even towards adults. Joshua's a little alarmed when Adam snatches a cigarette lighter from one of the small carts trading in the precinct, but doesn't say anything. Like the smoking, it's clearly something else at which Adam's well practised. Joshua's always been one to stick by the rules and to see them broken so blatantly holds a certain fascination.

During the first few weeks of their relationship,

Joshua's subjected to more of the same: contempt, cigarettes in the park, a few items stolen whenever Adam spots his chance. Underpinning it all is always the unspoken rule that Joshua will do whatever Adam dictates, without question. At first, though, everything's fine. He's content in his position lower down the pecking order, never noticing how the other boys avoid him now they've sussed he's Adam's sidekick. For Joshua, it's enough to have a mate to hang around with, someone different, someone daring and challenging, possessing all the fire and spunk he doesn't.

It stops being exciting a few weeks into their friendship, when Joshua challenges Adam for the first time. He's growing increasingly uneasy about the bunking off and the petty theft, concerned they'll get caught at one or the other before long. His mother's reaction if that happens won't be pretty.

'Aren't you worried someone will see you?' he asks one day after Adam lifts a cheap watch from a street vendor. The other boy snorts in derision.

'What are they going to do? By the time they catch on, I'll be long gone.' He studies Joshua intently. His scrutiny is unnerving, making Joshua wish he'd never raised the issue.

'Such a wuss. A mummy's boy, that's you all over. Too shit-scared of your own shadow to ever step out of line. That's where all the fun is, mate.' He punches Joshua on the arm, supposedly in jest, but it hurts, a reminder of how much bigger Adam is, how easy it would be for him to enforce his dominance should Joshua ever challenge him. He fingers the watch, acting grateful when Adam says he can keep it.

'It's crap. Wouldn't wear it if you paid me.' He punches Joshua's arm, too forcefully again, as he laughs, and Joshua's careful to conceal his wince. Adam's right; the watch is cheap and tacky, and Joshua tells himself he'll give it to some homeless guy. Clearly, the other boy doesn't steal because he wants the item; he does it because it's all a lark and he gets high on the adrenaline rush.

A few days later, Adam joins him in the park, his arm curled around something hidden under his jacket. They wander down to a secluded part under some trees. Adam pulls out a bottle of cheap cider.

'Got this earlier on,' he announces. 'Had to run like hell when the alarm went off but what a laugh! The wanker in the shop was old and fat, never stood a chance of catching me.' He unscrews the top, the cider fizzing inside the bottle, and draws a long draught into his mouth. Joshua's never tasted cider, but he knows he's about to; he prays it'll be easier to deal with than the cigarettes, the taste of which still revolts him. Adam passes him the bottle. Relief hits him as the cider pings off the back of his throat. Not bad at all; he could get to like the stuff, although he daren't risk going home to Joanna Barker tipsy. So he takes small swigs against Adam's large ones, never asking for the bottle, which Adam hogs anyway. They sprawl on the grass, Adam commenting on the tits of the women who serve lunch at school, enthusing over the firm, high boobs of one of them.

'Wouldn't mind giving the blonde tart a quickie,' he boasts. Pure bravado, of course, Joshua realises. Nothing but talk, aimed at reinforcing his hard nut image. For now, anyway. Thing is, though, Adam's physically way ahead of the game for eleven years of age, and Joshua doesn't think the loss of the other boy's virginity will be too far off. Sex. The idea seems repellent; girls are a giggling mystery to him, strange and alien, and he's content to leave the whole thing alone for now.

Despite his earlier resolve, Joshua feels the

alcohol gradually warming him through, relaxing him, giving him boldness he doesn't normally possess with Adam. He's drunk just enough to take the edge off the need to defer to the other boy. When the conversation gets round to what they'll do that weekend, Joshua seizes his chance. He's tired of playing underdog, desperate for once to do something with Adam he doesn't feel secretly ashamed of afterwards.

'We'll try our luck down town again Saturday. Been wanting myself a leather jacket,' Adam says.

'I don't think we should pinch any more stuff.' Joshua's voice comes out firm and strong.

Adam doesn't reply straight away. Then, his eyes drilling through Joshua's, he injects pure steel into his tone.

'What did you say, wussy boy?'

With that, Joshua's resolve hightails it out of the park, leaving him realising he's challenged Adam, a departure from the norm. When he replies, the strength has vanished from his voice, the words coming out too high in pitch.

'I said I don't think we should pinch any more stuff.'

Adam's gaze terrifies him but Joshua can't bring himself to break eye contact, although he dearly wants to. Snake and rabbit, deer and headlights, they stare at each other as Adam's boozed-up brain processes the fact someone's dared to challenge his dominance. Joshua realises Adam's drunk a lot more of the cider than he has. He's got no idea how it'll affect him, but he doesn't reckon it'll be in a good way.

And he's right. Quicker than a snake's strike, Adam's right arm shoots out, grabbing Joshua's throat, slamming him onto the grass, pinning him down with his bulk. His hand catches Joshua's windpipe in a powerful vice, but his eyes do the scaring. Some dark quality within them strikes Joshua as abnormal, although he's uncertain how he knows this. What he sees in Adam speaks of instability, of not being bound by conscience or any restraint from doing what he wants, whenever it suits. Combined with his size and strength, it's a terrifying mix, and for the first time Joshua realises he's scared shitless of the other boy, terrified of what those weird eyes say he's capable of doing.

His hand still constricting Joshua's windpipe, Adam never breaks eye contact.

'You'll do what I say.' Saliva flicks from Adam's mouth as he spits the words out. Fear overwhelms Joshua, his breathing laboured against Adam's grip. He gasps as he tries to force the word *sorry* past his constricted windpipe.

Adam reaches into his inside pocket with his spare hand. He brings out a flick knife and releases the blade. Joshua's eyes dart to Adam's hand, clasped tightly around the knife. He's sweating now with terror. Adam inches the knife up to Joshua's throat, the edge indenting the flesh without breaking the skin.

'You got that?' Joshua's head bobs up and down, his eyes never leaving Adam's face. Adam doesn't let go immediately, but he slackens his grip. Joshua's breathing gradually gets easier, less laboured. Adam clicks shut the flick knife, replacing it in his pocket, and moves back, still with his hand encircling Joshua's throat. He nods in satisfaction. Then he lets go, leaving Joshua gasping on the ground, more frightened than he's ever been in his life.

Adam passes him the cider. His voice is back to normal when he next speaks.

'Get some of this down you.' He leans back on his elbows, surveying Joshua with an amused expression, all trace of the rage of a few seconds ago erased. It's as if he shifted gear temporarily into something dark and horrifying and now he's back to normal, although Joshua later suspects the murky side is Adam's natural state. He gulps down the cider, the bubbles gliding over his bruised throat, as he attempts to process the incident.

Adam laughs. 'You're so easy to wind up. Should have seen your face. Priceless.'

Joshua sits up. He should be getting home but daren't risk saying anything. So he takes another sip of cider, staring at Adam, wondering how the darkness within can come and go so quickly, leaving no trace. Adam goes back to talking about boobs, coarse stuff about what he'd like to do to the dinner woman, and Joshua's safe. For now.

He's shaken up by the incident, though. That night, he lies in bed, unable to sleep, trying to decide what course of action to take where Adam Campbell's concerned. Best to back off, he tells himself, mix more with the other boys. Find some new mates. No more constant anxiety over whether his mother will discover he's been bunking off school. So far, his absences have gone unnoticed or unchallenged but his luck can't last.

The next day, he avoids Adam, opting instead to hang around near the other boys, hoping he'll be invited to join them at football practice, to eat with them, or whatever. It doesn't happen, despite Joshua's best efforts over the ensuing week. He's allowed to partake in conversations, but the invites for more don't come. By then, the friendship cliques are long established, their ranks firmly closed against outsiders, and whilst Joshua isn't left out, he's not exactly made welcome either.

He suspects the reason for his exclusion lies in his connection with Adam Campbell. The other boy isn't liked, not at all; instead, he's feared. Joshua is tainted by association, a stain difficult to wash off. By the end of the week, he's no further forward in establishing any meaningful links with the other boys; loneliness starts to seep back into the fabric of his life.

Adam doesn't attempt to rekindle their association during this time, which surprises Joshua. He's fearful the other boy won't let go now he's laid claim to him, worried there'll be a repetition of the knife at the throat incident. Nothing happens, though. Adam watches him, shooting cool stares of appraisal his way, but without attempting anything in the way of conversation. No mention of bunking off together or hanging out down town. The reason clicks into place in Joshua's brain. Adam's waiting for his sidekick to return by his own volition, realising Joshua won't be accepted elsewhere. When he comes back to Adam, as he will, the bonds will be a lot tighter. Stronger by far than if the other boy tries to force him back through overt dominance.

It doesn't take long. Worn down by his failure to break into any of the school cliques, tired of eating alone every day, weary of having nobody to hang around with, Joshua caves in. He spots Adam watching him one day and the dam of loneliness inside him bursts. Any company seems better than none, given how emotionally sterile his home environment is, and he finds himself walking over to Adam, despising himself for his weakness but desperate to end his solitude.

'Want to hang out down the park?' he asks. Adam nods; a grin, a smug and self-satisfied one, forms on his mouth, sealing with it Joshua's role in their double act.

A few days later, it's the weekend. Adam's parents have gone out; he's sprawled with Joshua on the floor in his bedroom, swigging Coke and talking football and girls. Adam's room's a tip, of course, dirty laundry strewn around, drawers open, plates with toast crusts turning green shoved under the bed. The smell of furtively smoked cigarettes and unwashed bedding pervades the room. Adam's banging on about tits again and Joshua's attention wanders to his chest of drawers, one of which is pulled open and half-full of clothes. His eyes go to something tucked underneath the mess, something distinctly out of place. Sugar pink, a colour far removed from Adam Campbell's tastes. Either thick cardboard or plastic, a right angle shape peeking out from under some socks.

'What's that?' The words are out of Joshua's mouth before he has a chance to consider whether they're wise. Adam glances over, and a smug grin etches itself on his face. He reaches towards the item and pulls it out, his fingers caressing it.

It's a girl's diary, the current year embossed in gold on the cover, matched by a flimsy lock on the side. A flowery pattern sprawls across the front. Joshua's bemused. Adam's an only child; he's never spoken of any female cousins and certainly doesn't have any girls as friends. All females are stupid, weak and ripe for abuse, according to the law of Adam Campbell. So who...?

'Whose is that?' he asks.

Adam sneers. 'Wouldn't you like to know?'

Joshua waits. He's familiar enough by now with the way Adam operates to realise the other boy's dying to tell him. He'll have something to boast about in connection with the diary, some story to demonstrate how strong and powerful he is.

Adam grins. 'Ran into her a while back. Got bored with being dragged along every time my parents visit my uncle. Went off by myself, had a mooch around.'

He tosses the diary across the floor, where it lands beside Joshua, open. The flimsy lock has long since been broken. At the front, someone's written a name, the exotic syllables of which sink into his memory. With a surname like Abruzzo, the diary's owner is clearly Italian. He flips the pages, puzzled. Childish handwriting, the entries often doodled around with hearts and stars. Joshua can decipher the more obvious ones, despite the fact they're all in Italian. *Cinema con Gina. Dentista. Vacanza in Sicilia.* He doesn't have much interest in it, however strange Adam's possession of it is, but then he notices the expression on the other boy's face. His grin bears a smug hallmark of satisfaction, and Joshua twigs the diary's owner must be another child who's fallen foul of Adam's need to be top dog.

Joshua fingers the diary, picturing a young Italian girl, someone even smaller and weaker than himself. All the more attractive to Adam for being less able to fight back. The girl to whom the diary once belonged.

'Took myself a little something to remember her by,' Adam says, his mind clearly roaming in the past. A sigh of satisfaction escapes him. Joshua sets the diary down on the floor, switching the conversation back to who has the best mid-fielders, Manchester United or Liverpool. They swig more Coke and Joshua lines up his opinion with Adam's. Far safer that way.

An hour passes. It's nearly time for Joshua to head back to Joanna Barker's frosty maternal care. Scrambling up from the floor, he forgets his half-empty can of Coke. The tin topples over, flooding dark streams over the pink diary that's open beside it.

'Hey! Watch what you're doing!' Adam seizes the diary, shaking rivers of Coke from it. The cheap cardboard cover is already puckered, the pages stained a dirty brown.

'You've ruined it, you stupid idiot.' Adam turns the diary over in his hands, before tossing it into the nearby rubbish bin, clearly judging it unsalvageable. Whatever fond memories he harbours about its acquisition, Joshua seems to have sullied them with his clumsiness. The other boy's expression is dark and shuttered. Joshua realises what's coming.

The first blow slams into his belly, folding him in two as he doubles over, bracing himself against the pain and the other punches that follow. Adam smashes his fists against Joshua's arms, his chest, wherever he can land a blow. Not his face, something that strikes Joshua later with its significance. Even in the midst of his rage, Adam exerts control. Joshua doesn't return home that day with any obvious signs of having been in a fight. Nothing to arouse questions. Given Joanna Barker's maternal indifference, it's simple enough for him to conceal the livid bruises covering his body.

Later on, when Joshua's banged up in Vinney Green, he has time to think over every nuance of his relationship with Adam Campbell, and the pink diary slides back into his brain, worrying away at him. Only one interpretation comes to mind, and it doesn't bode well for the young Italian girl who records her life between the diary's garish covers. The thought tortures him, tugs at him, making him wonder: is she Adam Campbell's first victim? Has he killed before Abby Morgan?

Is that why Adam explodes into rage when his cheap souvenir gets damaged?

Once the idea takes root in his head, it worries him constantly. Something about the way Adam's face oozed smug satisfaction tells Joshua the Abruzzo girl came off badly in her encounter with Adam. If he's killed another child, he's obviously got away with it. Joshua doesn't recall ever hearing about a missing girl with such an unusual surname, although what with being preoccupied back then with football, Adam and pleasing his mother, he's likely to have missed such an event anyway. The fact Adam took her diary disturbs him; the other boy clearly gets off on seizing trophy items from his victims. Abby Morgan's green hippo proves the point. Joshua attempts furtive searches at Vinney Green whenever he gets Internet access, searching for missing children with the surname Abruzzo and slamming hard against a dead end. Reassuring, he supposes, but his obsessive-compulsive nature won't let the matter drop. The whole thing boils around in his head whilst he's in detention until it becomes vitally important to find out who the Abruzzo girl is and what happened between her and Adam Campbell. Until he finds her, he'll always be uneasy, wondering if he shouldn't have realised what the diary signified, what Adam was capable of doing. He'll perpetually fret over whether it was a warning of what would happen to Abby Morgan, a sign he should have heeded.

After he's released, his obsession with the Italian girl fades in comparison with his immediate priority to adjust to life outside. Gradually, though, the old fixation returns. He needs to dispel, finally, his anxiety over the Abruzzo child, but fear of rocking his newfound stability holds him back initially. A long time passes through Mark's life before he makes a promise to himself. He's going to find out, once and for all, what Adam did to the little Italian girl and whether she survived.

11

HER SHAME REVEALED

Rachel doesn't hear from Mark for a couple of days, during which time every one of her insecurities kicks in. She's too pale, too skinny, too unattractive for him to fancy her, the way she does him. She logs onto Facebook obsessively, her hopes crashing each time she doesn't find a friend request from him.

When she eventually does, she's ecstatic. Her first priority is to scan his profile. Relationship status: single. Rachel's pleased, but not surprised; Mark carries an air of solitariness about him, good-looking though he is. She's prepared to bet he's not had many girlfriends. So far, she's his only friend on Facebook. Again, no surprise. She's already sensed a certain isolation about him, as if he doesn't make friends easily, something she can identify with.

Should she send him a message? She's debating whether to risk it when Fate decides for her. Mark is now online.

'Hi how r u thanks for friending me on fb,' she types.

He takes a minute or so before he replies, and when he does, she notes he's definitely not into text speak.

'No problem. Been looking at the page for the fun run.'

'U free? Gonna join me?'

When he doesn't reply, Rachel's insecurities kick in again, intense and insistent. After a couple of minutes, she types another message.

'Wld be gd to c u again and hv sum1 to do run with. Can u make it?'

Eventually he replies. 'Not sure at present. I'll get back to you.'

His closing words soften the perceived blow a little. 'Will be in touch. Bye for now. Good to catch up with you.'

Hmm. Far too brief a chat for her liking. Does he fancy her? He's certainly made a strong impression on her; an unspoken bond seems to have sprung up between them. She can't name it, but it exists, and she wants to deepen it, strengthen it. Mark seems familiar to her in some strange way, as though she knows him somehow, although she's sure they've never met before.

Mark Slater. Not exactly handsome, but his hair has finger-run-through appeal, his mud-brown eyes are soft and warm, and his athletic build is definitely attractive. So, too, is the dark tuft she noticed peeking over the top of his sweatshirt when they last met. She goes for hairy men, always has. The rugged masculine look. Don't get your hopes up, she warns herself. He may already have a girlfriend, no matter what his Facebook status proclaims. The gremlins of self-doubt within her start shouting. *You're too small, too ginger, too freckly. Too tainted, what with your murdered sister and your alcoholic father. Who do you think you are, setting your sights on Mark Slater?*

He's back on Facebook the next evening, as promised – *will be in touch* – saying how he's still unsure about the fun run, mentioning a prior tentative arrangement for the Sunday in question, how he won't know until nearer the time whether he'll be free. He doesn't elaborate and Rachel doesn't press the issue, too frightened of scaring him away. By the third time they chat, he's more forthcoming.

'You free this weekend? Fancy meeting up?'

She agrees straight away. He suggests lunch in Exeter on Saturday. Thankfully, Rachel doesn't have any events booked for her catering business that day. She punches the air in triumph before typing in: gr8 idea. Then: I no a gd pub we cn go 2.

Will leave choice of venue up to you, he replies. They decide on a time, swap mobile numbers, chat some more. Rachel's ecstatic when she eventually logs off.

She buzzes through the next two days on a fantasy-driven high. The time drags unbearably, despite the fact she revels in the anticipation. Saturday arrives at last. Rachel wakes up early, shot through with excitement. Today she has a lunch date with Mark Slater. She turns his name over in her head, approving of it. It's solid, permanent, strong. The name of somebody who could make his mark on her emotionally, and Rachel's ready for such a man, she really is. Mrs Rachel Slater. Sounds good, she thinks. The gremlins of self-doubt invade her thoughts immediately, ordering her not to set her sights too high. Don't get your hopes up, they shout.

Is it so wrong, she wonders, to want normality, a boyfriend, children? A stable home life? One without rows reverberating through a house that is supposedly a home but isn't? A marriage in which the husband doesn't stagger through the door late at night incoherent and stinking of beer?

Rachel sighs. She understands why she needs these things. They've been noticeably lacking in her life, all twenty-four years of it, so far.

She breathes in deeply, willing her nerves to subside. If only their initial meeting had taken place under different circumstances. Sometimes - no, often -

it's as if her life is ruled by the abduction and murder of her sister. Recently she's had to endure the anniversary of Abby's death along with the dreaded annual vigil. Not to mention dealing with her mother. Thank God for Shaun. He's been there for her, as he always is. Her brother, her rock. Every year, Rachel contemplates not attending the vigil. She forces herself to go, terrified that if she doesn't, her mother will disown her completely. A thought too painful to bear. In order to cope, Rachel always performs her own private homage to Abby the night before the vigil. Something of which only Shaun is aware.

Enough of dark thoughts. Rachel turns her attention to what she's going to wear today. Something stylish that'll emphasise her figure; although slim, Rachel's curved like a Coke bottle. She'll go for smart casual, as befits a lunchtime pub date. Her new jeans, teamed with black suede ankle boots. She dithers over choosing a top, eventually selecting a slash-necked one with long sleeves in pale mint. It skims her hips, hugs her waist. She twists and twirls in front of the mirror, frowning. Her head tells her she looks good, before self-doubt rushes in to tell her she's plain, ordinary, nothing special.

Gold dropped earrings, a beaded bracelet. A slick of lip-gloss, a touch of mascara, and she's ready. She pulls on her leather jacket, grabs her handbag and car keys and heads for the door.

They've arranged lunch at The Thatched House pub in Exeter, a favourite with Rachel. She arrives ten minutes early, concerned Mark won't show up, worried he'll have forgotten or found somewhere else to be. Met another woman who's more to his taste. She avoids the cramped area near the toilets, with its busy pool table, and settles for the alcove opposite the bar. Near the door, so she'll spot him when he walks in. Rachel hopes he'll approve of her choice of venue. The management of The Thatched House have gone for the old-fashioned touch with the décor, in keeping with the image invoked by the name. Thick oak beams traverse the ceiling, a few obligatory copper kettles hanging from them. Old books stacked on high shelves, flanked by china dogs. The effect of all the piled-on kitsch is beyond cheesy, but for Rachel it's familiar, soothing, comfortable. What's more, the food is outstanding.

Mark's five minutes late. The insecurities in Rachel's head grow ever more macabre; he's been mugged, suffered some terrible injury, died in a car crash. Right at the point where her mental scenarios are spiralling out of control, he walks through the door.

He doesn't see her at first, affording her the luxury of being able to give him the once over, and he's every bit as delicious as she remembers, dark and spicy and carrying an air of mystery about him. He eventually spots her and heads over to the window table she's bagged, his expression flustered.

'Sorry I'm late. Traffic was terrible.'

'Don't worry. You're here now.' He flops into the seat opposite her, shrugging off his jacket, and she glimpses again his chest hair making a bid for freedom over the top of his sweatshirt. Sexy. Very. Rachel's immediately bitten by shyness, so she buries her face in the menu. They make small talk – *how have you been? I'm good, thanks* - whilst they study the options.

'Steak and chips for me. I'm a meat and potatoes kind of guy, apart from my love of Chinese food,' Mark announces. 'What about you?'

'I'll go for the fish lasagne. Sounds intriguing and a change from the ubiquitous beef ones. If it's any good, I'll make my own version sometime.'

'You like to cook?'

'It's my job.'

'Really?'

'Got my own business. Started last year after catering college.'

'I'm impressed. An entrepreneur.'

Rachel laughs. 'I love it. I'm keeping it small for now, working from home, but watch this space.'

'You do dinner parties, that sort of thing?'

'Anything clients require. What do you do work-wise, Mark?'

His gaze slides away. 'Assistant manager for a building supplies company.'

She senses he's embarrassed for some reason. 'You don't enjoy your job?'

He shrugs. 'I do, actually. It's just that, well, it's not very glamorous, is it? Not like you, with your own business, dinner parties and all that. But I guess it suits me.' He lays down the menu. 'Can I get you a drink whilst I place the orders?'

'Small glass of dry white wine, please.' She watches him as he moves to the bar, this man to whom she's taken such a shine, and reminds herself to relax. He returns with a pint for him and the wine for her, and she fishes around for some topic of conversation. Of course. The fun run. Time to pin him down.

'Thought any more about doing the charity race?' She's afraid to look at his face to gauge his reaction. His reply doesn't come immediately and when it does, he's non-committal.

'Still not sure. Waiting to see if I'll be free on the day.' Best not to push it, Rachel tells herself. She mustn't be paranoid; he probably does have some other arrangement that clashes. She forces herself to shrug. 'Fine.'

He nods. 'So what's been going on with you? The other day, you weren't having too good a time. Not surprising, in the circumstances.'

'You're not wrong there. Sorry again for being a bit rude when you first spoke to me.'

'Understandable. Don't worry about it.'

Rachel sips her wine. 'The vigil is always pretty tough on all of us. Mum especially, but me too. Shaun as well, although he does a great cover-up act.'

'He's the strong silent type?'

'Definitely strong. Not so silent, though. Shaun's a master of straight talking at times.' Rachel remembers some of those occasions. 'Particularly where Abby's killers are concerned.'

She notices Mark's gaze sliding away.

'You think about your sister a lot?' he asks.

Rachel nods. The conversation is moving into uncomfortable waters but somehow Mark seems to understand. As though he's able to empathise with how life after the murder of a family member continues, but never down its previous track. She wonders briefly if his empathy is born out of suffering something similar, but lacks the courage to ask. Too soon for such questions, probably. Her situation is public knowledge, whereas his, if it exists, will be private, something to prise out of him when they know each other better. She likes the thought of unravelling the mysteries of the man sitting opposite her.

She realises he's waiting for an answer. 'Every day. Hard not to. I wonder what she'd look like now, what things she'd enjoy doing, how she'd be. She was so pretty, you see. Like a stereotypical princess, all blonde curls, with a really determined character starting to shine through, although she was only two when she died.' Rachel drains her wine. 'Her murder tore the family apart. Something so terrible has to. None of us have been the same since.'

'I can imagine.' He takes a sip of beer; she notices his hands are shaking slightly as he sets the glass down.

'It's like being branded. We're marked out, in both Exeter and Moretonhampstead, because of what happened. People stare, they talk, they ask terrible questions and make insensitive comments. Not one of them has any idea what we go through. Day in, day out, living with something so awful.'

Mark is silent. Rachel appreciates a murdered sister is a weighty subject for a lunchtime discussion. She decides to switch tack. Before she's able to, though, Mark clears his throat.

'Those two boys who were convicted of killing your sister.' His gaze is on his pint, his hands slowly rolling his glass between his palms. 'They were eleven at the time, weren't they? Wasn't there a lot of fuss about their ages, how they couldn't have known what they were doing?'

'You should hear my mother on the subject. Sorry, I forgot; you already have.'

'She seems to reckon they were fully culpable. Like adults. Both of them.'

'Yes. She does.' Rachel fiddles with her fork. This wasn't what she came here for, although she appreciates Mark's obvious empathy. 'Listen, do you mind if we don't discuss it anymore?'

He pulls back immediately. 'Of course. I didn't mean -'

'It's just that it's still kind of raw. After the vigil and all that.'

'I understand. Sorry.'

An awkward silence arises, broken by the arrival of Rachel's fish lasagne and Mark's steak. Mark gets himself another beer and she allows herself a second glass of wine. They discuss running, music, food and favourite films; with the tension now eased, somehow the time slips away. The lasagne is sublime; lemon sole, prawns, cream and pasta combine into a piscine taste sensation. Across the table, Mark quickly disposes of his sirloin. Dessert for both of them is a superb raspberry and rhubarb charlotte. Rachel can't remember when she last enjoyed herself so much. An idea is forming in her head. Emboldened by the wine, she plunges ahead.

'Do you want coffee?' she asks.

'A shot of caffeine wouldn't go amiss.'

Right answer. 'We could go to my place.' Unable to maintain eye contact, she ploughs on. 'Unless you need to get back to Bristol?' There it is: the get-out clause, the one she hopes he won't take.

He doesn't. He seems surprised, but pleased. 'That would be great. Thank you.'

Job done. Rachel's happy. Mark insists on settling the bill, his old-fashioned approach both amusing and gratifying to her, and they head towards the car park. Rachel gestures at her Fiat. 'Follow me. It's not far.'

Back at her flat, she's conscious of the fact she's not tidied away her breakfast dishes from the coffee table in the lounge. A whiff of bacon lingers in the air, along with the bread smell from the loaf she made earlier on. Thing is, she had no notion she'd be inviting Mark back here this afternoon. She notices him glancing around, taking in the blank walls, bare of pictures or photos, the lack of any ornaments, any personal effects.

'You've only just moved in?' he enquires.

'No.' She's embarrassed. How best to explain this? 'Been here a few years now. It's just that - well, I've never really felt at home here. So I haven't got round to doing all the homely stuff, pictures, plants, those kinds of things.'

She sees he's still puzzled. 'This place was my bolt hole originally, you see. When I moved out from home, in Moretonhampstead. When life there got too difficult.' *Please, please,* she prays silently, *don't ask me to elaborate what too difficult means.* She can't deal with questions along those lines, not when she wants him to like her, not see her as weak and needy.

'I can't afford to move, not yet, anyway.' She turns away. 'Coffee coming up.' She injects a breezy tone into her voice as she walks into the kitchen. 'Got some lemon cheesecake too. Made it myself. Think you can squeeze any more food in after that humongous dessert?'

He laughs, and she realises he's following her. 'Not an offer I can turn down. Thanks.'

He lounges against the doorjamb, watching her, but it doesn't make her nervous. Rather, she likes it. She forces her mind to concentrate on the task in hand. Coffee, sugar, milk. Mugs, spoons, kettle. Oh, and plates for the cheesecake. Top shelf of her cupboard. At times like these, she wishes herself taller, better able to reach, but she's keen not to play the helpless female. No asking for help.

Rachel opens the cupboard door, stretching up. The sleeves of the pale mint top flop down to her elbows and before she has time to do anything, it's too late. Mark will have seen her shame. Her body freezes in its stretch before contracting back, her arms falling against her sides, her hands tugging down her sleeves. Right now, she doesn't possess the courage to turn around, face him, check his face for judgement, condemnation, contempt.

He's only a couple of feet behind her. She's acutely aware of the tension that's arisen in the small kitchen. He's seen her arms; he must have done, unless by some miracle he wasn't looking as she stretched upwards. He'll never fancy her now, never want her the way she wants him. Mrs Rachel Slater is over before she's even begun.

Then he's beside her, reaching into the cupboard, bringing down two plates. He opens a drawer, taking out forks and a kitchen knife, before pulling the fridge door open. His hands reach in and take out the cheesecake. He cuts two generous wedges, sliding them onto the plates, adding a fork at the side of each. So neat, so precise, she notices, the slices identical in size. She's not yet dared look at his face but his actions don't suggest judgement. He hands her one of the plates.

She'll have to explain, of course. Even if he rejects her, even though they might never see each other again, she's unable to bear the idea of what he might think if she doesn't. Perhaps it's better this way. If anything worthwhile is to develop between them, he'll have to accept her the way she is. If, by some miracle, he's still unaware of her shame, he'll find out the minute sex comes on the agenda. Heat rises into her face at the thought.

'Shall we go and sit down?' She gestures towards the living room. She's still not able to meet his eyes.

12

ONE, TWO, BUCKLE MY SHOE

Fourteen years ago. March 21, to be precise.

It's the Easter holidays; Joshua and Adam are bored, restless. There's only so much hanging around the park and the shops they can do. Joshua's relieved Adam hasn't suggested any more stealing expeditions. Although he's aware it's only a matter of time, he's grateful for the respite.

'We'll go over to Moretonhampstead,' Adam announces. Joshua's surprised. Nothing against the place, but he can't imagine why they'd want to visit, unless Adam sees it as fresh ground for nicking stuff.

'Why there?' he asks.

Adam shrugs. 'Somewhere different to hang out. I'm bored with the same old crap around here. Aren't you?'

'Well, yeah, but…'

'That's settled, then. We'll go, check out what's there. Been before. A few times.'

'What for?' Joshua's reckons Adam's probably been to suss out the shoplifting potential, and he's unnerved.

'Stop asking stupid questions. Come on.'

By now, he's too scared of Adam even to think of saying no or suggesting something else. They trudge off to the bus stop. Adam is unusually quiet on the way. His silence unnerves Joshua because it's so uncharacteristic, although he can tell the other boy isn't in a bad mood. Rather, he projects understated elation, as though he's anticipating some future treat, which Joshua surmises must be some high-value item he's intent on stealing. The thought increases his anxiety; he forces his mind away from the seemingly inevitable prospect of store detectives, being caught, his mother's reaction.

Once in Moretonhampstead, Adam steers them in a certain direction, clearly knowing where he's going. To Joshua's relief, they don't appear to be heading towards any shops, but into a residential area. He's baffled, but follows Adam without question.

They walk for a while, until they're not far from the edge of town. Adam's striding on ahead, leading the way. Joshua's following, concerned about what the other boy has planned. To his right, he sees a silver Mondeo, facing away from him, parked in a nearby street. A man is unlocking the driver's door. A woman waits by the passenger side. Both the man and the vehicle's registration plate appear familiar.

Something clicks in Joshua's brain.

He's seen the car parked in the driveway of Adam's house.

The man is Adam's father.

The woman is not Adam's mother.

Jon Campbell and the woman get in the Mondeo. They kiss, long and hard, their bodies an inverted V-shape straddling the gear stick. Eventually Joshua hears the engine start. The car drives off. Joshua's unsure as to what he's just witnessed or its significance.

Adam turns round to see him still looking down the side road.

'Hey, arse-dragger! What the hell are you doing, standing there gawping at nothing?' He strides back to Joshua, grabbing his arm. 'Come on,' he says. 'Get your butt in gear, can't you?'

Joshua complies. It's plain Adam didn't spot either the car, his father or the woman, so intent is he on getting to their destination. Jon Campbell obviously has a girlfriend on the side. Not an unusual occurrence, from what Adam's already let slip. Apparently, his father changes women almost as frequently as he does his socks, despite still being married to Adam's mother.

Joshua shrugs. None of his business. He dismisses the incident from his mind.

They walk until they come to a row of ageing nineteen-thirties semis. Adam stops at the end house. It has an air of neglect about it, beige paint peeling from the windowsills, the plastic gutters sagging. Most of the garden's not visible from the other houses, wrapping as it does around the house at the front, back and side. Mostly grass, with a few token flowerbeds bordering the edges. A low wooden fence, over which Joshua can easily see, surrounds the garden.

It's then he gets his first glimpse of Abby Morgan.

One of the most important moments of his life, but at the time he thinks nothing of it. He's an eleven-year-old boy, with no interest in girls of any age, let alone toddlers, who, if he considers them at all, he imagines to be whiny creatures, prone to tantrums. So his gaze merely skims over Abby as she plays on the grass in the side part of the garden. It comes back to rest on Adam, who's staring at the child. He risks a question.

'You know this kid?'

Adam's answer is dismissive. 'Nope. Seen her once or twice out playing, that's all. When I come with Mum and Dad. My cousins live nearby.'

The child is sitting on a play mat spread on the grass, her attention absorbed in her toys. The green hippopotamus, the one Adam later steals as a trophy, lies beside her. She's busy playing interior designer with a large plastic dolls' house, her bottom lip pushed forward with her concentration. A tinkling tune sings forth from the Fisher-Price CD player by her side, a high-pitched female voice delivering the words of *One, Two, Buckle My Shoe* with determined enthusiasm.

She's obviously a girly kind of girl, this child before him whose name he's ignorant of for now. Blonde, with soft curls reaching to her shoulders, pretty in a way that will stretch the nation's heartstrings when they learn of her murder. She's dressed completely in pink; a fuchsia-coloured jacket with the slogan 'Pretty Princess' slashed across the back, pink T-shirt and trousers, the theme extending to her carnation-hued trainers, with matching Velcro fastenings. The pink beads of a bracelet circle one of her tiny wrists. A white plastic Alice band provides the only relief in a sea of Barbie tones.

Years later, as an adult, the former Joshua Barker wonders if the child's fragile beauty intensifies the national loathing for him and Adam. Whether it's worse to kill a Pretty Princess, someone like Abby Morgan. Would the death of a plainer child have aroused less public wrath? He suspects so. Looks matter, whatever political correctness likes to assert.

Adam's still staring down at the child. Joshua's not interested in her after his initial appraisal. He glances past her towards the side entrance to the house, and that's when he gets his first glimpse of Rachel Morgan. A little younger than him and Adam. Her pale red hair is tied in a loose ponytail, her attention focused on the book she's holding in one hand. With the other, she's stroking a black kitten nestling on her lap. Earphones are clamped to her head, blocking out the world around her. She doesn't glance up towards the two boys, partly concealed by the fence at the other end of the garden.

Joshua becomes aware of Adam leaning over towards the child.

'Hey, Barbie girl,' he calls. Her eyes flick up, then back to her dolls' house. Adam stretches further down. He reaches an arm out, clutching something in his palm.

'Psst,' he whistles softly. She looks up again, this time keeping her gaze on him. 'Barbie girl. Princess in Pink. Want some choccy?'

He unfurls his fingers to reveal a packet of Smarties, flicking the top off, easing an orange one onto his palm. Without taking his eyes off the girl, he brings his hand to his mouth to eat the chocolate. 'Mmm. Tastes good. Want one?'

She nods slowly but doesn't move. Adam extends his hand back down. 'Gotta come and get it, little girl. They won't come to you. Here.' He selects a red one, balancing it on a fingertip. 'Just for you.'

The child peels herself slowly from the plastic mat, with her eyes fixed on the chocolate a couple of feet from her face. She extends a hand, uncertainty apparent in her dilatory response. Then her fingers move rapidly to seize the prize, throwing it quickly into her mouth, before taking a step back, her gaze never leaving Adam's face.

Adam laughs. 'Want another?'

Her confidence growing, the child toddles forward to snatch a couple of Smarties, smearing chocolate around her mouth and on her fingers, all thought of her dolls' house clearly forgotten. Beyond her, lost in her world of music, book and kitten, the girl on the doorstep reads on, unaware of the insidious seduction taking place at the other end of the garden.

'You want to go on an adventure with us, Pretty Princess?' Joshua is startled, confused, rattled. Adam, like him, has never shown the slightest interest in small girls. He's imagined the other boy intends to steal something today, but he hasn't pictured a tiny child as the booty. What Adam has in mind, Joshua has no idea. Certainly it never occurs to him - why would it? - that Adam is contemplating committing a violent murder. How he's planned this, enjoying having the ever-obedient Joshua as his sidekick. So he says nothing, waiting to see how this curious new development will unfold, although unease is uncoiling deep within him.

'Gonna go look for buried treasure. Wanna come?' The child nods, her eyes fixed on the Smartie tube. Adam unlatches the gate, slowly and stealthily. Joshua glances back at the girl on the doorstep. She hasn't moved. Behind Abby, the Fisher-Price CD player loops back to start again. *'One, two, buckle my shoe...'* Adam eases the gate open, beckoning to the child, his hand still extending the Smarties towards her. He's Abby Morgan's Pied Piper, his tune promising chocolate heaven, and she's hooked on the bait.

She reaches out for another Smartie and Adam bypasses her hand to pop it into her mouth. Her laugh sounds out, high and happy, unable to penetrate the earphones her sister is wearing, and she moves towards the open gate. Then she stops, reconsidering. She goes back to fetch the green hippopotamus, tucks it under one arm, and edges back towards Adam.

Joshua's about to take a risk, he's aware of that, but this is all too weird. He's got to say something, find out what the hell's going on. Afraid though he is of the other boy's innate violence, he's none too keen on spending the afternoon with a small child in tow. Besides which, he *knows* this is wrong on all kinds of levels. The child belongs here, in the garden of what Joshua assumes is her home, safe with her toys, not wandering the streets with two strange boys. Joshua wills the girl on the doorstep to look up, see them, challenge what they're doing, but she doesn't. One hand continues to stroke the black kitten whilst the other holds the book. Whatever world she's lost in, she won't be returning for some time.

Joshua opens his mouth, forcing the words out.

'Adam, what the...?' He doesn't get any further than three words before Adam's head twists round to transfix him with a look, only this time his stare is angrier and more intimidating than ever before. Whatever the other boy has planned, Joshua can't imagine it'll be for the girl's benefit. He most likely wants to tease her, make her cry, give her a bit of a scare, the child's fright feeding his inner bully. Adam gives her another Smartie as she walks past him, her chocolate-coated hand smearing brown streaks on the plush material of the green hippo. He pulls the gate closed behind him with the same care and stealth he used to open it. He places his hand on the child's back, steering her towards the small lane nearby. Beyond it, Joshua sees what appears to be farmland.

'Come on,' Adam says. 'This way.'

They walk for a couple of minutes, heading away from the town. Eventually the lane opens onto the outskirts of a farm. Joshua sees a wooden shack, in bad repair, to one side of them. They turn right across the field towards it, the child starting to grizzle, tiredness clearly biting at her.

'No,' she whines, as Adam drags her forward.

The three of them enter the shack. Joshua sees it's been used for storing various implements and tools, although it doesn't look as though anyone's needed what's here for a long time. Everything is filthy, rusting, covered in grime and spiders' webs. Joshua's not even sure what some of it is. It's approaching late afternoon now, the weak March sunshine filtering through the gaps in the wooden slats of the shack, highlighting the mess within. Next to Joshua, the child upends the Smarties tube, shaking it, convinced if she jiggles hard enough she'll get more chocolate treasures. She shoots a pleading look at Adam.

'All gone,' she says. 'Want more.'

Adam shakes his head. Joshua doesn't like the smile playing around the other boy's lips. His unease is growing by the second. This is all too weird. What are they doing here, in the middle of nowhere, in this filthy shed, with a child who doesn't seem to have any connection to Adam, one who should be back in her garden, playing with her dolls' house? The green hippo falls from the child's hand, unnoticed, onto the mucky floor, as she renews her pleas for more chocolate. Adam shakes his head again. Something lurking in the other boy, the darkness Joshua can't put a name to, the evil coiled deep within, is about to unfurl. He summons whatever grains of courage he possesses where Adam's concerned in order to speak.

'Shouldn't we be getting back?'

Adam ignores him. Joshua tries appealing to the shoplifter within him.

'If we hurry, we can check out the shops before they close.'

'Shut it.' Adam's voice is terse. Whatever is uncoiling inside him is doing so rapidly. He turns back to the child. 'Would you like to play a game, Pretty Princess?'

The child's head bobs up and down. She smiles, her trust complete in this unknown benefactor who provides chocolate and fun.

Adam grins back at the child, but nothing benign warms his expression. He pulls the sleeves of his jacket down over his hands, before reaching behind him to pick something off the floor. Joshua sees it's a rake handle, with a metal casing on the end, which originally held the prongs. The two have become detached at some point, so now all Adam holds in his hand is the part with the rusty casing. He's grasping the other end, so the brown erosion of the rust is highlighted in the stream of sunlight.

'Ready to play?' Adam asks the child. She nods again.

Everything that happens next imprints itself on Joshua's mind forever. Adam raises the rake handle, swinging it through the air to crack it down against the child's body. She screams, a thin high-pitched keening sound, slumping to the ground, as Adam hits her repeatedly. Joshua's horror and disbelief freeze him. The metal casing bites into the child all over: head, legs, arms, torso. Blood runs from her wounds, soaking her pink clothes, dyeing them red. She carries on screaming, but then stops; Joshua realises she's not moving anymore. The child's inertia unfreezes him; he finds his voice, not caring about Adam's reaction, yelling at him to *stop, for God's sake stop, what the hell do you think you're doing, she's just a little girl*. His words come out a chaotic, desperate jumble. They seem to reach their mark, though, because Adam ceases whacking the child.

He drops the rake handle to face Joshua. Tension sparks through the air.

Adam takes a step forward.

Never has his size been so intimidating.

Never has Joshua seen such darkness in the other boy's eyes.

Adam pushes himself right into his face.

'Told you before.' Joshua's feet instinctively shuffle backwards, away from the dark something in Adam that's now completely uncoiled and in full strike.

'Shut the fuck up. Or I'll give you some of what she's getting.'

Joshua is silent, finished. Adam bends over the

child. 'Still alive,' he says, whilst reaching into his pocket. Joshua realises what he's going to bring out. The flick knife. As well as what he intends to do with it.

Another pivotal moment in Joshua's life. When, despite the threats, regardless of the hold Adam has on him, he has the chance to save Abby Morgan's life. He's smaller than Adam is, not as strong as the other boy, but he can take some action, surely? Grab something. The rake handle, maybe. Clobber Adam and spare the life of the child who lies unconscious and bleeding on the filthy floor of the shack.

He doesn't, though. The fear of Adam is too ingrained, his dread of the flick knife too potent. He does nothing, thereby sealing Abby Morgan's fate. Adam bends over the child, plunging the blade into her, again and again, doubling, trebling the amount of blood that's everywhere.

The child is motionless. No way can she still be alive, thinks Joshua, not after so many blows, several aimed at her throat and heart. The rake handle lies, bloodied and spent, beside her body.

Adam stands up and walks outside the shack. He plunges the knife repeatedly into the earth to clean it, in a grotesque parody of what he's just done to the child. Then he retracts the blade and wipes the handle before replacing it in his pocket.

'Gonna sling it on the way back.' Such calm in his voice. Whatever uncoiled itself in Adam has retreated, although Joshua senses it's not as deeply hidden as before.

'I'll kill you if you tell anyone.' No emotion in Adam's voice or expression. Just a bald statement of how it is. Joshua doesn't even consider the possibility the other boy's fooling around. How can he, when the corpse of a child lies at his feet, the bloody evidence sprayed over his jeans? Of course Adam will kill him if he talks.

Moreover, being found out seems inevitable. How the hell can they hope to get away with it? The knife will be discovered, despite Adam's plans to ditch it. Joshua's watched enough crime dramas on TV over the years to picture police officers raking through waste bins, combing the surrounding countryside, when they don't find a murder weapon at the scene to explain the stab wounds. Something, Joshua doesn't know what, will inevitably lead back to them.

Being found out means the distinct possibility of being sentenced to the same punishment unit as Adam, giving the other boy every chance to carry out his threat. His only option is to shut up and stay that way, no matter what happens. It'll be his word against Adam's anyway, without fingerprints on either the rake handle or the knife.

Adam's laugh startles Joshua from his thoughts. 'Seen our Pretty Princess a couple of times before today. Decided to find out how much fun it would be to stick a knife in her. Make her bleed. Hear her scream.'

The murder's been premeditated, then, but Joshua's not surprised. The child's killing lacked the ferocity of a sudden loss of control, vicious though it was. No, the blows rained down on Abby Morgan were brutal, sure, but they bore the hallmark of someone with iron self-command, who understood - and enjoyed - what he did. Joshua's not certain how he knows this - perhaps he's absorbed more than he's realised from those crime dramas - but he believes Adam planned this, in every detail, before they came here today. Adam's next words confirm this.

'Found this place a couple of weeks ago when I was last over here. Saw its potential straight away.' He laughs again. 'A ready-made toolkit on hand as well, although I brought the knife along for a bit of extra fun.'

He pulls the weapon from his pocket, his fingers wrapped carefully in his sleeve. 'Be a shame to ditch it. Easy enough to get another, though. A bigger one next time.'

He thrusts the knife towards Joshua. 'Unless you'd like to keep it? Be a great souvenir of a good day out. Nah, didn't think so,' as Joshua recoils. 'No idea why I bother with you.'

He slides the knife back into his pocket. 'Did it too quickly, though. She died too easily.' Regret sounds in his voice. Adam has clearly enjoyed every single blow and scream of killing the child. How such a thing is possible, Joshua can't fathom; he experienced nothing but revulsion on watching Abby Morgan's life being beaten and stabbed out of her. When Adam's next words filter through the fog in his brain, they're so terrible he thrusts them away, refusing to believe the boy in front of him, dark and twisted though he is, can mean them.

'Next time, I'll do it more slowly, have more fun.'

The unspeakable horror of *next time* pounds through Joshua's brain. He stares at the child's corpse. She's laying all crooked, blood matting her hair. One small trainer has come away from her right foot. Joshua registers the pink plastic of the shoe with its Velcro fastening. He hears again the tinny female voice singing *'One, Two, Buckle My Shoe,'* and it becomes imprinted on his brain forever. Strange how the silly song associated with the worst day of his life comes to represent comfort when he's stressed, but the human psyche can be anything but rational. The song tinkles its happy tune in his brain, and as he sees the bloodied rake handle the words *'five, six, pick up sticks'* echo in his head.

'Time we were getting back.' Adam reaches down to pick up the green hippo, smoothing the soft material, the fabric browned with blood and chocolate. 'Think I'll take this, have myself something to remember the fun we've had together.' He grabs Joshua by the arm. 'Let's go. We're done here.'

13

SILENT SCREAM

Mark and Rachel carry their plates into her living room, her offer of coffee forgotten. They sit on her sofa, Rachel's fingers playing with her fork. Flipping it through her fingers, back and forth, the rhythm strangely soothing. The idea of lemon cheesecake, so tempting a few minutes before, now revolts her. Beside her, Mark is eating his slice, making neat incisions with his fork, tackling the cheese filling and biscuit base with precision. A thick wall of tension separates them, even though her arms, having betrayed her shame, are now safely hidden beneath her sleeves. She's silent, allowing him to eat his cheesecake, before she risks broaching the subject.

'I expect you're shocked,' she says. She'll find out now. If, by some miracle, he didn't see, he'll give her the surprise, the *what do you mean?,* and her secret will be safe, at least for now.

He shakes his head, and all hopes of him not having seen evaporate, adding to the tightness in the air.

'No,' he says as he swallows the last mouthful of cheesecake. 'Not shocked, Rachel.'

'I can't help it,' she whispers.

'I understand.' He does, too, she gets that, although she's no idea why or how he can comprehend something that Shaun, however supportive, never has. Empathy implies understanding, which in turn suggests suffering on a commensurate level. She wonders what Mark's particular sorrow has been and whether he'll ever tell her. Sadness stabs her that he's had pain in his life but right now, it means he won't judge her, and that's the most important thing.

'I'm sorry you saw…what you did. But thank you for not getting on my case about it.'

She's able to look at him now, registering the empathy in his expression. He shifts a little closer to her on the sofa, his eyes on her sleeves.

'How long?' he asks.

'Years. Since I turned fourteen or thereabouts, I guess.'

'It takes whatever is hurting you inside away.' A statement, not a question, and Rachel again thinks: *he understands.*

'Yes. How did you -'

'I know. Believe me, Rachel, I do.' His gaze is averted now. She gets why. It's too soon to ask, and if he's not volunteering the information, she's not going to push things.

'I use a sharp kitchen knife.' Her voice is a whisper.

'Just on your arms? Or elsewhere?'

'Legs as well. My stomach, too, once or twice, but not often. Arms and legs are better. Not sure why. Each to their own, I guess.' She lets out a tiny laugh, without any mirth in it.

'So you always wear long-sleeved tops. And trousers.'

'I have to. Even when I run. It's bad, Mark. The scarring.'

'I wondered why you pull your sleeves down a lot. Now I understand.' Rachel reaches for her sleeves as he speaks, tugging them forward. A nervous habit, learned over many years of concealing her shame from the world. 'Yeah. Like that.'

He leans towards her, slowly, and at first, she thinks he's going to kiss her. Instead, his hands reach for her sleeves, and she pulls away, drawing her arms back, hiding them behind her. It's asking more than she's willing to give at this stage. Nobody has ever seen the full extent of her scarring. Sex is always a furtive, clothed affair for Rachel. She's taken care to avoid hospitals, with their potential talk about professional help, counselling and the like. She won't be going down that route anytime soon.

'I'm sorry.' He moves away from her, giving her space. 'I didn't mean to upset you.'

'I can't show you. It really is bad, Mark. Ugly.'

'You don't have to.'

'They're partly bandaged anyway; well the left one is, as you must have seen. That's the worse one, because I'm right-handed. But my other arm's one hell of a mess too.'

'You cut the left one recently then?'

'Yes. The night before the vigil.'

He nods in understanding. 'Of course. Makes sense.' She can't fathom what's lurking in his voice besides the obvious. Concern, yes; empathy, definitely, but what else? It's a kind of sorrow, as though he regrets something, and deeply, but what it might be she can't tell.

'I was so stressed, you see. I knew all the reporters would be there. Not to mention the television crews. It's hell every year, but I can't not go. She was my sister. I loved her.' Tears threaten to overspill her eyes; she forces them firmly back. She won't cry in front of Mark, even if it means adding another scar to her collection later.

'Is it worse when you get stressed?'

'Definitely. If I get wound up, or something triggers it, like the vigil, I cut myself. It's the only way I can deal with…stuff.' She glances up at him, braver now the tears have retreated. She registers the same sorrow in his face as she noticed in his voice earlier. As her eyes meet his, he gives her a strained smile.

'I tried not to do it this year. Promised myself I wouldn't. But the night before…it all got too much for me. Shaun knows what I'm like, what makes me worse, but he couldn't be with me that night. Away with work. If he'd been around, I wouldn't have done it. He'd never let me cut myself in front of him.'

'He takes care of you.' Again, it's not a question. He must have seen at the vigil how protective Shaun is of her.

Rachel nods. 'He's always been very supportive. Never gets angry, never lectures me about how I should get help. Just listens as I rabbit on about whatever's bugging me.'

'You've never thought about counselling, doctors, that kind of thing?'

'No. I've always been too ashamed; too scared they'll judge me. They wouldn't understand, I don't think. How can they? Unless you do this kind of thing yourself, it must seem so weird. But it's the only way I can cope.'

Rachel gestures towards his arms, bare beneath his rolled-up sleeves. 'You, though…you don't cut, at least not there. It's more of a female thing, anyway. So how can you…?'

He gives her his sad smile again. 'I understand, Rachel, I really do.'

'I don't want you thinking I'm some kind of weirdo. I'm not. You see, it makes all the badness inside me go away. When I cut. What's strange is, it doesn't hurt, not when I'm doing it.'

He seems surprised. 'It doesn't?'

'No. It's like cutting's its own anaesthetic, taking away the pain so it doesn't give any back. Like I'm in some kind of a zombie state. What I call my silent scream.'

He nods. 'When you want to stop the world and get off, but can't.'

How does he *know*? 'Yes. Exactly. Shaun wasn't around the night before the vigil, as I told you. Usually I phone him if things get bad, and he's so good, he really is, but sometimes I cut myself before I think of calling him. We no longer live together, now we've both left Moretonhampstead, and he can't be expected to watch me all the time.'

'What about your mother? When you were living with her, I mean?' Rachel freezes. *Don't ask about my mother*, she begs him in her head.

'I've not lived at home for six years now. Since then, Shaun's been my main support system. He's always so patient, never complains.' She prays her tactic of switching the conversation back to Shaun will deflect Mark from asking about her mother. She doesn't think he'll be fooled, but she hopes he'll take the hint not to probe further. 'I've read plenty of books about self-harm. Along with getting help from the Internet. Websites, online support groups. They've all been useful, especially the forums I've joined. I can hide behind a different identity on them.'

'A different identity. Yes, I get how that would help.' The strain in his voice seems magnified. 'Rachel, can I ask - you don't have to tell me, of course - what triggered all this? Was it - I know I'm stating the obvious here - was it your sister's murder?'

Crunch time. Will she tell him? The answer is yes, she will. She's come this far, he's not judging her, and she feels safe with this man. If they end up together, he'll have to know anyway. Why not right here, right now?

Not easy to do, though. She draws in a deep breath.

'It's hard to explain.'

'Isn't your sister's murder the root cause, though? Plus your father turning into an alcoholic. Tough enough for anyone to deal with, let alone someone your age. You were, what, twelve when he left, you said?'

She nods.

Her evasion clearly puzzles him, his confusion evident in his face.

'Does something else make you cut yourself? I don't mean to pry, Rachel. Like I said, you don't have to tell me if you can't deal with it.'

Oh, God. Presented with the perfect opportunity, Rachel chickens out. Time for more deflection tactics. Back to the events of fourteen years ago.

'Abby dying the way she did came as a huge shock,' she says. 'Until you've been through something like that, it's impossible to grasp what it's like. One minute she was there and then she was gone. The part before she was found was awful for all of us. The not knowing was torture. Dad retreated into alcohol, as usual, and Mum - well, she was like a zombie. Then they found Abby, dead in that old farm shack. When they did, at least the not knowing part was at an end.'

The tears are threatening her again. In her head, she's ten years old once more, bewildered and frightened. 'The police were scary. They questioned me after Abby went missing.'

Mark nods. 'Being stuck in front of police officers can be very intimidating to a child.' His expression seems strained again.

'Yes. I got the impression the policewoman who did most of the questioning blamed me for what happened.'

'Blamed you? Why?'

'For not paying attention to Abby. I was in the garden at the time she was abducted, you see. I wasn't taking any notice of her, though. I dumped her on her play mat with her favourite toys and left her to it. Thought she'd be safe enough. Thing was, although she was my little sister and I loved her, I was still only ten years old. Most of the time, Abby was simply a nuisance.'

'The police were hard on you? They frightened you?'

'Yes. Being grilled by them was sheer hell. She was still only missing at that stage. I remember praying so hard she'd be found. The questions from the police dragged on and on, but I had nothing useful to tell them.' Her voice sinks to a whisper. 'I wish to God I had. But I didn't see or hear anything. Not a thing.'

'Your mother sat in on the questioning, though, didn't she?'

'Yes. Not that she helped at all. As I said, she was in some weird zombie state, at least whilst Abby was only missing. When her body was found, she went totally the other way.'

'Like she is now? The anger took over?'

'You got it. Dad, well, he retreated into the drinking; he either spent most of his time down the pub or crashed out on the sofa. He stank, Mark. Didn't wash, had a constant reek of booze about him. On the rare occasions he was sober, Mum would pick fights with him. The rows seemed never ending. I was grateful, in a way, when she eventually kicked him out. All the while, I felt so alone, even though I had Shaun. I'd lost my sister and for all practical purposes I was losing my parents too.'

'What about your brother? How did he cope with it all?'

Rachel smiles. 'Brilliantly. In many ways, he's the strongest one in the family by far. Mum couldn't even do the basics of looking after us, so he took over. Between the two of us we cooked the meals, did the laundry, all that sort of stuff. It was like he dealt with grieving for Abby by throwing himself into practicalities. He loved his baby sister like crazy, was gutted by her death, but he's not the weeping and wailing type.'

'He seemed to have his act pretty much together at the vigil. Came across as very supportive of you and your mother.'

'Yes. He was even good in other ways as well. Dad wasn't going to work, of course, not once he started hitting the bottle so hard, so he ended up being fired. Things weren't getting done, like bills being paid or routine maintenance around the house. All that was the least of Mum's concerns. She got her act together once Abby's murderers were put away, but in the meantime Shaun helped sort out the finances, dealt with minor repairs and so on.'

'As well as supporting you. Rachel, can I ask you something?'

She nods.

Mark clears his throat.

'The cutting,' he says. 'OK, so your sister's death and your father leaving played a part, but I'm still curious about what else did. Thing is, you seemed evasive earlier on. Like I said, I don't want to push you. Not if it's something you don't want to discuss.'

'It's OK.' She fiddles with her sleeves again, hooking her fingers inside the fabric to draw them down and keep them in place, playing for time, unsure how best to tell him.

No more chickening out. Deep breath in. 'I do it because I hate myself for what happened to Abby.'

He seems taken aback. 'But why? You weren't to blame.'

'Yes, I was.'

'Why do you say that? Because the policewoman who questioned you seemed to be judging you?'

'Yes. Well, partly, I suppose.' She's unable to look him in the eye. The conversation is growing more difficult by the minute. Her guilt and self-hatred are battering her with full force, as they do on a frequent basis. He doesn't press her to continue, for which she's grateful, although they can't leave things hanging on the word *partly*.

'I cut myself because I'm responsible for what happened to Abby,' she continues. 'When I see the blood flow out, it's not blood anymore, but the guilt I carry inside about her murder. Like I said, I don't feel any pain, only a welcome relief. To me it's a good thing, an incredible release. I cut when I get stressed, say if my business isn't going well, but as I start to do it, it's not about work or anything like that anymore. Whatever may have triggered it, it always ends up being about Abby. And the overwhelming guilt I've always carried because of her death.'

Mark edges closer, grasping her wrists, taking her hands in his. She's terrified he's going to push her sleeves up to reveal the slashed mess underneath, but quickly realises he won't abuse her trust that way. Not after her earlier refusal to show him her arms.

His voice is gentle when he speaks. 'Listen. You were ten years old at the time. Still a child. No way were you to blame. Shaun must have said all this to you, surely, and you've got confidence in him, so why not believe him? Why carry guilt, when you don't need to?'

'I'm not the only one who thinks I'm guilty, that I'm to blame.' She pulls her hands away. Mark's empathy is wonderful but she's unworthy of it; his touch is an absolution she doesn't deserve.

'The policewoman?'

She's silent, unable to reply.

'No,' Mark says. 'Not the policewoman.'

She shakes her head.

'Tell me who else blames you.'

Rachel raises her eyes to his, but still can't speak.

'Say it,' Mark urges.

'My mother,' Rachel replies. 'Mum blames me for Abby's death. She hates me for what happened. She always will.'

14

KINDRED SPIRITS

There. She's said it. She's silent, drained by the effort of getting the words out. They hurt. It's beyond painful for Rachel, having her mother condemn her, however justifiable her censure. Knowing how, since that day, Michelle Morgan has retreated, taken back the love she used to bear towards her daughter. Thing is, she's withdrawn from pretty much everything except her campaign against Abby's killers.

Mark's voice interrupts her thoughts. 'What do you mean?' She glances up at him. 'I guessed it must be your mother you meant, but honestly, Rachel, I can't understand why she would blame you. Although she obviously does. I mean, I noticed at the vigil how she was with you. More to the point, how you were with each other.'

'She blames me because I let it happen. I wasn't doing what I was supposed to.'

'Minding Abby, you mean?'

'Yes. Mum had to go out. Shaun was busy upstairs, doing homework, so she said I shouldn't disturb him, how he needed to be left in peace. She asked me to keep an eye on Abby. We were in the garden. I remember it was a sunny day, unusual for March, and Abby had been playing up. Tantrums, being difficult, more so than usual. Mum decided some time outside in the fresh air might do her good.'

'You didn't mind being asked to watch over her?'

'No. Well, a little. See, I was only ten myself, so Abby often seemed a bit of a nuisance, what with the tears and wanting everything her own way, although I loved her, I really did. She'd been a pain that morning, constantly demanding attention. I needed a break from her, so I left her on the grass, playing with her toys.'

'You must have thought she'd be safe enough.' Mark's voice seems strangled, as though the words are trying to squeeze through too tight a space. She doesn't blame him if he finds this hard to deal with. They barely know each other, after all.

'Well, yes. Moretonhampstead's a small enough place, after all. Nothing ever really goes on there, and besides, you always think that sort of thing happens to other families. Not yours. She seemed happier by then and I didn't think she'd be in any danger. Except she was, and I should have prevented her getting hurt. What she must have suffered...' The tears come now, sliding down her cheeks, at the image of her sister being stabbed to death to provide two boys with some kind of sick entertainment. She needs time out, she realises. Paper towels; she'll grab a handful to blow the snot from her nose. When she comes back from the kitchen, Mark's face is pale. He doesn't look well.

'Are you OK?' she asks.

He nods. 'Shouldn't I be asking you that?'

She wipes her nose again. 'I'm fine. Good job you're here, though. I'd probably be cutting myself otherwise.'

'So let me get this right. Your mother blames you because your sister got taken whilst you were supposed to be minding her?'

'You got it. Abby was down the end of our garden, wrapped up in whatever she was playing with. Her dolls' house, probably, or that damn Fisher-Price CD player she loved so much. We all got sick to death of hearing *One, Two, Buckle My Shoe* all the time. Anyway, I was sitting on the doorstep, on the same side, but much further up the garden. Listening to music. Christina Aguilera. Never been able to stand her since. I had my headphones on, reading. Harry Potter. I got totally absorbed. Lost myself in a fantasy world, never realising what was going on. When I did look up, Abby had gone.'

'You were just a child, though. Your mother placed a lot of responsibility on your shoulders.'

'And I didn't live up to it. I failed her. I get why she blames me, I really do. When I did put down my book, and couldn't see Abby, it was as though it were all unreal. As I said, murders and child abductions aren't commonplace in Moretonhampstead. I thought at first that she'd managed to unlatch the gate and wander down the lane. How she couldn't be far away. But she wasn't anywhere to be seen, and I shouted her name, over and over, checked everywhere I could think of, and that's when I ran back and got Shaun.'

'And he phoned the police?'

'Not at first. We called Mum's mobile, but it went straight to voicemail. Dad was out boozing somewhere, as usual. In the end, Shaun ran to find our next-door neighbour, Mrs Frinton, and she called the police once we told her Abby had disappeared. Said you couldn't take chances with a missing child. She said not to worry, though; Abby was probably safe somewhere I'd not yet looked. Except I'd searched everywhere, and I realised then something terrible must have happened to her.'

Mark shakes his head. 'I can't imagine what that must have been like for you.'

'It was beyond awful. Right from the start, before Mum said anything, the guilt I felt was overwhelming. All I had to do was keep an eye on her. Make sure she was safe, in our own garden of all places, and I didn't even manage to do that. Too wrapped up in Christina bloody Aguilera and Harry Potter.'

'Your mother actually said she blamed you, then?'

'Made it crystal clear.' In her head, the memory floods back to Rachel. She sees her mother, standing before her, face distorted with grief; hears the accusations cascade from her mouth, drenching Rachel in a torrent of guilt. Which, after it's had time to fester within her for a few years, twists itself into the urge to slash her arms and legs with whatever sharp instrument she can find. Rachel yearns to go back in time, to when she's asked to watch over Abby, when she has a mother who behaves like one, because after that day Michelle Morgan is never the same towards her. A gulf has split the two of them asunder, forcing them onto different tectonic plates, inching ever farther apart.

'She screamed at me, her face all contorted, demanding why I hadn't taken better care of my sister.'

'No-one can blame you. She shouldn't have placed such a responsibility on a child.'

'It was such a simple thing she asked of me, though. But I messed it up.'

Mark's fingers drum a nervous beat against his thigh. 'Did she say where she'd gone off to?'

'Yes. She was a couple of streets away, with a neighbour. A woman with early-onset Alzheimer's. Mum used to do the housework, bring in groceries, deal with whatever needed doing.'

'She did that often?' Mark's voice seems oddly constricted. She glances at him, catching a fleeting expression of – what, exactly? – before his face resumes its normal mien.

'Yes. Started going regularly a few weeks before Abby's death. She'd give up hours of her evenings, weekends too, helping this woman. Although all that stopped when Abby died. See, Mum's such a good person, she really is, despite all the anger.'

'You love your mother. Even though she blames you for what happened.'

Rachel's nod is sad, resigned. 'Yes. It makes it worse, her doing something so kind when Abby was dying, whilst I was being so selfish and stupid. Reading and listening to music instead of minding my sister.'

'Rachel, you were only ten years old.'

'That's never cut any ice with Mum. The way she sees it, I was old enough to load the washing machine, help round the house, do whatever she asked, so in her eyes I was certainly responsible enough to keep tabs on my sister. She's right.'

'No.'

'Yes. Remember, Mark, what she said at the vigil. How she's never accepted how the two boys who killed Abby were too young to understand what they were doing. She's always said both of them must be evil, through and through, in order to kill Abby, so they must have been aware of what they were doing. Her killers were eleven years old, and Mum's never cut them any slack. She's hardly likely to do it for me, when I was only a year younger.'

She notices how Mark's face has blanched again. He really doesn't appear well.

'The two boys,' he says, hesitancy shot through his voice. He seems nervous, Rachel thinks. Not surprising really. They're discussing terrible things here.

'Do you...?' He swallows. 'Do you agree with your mother? That they're evil, I mean?'

Rachel weighs up her answer. She's thought repeatedly throughout the years about this question. One about which she's never come to a definite conclusion, because the issue involved is too complex.

She knows little about the two boys concerned. Their boyhood faces are familiar to her from the photos made public at the time. Sometimes she wonders how they might look today, now they're grown men. Not just their physical appearance will have changed. They'll have altered mentally as well. Have they confronted the magnitude of their crime? Do they carry guilt for Abby Morgan's death around with them every day, the way she does?

Questions to which she'll never get the answers. Both boys are men now, hidden from public view, shielded by new identities. Their backgrounds are a mystery to Rachel too. She remembers how much was made of how ordinary their family lives were; no obvious signs of abuse or neglect, although as she knows with her own mother, these things are often masked. Hidden away, only revealing their ugly faces in private. What was the driving force behind these two boys? Joshua Barker, she recalls, had lost his father when young, aged nine or thereabouts. The other boy, Adam Campbell – wasn't there some talk about him being prone to aggression, being difficult to handle? Did nature trump nurture where Abby's killers were concerned, or was it vice versa?

'I don't know,' she admits. 'Sometimes, yes, I think she's right. I mean, how can one human being do that to another? So brutal, the way she was beaten and stabbed, and her so small, so pretty, too. Who could do such a thing? Except someone did, and not just anyone, but two other children. When I hear about stuff like all the looting that went on after Hurricane Katrina, it seems like we're all only a thin layer away from reverting to primitive behaviour. At times like those, I reckon Mum's got the two of them sussed. That they're evil and they realised exactly what they were doing, but simply didn't care whether it was right or wrong.'

Mark's fingers resume their rhythmic drumming against his thigh. His face is still unnaturally pale. 'You said you only agree with her sometimes?'

Rachel shrugs. 'Other times, I think, yes, they were only eleven; they might have been young for their age, perhaps playing a game, something that went horribly wrong. How they didn't mean to hurt her, or kill her, but somehow it ended up that way.'

'Or one of them might have influenced the other one.'

'Perhaps.'

'Forced him into taking part, I mean.'

'I suppose that's possible, although they admitted equal guilt, received the same sentence. Anyway, Mum's been consumed by anger ever since. Totally preoccupied with Abby's death. Her life's on autopilot, really; she goes through the motions of living, but nothing gets through to her unless it's connected with Abby. The bitterness she harbours about those boys being released, given new identities - it's as if it's chewing her up inside and she doesn't have room for anything else. Certainly not me.'

'I guess she's not going to change her tune, not after all this time, not towards the boys responsible or you either.'

'No. It's as though the anger, the bitterness, are all she has to live for, so she can't let go. I don't imagine for one moment you do ever move on from having your child murdered, but she could at least make peace with it. She can't, though.'

'Being rejected by your own mother...' Mark shakes his head. 'Hits you right in the gut, doesn't it? Hurts you like nothing else.' The depth of emotion in his voice tells her what he hasn't so far. Now she gets why such a bond has sprung up between them. He's also been spurned by his mother. Hence his understanding of where she's coming from with all this. She resolves to unearth the reason for his rejection, and soon.

Rachel's spent, drained, exhausted, by the emotion needed to tell him all this. Perhaps now she's talked so much about her dysfunctional family, he'll be more open about his. Especially his mother.

'Enough about me. Tell me more about you.'

Mark shifts uneasily. His fingers twist the hem of his sweatshirt. 'What do you want to know?'

'Are your parents still alive?'

'My father's dead.'

'That's sad. Were you very young when it happened?'

Rachel senses his discomfort. 'Pretty young, yeah. We were close, Dad and I. Came as a shock.'

'An accident?'

'Car crash.'

'And your mother?'

'Not in contact with her anymore.'

His words come as no surprise. Rachel chooses her words carefully. 'I don't mean to pry, Mark. If you want to tell me, then I'll listen. If you don't, that's fine. It's just that, well, I've been rabbiting on for ages about my weird family set-up. Figured we should move on to yours.' She attempts a laugh, but it comes out sounding forced. 'You can say it's none of my business if you like.'

Unease is pouring off him in waves. He doesn't reply, glancing at his watch instead. 'I really ought to head back to Bristol.'

'OK.' She's disappointed, but reluctant to press him if he's uncomfortable. Really, it's understandable, him not wanting to talk. Give him time, she reasons. With no family to speak of, he's probably as lonely as she is. They have so much in common, and all the time in the world to discover it together.

'Shall we meet up again sometime?' The words are out before she can stop them. 'I mean, we didn't exactly talk much about the fun run, did we? If you're free one weekend...' She's not used to taking the initiative with men, so she stops before she says too much, scares him off.

'OK.' Reluctance in his voice. She's disappointed.

He grabs his jacket and turns towards the door. 'Good talking with you, Rachel.' He moves as if to hug her and it's then she stretches up on her toes and kisses him.

Pure impulse. She hasn't planned any such thing. Her mouth meets his but he doesn't respond. She pulls away, about to stammer an apology, when everything changes. His arms tighten around her and he's kissing her back, hungrily. As though he's sucking something he desperately needs from her. Their kiss is one between kindred spirits, Rachel decides. Mark's every bit as damaged as she is; he's hunting some small shred of comfort through her mouth. Isn't that what she's seeking too? They kiss, long and hard, before he abruptly breaks away.

'I must go, Rachel. I'll be in touch about the run.'

'Promise?' God, she doesn't mean to sound so needy.

'Yes.' His fingers twist the door latch. 'I mean it. I'll text you.'

'OK.' A text. Not a phone call. She's disappointed again.

He pulls open the door. Then he's gone, leaving her confused as to why he's mixing hot and cold, fire and ice, chalk and cheese. It hurts.

At least his empathy, the touch of his hand on her sleeve, the kiss - they all fuel the hope within her. She won't dwell on him pulling away from their kiss.

Because if she does, she'll end up with her right arm as bandaged as her left.

15

JUST DO IT

The usual road works are clogging the M5. Mile after mile of cones, slowing traffic to a crawl. Heavy rain lashes the windscreen as Mark drives back to Bristol. Anxiety presses hard against his chest. Hardly surprising after the afternoon's emotional intensity, but for once he manages to shove his angst aside. He doesn't want to count, not now, when he has so much weird shit to process in his head.

First up, he's battling mixed emotions about the meeting with Rachel. On the plus side? Sure, he's now got a much clearer idea of the damage he's caused the Morgan family. Thing is, though, he doesn't care to examine the image too closely. If he does, the reality of the harm he's inflicted will deliver a truckload of pain to his doorstep, far more than he can bear right now. It's one thing to watch the Morgan family on television at a safe distance, another altogether to have Rachel's slashed arms shock the shit out of him. Along with finding out about Michelle's cruel withdrawal from her remaining daughter. Not to mention having Matthew Morgan's descent into alcoholic oblivion thrust down his throat.

Mark reflects on the parallels between Rachel's mother and his own, and they're not good. Things aren't as black and white as Michelle Morgan makes out;

moreover, her treatment of her remaining daughter stinks.

He recalls Rachel reaching into the cupboard, replaying the exact moment her falling sleeves reveal her shame. One arm bandaged, with old scars from previous cuttings scoring the flesh either side of the dressing. The other one bare to his gaze. Exposed. Vulnerable. Sporting livid slashes where she's used a kitchen knife on them. He pictures her legs, equally sliced and scarred, destined to be hidden forever under trousers. No short-sleeved dresses are on the agenda for Rachel Morgan, not ever.

Seems she sports more than a few mental scars as well. Her guilt about her sister. Her rejection by her mother. Her father's alcoholism. She's twenty-four and already she's been pretty thoroughly fucked by life, or more accurately, by Adam Campbell and Joshua Barker.

Mark attempts to breathe out the tightness in his chest. *One, two.* It helps a little. He's treated Rachel badly, of course. Something he regrets. His connection with her is selfish, wrong, warped, but Mark can't let go, not yet. Above all, he decides, he mustn't do or say anything to fuel her hopes. She's so needy; her air of vulnerability has already led to the two of them maintaining their fragile contact beyond what's wise. A mistake, but she's so blatantly hopeful it's hard to refuse her.

One more meeting, he promises himself. Shaun Morgan is the reason. The last unanswered question Mark has. He'll drive down for lunch with Rachel again. Once there, he'll steer the conversation round to her brother, see if he can get a handle on what makes this man cope so well with the crap life's thrown at him. What lies beneath the stoic veneer? Has this man, so calm on the surface, been damaged inside by Michelle Morgan's obsession with her daughter's killers? By having to parent Rachel whilst still a kid himself? In having an alcoholic for a father?

Shit like this must have left its mark somehow, even if Shaun doesn't self-harm with knives or alcohol like his sister and father. What his particular mental sticking plaster is, Mark can only speculate. Perhaps some people are simply more resistant to life's javelin throws than others are, with him and Rachel down the weaker end of the resilience scale. The man who has supported Rachel through the trauma of her self-harming is to be admired, he thinks. No apparent judgement of either his sister or their mother. Mark, used to being judged his whole life, finds Shaun Morgan an enigma. Chances are he can learn lessons from this man, if Rachel can be persuaded to reveal what drives her brother.

Once Mark's questions about Shaun have been answered, there'll be no glue binding him to Rachel Morgan. He'll delete his Facebook account and ignore any text messages from her. Their pseudo-relationship will then be over.

His mind veers towards their kiss. Madness, sheer madness, although they both have very different reasons for locking lips. Rachel clearly views him as potential boyfriend material. In this respect, going to Exeter today hasn't proved a good idea, not if it's encouraged her attraction to him. She's not his type physically, despite her undoubted prettiness. No, sex doesn't explain him returning her kiss. Hell, when it happens, his first reaction is to pull away. She's Abby Morgan's sister, for fuck's sake. What eventually leads him to reciprocate is something very different from lust. For Mark, their kiss is a plea for forgiveness, an attempt at atonement. It doesn't stem from desire. Never that.

The M32 into Bristol. He's almost home now. His flat, where he can pour himself a beer and try to unscramble the mess in his head. The rain is still driving down, the steady flick-flack of the windscreen wipers oddly soothing, keeping the tightness in his chest under control until he can reach the sanctuary of his flat. He guides the car over to his exit. He'll be home within five minutes.

Beer. Mark remembers his fridge is devoid of alcoholic comfort. A bottle or two of Black Sheep ale is necessary before he contacts Rachel again. He parks up near his flat, braving the rain to cross the road to the corner shop. The sullen girl behind the counter is clearly irritated by the arrival of a customer to interrupt her reading. Her gaze bounces swiftly back from Mark to her magazine. He deliberately lingers over his choice of beer to annoy her. No Black Sheep on offer; he'll have to make do with Tetleys or London Pride.

Behind him, he hears the sounds of another customer coming in. He turns to check how Ms Sullen reacts to this additional fly in her ointment, and freezes.

Abby Morgan is in the shop with him.

A golden-haired girl, about two years of age, clutching a man's hand. Her father, presumably. She's pouting, clearly on the verge of tears, with the man's patience seemingly poised to plunge off its tightrope. He's brusque, impatient, obviously keen to get whatever he's come for and go. Mark takes in the pink of her jacket - thankfully, she's wearing jeans, so no reminder of Abby Morgan there - and his chest constricts, hard.

It's all too much, on this crazy Saturday when he's already had a surfeit of emotion piled on him. Now he has to deal with this small blonde child a mere couple of feet away, rubbing tiredness from her eyes. Don't cry, please don't cry, he begs her in his head. She does, though, fat tears oozing from beneath her fingers, a thin wail shredding the air. Her father yanks on her arm, his exasperation ready to burst. The wail swells into a shriek.

Mark's catapulted far beyond his emotional limit. He wrenches at the fridge door, thrusting the four-pack of London Pride back on the shelf. Ms Sullen glances up, mildly alarmed, as Mark pushes out of the shop, past his blonde nemesis. His heart thudding, he leans against the window, forcing oxygen into his lungs. Shit. He needs the sanctuary of his flat. Now. Otherwise, the child might leave the shop at any minute and he'll have to endure her tears again. Impossible to move, though, not with the pounding in his chest. He begins to count. *One, two, buckle my shoe*, onwards towards the safety of the higher numbers, his mind skating over the pictures brought to him by *five, six, pick up sticks*. Mark squeezes his eyes shut, willing the mantra to take effect.

Too late. The door jangles open as the man drags the child out of the shop. She's in full crying mode now, broadcasting her anguish to the world, her father shushing her impatiently. Too much by far for Mark. He turns away and vomits up steak, chips and cheesecake, not caring if anyone sees him, the stream of half-digested food purging his crappy day from him. Even when his stomach signals it's empty, he carries on heaving, desperate to spew out every last remnant of guilt.

Ashamed, he moves away from the stinking mess at his feet to sit on a nearby wall. The nausea slowly passes. Mark watches the rain pound into the pool of vomit. A sour taste of puke lingers in his mouth. His thin jacket's already soaked through, his hair plastered against his skull, raindrops rafting down his cheeks. Mark doesn't care. Once the spasms in his stomach cease, he makes his way back to his flat.

Inside, he's safe again. Screw the beer; he'll have to get by without an alcoholic crutch tonight. Into the washing machine with his soaked clothes; Mark grabs a towel from the bathroom and rubs hard at his head. Back in the kitchenette, fully dressed again, he pulls open the fridge, pouring himself a glass of filtered water. The coldness draining down his throat relaxes his tight shoulders, sweeping away the angst of before.

Shit. He needs to get his act together, and fast. No way can he carry on this way, allowing every blonde two-year-old to shellshock him out of control. Moreover, the kiss with Rachel torments him. In Mark's mind, he's betrayed Natalie. Strictly speaking, as she's his ex, it's not infidelity. Thing is, Mark's a purist, all part of his obsessive nature. He's been unsuccessful in detaching himself emotionally from Natalie. A failure that means kissing other women is off the agenda.

He still has strong emotions where she's concerned, a yearning to pillow his head against her generous breasts once more. Discover how the soft, warm comfort they provide can obliterate the Morgan family from his mind. Taking with them Joanna Barker, Tony Jackson and, most of all, Adam Campbell. Natalie's the one person who's managed to breach his defences, even though she's chosen to walk - no, run – away. Not that he blames her.

Mark wonders where she is, what she's doing. Saturday evening; she'll almost certainly be at her mother's, probably watching television whilst demolishing a takeaway Chinese. Using food the way she always does, plugging a physical gap to disguise the emotional one underneath. Natalie's insecure, a trait that's usually a precursor of jealousy and one his ex-girlfriend possesses in truckloads. She'd never understand the whole crazy scenario with Rachel.

Does she miss him, though? Is she sorry she ended their relationship?

Mark's self-loathing, always close to the surface of his mind, rebuffs his questions with a sharp *no*. He's a convicted child killer. Natalie can't possibly regret breaking up with him.

God, how he wishes he had a cold bottle of Black Sheep to wash away this shit. He's jangled after the encounter with the kid, antsy, desperate for change in his life. An impulse seizes him; he'll reach out to Natalie, bridge the gulf between them. Before he can think through what he's doing, he's pulled out his mobile. A hastily composed text. 'Missing you. Been thinking about us. Hope you're OK. Couldn't tell you the truth. X.'

His fingers hesitate over the send option for a second, before he decides. What the hell. He'll live dangerously for once. *Just do it, Mark.* His fingers dispatch the text. Even if she never wants anything to do with him again, at least he's been straight with her. No lie in saying he's missing her. And he's sorry all right. About everything.

He waits a few minutes. No response from Natalie. Has she even read his text? Will she angrily delete it or is she composing a reply right now? He sighs. Where Natalie is concerned, it might go either way. All he knows is, he wants another chance with her.

Time to honour his promise to Rachel. No text message; he'll use Facebook instead. With any luck, she'll be offline. Less chance of connecting with her.

Mark goes into his bedroom and grabs his laptop. Once it's switched on, he logs into his Facebook account, relieved to note Rachel doesn't appear to be online. He'll set up another lunch meeting for the following weekend, making sure he turns down any offers of coffee afterwards at her flat. If she asks, he'll tell her he can't make the fun run. Once lunch is over, he'll make his excuses about getting back to Bristol, in order to exit her life for good. Best for everyone, Mark thinks. Especially her.

He taps out a quick message, intending to be off Facebook straight away, but Rachel comes online as he's typing. Shit. Mark keeps their interaction as brief as possible. The result is an arrangement to meet at her flat again, same time a week tomorrow. A Sunday. Mark notes the eagerness with which she suggests this, along with the way she attempts to string out the conversation.

'Wll cook sumthg 4 u. Show off my culinary skills,' she types.

'Remember I'm a meat and potatoes guy. No green stuff, please.' A few more back and forth exchanges take place before Mark's able to make his exit.

Shit. After he's logged off Facebook, he remembers something. Seems he's fallen for the whole vulnerability thing again with Rachel. Didn't he promise himself not to go to her flat again? And now he's arranged a home-cooked meal with her. More intimate by far than lunch at a pub. Not a wise move.

At the thought of food, his stomach growls, pronouncing its emptiness, his nausea gone. Time for something to eat. He walks into the kitchenette, pulling from the fridge bread, butter, ham, tomatoes. From the cupboard, a chopping board, a knife for slicing. Mark's fingers cut precise segments through a tomato, before he remembers Rachel. Her arms.

Mark tests the tip of the blade against his thumb. It bites in, sinking a dent into the flesh without piercing it; Mark's not pressing hard enough. Even so, the knife's edge hurts. He wonders what it must be like to draw a blade across one's arm, experience it slicing through the skin, watch the blood well up from the wound. Rachel's silent scream, along with her claim not to feel any pain. Only the subsequent relief.

Her ruined arms flash before his mind again. Jeez. This woman's locked her pain deep inside her for fourteen years, unseen by any psychiatrist or counsellor. Rachel Morgan probably won't ever slay her demons without professional help. Hell, though, maybe she's not the only one who needs a shrink. He kissed her, didn't he? Plenty of people would judge such madness sufficient grounds to warrant him seeing a psychiatrist himself.

Easy enough to recommend for someone else. Impossible to do himself. Mark's also been fucked by life, but he intends the psychologist at the detention unit to be his sole visit to Shrinkland. He'll make do with the neatness and counting rituals, thanks all the same.

Their forthcoming lunch. Don't fuck this up, Mark warns himself. Hasn't Rachel Morgan been hurt enough already?

16

CHOCOLATE AND WINE

Callie Richards passes a packet of McVitie's to her daughter. 'Want one?'

'Thanks, Mum.' Natalie takes a biscuit and bites into it. Chocolate chip, her favourite. She's spending the evening at her mother's house. Their Saturday nights together, along with Callie's Sunday roasts, have been a ritual ever since Natalie, aged twenty-two at the time, left home. Natalie always visits her mother, never the other way around. Callie Richards has never once been to her daughter's flat. For the simple reason she can't.

The day her philandering husband walks out on her for good, Callie takes to her bed, pulling the duvet over her head. She remains there for the next month. Natalie, aged eleven, is forced to cook their meals, clean the bathroom and do the laundry, at the same time as struggling with hours of homework from Bristol Grammar School. Not to mention the unwelcome novelty of monthly cramps. Her mother eventually leaves her bed, but not the house. Callie Richards has never ventured outside since, the four walls of her home protecting her from the world's dangers. Once her savings are gone, she survives financially – just - on state benefits and her ex-husband's sporadic child support payments. Television's her only source of entertainment. Callie devours every reality show, watches all the soaps, vicarious living through onscreen pap becoming her substitute for real life. Like Natalie, eating is both her comfort and her curse. Her life reduced to TV and junk food, Callie Richards has swollen to a dress size greater than her daughter's age. Natalie, now twenty-five years old, hopes the trend won't continue.

'Of course, women like that are so vulnerable. Mind you, men are the real problem.'

'What are you talking about, Mum?' Natalie pulls her attention back to her mother. She glances at the TV. Crimewatch, one of Callie Richards's favourites, a recording from the previous Thursday.

Callie jabs a finger towards the screen. A photo of a woman fills it. She wears her profession on her face. 'Working girls, that's who.'

Callie warms to her theme. 'Men. They're the ones responsible for women like that being on the streets in the first place. If they weren't all so dick-driven, the world would be a better place. Poor girl. Some bastard's murdered her.'

It's a familiar tune, one Natalie's heard often. Bruised by her ex-husband's inability to keep his penis in his pants, Callie Richards herds all men into one category: arseholes. Divorce has grown her a pair of lady balls at last, her former passivity replaced by a fiery contempt for men. Her frequent tirades about the male sex have influenced Natalie to some degree over the years, even though she tries hard not to be affected by her mother's issues. Men, Natalie has long ago decided, are what her mother really fears to encounter beyond the walls of her house.

'Chop the murdering sod's dick off, is what I say.' Callie shakes her head. 'Although I doubt they'll ever catch whoever did it, not now. Trail's getting colder by the minute. Look, Nat, here comes the re-enactment.'

On the TV, a woman walks along a dimly lit street. She's dressed in the standard working girl attire; a skirt wrapped tightly around her thighs, high-heeled strappy sandals, a fake fur jacket. The footage is dark, grainy, typical CCTV quality. The screen switches to the presenter in the TV studio.

'Kayleigh Thomas was last seen alive at 9.30pm in Deaver Street. Her body was discovered the next day by children on a nearby patch of waste ground. She had been badly beaten and suffered from multiple stab wounds. Police say…'

Natalie remembers now. A couple of weeks ago, Southampton, wasn't it?

'Never got whoever killed that other one a while back, did they?' Callie reaches for the packet of biscuits. 'Some other city, that was. Can't remember where.'

An image, dark and unwanted, intrudes into Natalie's brain. Hot breath against her ear, a heavy body pinning her down. Fingers inside her, making her bleed. The face of her attacker, unseen yet always in her mind.

She forces the memory away. *Totally different*, she rebukes herself. *I lived. Those women didn't.*

Natalie's phone vibrates into life. A text coming through.

Mark, is her first thought.

She's right. Before she's able to do the sensible thing and delete it, her fingers open the text.

'Missing you. Been thinking about us. Hope you're OK. Couldn't tell you the truth. X.'

Oh…my…God, Natalie's brain says. Her emotions surge back and forth as she tries to decide why he's texted her. The dominant response in her head ends up being anger, in a replay of her self-righteous rage when she dumps him. Her fingers hit the delete icon.

Callie Richards's eyes narrow as her daughter stuffs her mobile back in her handbag. 'That the guy you've been dating? Mike, Mark, whatever his name is?'

'We broke up.' Natalie dreads what's coming.

'Another worthless bastard, then. Like all the others you've been out with. Been greasing his pole elsewhere, I expect.' Satisfaction echoes in Callie Richards's voice at having her theories about the male sex confirmed. 'No idea why you bother. More trouble than they're worth, the lot of them.'

Thing is, maybe Natalie prefers the idea of Mark being a love rat. Men cheating on their girlfriends are commonplace. Something she can admit to other people without it sounding weird. Not child murder, though. Impossible to reveal she's been dating one of the nation's most hated men.

Normally such tirades skate over her head, but Callie's comments have caused the wounds inflicted by Mark to bleed afresh. Natalie needs solitude, time to reflect, away from her mother's bitterness.

She stands up. 'I need to get home, Mum. Bit tired. Could do with an early night.'

'Don't even think of texting the bastard back.' Callie Richards wheezes as she struggles to her feet. 'You're well shot of him, mark my words.'

Back at her flat, Natalie plumps herself down in her overstuffed beanbag, snuggling into its corduroy depths. She pulls open a bag of cheese Doritos. Perfect with a salsa dip. She's piled on even more kilos since the split with Mark, but she doesn't care. Food's her only comfort these days, now she's lost contact with her mates from school. A mistake, engendered by the notion that her first proper boyfriend at the age of eighteen is all she'll ever want or need. Wrong. Very. When Natalie, devastated by their split, needs a friend, she finds they've all moved on.

So she slouches in the beanbag, alone, scoffing the Doritos, Mark Slater on her mind. Wise to her mother's prejudices, she's never said much about him to Callie Richards. What can she say? How she's met a guy, who's good-looking, serious, hard-working, all the things she's after, but who never quite gives her his all, who always keeps her at arm's length? Callie won't hold back with her condemnation if she does, which will only increase Natalie's angst. As to that, she recognises where her issues stem from, of course. Her womanising father, who has proved himself a liar, a cheat and as shallow as a pond in the African sun. Her mistrust is coupled with a desire not to repeat her mother's enabling behaviour.

Callie Richards's voice sounds in her head. 'Bastards, the lot of them. Can't trust a single one.'

Stop, she tells herself. *Don't let yourself get as twisted as Mum is about Dad.*

Ah, dysfunctional families. Are theirs what drew her and Mark together in the first place? The recognition that they're both loners, not by choice but by circumstance? Two people with lives lacking in friends and family? She's unsure whether Mark has any relatives at all. Father dead, no connection with his mother. As for Linda Curtis, it's anyone's guess as to whether he's still in touch with her. Most likely he's not.

The bag of Doritos is empty now. More carbohydrates are required; the bar of Dairy Milk nestling in her fridge is calling her. Along with toast. She hauls herself out of the beanbag, walking into the kitchen, taking two slices of bread from the freezer. Butter, jam, Marmite, knife, plate. A glass or two of wine won't go amiss either. She pushes down on the toaster handle then opens a bottle of Pinot Grigio that's been chilling in the fridge. She returns with the toast, chocolate and wine to the comfort of the beanbag.

The food soon disappears. Natalie's bloated, more than a little nauseated, but she's past caring. The Pinot Grigio soothes her, starting to unravel the mess in her head. Can she accept what Mark's done, or at least find the courage to discuss it with him?

'Missing you.' His text has warmed her right the way through; Natalie now wishes she'd not deleted it. Too hasty by far. She wants to read it again, analysing each word for hidden nuances. Although she can pretty much remember the message. How he's been thinking about the two of them. Hoping she's OK. His regret about not being able to tell her the truth. Hardly surprising he didn't, she supposes.

She tries not to read anything into the kiss at the end. A standard way to finish texts, nothing more. It means zilch.

What has prompted him to text her, though? Her rejection of him? Is he trying to deal with their break-up on his own terms, his words his way of saying goodbye? Mark's final stab at closure before moving on with his life?

Perhaps there's another explanation. Is the text the opening salvo in an attempt to win her back? To convince her he's not a vicious child killer? *That's not how it was, Nat.* The memory of his words wash over her, bringing with them the desire to believe him, to marry up the man she's been dating with the reality of what Linda Curtis's letter reveals. Does Mark want a chance to explain, make things right between them? Has she been too hasty, too quick to condemn?

That's not how it was. The words bounce off the inside of her skull, teasing her, delivering hope. Thing is, if he's telling the truth about being coerced by the other boy, doesn't he deserve another chance? He's served time in prison, been judged worthy of release by the system, is being monitored by the police. He holds down a steady job, keeps himself out of trouble. All signs pointing to him being repentant, rehabilitated, responsible, his crime folded neatly away in the past. Should Mark really be forever an outcast for a mistake he made so long ago? When only eleven years old?

The least she can do is meet with him, talk with him, ask him these questions in person. Better than supplying the answers in her head. *It's the only way to get the truth,* the voice in her brain insists. *It won't commit you to anything. If he bullshits you, simply walk away.*

She misses Mark, or Joshua, or whatever the hell he's called; she recognises that much. Sometimes, at night, she reaches for him, only to be met with the coldness of the unoccupied side of the bed. Occasionally a thought comes into her head and she thinks: I must remember to tell Mark. Then reality hits, and she regrets the loss of him, every minute, every second. Not having anyone to confide in accentuates his absence from her life.

The thought of Mark is temptation on a plate. Natalie pictures his smile, the spiky tufts of his cropped hair, his broad chest. In her mind, they're having sex, his body slippery with sweat against hers. He's rubbing her nipples between his fingers, telling her she's one hell of a hot fuck before his mouth becomes deliciously busy elsewhere. She loves the way he flips her self-image in a second from overweight to sexy. The memory causes a twitch between her legs; she'll relive his hands on her body once she's in bed, her fingers moving in time with the scenes in her head as she makes herself come. The pictures in her brain are potent, steamy, arousing. Enough to convince her she's a fool if she doesn't give Mark the chance to explain.

Decision made. She'll contact him and, at the very least, they can talk. First, she'll get his explanation of Abby Morgan's murder. Her gut instinct will be tuned in for any hint he's lying. When he's done speaking, she'll pose her questions. Some of them may have been answered by what he says, of course, particularly whether he's repentant about the murder. He won't be able to fake remorse, not well enough to fool her. If her bullshit radar lights up, she'll walk away. If it doesn't, she'll ask him if he wants to be with her long-term. A bold question, the sort for which she's never had the guts before. Again, if he's not straight in his answer, her crap detector will sniff him out. She won't go any further with the commitment issue beyond that, not at this stage. They can work the rest out further down the line.

He'll probably have questions for her, too. He'll want to know things like *can you accept what I've done, do you promise not to tell anyone who I am, will you ever throw my past in my face,* and she hopes she'll be able to answer *yes, yes* and *no.*

His message gives her some reassurance he wants to be with her. Surely to God he wouldn't have sent it if he didn't? Now it's up to her to respond.

Natalie pulls out her mobile. She'll suggest lunch, down at the Watershed perhaps, or somewhere out of town, like The Rose and Crown. A place they've been before, familiar yet neutral territory. Her text will be brief, non-committal, a simple statement of how she wants to meet up, hear what he has to say.

Wait; she needs more wine, before she does this. She slugs back a generous measure of the Pinot Grigio, now lukewarm, and settles back into the beanbag.

Do it, she tells herself.

Her fingers obey. 'Miss you too. Can we talk?' Before she has time to backtrack, she sends the text.

Natalie gulps down the remainder of her wine before pouring herself another large glass. She cradles her phone in her hands, willing him to respond straight away.

He doesn't disappoint. Two minutes, tops, go by before her mobile vibrates with his reply coming through. Her fingers can't open it quickly enough.

'Desperate to see you, explain things. Miss you like hell. X.'

17

A WHOLE POUND COIN

Sunday, just over a week since his last visit to Rachel Morgan, and Mark's travelling down the M5 again for lunch at her flat.

He's optimistic, upbeat, buoyed up by the texts he's been exchanging with Natalie. Both of them are playing it cool, not straining their fragile truce. They've not spoken on the phone so far, simply swapped messages. What they have to discuss needs to be said face to face, not via their mobiles. She's agreed to meet him, though, which is the main thing. Tuesday evening he'll go to her flat. Better than Natalie's suggestion of a pub meal. Their conversation will be too intimate, too personal, to risk it being overheard. Besides, if things go well, he'll want to touch her, hold her, take her to bed. Somewhere public doesn't fit that particular bill.

He's praying he'll find the words to convince her he's no vicious child killer. Natalie Richards, with all her insecurities, is the woman he wants, despite her being every bit as damaged, as flawed, as he is. Jointly, though, they can synergise something better. He doesn't ask for much; people as scarred as he is tend not to. A loving relationship, his job at the building supplies firm, a home together. Children one day, perhaps. Natalie wants them, he's well aware, and he won't deny her, however strange the idea of him being a father is. The chances seem fair his life will morph, slowly but firmly, into what he's always wanted. Stable, solid and good.

Before any of this can happen, though, Mark's priority is to resolve things with Rachel. Today will be the last time he has any contact with her; they'll meet, he'll find out what he needs to and after that it'll be over between them. Then, slate wiped squeaky clean, he'll be able to meet Natalie on Tuesday, minus the guilt of Rachel Morgan hanging over his head.

He's nearly at her flat now, the journey having passed without him needing his counting rituals once. He's early, as he always is, but the extra few minutes will give him time to breathe, prepare himself for the afternoon ahead.

Five minutes later, his energies recharged, he presses the bell for Rachel's flat. Her face is overly eager when she opens the door; he composes his features into a suitably warm expression, a warning sounding in his head. *Don't fuck this up.* As both their smiles fade, a moment of awkwardness raises its head. The kiss surges into Mark's mind, and he's damn sure it does in Rachel's, too.

'Come on in.' Rachel waves him inside. A hot smell reaches him, a delicious aroma of cooking meat, cheese and onions. His stomach growls at the prospect of food; it'll also be welcome as a way of easing any lingering tensions between them. She's suitably garbed in a striped apron, hands encased in oven gloves, sleeves rolled down over her scars.

'Beer?' Rachel gestures towards the fridge. 'Got some Budweiser in. Wasn't sure what you'd like. Or I've got red wine, if you prefer?'

'A Budweiser would be good. Just the one, though, as I'm driving.' Not to mention he wants to keep a clear head for any discussion they have about Shaun.

She shucks off the oven gloves, pulls open the fridge, handing him a can. 'Sit down. Make yourself at home. I've put a glass on the table for your beer. Lasagne's the dish of the day. I hope that's all right?' Her forehead is puckered with concern she's made the wrong choice.

'Can't wait. Smells wonderful.' He watches the relief wash over her face.

'Oh, good. I wasn't sure, what with you saying you're more of a meat and potatoes guy. Wanted to cook something other than a roast, though. I'm doing chips with the lasagne, so one way or another you'll get your meat and tatties today. It's all been rather rushed this morning. Had to miss running with the Hashers. Shaun's been here.'

'Is everything OK?' He's concerned. Has she been cutting herself again, or wanting to?

She shrugs. Her back is towards him as she bends down at the oven, her gloves back on, pulling out the dish of lasagne, so he can't read her expression. 'I guess so. No, not really. It's Dad. Shaun goes down to Taunton every so often, to check up on him, see how he's doing. No change, unfortunately.'

'Still drinking?'

'Yeah. Can't see him getting off the booze, not now. He's too far gone, with no compelling reason to stay sober. He's not spoken to Mum in years, and it seems his remaining children aren't enough of an incentive to ditch the drink.' Weary resignation leaks from her voice. Mark can tell she's long ago accustomed herself to the reality of having an alcoholic for a father. 'He'll drink himself to death and there's not a lot I, or Shaun, or anyone, can do about it.'

'I'm sorry, Rachel.' Such inadequate words.

'Not your fault,' she replies, unaware of how wrong she is, and tips a generous helping of chips onto his plate before handing it to him. She pulls out a chair to sit down, pouring herself a glass of Chianti. Her portion of lasagne is very much smaller than his one, and she's gone for salad rather than chips, he notes. 'Dig in.'

The food is sublime, a perfect blend of meat, cheese and pasta. 'This is bloody good,' Mark says. 'No, scrub that. It's great. You should do this for a living.'

She laughs. They eat in silence for a while, with Mark unsure whether to pursue the conversation about her father in the hope it'll lead back to Shaun. In a way, he's like a vulture, picking over the bones of her wrecked family life. It doesn't make him feel good, not at all.

'I miss him.' Mark's head jerks up as Rachel's words pull him from his mental quicksand.

'Your father?'

'Yes. I was always a Daddy's girl, at least when he was sober enough to notice me. He wasn't so bad with the booze, not when I was younger, before Abby's death. I blame myself for him leaving, the drinking getting worse, everything.' Her hands shake slightly as she forks lasagne towards her mouth, drips of béchamel sauce falling onto her plate. She gulps some Chianti, her gaze fixed on her food.

'Abby was every bit as much a Daddy's girl as me. It tore him up not doing the fatherly thing. Not protecting her from what happened, I mean.'

Mark can't dredge up any words that don't seem entirely inadequate. Rachel spears a slice of tomato, contemplating it. 'Sorry to bring up all this crap, Mark. What you must think of me and my dysfunctional family, I hate to imagine.' Her fork disappears into her mouth.

'I grew up in a glass house where screwed-up families are concerned. No throwing of stones here.' Mark smiles, attempting to loosen the tension a little.

Silence settles down around them again as they eat. Despite the excellence of the lasagne, the heavy combination of meat and cheese sits like an iron bar in Mark's stomach, weighed down as he is by the revelations about Matthew Morgan's booze-filled existence. He's not been able to touch his Budweiser; drinking alcohol seems an insult to the man whose life and family he's contributed to ruining.

Rachel finishes her meal first, eyeing his half-eaten food with alarm. 'Too rich for you? Too much seasoning?' Every one of her insecurities is clearly kicking in, and he hastens to reassure her. 'Just a slow eater, that's all.' He vows to finish every morsel of it, even if he vomits, rather than inflame Rachel's self-doubt any further.

Time to bring up the topic of Shaun.

'You said your brother checks on your dad occasionally? Can't be easy for him.'

She shakes her head. 'No, it's not. He can't be sure from one visit to the next how Dad will be. Never lets on if it bothers him, although it must do. Not many people are as strong as Shaun.' Sisterly pride infuses her words.

'Sounds like he's your rock.'

'He is. I guess some of us are simply born tougher than others are. Mentally, I mean. Shaun being one of them.' Her words echo what Mark has already thought. 'He loved Abby, of course, but somehow he dealt with her murder better than any of us. He grieved for his sister, he missed Dad when he left, still does, but he's always been able to stay on top of it, rather than getting dragged under like Mum and I do.'

'Does he really cope? Or simply bottle up his emotions?'

Rachel pulls a face. 'Hard to say. He's not always an easy fish to fathom.'

'Like you said before, he's the strong, if not so silent, type.'

'Definitely.'

'Thank God he is, though. For you and your mum, I mean.'

'Don't know how he does it. When I ask him, he just shrugs and tells me that's life, how it throws rocks in your path at times. Seems like he leapfrogs over them, whereas I fall flat on my face.' A shadow of a smile hovers round her mouth.

'He's never been treated the way you have by your mother, though. Rocks? Seems she's more like one hell of a mountain.'

'But that's partly why I think he's always dealt with everything so well. He won't admit it, but I reckon it's because his conscience is clear. Unlike me, he has nothing to feel guilty about where Abby's death is concerned.'

Mark leans over, briefly touching her left arm. A gesture of support, of empathy. Even though the pressure of his fingertips is feather soft, he can feel the ridging of her scars through the thin material of her sleeve. An awkward moment passes between them before she pulls away.

Embarrassed, he seeks to smooth over the tension. 'None of you has any reason to feel guilty, Rachel. If only you could understand how it wasn't your fault, any of it.'

She chooses to ignore his words, not that he's surprised. Self-blame as deeply entrenched as hers requires more than a few glib sentences to lever it out of place. 'Shaun was upstairs, remember, when Abby was lured out of the garden by those boys. Doing his homework. He wasn't drinking alcohol or too busy reading, like Dad and me. Just boring old schoolwork.

So he has no reason for guilt. That's my opinion, anyway.'

'Neither do you.'

Her mouth twists bitterly. 'You reckon? I had my headphones clamped on tight, Christina Aguilera booming in my ears. Couldn't hear anything else. I wasn't even watching her either, like I'd been told. Had my head in my book, oblivious to the world.'

'Apart from your cat. I remember now. You were stroking your kitten.' Mark smiles at his mental picture of the pretty ten-year-old, absorbed in another world, her right hand smoothing the animal's black fur, the sunlight striking fire into the pale copper of her hair. He smiles, and the memory almost blots out the remembrance of what follows. Not quite, though, because nothing can ever erase Abby Morgan's death. He's lost, back in time, fourteen years ago, and so he doesn't realise, not at first, the significance of what he's just said. Neither does Rachel.

Time slows down to a crawl as awareness pulls him back, sharp and sudden, into the moment. His words echo through his head, plucking the mask of Mark Slater away to reveal Joshua Barker. What he's said should never have been said, and he can't claw the mistake back inside. His only hope is for Rachel not to connect the dots, a faint one admittedly, but perhaps she's too immersed in her thoughts to register his words. To understand the implication of his knowledge of her black kitten.

At first, he doesn't see any change in her expression. She's still lingering in her head over Christina Aguilera and Harry Potter. Then Mark notes the exact moment when her mind shifts to the soft black fur of her cat, when not a penny but a whole pound coin drops in her brain. Her eyes stretch wider and her face, always pale anyway, takes on the colour of chalk. Her gaze slams into his, and he's unable to hide behind the mask any longer.

'How do you...' Her voice sounds as though it's fighting its way through treacle in her throat. 'You mentioned me stroking my cat. How did you know about that?'

Mark's aware of his breath, coming rapid and shallow, his chest tight. No words can explain the unexplainable. He takes refuge in a lie.

'I...' He swallows, trying to stifle his dread of what's to come. 'I must have read about it or heard it on the news.'

'None of those details were ever released to the media.' Her voice manages to be both hoarse and high at the same time. 'I told you about listening to music, and reading, but not the cat. I never mentioned the cat. I know I didn't.' She staggers to her feet, pushing back her chair with one hand, the other grasping the table to steady herself. Mark aches to hold her, pour out what happened, receive her understanding, her absolution, whilst recognising the sheer impossibility of such a notion. She's on the verge of guessing who he is; he's the last person she'll ever allow to touch her.

'You'd only know that if...' She's pressed back against the wall now, hands in front of her to keep him at bay. He sees her swallow, her breath audible, as rapid and shallow as his own. 'Oh, God. My God. Which one are you?'

A question he's able to answer, yet he doesn't. If he admits his identity, if he says his birth name, it will make all this real, and he's unable to cope with it. *One, two...* He starts the familiar count in his head, abandoning it seconds later as she speaks again.

'Why?' She's crying now, the chalk of the previous moment replaced by red staining in her cheeks as the sobs come. 'Why did you seek me out? How *could* you? I thought....' The words fight with her breath in her throat, her syllables strangled. 'We talked about going running. You asked to meet me for lunch.'

Mark can only nod, still silent.

'You *kissed* me.' She flings the word out, as though by even saying it she's defiled.

Mark doesn't respond. What, after all, can he say? No words exist to vindicate why he's here, why he approached her after the vigil. She'll be attributing all sorts of twisted motives to his behaviour, how he must have drawn sick gratification from kissing his victim's sister, how he's revelling in turning the blade deeper in her wounds. How can he possibly explain the kiss being a cry for understanding, a gesture of repentance?

Rachel's face is contorted with disbelief, denial, rage. She's regarding him as one would a fully-fledged incarnation of the Devil, standing before her reeking of brimstone and brandishing a pitchfork. He doesn't blame her. It's even worse than being back in the courtroom before the handing down of his sentence by the judge. So he sits in front of his half-eaten plate of lasagne, too agitated even for his counting rituals, waiting for whatever she has to say.

'Which...' She swallows, clearly attempting to get her mouth to work. Her voice still sounds as though it's being pulled through razor wire. 'I asked you before. You owe me that much. Which one are you? You're Joshua Barker, right?'

'Yes.' He doesn't even attempt to prevaricate. All traces of Mark Slater have been stripped away. The events of fourteen years ago arise in front of him and Rachel, their sting uncurled and ready to strike.

'Rachel, please listen to me...'

'You're fucking joking, right?' She's found her voice now, and it's more of a scream. 'Why the hell should I listen to you? Mum's been right all along when she says the two of you are evil, how neither of you has any conscience, how you should rot in jail for the rest of your miserable lives. I thought you were genuine. That you liked me. We *kissed.*' Again, the words are spat out. Mark's shocked by the profanity. Rachel has always been so polite, so well-mannered.

'Do you get some weird kick out of this?' A bead of spittle flies from her mouth, landing on the table between them. 'Enjoy this, do you? Leading me on, making me think...' It's then that she breaks. She sinks back into her chair, pillowing her head on her arms as she leans on the table. Sobs hiccup from her, her scars lividly in view where her sleeves have ridden up. For once, she obviously doesn't give a toss. Apart from her tears, she's silent, spent, finished.

'Rachel.' He has to try to gain her understanding. 'I'm sorry. For your sister's death, for what I've done to your family, for everything. I should never have approached you after the vigil. I did it...' He swallows hard. 'Because I needed to make sense of Abby's death. I've always been so sorry, Rachel. You must believe me.' Why should she, though? Even as he says them, the words sound cheap, easy, the kind liars always use to justify themselves.

'You fucking bastard. Don't you even dare say her name.'

Mark tries again. 'I didn't hurt her, Rachel. It was Adam Campbell, the other boy. He did it all. It was impossible to stop him. He was so...' Adam muscles his way into Mark's mind, his size, his innate aggressiveness. Above all, the sense of the other boy harbouring inside him something warped, twisted, beyond redemption.

'I've always been desperate to make amends. I just don't have a clue what to do. That's why I approached you after the vigil.' Is she taking any of this in? She's a foot or so away physically but emotionally she's light years distant. Mark has no idea whether anything he says can bridge the gulf between them. 'I hoped if I could talk to you, find out how it's been for you, for your family, I might get some pointers. I never meant to hurt you, honestly I didn't.'

What he's just said bridges the gap between them all right, but not in the way he intends. She raises her head, spearing him with the loathing in her eyes. It's so strong he flinches, as though her hatred might shoot forth to stab him, cut him, slice and dice him into shreds.

'Is that the best you can come up with? He made you do it? How fucking feeble.' She's getting into her stride now. 'I don't believe a word of your shit. You're evil, pure evil, the pair of you. You beat and stabbed a two-year-old child to death, for fuck's sake. Only someone completely without any conscience would do such a thing. You've breached the terms of your release, not that you should ever have been paroled in the first place. By going to the vigil. By even daring to look at me.'

'I know.' He's the one sounding hoarse now. 'It was wrong. I thought -'

'You didn't think at all. You bastard. All you cared about was getting your kicks out of tormenting me. As if I've not suffered enough, every fucking day, since Abby's death.' She pushes back her chair violently, the legs scraping against the carpet, pulling herself to her feet. 'Get out. Get the fuck out of my flat. You're scum. Fucking scum. Don't think I won't tell the police you've broken your parole. I'll make damn sure your arse gets thrown back in jail where it belongs.'

18

STUPID AND WEAK

Mark has no idea how he manages to unlock his car door, let alone start the engine. He drives a mere couple of hundred yards from Rachel's flat when he has to pull over or risk a crash. The pain in his chest squeezes tight, constricting his breath, far worse than when Natalie walked out on him. *Breathe, just breathe through it*, he tells himself.

Rachel's tortured face flashes before him, white and terrible, with its accusatory gaze. Her words slice through him. How she concurs with her mother about him being evil. How he's scum, wicked, should be rotting in jail. Mark's inclined to agree. Wrong, ill-judged, selfish, to have ever talked to her that day in Moretonhampstead, to burst the bubble of her grief by foisting his own issues on her. Hell, he needs to confront the damage he's caused to the Morgan family, sure, but piling more hurt on top of what already exists isn't part of his game plan. Desperate to drive out his own demons, all he's succeeded in doing is sending them Rachel Morgan's way.

With eyes squeezed shut, he begins to count. *One, two, buckle my shoe,* and Abby Morgan's wrenched-off trainer flashes into his mind, transporting him back to the shed floor, with the streams of sunlight bouncing off the pink Velcro. God, oh God. He'll never be free of the horror of his past. He's at liberty when it comes to his physical self, but his mind's forever imprisoned in the abandoned farm shed of fourteen years ago. *Three, four, knock at the door.* Onwards and upwards, his brain moves through the numbers, seeking the safety of the higher ones, except this time the comfort doesn't come. The anguish, the memory of Rachel's face, her voice, as the realisation slams home of who she's kissed, stays firmly wedged in his mind. It's all too much, and for the first time since he was a child, Mark cries. He rests his forearms on the steering wheel, the unfamiliar sensation of tears on his face, as the wounds inside him split open, raw and deep.

Joanna Barker strides into his head, the pain of her rejection chilling him. She's followed by the fury that overwhelms him as he drives his fist into the wall at Vinney Green. Natalie walking out on him. Rachel's slashed arms. His fault, all of it, and crowding out everything else is the memory of Abby Morgan's broken and bloodied body, accusing him of cowardice for not preventing her death.

Knuckles rap on the glass beside his ear, jolting his head off the steering wheel.

A policewoman is bending towards the window, her hands motioning for him to open it. Panic kicks into Mark, sharp and instantaneous. Immediately he's eleven years old again, cowed and confused. Impossible not to obey this woman. His fingers fumble for the down button.

'Sir, are you all right?' The woman's voice is concerned, kind, but Mark needs her to get the hell away from the car, right now. No police, not today.

He nods, unable to speak.

'Is something wrong? Do you need help?'

Mark shakes his head, trying to find his voice. When he does, it's croaky. 'No. I'm fine, honestly. It's just that...' He clears his throat. 'I've got some shit to deal with, that's all.'

She nods in sympathy. 'Where are you heading for? Do you have a long way to go?'

'Bristol. Not far.'

The woman's mouth purses a little. 'You shouldn't attempt to drive a car. Not whilst you're...' She's clearly searching for the right word. 'In a distressed state.'

Desperation to get rid of her grows ever more urgent in Mark. 'You're right. Thing is, I just need to sit for a while and get myself together, you know?' He manages a weak smile. 'I'll be fine. Honestly.'

She's clearly unconvinced, but as Mark's not breaking any laws, all she can do is reiterate her warning not to drive until he's safe to do so.

Once the policewoman's gone, Mark leans back against his headrest, incapable of further tears. He's spent, finished. Exhaustion born from the strain of recent weeks slams into him; he's weary all the way down to the bone and into his marrow, tired of everything. Somehow, he has to drive to Bristol, back to his life. Such as it is. Recollection hits him. Hell, he's supposed to be seeing Natalie on Tuesday. Their big talk is in the evening, the one supposedly to sort things out between them, convince her he's worthy to share her life. Well, that's fucked up now, for sure. The contempt in Rachel Morgan's face has hammered a basic truth home to him: he doesn't deserve happiness.

Drive, Mark, drive, he tells himself. *Get a grip on yourself.* He peels himself off the steering wheel, fumbles for his keys, starts the engine. The journey will have to be done on autopilot; thank God it's not far. He'll count, and breathe, one, two, in, out, allowing the rhythmic disappearing of the road beneath his wheels to hypnotise him, numb him until he reaches the sanctuary of his flat. He recalls Natalie telling him about Callie

Richards's agoraphobia. Right now, he understands the appeal, although he's not planning to add it to his list of compulsions. To stay indoors, making one's home a haven against the outside world - he gets why people go down that route.

He sets the car in gear and drives away, heading towards the M5 junction, counting as he goes, batches of seven, repeatedly, getting a rhythm in his head. He takes the journey slowly, sticking to the inside lane all the way, too exhausted to deal with the logistics of mirror, signal, manoeuvre. The self-medication works; eventually he's in Bristol, back at his flat, before he's aware of how he got there.

At home, he pulls a bottle of Black Sheep from the fridge before slumping on the sofa with his beer. What he can't understand is how things ever got this far. The impulse to speak with Rachel after the vigil was bad enough, but this? Facebook messages? Lunch, not once, but twice? What the hell was he thinking? The pain of Natalie's rejection is no excuse for his behaviour. He's managed to screw things up, which means retribution won't be far behind. People like him always get caught and punished. It's the consequence of being born lower down in Nature's pecking order.

Mark swings his legs off the sofa. He's wound too tightly to sit still. One, two, he paces across the floor, nervous energy surging through him. Back and forth, four strides taking him from one side to the other of his living room. He settles into a rhythm as he walks, beer bottle in hand.

It looks as though his subconscious has sabotaged him, leading him to press the self-destruct button. Was that what he wanted to happen? Was the mention of Rachel's black kitten deliberate? Some weird kind of Freudian slip? Did he delude himself about seeking answers from her whilst all the while intending to reveal himself as Joshua Barker? So she would either absolve or condemn him? After all, Michelle Morgan has already judged him, whereas Rachel's verdict on him has been an unknown before today. He's unsure of the answer, but he suspects he's pretty close to the truth.

How she'll react to the knowledge of who he is seems inevitable. She'll resort to the knife. Mark pictures the blade, slicing through the flesh of her arms, her legs, her senses oblivious to the pain, the silent scream sounding out through the blood, the open wounds. She'll cut, and it'll be deep too, in an attempt to carve out the memory of their kiss. After all, he's branded himself on her with his lips. One more in a series of never-ending punishments for her supposed neglect of her sister fourteen years ago.

Besides the inevitable self-harm, Rachel will also seek revenge, of course. She's too furious, too insulted, to do otherwise. *Don't think I won't tell the police you've broken your parole.* On the slim chance she doesn't, perhaps through shame or embarrassment, then Shaun definitely will. She'll get the itch to cut and then call her brother. He'll demand answers about what's triggered her latest urge for the knife. Rachel will eventually confess how she's unwittingly been seeing Joshua Barker. *I hadn't a clue who he was, I swear*, she'll say. Enough, surely, to shatter this man's seemingly unshakable cool at last. Shaun will inevitably erupt with anger and the police will be informed within the hour.

Perhaps Rachel won't turn to her brother, though. Second, less likely, scenario. She'll cut, releasing her pain with yet another silent scream. More scars for her collection. Then she'll lock the knowledge of their connection inside her, too ashamed to confess she's kissed one of the individuals convicted of her sister's murder. The police will never find out. He'll keep his job, his flat, his life, such as it is. It's more of an existence, really. He doesn't kid himself he'll be able to reinstate Natalie in his life, not now, not after this. He'll continue to get up, go to work, come home, eat and sleep as per usual. All without the embellishments that add depth to living. Like friends, warmth, love. He'll never have those, so what he'll be left with is worth fuck all anyway.

The most likely scenario, though, will be the first one, in which Rachel seeks revenge. Hell hath no fury like a woman scorned, after all. She's definitely that all right, humiliated as she'll be by her former hopes about him. She'll turn into her mother, all fire and brimstone, her mission to throw his arse back behind bars for the rest of his life. No, one way or another, the police will come for him. He's unsure how much time he has left, but he won't be free for long. The rapping of the policewoman's knuckles against his window now seems a warning, a foreshadowing.

When the police do arrive, he won't be able to deny his connection with Rachel. Their shared history on Facebook is a giveaway; even if he deletes his account, some techno-whizz will be able to recover it. Mark's sad about the prospect of disappointing Tony Jackson; he's a decent enough guy who's come to expect Mark will always toe the line, not give him any trouble. Now Jackson gets landed with this shit. The poor bastard's simply another in a long line of people he's let down.

Back to jail. Really, it's not such a bad prospect. He'll forfeit his job and his liberty, sure, but he's used to prison life. No, it's the loss of Natalie that hurts the most. A sense of inevitability follows the pain. Did any chance of making things work with Natalie ever exist, tainted as he is? No is the answer.

She tugs at the back of Mark's mind, though. Natalie's messages have been guarded but she's made it clear she's open to listening to his side of the story about Abby Morgan. How reconciliation between them might be possible. He's been so stoked up about their forthcoming meeting on Tuesday, but now the idea is unbearable. All that seems lost now. He should never have texted her in the first place. Someone else he's hurt by being the total fuck up that he is. He's failed Natalie. If he ends up back in prison, then they're over anyway. If he doesn't, he still can't see the two of them being able to work things out, for the simple reason she deserves better than him.

Enough is enough. He's acted like an idiot recently, too much impulse and not enough thought or consideration. Time to stop, right now, and grow some balls. He's fucked up once too often and whatever he does or says from now on, he has to get it right. Too many people have been hurt by him already. Whilst he can't do anything to influence Rachel, he can do what's right by Natalie. The kindest thing will be to set her free from him.

So, then. Decision made. He'll go to her flat on Tuesday as they've arranged. No talk of reconciliation, no holding out false hopes of a shared future. He'll simply tell her they can't be together.

Shit. He remembers Rachel's threat. All this assumes he'll be granted the chance to meet up with Natalie. Rachel Morgan might be talking to the police right now. If he remembers correctly, once his name is logged into the criminal database, it'll trigger an alert, warning the few individuals who know his new identity, flagging up his breach of the rules to Tony Jackson and his superiors. After that, they'll arrive swiftly at his door. Extinguishing all chances of him ever explaining anything to Natalie.

A circle of pain is clamping down around Mark's head. Too little time, too much to do. He could call

Natalie, ask to go over there now, but his brain is too fried, his nerves too shredded; he'll end up getting what he needs to say all wrong, making things worse rather than better. No, this has to be done right.

A thought occurs to him. Perhaps he should text her, ask if they can bring their meeting forward, to Monday evening. Then he remembers. They arranged it for Tuesday for a reason. Natalie's away all day tomorrow. Some television production she's working on up in London. A slap-up meal afterwards. She won't be home before midnight.

Shit. He'll have to take his chances as to whether he's granted sufficient time to explain things to her.

Mark stops his pacing, tossing his empty beer bottle in the bin. Time for a shower. Once in his tiny bathroom, he turns the water on as hot as it will go, willing it to wash away the stress of the day. He doesn't hurry; this may be his last shower as a free man. The heat steams through the cramped space, enveloping him with comfort. Mark closes his eyes, leaning against the tiles as the warmth cascades over him.

Without warning, a memory surfaces; Joanna Barker's voice sounds in his head. It's fourteen years ago, not long before Abby Morgan's death. His mother's outside the bathroom as he showers before school, shouting at him not to waste so much water. A frequent complaint of hers. For a second, her irritation works its usual effect in the present day, causing Mark's fingers to stray towards the off knob on the shower. He stops himself, struck by how pervasive, how powerful, the maternal influence is. All these years, and she's still able to cow him.

His mother. She'd not be surprised, not at all, if she knew about his latest fuck up. She always did consider him stupid and weak. Unworthy to be her child. *You're your father's son.* Along with *can't trust you to get anything right.* Her favourite mantras when annoyed, making it clear his paternity isn't something of which to be proud.

Thing is, her voice in his head has a point, given how badly he's screwed up this time. Perhaps it's not so hard to explain why she didn't love him. The answer is so obvious, really. Joanna Barker sniffed out his weakness, his unworthiness, as soon as he made his entrance into the world. Maternal rejection is hardly unknown in the animal kingdom, after all; why shouldn't humans act the same way? Abby Morgan was the excuse his mother needed to oust him from her life completely and finally, a thorn pulled from her flesh at last.

Is it so complete and final, though?

Somewhere inside, Mark's still a young boy, one who craves his mother's approval. As well as wanting one last attempt at shattering her icy defences before he's arrested. Not unreasonable to hope fourteen years may have changed her. People often mellow as they get older. Why not his mother?

For the first time ever, he considers attempting to find her. Not impossible, not at all, to contact Joanna Barker. Wherever she is.

Whether it's advisable is another matter.

Your mother has decided to move away from Exeter and change her name.

Shit. Should he even be contemplating tracking her down?

He stands under the cascade of water, desperate for an answer.

The child inside him, the one still craving his mother's love, ends up victorious. Sod taking the easy way out. Joanna Barker is a ghost he needs to exorcise, one way or another.

He'll do it. With the possibility of arrest an imminent one, he'll have to act fast. Hanging around isn't an option. He'll call in sick to work tomorrow. Put the enforced delay in seeing Natalie to good use.

Mark turns off the shower. Time to make a long-overdue phone call.

19

IN HER OWN WAY

Rachel's hands are grasping the edge of her kitchen unit so tightly, she's amazed she doesn't snap either it or her fingers off. The slam of the door to her flat echoes in her head, taking with it Mark Slater and her hopes for the two of them. He's gone, leaving her alone, fighting to get a handle on the emotions churning inside her.

Wine. Always a good idea. She gulps back the remainder of her glass of Chianti before pouring herself a second measure, her fingers shaking, red splashes spattering over the table. She doesn't care. At times, she understands why her father drinks the way he does. Why he depends on the booze to blur the sharp edges of reality, transport him to a world where children don't kill each other. Rachel's confident she'll never walk down that road herself - for her, a sharp knife provides the release, not alcohol - but she reckons the principle's much the same. She swallows another large mouthful, coughing as the liquid goes down the wrong way, gasping and spluttering as the tears come.

'Oh, God.' Her words come out as a moan. She might as well have said *why me*, because it's what she's thinking. Hasn't she suffered enough? Been sufficiently punished already?

She underestimates her own capacity for mental self-flagellation. The self-torture commences.

He gave off enough clues about his identity, except you missed them all, you stupid bitch.

Now Rachel realises why Mark seemed somehow familiar to her when they first met.

Mum will go berserk when she hears about this. She'll jab her fingers in my face the way she always does when I've pissed her off. She'll scream how stupid I've been. She'll tell me I should have realised who he was. How it must have been obvious. And it was. I ignored all the signs, though. How he approached me after the vigil, with his lies about coming across it by chance. The way he steered most of our conversations around to Abby's murder, the effect it's had on us.

Oh God. Time to sift the mess in her head into some semblance of order, before she decides what to do next.

She has three options.

One, the tried and tested route of cutting herself.

Two, call Shaun and tell him what she's discovered.

Three, show some spunk for once in her life and make good on her threat. Notify the police about what's happened.

Number one is her favourite. The second option will inevitably lead to the police being informed anyway. Shaun is bound to insist on it. She can't bring herself to contemplate how swiftly their involvement will unleash her mother's contempt. For not realising sooner she's been hanging out with Joshua Barker. The third – well, no matter what she screamed at him, right now any spunk she possesses has barricaded itself behind the walls of some inner fortress. Impossible even to contemplate the police, not on her own, not without Shaun's support.

Before she decides, Rachel needs more wine. She drains her glass. Her fingers reach out to pour herself another, before she checks herself. She's eaten enough of the lasagne, along with bread and salad, to be reasonably full, offering some protection against the alcohol. If she keeps downing it at this rate, though, getting pissed isn't far off. Best to slow down a little, so she can think things through; she's certainly drunk enough already to sand the rough edges off the shock of it all. Thank fuck for that.

She sinks into a chair, resting her head in her hands, her fingers blocking the light from her eyes. Can she put a name to the emotions at war in her head? Shock, yes, coupled with disbelief. Anger at herself for not realising sooner who she's been seeing. Above all, though, Rachel decides, she's been violated. Not only her trust but her body as well. She kissed this man and he kissed her back. Now Rachel knows locking lips isn't always a sign of love, of caring; it can mean treachery, too. No finer example than this of a Judas kiss. She's betrayed Abby along with the rest of her family by touching her mouth to Mark Slater's. Or Joshua Barker, as he really is.

Why the hell did he seek her out after the vigil? His words about being sorry and seeking atonement ring in her head, but a hollow note echoes through them. Her mother's speech, spoken after Joshua Barker and Adam Campbell's release, returns to taunt her. 'Leopards don't change their spots. Once a killer, always a killer. Those boys will be every bit as evil now they're men, worse in fact. The killing instinct in them will be stronger now. They were just practising when they murdered Abby. Now they're out of prison, they'll murder again. Mark my words.'

Her mother's right. When Joshua Barker approaches her disguised as Mark Slater, atonement is obviously the last thing on his mind. No, what he's seeking is a chance to twist the knife in her. How he must be laughing at her gullibility. The way she tells him to friend her on Facebook, asking him to do the fun run with her, cooking him lunch. How he pretends he gets involved in charity events, as though he cares about kids being abused. Lies, all lies. He's been chasing gratification of his sick impulses instead. He's made a fool out of her and he'll have enjoyed every minute.

She might as well erect a flashing neon sign above her head, proclaiming: *roll up, roll up, check out this bitch's low self-esteem*. Her body language, her clothes, her expression, must shout out the message loud and clear. A beacon to the likes of Mark Slater. He must have marked her out as an easy victim when he saw her at the vigil, perhaps even before. She's worthless, and he's relished playing with her.

Rachel agrees with him, of course. After all, Mark Slater's not the only one who considers her to be trash. Take her mother. What better way to understand how utterly valueless you are, if not through rejection from the woman who helped create you? Who is more qualified to pronounce judgement as to your worth than the person who raised you? Michelle Morgan's antipathy constantly castigates Rachel, every time she speaks coldly to her daughter or simply ignores her. Nothing Shaun can say ever eradicates Rachel's unswerving sense of her own unworthiness.

'Telling yourself if only this, if only that, is pointless. You weren't to blame; those two boys were. The responsibility for what happened is theirs alone.' Impossible for Shaun's words to penetrate the barrier created by her mother's rejection. Rachel always nods when he says these things, dismissing them immediately. Shaun's wonderful, the way he supports her, but he's wrong. Rachel's every bit as much to blame as Joshua Barker and Adam Campbell. No way around the truth; had she been paying attention, watching her sister properly, Abby would still be alive today. Her mother wouldn't be a frigid stranger, a relative in name only, and perhaps her father wouldn't have degenerated into a hopeless drunk.

Mark Slater, a.k.a. Joshua Barker. The thought, intrusive and unwelcome, forces its way into Rachel's mind: *at least I didn't sleep with him.* A small mercy, but she's grateful for it. The horror of finding out later on she's entrusted her body to one of the men who have destroyed her family would be a violation so huge she'd never recover. She thrusts the idea far behind her, where it can't soil her any further, locking it away in her mind, along with the kiss. She's certain of one thing. Whatever she tells anyone about what's happened, whether it's to the police or to Shaun, she'll never mention the kiss. It's her secret shame; she'll have to deal with it in her own way, which means the knife.

Every time she cuts herself, she swears she won't do it again. She promises Shaun too, hating herself for piling her crap onto him. He deserves better than having such a total fuck up for a sister. She means it, too, always thinking: *no more.* It's an empty pledge, because she never keeps it. When her catering business stresses her or if her mother speaks coldly to her, the knife becomes her refuge from the pain.

This time, though, she's had more than sunken cakes or a rebuke from her mother to stress her. What's happened here today is major stuff. She'll struggle to survive the next hour without cutting herself.

Although Rachel does her best. She can control it, she tells herself; she doesn't have to do this. Her left arm has now healed enough for her to ditch the bandage. Why add to the damage already scored there? Why not take this opportunity to transcend her compulsion? After all, if she can make it through something as big as this without cutting, she'll be one step further towards recovery. Besides, if the impulse gets too great, Shaun is only a phone call away. He'll drop everything if she asks him to. No way will he allow her to injure herself whilst he's around.

'Bloody knives,' he's often commented, angry at how impossible it is to rid Rachel's life of them, given both her chosen profession and the basic need for them in any kitchen. Even if she does change jobs and live entirely from ready meals, it won't solve anything if she can walk into the nearest supermarket and buy a knife anyway.

The impulse to draw blood, release her inner pain, is growing stronger. Should she call Shaun? It's then she realises she doesn't want to. The shock of discovering she's kissed her sister's killer has been too profound. Shaun's support isn't what Rachel needs right now. She's being punished, so she intends to submit to it. The urge becomes overwhelming. She's going to cut herself.

Rachel has a well-established ritual for these occasions. She pushes back her chair, walking into the kitchen, towards the knife block on the worktop. She draws out the vegetable knife, the smallest one. She used something similar when she first self-harmed, setting herself a precedent. It's a dedicated knife, kept solely for this purpose. All part of the ritual. She pings the blade against her thumb. Sharp, but not enough.

Rachel rummages in a cupboard, drawing out an electric knife sharpener and plugging it in. She draws the knife through the slots, three times on each side, and tests the blade again. A small fissure opens on her thumb from the lightest of pressure, followed by a tiny ooze of blood. Her chosen instrument of punishment is now as keen as a fresh razor. She sucks her thumb, licking away the blood summoned by the blade's kiss against her flesh, and closes her eyes, breathing deeply for a few seconds. Then she walks towards her bedroom, the knife in her hand.

Rachel perches on the edge of her bed and opens her bedside cabinet. She takes out a large green first aid box, containing bandages, gauze, scissors, tape, antiseptic cream. The phone she keeps by her bed reminds her it's not too late to call Shaun, but she ignores it. She positions the knife against her left arm, avoiding the area still barely healed from her last cutting session. A sensation almost akin to happiness shoots through her as she anticipates the release to come, how bleeding herself will alleviate the torment inside. Rachel closes her eyes, breathing rhythmically, one, two, in, out, closing her eyes as she counts. Her heartbeat gradually slows as she relaxes.

The perfect moment eventually arrives. She presses the blade down, drawing it across her arm in a steady, measured movement.

Her eyes ping open on the initial application of pressure from her right hand. For Rachel, the first cut isn't the deepest, no matter what the song says. It's a preliminary, a test run, for the real thing. So she doesn't press too hard, creating the narrowest of grooves to add to her collection, only a thin sliver of blood visible against her scars. Then she waits, breathing deeply again.

When Rachel's ready, she positions the knife in a fresh area, preparing for the main event. Over the years, she's perfected her technique, gauging exactly how much pressure to exert in order to achieve the desired result. One last breath and she's all set. Slowly her right hand presses down then draws back, deeper this time, her gaze fixed on the way her flesh parts under the knife blade. It's always been important to witness her self-mortification, watch the blood as it flows from her body, rich and red, delivering its welcome release. The gully she's creating fills with sweet fresh blood. No pain, as she told Mark. She lets out the breath she's been holding, anticipating the relief to follow.

It comes, but it's not enough. Shit. Why is this happening? She's always been able to gain the release she craves, but today is different. Oh, a small measure of relief exists, sure, but nowhere near sufficient. Normally by now, she'd be allowing herself to fall back on her bed, a gauze pad pressed against her flesh, savouring the pleasure before she attends to herself with bandages and tape. This time she needs more.

Rachel gazes down at her left arm, seeking a new spot to cut. The most recent wound appears to link with those around it to shape the letter A. How apt that her dead sister's initial has found its way onto her flesh, forever marking her, reminding her of her guilt. Then another, more disturbing, letter reveals itself to her. The fresh cut also forms an M with some of her other scars. M for Mark. Something else occurs to her. A can be for Adam as well as Abby. Which means she now has a reminder on her arm of both the bastards who have ruined her life.

Something that can't be allowed, not even for a second.

Once more, she places the knife in position.

The blade slashes angrily through the M and the A, repeatedly. Rachel's breath comes hard and fast. This new persona frightens her; she's normally so in control, so aware, when she cuts herself. This time her self-disgust over the kiss drives her, forcing the knife to carve harder, deeper, faster. She slices through her flesh with desperation, willing the familiar sense of release to show itself, but it remains elusive. She wants to die, she thinks, the only way she'll ever be free from her demons. Dead, but at peace.

Several frenzied strokes of the blade later, some deeply buried sense of self-preservation asserts itself, causing her hand to stop its obsessive slashing through her flesh. She stops, trembling from the emotions battling inside her head. To her shock, she realises her arm hurts, and badly. No, scrub that, severely. Never has she made such a mess of herself as she has today. She's never cut as much, or as deeply, in one session before. Blood seems to cover everywhere, her hands, the bed, the knife, with more coming.

Rachel grabs the gauze and bandages, packing them tightly into her wounds, the white lint turning scarlet immediately. There may not be enough in the box for what she needs; it's getting saturated, and fast. She rips open more packages of gauze with her teeth, dragging the contents out with her good arm to staunch the flow. What to do, oh God, what to do? She can continue what she's started, succumbing to the demon tempting her, the one saying how much better it'll be for everyone around her, especially Shaun, if she dies. She's a burden he's carried for too long; he deserves to be free.

Her newly aroused sense of self-preservation forbids that option, reminding her the death of a second sister is an extra blow she can't deal to Shaun. She'll live, then, which means dealing with the blood. She grabs her duvet, pressing a fistful of it down against her arm, whilst her right hand snatches the phone from her bedside cabinet. Shaun's number is the first in her speed-dial list. She checks her alarm clock on the cabinet. Nearly three o'clock on a Sunday afternoon; Shaun will either be weight training at the gym or out for a run. Wherever he is, Rachel knows he'll have his mobile with him, switched on. It's been that way ever since she started cutting regularly.

Her fingers hit the button.

He answers on the second ring. 'Rachel? Are you all right?'

'Come quickly.' She shifts her pressure on the duvet, now as bloodied as the gauze pads. 'It's bad this time. Really bad.'

20

JUDGEMENT

Time slows down for Rachel whilst she's waiting for the sound of Shaun's key in the lock, as though she's dazed, drugged, by the cutting session. The clock by her bed tells her ten minutes, no more, pass before she hears him arrive. He's had his own key to her flat ever since she moved in, with occasions like this specifically in mind.

Rachel's still perched on the edge of her bed, the duvet pressed tightly against her arm, her emotions deadened; she rocks herself slowly back and forth, hoping the rhythmic motion will comfort her. So far, it's not worked. Shaun is what she needs, with his ability to take control of situations. What's worrying her is the certainty she'll need medical attention this time, something she's always avoided in the past, but then she's never cut herself this badly before. Besides, if Shaun insists on a hospital, which he will, then hospital it will be. She's too numb, too emotionally bruised, to argue.

He strides into the bedroom, knowing where to find her because of her ritual, the way she always cuts herself there. He stops short for a second in the doorway, his expression stricken, before coming to sit beside her, and she realises he's never seen her this bloodied before. Not once has she been so bad she's needed her duvet to halt the damage. He squeezes her against him briefly before his hand reaches for her left arm.

'Jeez, Rachel.' He sounds tired, which he probably is, she thinks. Exhausted by having to clean up her emotional messes all the time, fed up of continually being strong. Shaun is the one his dysfunctional family turns to for help, but who cares for him when he needs someone? They all expect him to support them, without giving anything back. Shame and remorse prick her and if Shaun weren't here beside her, she'd pull off the duvet and cut herself again.

His arm tightens around her. 'Is it as bad as it looks?'

She nods. He starts to haul her to her feet. 'Come on. We're going to the hospital, get you stitched up. No buts,' as Rachel shakes her head, panic rising within her. 'You need to see a doctor, get proper help. This can't go on, Rachel.'

She tries, although she knows it's probably useless. 'No doctor. No hospital. Never needed one before, Shaun. Always managed with being bandaged up. I don't want -' She swallows hard. 'I can't bear anyone finding about this. They'll think I'm crazy. They'll say I need psychiatric help.'

'You do.'

'But, Shaun -'

He reaches over to grab the pillow behind her, before rummaging in the first aid box for the scissors and tape. 'I'm going to put this around your arm. We can't go to the hospital with you trailing a duvet behind you.' He cuts off lengths of tape, laying them ready on the bedside cabinet. His touch gentle, he eases her fingers from the duvet and peels it away from her wounds. She averts her gaze, not wanting to see the damage she's inflicted. A shocked sound hits her as Shaun draws his breath in sharply before slamming the pillow down on her arm.

'Jeez, Rachel.' He huffs air from his lungs in

weary resignation. 'Do you have any idea of how badly you've cut yourself this time? Your arm's one hell of a fucking mess.' Practised hands wrap tight hoops of tape around the pillow, securing it in place. He pulls her to her feet. 'Keep your hand on that. Press as tightly as possible. We need to get you to a hospital. Now. Don't give me any grief on this one, Rachel.'

She's past the point of protest. It amazes her she can put one foot in front of the other when she's so numb, so frozen, inside her head. Her fingers tightly clutch the bloodied pillow strapped around her left arm, like she's been told. Once outside her flat, Shaun leads her to his car, unlocks the passenger door, propels her into the seat, pulls the safety belt across her and fastens it.

The Royal Devon and Exeter Hospital's not far and it's Sunday afternoon; not much traffic on the roads. Shaun doesn't talk, for which she's grateful. He'll be grilling her later as to what's caused this worst-of-all cutting episode; whether she can bring herself to tell him, she's not sure. Spilling the whole sordid story will be torture enough, without dealing with his inevitable insistence on informing the police immediately. Rachel's not sure if she's mentally able to handle what that will entail. In her mind, she reverts to her ten-year-old self, sobbing and scared before the police officers who question her, and the memory is painful enough to make her leery about revealing Mark Slater's duplicity.

'We're here.' Shaun parks the car, getting out to open her door, so she can keep her right hand clamped on the pillow. 'This way.'

Rachel allows herself to be guided into Accident & Emergency, her gaze on the floor. Eye contact with anyone is more than she can cope with. She's afraid anyone looking into her pupils will see straight through them to the ugly mess in her head; it's not something she wants anyone to glimpse, especially not a psychiatrist.

Thankfully, Shaun deals with everything, allowing Rachel to speak only when necessary. They wait in A & E for someone to stitch her up; Rachel's unsure how much time passes. Time is meaningless right now. Shaun's still silent, his arm around her; he'll have plenty to say later, though. She's aware his priority is to get her physical needs sorted, and then he'll be demanding answers from her. She doesn't have a great deal of time left to decide what to tell him.

Shaun's on his feet now, pulling Rachel to hers. She's dimly aware of someone, a doctor, standing in front of her, telling her to come with her. She's propelled into a cubicle, exposed and vulnerable without the protective presence of Shaun.

The woman motions her towards a waiting gurney. She removes the tape around Rachel's arm, taking the pillow with it. Rachel hears the same rapid inhalation of breath as she did with Shaun.

'How long have you been doing this to yourself?' Disapproval is evident in the woman's tone. Rachel's stomach clenches.

'Since…' She swallows. 'Several years now.'

Thankfully, the doctor doesn't respond, for which Rachel is grateful. Her worst fear about revealing her self-harm to anyone is their condemnation, their lack of understanding. She can't blame them. How to explain how good it feels to slice through your own flesh? The relief it brings? Impossible to defend her actions to anyone whose own arms don't also bear witness to their inner demons. Shaun's been the only one she's ever trusted with her shame.

No, not true. The memory of telling Mark Slater about the cutting squeezes past her defences, mocking her. A tear slides down her cheek.

The doctor leans over Rachel, instantly drawing

back. 'Have you been drinking?' Her disapproval has morphed into condemnation.

Of course. The wine with lunch, as well as the huge glassful she gulped down afterwards. Her breath must stink of alcohol. Rachel is mortified, so much so she's unable to think straight, and not just because of the booze. The doctor is scrutinising her, awaiting her answer. A picture of the bottle of Chianti comes into her mind. Is it half or three-quarters empty? She can't be sure of anything anymore.

Rachel finds the words from somewhere. 'Yes. A few glasses with lunch.' Does the woman believe her? By now, she's past caring. All that matters is getting out of here, and fast.

The doctor doesn't reply. She opens a cabinet, taking out gauze, sterilising swabs, a dark-glassed bottle of liquid. Her movements are crisp, brisk, efficient, her attention focused on the task in hand. The doctor's silence bothers Rachel, although the deftness of her hands as she cleans, stitches and bandages the damaged arm is reassuring. The worry remains, though. Is the woman judging her? Is she impatient with Rachel, thinking about all the people waiting in A & E who have suffered injuries through no fault of their own? Is Rachel viewed as a time waster because her wounds are self-inflicted?

The answer comes once the doctor has finished. The woman types some notes into a computer, before turning back to Rachel. Her face is unsmiling, her expression sour. When she speaks, it's in full-on headmistress tones.

'You need to get some help.'

Rachel flinches before the doctor's unyielding stare.

'There are leaflets I can give you, helpline numbers. Your own G.P. - '

'No.' Rachel's aware of the scared *please don't do this* tone in her voice. She's unable to say any more. Whatever words she has, they will wither before this hard-faced medic, whose tightly pursed mouth proclaims her opinion of weaklings like Rachel Morgan.

'Nobody can help you if you're unwilling to co-operate.' The doctor doesn't attempt to conceal her impatience; it's evident in every syllable. 'At least - '

Rachel shakes her head. She's desperate for Shaun, for the comfort only he is able to deliver. She needs to escape from this place, where all her worst fears about being judged have been proved correct. She slides off the gurney and walks quickly from the cubicle, heading back towards where Shaun is waiting in A & E. The doctor doesn't follow or try to remonstrate further with her. She obviously believes she has worthier patients waiting.

Shaun gets to his feet as Rachel approaches, his eyes on her left arm, now neatly stitched and bandaged under the bloodied sleeve.

'Let's get out of here. Now,' Rachel tells him.

Shaun's silent again as he drives back to her flat. Rachel reclines her seat as far as it will go, a sudden lassitude rendering her incapable of speech. Her left arm throbs and stings, as well as itching under the bandage. She cradles it with her right one, half of her vowing this will be the last time she cuts, the other part being realistic, reminding her that without something to break the pattern she'll do it again. Her eyes drift shut as she leans back, her exhaustion overwhelming her. She's almost asleep when Shaun switches off the car engine in front of her block of flats.

Once inside, he busies himself in the kitchen, making coffee for them both.

'Go and lie on the sofa,' he says. 'Put your feet up on the arm rest. Make sure they're above your head.'

Ever the practical one, her brother. Rachel's dreading what's to come. What to tell him? Then she remembers how good he's always been to her, how he's dropped everything to rush her to the hospital this afternoon. He deserves the truth, however difficult it is; anything less is tantamount to taking the piss.

He strides into the lounge, handing her a mug of Kenco and a biscuit, before sitting down in the armchair opposite her.

'So.' He sips his coffee. 'What triggered it this time?'

Rachel looks away, unable to bear the directness of his gaze.

'I thought you were getting better. Moving past...' He gestures towards her left arm. 'All this. What happened, Rach? Did Mum have a go at you again?'

She shakes her head. 'No. Nothing like that.' Her voice is a mere whisper.

'What then? OK, so you cut yourself the night before the vigil, and I get that, but before then, you'd managed to go quite a while without hurting yourself. You'd started to call me every time you got the urge.' His voice is puzzled. 'Why not today? What was so bad you needed to slash yourself to pieces?'

'It's hard to explain.' Tears start to come, but she blinks them back.

'Try, Rachel. Because I'm scared for you, I really am. Your arm was a frigging mess. Cut to ribbons. Deep cuts, too. This can't go on.'

'No. I'm sorry, Shaun. About putting you through all this today.'

'If you won't talk to me, then you should get professional help. Go to your doctor, ask to be referred to a counsellor or whatever.'

'No doctors.' Rachel recalls the hard face of the woman who dressed her wounds earlier. No counsellors, no psychiatrists. She doesn't want people like that poking around in her head. Shaun's grimacing with frustration; she tries to explain. 'The doctor who stitched me up today, Shaun. She made me feel like some sort of lowlife, as if I were wasting her time. I can't go to a doctor, I just can't. My G.P.'s nice enough, but he'll send me to a psychiatrist, I know he will. I'm scared I'll end up in some awful mental hospital somewhere.'

Shaun's impatience is evident in his face, although when he speaks he's obviously trying to keep a tight leash on his emotions. 'Won't happen, Rachel. They'll talk to you, help straighten your head out, nothing more sinister than that. You can't go on like this.' He sets his mug down, leaning towards her. 'What happened today, Rach?'

She swallows down the dryness in her throat. 'Promise me you won't shout. This is hard enough as it is.'

'I promise. Tell me, and we'll get it sorted.'

Her rock, as usual. She drops her gaze. This will be easier if she doesn't have to look at him.

'I met a man. After the vigil, in Moretonhampstead.'

From her peripheral vision, she sees Shaun nod encouragement at her. Rachel's conscious he must be getting the wrong idea, how some broken fledgling romance has hurt her. True up to a point, she supposes.

As quickly as she can manage, she spills out the rest. How, at first, the man seems genuine, nice, easy to talk to. How they share an interest in running. The messages they swap on Facebook. Their lunch at The Thatched House the previous weekend. Rachel makes no mention of the kiss. Her shame will stay a secret, however much she owes her brother the truth.

She's coming up hard against the difficult bit, where she has to reveal Mark Slater's former identity to

Shaun. When she does, nothing will ever be the same again. Oh, to be able to cling on to the present moment, when although her life is crap, she's the only one able to smell the shit smeared all over it.

She pauses to gather mental strength.

Shaun seizes the opportunity to speak. 'So, you met some guy. Has he messed you around, Rachel? Been seeing other women, that kind of thing?'

'No.' She breathes in deep. 'I didn't realise who he was, Shaun, I swear I didn't. I thought he was just an ordinary guy. And, of course, I didn't recognise the name. Mark Slater. That's who he said he was.'

Shaun doesn't understand; not surprising, she supposes. 'I don't get it, Rachel. Who is this guy? What's he done to upset you so badly?'

The tears are flowing now, despite her best efforts. 'I believed him, Shaun. I swallowed every lie he threw my way.'

'What lies, Rachel?'

'About who he was.'

Shaun's impatient again. 'I still don't understand. You said he told you his name's Mark Slater. Was he lying about that, then? Who is this guy?'

'He's so different now he's a man, nothing like his picture. How was I to know?'

'What the hell are you going on about, Rachel?'

Rachel chews her bottom lip. The information Shaun's seeking bubbles up onto her tongue. Ready. Waiting.

'For Christ's sake. I'll ask you again. Who is this guy?'

'Joshua Barker.' The name slips out of her, bringing sweet relief.

'What did you say? I didn't catch that. Speak up, Rachel.'

Now she's done it once, the second time isn't so

hard. She's even able to meet Shaun's eyes. 'Joshua Barker,' she says, and this time her voice is clear and strong.

A stunned silence. Rachel watches as various emotions battle for dominance in Shaun.

'Joshua Barker? The one who killed Abby?'

'Yes. I didn't know who he was, Shaun, I swear. If I had…'

'You're telling me Joshua Barker went to Abby's vigil?'

'That's right. You see …'

'He spoke to you, despite being fully aware you're Abby's sister?'

'Yes. I didn't realise…'

'Of course you didn't.' Shaun's breathing is slow, measured, as if he's struggling to gain control over himself. Then he curls his right hand into a fist, draws it back, slams it hard into his left palm. Rinse and repeat. *Whup, whup, whup,* a steady pounding out of anger, one hand against the other.

'Fucking bastard.' Shaun shakes his head.

Rachel instinctively shrinks into the sofa. She doesn't recognise the man opposite her as her brother, normally so calm, so controlled.

'Sorry, Rach. It's him I'm mad at, not you. Never you. The arsehole. The fucking arsehole.'

'I can't believe he'd do something like that.'

'He's sick in the goddamn head. That's why he did it. The prick gets some sort of twisted thrill out of sticking the knife in once again.' Shaun's still pounding one hand against the other, fast, furious, as if to vent what's boiling up inside him. 'Can't believe you had to suffer such shit. No wonder…' He gestures towards her bandaged arm.

Then he stands up. 'I'll get your jacket. We're going to the police. Sooner the better. They need to be informed, so they can arrest the bastard and throw his fucking arse back in jail. Where it belongs.'

'No.' Rachel presses herself against the sofa, as if to beg its protection. She can't deal with the police, not straight after Doctor Judgement. A limit exists to how much crap she can handle in one day; right now, she's hard up against that boundary.

'We have to, Rachel. We can't let this go, no way. He's breached the terms of his release.'

'Not yet.' A plea for time.

'Mum wouldn't want us to waste a second. You know how she gets about all this.'

Her mother, her Achilles' heel. Shaun's not above a spot of manipulation, it seems.

'It's just that…I can't deal with this right now, Shaun. The doctor at the hospital - she was awful to me. My arm hurts like hell. And I'm worried the police will blame me. Say I ought to have realised it was him. But I didn't. How could I, when he's fourteen years older now?'

Shaun sits back down. 'Nobody will blame you, Rachel. I'll be there, with you, when you tell them.'

'I can't.'

'The police will understand you needing time to get your head together, but any longer and yeah, they'll blame you. For dragging your feet in coming forward.'

'A few days.' He starts to shake his head, and she presses on before he can speak. 'Give me some time, then we'll tell them, I promise.'

'We need to go today, Rachel. Immediately. Now his identity's been uncovered, you're not safe from him. Or he might be planning to do a runner, leave the country.'

She hasn't considered that possibility. Then a thought strikes her. 'He won't have a passport. He's supposedly being monitored since his release, so there must be some way of preventing him getting one, even with his new identity. Besides, if he were intending to hurt me, he'd have done so by now. He's had every opportunity.'

'I suppose so.' Shaun doesn't sound convinced.

'A few days. That's all I'm asking.'

He doesn't reply.

'Please, Shaun.'

'OK.' He sighs heavily. 'I'll go along with you on this, but only so far. You asked for a few days, so I'll give them to you.'

She smiles her gratitude at him.

'You've got until the end of the week.'

Rachel nods. 'That's fine. Thank you.'

'After the week is up, you'll either come with me to the police or else I'll go alone. That's the deal, Rachel. It's not open for negotiation.'

21

THE UPPER HAND

Monday morning. Mark's called in sick to work. He's sitting in his car, parked outside an imposing detached house whose size proclaims its occupants as being very comfortable indeed financially. Eyes shut, he leans back against the headrest, digging deep for the last dregs of his courage, although the search is proving difficult. His self-worth has taken a heavy beating already from the episode with Rachel Morgan.

Mark's about to subject it to the likelihood of similar treatment from a different woman.

His mother.

He's read his grandmother's letter so many times he knows every loop, slant and curve of the handwriting. Each word has burned itself into his memory.

...your mother has decided to move away from Exeter and change her name, and it is her intention to begin a new life, a life without you...

After fourteen years, the emotions sparked by the words still chill Mark. This is a long overdue visit, though. One final attempt to shatter the frost of her exterior. Discover if a real woman exists anywhere inside. One who experiences some kind of warmth towards her son. Even if she can't manage love. Of course, the chances are slim she'll have grown a heart over the last fourteen years, but, hell, this is his mother. Hope hasn't completely died within him. Joanna

Barker's rejection has eaten steadily away at Mark over the years. He's no longer a cowed boy; he needs to confront her.

So here he is, on a damp Monday morning in Cardiff. Taking advantage of the fact Natalie's in London, using the delay to reconnect with his mother. She lives, along with her second husband, in the house he's parked outside. Mark knows she's remarried, in the same way he's aware they own this quasi-mansion in the affluent suburb of Cyncoed. Because last night he spoke with his grandmother for the first time in fourteen years.

Linda Curtis. A woman whose warmth of soul makes her an unlikely candidate for having such a flinty daughter. Easy enough to track her down. His grandparents have always been stable people, not prone to moving around. When Mark starts his search on Sunday evening, he's hoping they won't have moved house. Sure enough, when he types their old address into an online telephone directory, there they are: R. and L. Curtis. Roy and Linda. Still in Exeter. Mark even recognises the number, long forgotten by him. He punches the digits into his mobile straight away.

The phone rings for a long time. Mark's on the point of ending the call, and then his grandmother's voice comes on the line. Older, to be sure, less firm - she must be in her eighties now, he thinks - but it's his grandmother, no doubt about it, and for a few seconds he savours the sound of her.

'Hello? Is anyone there?' Speak, Mark, say something, he urges himself.

'It's me.' He curses himself for the stupidity of his words. Ridiculous. She won't recognise his voice when all she remembers is his pubescent treble.

He tries again. 'It's Joshua, Gran.'

She's silent. Well, his call must be one hell of a shock after all this time, when no verbal communication's taken place between them for fourteen years. His grandparents always found the idea of visiting him in Vinney Green or prison too disturbing. Angry and despairing whilst locked up, he's unable to bring himself to contact them by phone or letter, figuring what's left of his family will do better without a loser like him. Stupid, really. Both Roy and Linda Curtis are people of warmth and emotion, unlike their only child. After his release, his new identity prevents him from getting in touch with them. So many wasted years, he thinks.

'It's me, Gran. Remember? I used to play Go Fish with you when I came to visit and you'd bake me chocolate brownies.' Perhaps he's taken her too much by surprise, or maybe she's beginning the slow decline into dementia. What else can he say to convince her? He pulls memories from his brain, searching for the right one, the one to prove his identity conclusively, when at last she speaks.

'Joshua.' Surprise and wonder mingle in her voice. 'Is it really you, my love?' Her words are like a hot shower on a cold day for him, especially the endearment.

'Yes, it's me, Joshua. Or Mark, as I'm called these days. My new identity, you know.'

'Always Joshua to me,' she says. 'Always my lovely grandson. Your conviction was a terrible injustice, my darling. All the fault of that other boy. You were never capable of anything so vicious.'

Mark doesn't reply, because he's too choked up.

'Always such a gentle soul, you were.' His grandmother's fond tones warm him even further. 'Like your father. Not a bad bone in either of you.'

'I didn't do it, Gran.'

'I know, my love. Your granddad, he always believed you innocent as well.' Mark registers sadness in her voice, along with her use of the past tense. *Please God, no*, he thinks, whilst preparing himself for the worse. Roy Curtis, seven years older than his wife, stands a fair chance of being no longer alive.

'Is he...' Mark can't ask if he's dead. 'Can I speak to him, Gran?'

'No, my love. He died.'

He closes his eyes against the pain. ''When?'

'A couple of years ago now, it'll be, come the summer.'

'I'm sorry, Gran.'

'You'll be wanting to ask about your mother.' Sharp, is Linda Curtis. She's guessed the underlying reason he's called.

'Yes.'

'She's remarried. Joanna Stone, she is now. Married a property developer and moved away. Lives in Cardiff these days.'

Mark poses the question that's tormented him throughout the years. 'Why didn't she want anything to do with me afterwards, Gran? When I got sent to the detention centre?'

Linda Curtis sighs. 'You know how she's always been. She's a hard one, my daughter. We tried to persuade her otherwise, but she was adamant. Changed her name back to Curtis, then moved away to escape all the media attention. Said she...' Mark can imagine what his grandmother's unwilling to say. How Joanna Stone considers her son an embarrassment, and worse. 'We told her you couldn't have done it, how it was all a dreadful mistake, but she'd have none of it. I don't see much of her these days.'

'I need to contact her, Gran.' No need to mention his likely return to jail or the underlying reason. 'Can you give me her address?'

'She's not changed, Joshua.' He gets she's trying to warn him, prevent him from disappointment, but he's a man now. When he sees his mother again, it'll be as an adult, on equal terms, and it's a risk he needs to take. He writes on a pad the details his grandmother gives him, and they chat for a while. Mark ends by telling Linda Curtis he can't promise to keep in touch. She understands. She's fully aware of the restrictions posed by his new identity. No need for Mark to mention he may soon be back behind bars.

Now, the morning afterwards, his resolve of the night before is entirely absent. 'She's not changed.' His grandmother's words make him consider heading back to Bristol; hasn't he suffered enough maternal rejection? He doesn't, though. This is too important. His mother has been a festering wound for too long. Time to prise off the scab.

A BMW 740i sits in the driveway, its silver sleekness matching the wealth of the house, telling him somebody's home. With any luck, it's his mother. It's daytime on a Monday. Mark assumes Phil Stone – his stepfather, what a weird notion - is out property developing or whatever it is he does. Not that he gives a shit about the man. He'll ring the bell; if his stepfather comes to the door, Mark will make some excuse and return later. His reunion with his mother is something that needs to happen without anyone else around. Besides, Phil Stone almost certainly doesn't know he has a stepson. No way will Joanna Stone have told her second husband about her son, the convicted child killer, not if she's moved cities and changed her name to get away from him.

A deep breath in. Mark begins his counting ritual as he gets out of his car. *One, two, buckle my shoe.* He walks around the BMW, up to the front door. A brass lion's head knocker sits solidly in the middle. *Three, four, knock at the door*, he counts and then does so. Two loud raps echo out into the cold April drizzle.

No response. Mark waits. *Five, six, pick up sticks.*

He tries again. One more loud knock of the lion's head.

Steps sound in the hallway.

Breathe, Mark. One, two. In, out.

The door opens.

His mother stands there, staring at him.

She's not changed much. As bony as ever. Older, obviously, the lines between nose and mouth scored deeper than Mark remembers. More make-up than before; heavy foundation, set with powder that's caking slightly in the creases of her face. She's smartly dressed, the cut of her cream silk blouse proclaiming its designer pedigree. Better coiffured, too, her dark hair cropped into the latest style. Her perfume, a musky, cloying scent, drifts into Mark's nostrils. Overall, it's unmistakably her, but an enhanced version of fourteen years ago, equalling extra intimidation. Joanna Stone is more unapproachable than Joanna Barker ever was. A rattlesnake compared to the common viper of before.

She doesn't recognise him, of course. He's grown a foot in height since she last saw him; a man stands before her instead of a boy. He's the last person she expects to pay her a visit anyway. Hurt twists inside him. She's his mother, for God's sake. Shouldn't something trigger a maternal memory in her? The cast of his features, perhaps, or the resemblance to his dead father. Instead, she stares blankly at him.

'Yes? Can I help you?' Impatience in her voice.

Mark's unsure exactly how to proceed. He goes for the simple option.

'It's me, Joshua.' No change in her blank expression. 'Your son.'

Either displeasure or anger, Mark's not sure which, replaces the blankness. As well as something suspiciously like fear.

'Joshua? What on earth are you doing here?' She glances around, as though afraid his presence on her doorstep will somehow render her *persona non grata* with her neighbours. 'You'd better come in.' She opens the door wider, standing aside so he can enter.

She presses herself against the wall as Mark steps into the hallway, clearly unwilling for any part of her to make contact with him. He may as well be a leper. *Unclean, unclean.*

Joanna Stone doesn't take him into the lounge, ushering him into the kitchen instead. This one room alone is as big as his entire flat back in Bristol. No white marble in his kitchenette back there, either, unlike here. Her arms fold across her chest in a *keep away* posture as she leans against the fridge freezer. No offer of tea or coffee, no suggestion he should sit down. Clearly, she's not expecting him to stay for long. Mark leans against the large oak dining table, its solidarity a stark contrast to the apprehension chewing him up inside. He's unsure what to do with his hands; suddenly they're too big, too awkward. He thrusts them deep into his pockets, despite the overly casual appearance it must give him.

'She's not changed, Joshua.' A warning he'd have done well to heed. More rejection is heading his way; the knowledge he's volunteered for it only makes it worse. His awkwardness renders him mute, something his mother clearly interprets as proof of the weakness of which she's always accused him.

'What do you want, Joshua? Why are you here?' She folds her arms in tighter, shielding herself against this unwelcome intrusion. 'It's you all right. I didn't recognise you at first, but now I do. You look just like your father.'

Her tone makes it plain the resemblance isn't a desirable quality. Resentment at his invasion of her sanctuary proclaims itself from every line of her body.

'No need to ask how you found me. That loose-lipped mother of mine, of course. I told her not to say anything if you ever got in contact with her, but she's never listened to me. She's always thought me hard, uncaring, for not wanting anything more to do with you.' A snort of derision escapes her. 'Easy enough for her to say. She didn't have reporters, the television people, hounding her night and day like I did.'

'I'm sorry.' The words aren't adequate, not even slightly, but Mark has to try.

'Hordes of them, camped outside the house. All hours, day and night. Went on for weeks.'

Joanna Stone warms to her theme. 'Not just reporters, either. Other people harassed me too. I got abusive phone calls. Hate mail as well. Telling me it was all my fault, how I must have brought you up wrong. Turned you into a killer.'

'I never - '

'You haven't a clue. I had dog faeces pushed through my door.'

Mark's stunned into silence. *What?*

'You heard me. All the neighbours treated me like shit. Several times, they delivered a physical version of their opinion through the letterbox.'

'I'm sorry. That's awful.'

She shrugs off his apology. 'I'll ask you again. Why are you here?'

It's pointless, Mark realises, but he'll try anyway. 'I came to see if we could re-establish some sort of contact. You're my mother, after all.'

No response, simply the same cold stare.

'I didn't have any part in killing Abby Morgan, I swear I didn't. You have to believe me.'

Joanna Stone snorts in derision again. 'Of course you did. You were found guilty, weren't you? Along with that other boy.'

'It didn't happen that way.'

'Liar. I thought I'd already made it obvious I want nothing to do with you anymore. The shame of having my son arrested for murder. At eleven years of age, too. People posted shit through my door, Joshua. Do you have any idea what that's like? Of course you don't.'

Joanna Stone shakes her head. 'No wonder I moved, reverted to my maiden name.'

Her, her, her. As usual, Mark thinks, it's all about his mother. This woman has never once expressed regret over a child losing her life or entertained any notion of her son being innocent. Another thought strikes him. He notices she only mentions the reaction of her neighbours, not her friends. She didn't have any fourteen years ago and he doubts she does now. Some things don't change.

'You take after your father, that's your problem. Losers, both of you.'

Her words pierce him with their cruelty. He remembers his father, their visits to the park together, kicking footballs around. Andrew Barker may have been weak where his wife was concerned, but he was essentially a good man. Kind, caring.

'I've denied ever having a son since moving. Nobody's aware you exist.'

'You've remarried. Doesn't your husband know about me?'

Her horrified expression confirms his earlier supposition.

'God, no. The shame...he must never find out.' The thought is clearly repugnant to her. 'You need to leave, Joshua. Don't ever come back. If I have to, I'll move away again.'

'Please,' He hates to grovel, but she has to see how important this is. They don't have much time. Rachel Morgan may be sitting in front of a police officer right now, or perhaps Tony Jackson is searching his flat.

'You don't understand. Something's happened. I might be rearrested at any moment, be put back in prison. For years, perhaps. If you send me away now, we may never get another chance. Please, Mum.' The last word is deliberate, an attempt to remind her of her maternal role, appeal to any shred of motherly feeling dormant within her.

Joanna Stone's expression grows ever flintier.

'You've obviously done something bad if the police are looking for you. Don't tell me; I don't want to know what crime you've committed now. Everything you say simply confirms to me what a loser you are. Always have been, always will be.' She peels herself away from the fridge freezer, standing in front of him, arms crossed, legs planted apart. 'Get this into your head, once and for all. I want nothing whatsoever to do with you.'

The slap, when it cracks across her face, shocks both of them. Mark's hand smacks across Joanna Stone's left cheek before any conscious awareness of what he's doing hits him. The blow is hard, the force knocking her backwards against the fridge freezer again. A tiny puff of beige powder erupts from her skin as a red stain blooms on her cheek. Her mouth hangs open with disbelief as she brings her palm up to nurse her face.

A pivotal moment for Mark. For the third time in as many weeks, he's been rejected by a woman for what happened fourteen years ago, and it'll be the last time. He's finally shut his mother up, gained the upper hand, and it feels good. Very good.

Joanna Stone flinches as Mark steps forward. Time for him to deliver a home truth or two.

'You've got things arse-backwards. I'm the one who wants nothing more to do with you. I've been a fool to hope you'd be any different. You're the same hard bitch you always were.' No response, but he detects fear in Joanna Stone's eyes. 'My father was always way too good for you. Too bad he died before he found himself a decent woman to love, not a cold fish like you. You were a crap wife. Not to mention being shit in every way as a mother, as well as an all-round failure as a human being.' He spits the words in her face, each one an additional slap, piling on the punishment. 'Those people were right to post shit through your door. Wish I'd shoved a big steaming pile onto your fucking doormat myself.' He strides past her, out of the kitchen, into the hallway. The thick front door makes one hell of a bang as he slams it behind him.

Sweet liberation. At last.

No lingering in his car this time. Mark starts the engine and heads back towards the M4, his palm still stinging from the slap that's freed him. The burden he's been carrying, the weight of her rejection, has been lifted. He'll always be his father's son to Joanna Stone, a loser, someone who's messed up her life. Mark finds he simply doesn't care. If he's no son of hers, then she's dead to him as well. Time to move on. No time to waste. He doesn't know how much time he still has as a free man, and he has other matters to which to attend.

The miles seem few once he turns onto the M4. He's soon back in Bristol. No police at his flat when he gets there, thank God. Rachel can't have told them yet. So far, his luck's holding.

After Natalie tomorrow, only one thing remains to sort.

Mark pulls out his mobile. He's reached a decision on the journey back; now he intends to act on it. The contact he's after is at the top of the list. A single letter. A.

Time to call Adam Campbell and set up a meeting.

22

FINAL STRAW

Tuesday evening. Natalie's in her bedroom, getting ready for Mark to arrive. He's texted her to ask if they can meet earlier than originally planned. A good sign, she decides; he's keen to see her again, explain things to her, get their relationship sorted. Their communication so far has been solely through texts, but she's happy with that. What they need to say to each other is face to face stuff, however hard it might be. She hopes the result will be worth it.

So far, Natalie's tried on most of her small wardrobe of clothes in order to strike the right balance with her appearance. The numerous packets of biscuits, bars of chocolate and takeaways she's downed in the past three weeks have made their home on her hips and stomach, with a couple of extra stretch marks joining them. Sheesh. Mark will think she's fat, ugly, in need of salad and exercise. All too much effort, though. Besides, she reminds herself, Mark's always said how he likes her curves, her breasts, her belly. Not all men prefer skinny women, ones shaped like a floor mop. Her new jeans, the ones she bought at the weekend, fit her well anyway, plus she has the purple silk top to go with it, the one that clings like a wet tissue to her boobs. Not in a tarty way, but simply highlighting the soft breasts nestling underneath. Earrings, a necklace. Her make-up is minimal; Natalie dislikes the stuff, limiting herself to a lick of mascara and some lip-gloss. A squirt of perfume, and she's done.

Ten minutes early. She walks into the living room, sitting on the sofa, waiting for the bell to ring. Mark's due to arrive at seven. He'll be punctual, for the same reasons he's a neat freak. That's why he must be telling the truth about Abby Morgan's death. Something has to be very much out of control in a person, Natalie decides, if they can batter and stab a tiny child to death. Mark's simply too self-restrained to harm anyone. Blood, knives and murder don't go with this man, whose flat is always perfectly tidy and clean. So he can't be the brutal killer everyone portrays him as; it's simply not possible.

Skewed logic, a small voice inside her warns. *Remember Martin Burney.* Natalie tramples it down. She'll believe what she wants, thank you very much. The fantasy of their passionate reunion is too compelling. They'll talk; he'll explain, she'll listen and be so understanding, so forgiving. Once all this crap is out of the way, they'll be able to move forward. No wonder everything before has seemed stilted between them, stifled as it's been beneath the cloak of Mark's hidden identity. They can take things slow if it suits him, but eventually they'll move in together. They'll discuss marriage, starting a family, the way other couples do. Natalie will finally have the stability she's always wanted. OK, so she'll be living with a convicted killer, but to the outside world, they'll be Mark and Natalie, Mr and Mrs Ordinary. She reckons she's a misfit too, what with her dysfunctional family, her comfort eating and lack of friends, so they'll dovetail perfectly. Like meets like, two loners. It'll work, she's sure of it. Mark's a good person at heart, someone led astray when still a child by the evil in Adam Campbell. He deserves a second chance, the opportunity to be happy. They both do. Life is turning out sweet at last, and she's pretty stoked up about it.

The doorbell rings.

She can't answer it quickly enough. She wrenches open the door and he's there, standing before her, but something's wrong. The smile drops from her face. Why doesn't he kiss her, why is his greeting only a muttered *hi*? A sense of her hopes withering inside her washes over Natalie; unexpected tears prick her eyeballs. The need to pull away, tack her defences back into place, seems imperative, although it shouldn't be. He's probably simply nervous, she reassures herself.

Eventually, Mark moves forward. His body is stiff, reeking of tension, more so than she's able to attribute to nerves about their meeting. His arms come out as if to hug her, so she steps into them, robot-like. Their embrace is like two magnets of the same polarity being forced together. An awkward moment passes between them as elbows bump and hips clash. She breaks away, disappointment pooling in her gut.

'Come in.' She waves him into the lounge. 'Tea? Coffee?'

He shakes his head. 'I'm fine.' Natalie badly needs a caffeine hit but is reluctant to waste time on coffee just for herself. She sits down in one of the armchairs, Mark doing the same, so he's opposite her. His gaze is directed at the carpet, not at her.

Natalie clears the nerves from her throat.

'So.' How to begin, she wonders. 'What happened with the little girl...you said it's not what it seems? I need to know, Mark. How things were that day. You have to tell me,' as he begins to speak. 'We need to get this sorted, if we're to...'

'Natalie.' She's struck by the exhaustion in his voice. 'I've not come here today to talk about Abby Morgan or my conviction. I can't do a damn thing to change the past, however much I want to. I realise the texts I sent you…'

Why won't he look at her? She wills him to raise his head, return her gaze, but he doesn't. *Please,* she begs him in her head. *Don't do this to me.*

'How they might have made you think -' He pauses. 'At the time, I meant what I said. I still do. About missing you, wondering how you've been doing. I hoped…' A shake of the head. 'But that's impossible now.'

'What do you mean?'

No response. He's making no sense. She tries again. 'You coming here today – isn't it to tell me how it was with the little girl? So we can get it all out in the open, so there are no secrets between us. Isn't that why you're here?'

'No. It was, but not anymore.'

'I understand.' It's obvious, really. He's met another woman, someone slimmer, prettier, more stylish. She's surprised how calm her voice is, given the jealousy that's tormenting her.

Mark raises his head to look at her. His face is pale, tortured. 'No. You don't.'

'Then why have you come?' The words burst forth, her impatience overwhelming her. 'Why agree to see me, if not to discuss your past? Fill me in on what really happened? Straighten things out between us?'

'I did, originally. That was exactly what I had in mind.' Another shake of the head. 'But not now. I can't bear to talk about all that anymore. As for you and me - I'm sorry, Nat, I really am. You've no idea how much I wanted things to work between us. But they can't.'

'Why not?' Her voice is high, desperate. 'Why not, if that's what we both want, Mark?'

'Things have changed.' He leans towards her. 'I have stuff I need to tell you. Before I do, though, you should know I wish things were different. That we could put all this behind us, build something together, something meaningful. You getting hurt - it's not what I intended or wanted, Nat. You have to believe me.'

He's telling the truth; she can hear it in his voice, see it in his expression. Neither fit with a man who's been unfaithful, so it's not another woman causing him to be so withdrawn, so unhappy. What, then?

'I do.' Her mouth is too dry with nerves to form the words properly. 'I do believe you. What's changed? What is it you have to tell me?'

'Before I get to that, do you understand now why I've always been, well, a bit distant with you? Kept you at arm's length, when God knows it's the last thing I wanted?'

'Yes. Well, I do now. I'm sorry I reacted so badly before. It was just such a shock.' She attempts a weak smile. 'Not the sort of thing you find out every day. I couldn't deal with it, not at first.'

'I'm sorry, Nat. Finding that letter - I get how awful it must have been for you, I really do.'

They're able to look each other in the eye more easily now, although Natalie's still pent up with wondering what Mark has to tell her.

'And I've never been with anyone else whilst with you, Nat. You're the one I want, except my own stupidity has made us being together impossible.'

'Why?' Desperation bursts forth again from Natalie. She doesn't understand any of this. He's not making any sense.

'I'm getting to that. You're aware I was released from prison under certain conditions? Not to revisit where it happened, not to contact Adam Campbell or any of the Morgan family?'

Natalie nods. The articles she's read have mentioned the terms of Mark's release. He's told her himself about his ongoing monitoring by Tony Jackson.

'I've broken all three since I last saw you, Nat.'

She's stunned. 'What...? But *why*, Mark? Won't that get you sent back to jail?'

'There's a strong possibility I'll be arrested, yes.'

Whatever she's been expecting he might say, it isn't this. He's talking like a madman.

He sighs. 'It's hard to explain. I suppose I should talk about Abby Morgan, however hard it is. What really happened that day. I said I would, after all.'

'Tell me.'

'You see, I may have been convicted on an equal basis as Adam Campbell, but no way was I as guilty. He beat Abby Morgan with the rake; he was the one who stabbed her. I didn't do any of it. He was bigger than I was and much more aggressive; it was his idea. Planned it all in advance. Took me along because he liked having an obedient sidekick as an audience.'

Her theory is right, Natalie thinks. Joshua Barker was a kid in the wrong place at the wrong time. Forced into an inconceivable act of brutality by the other boy. 'He bullied you?'

'From the word go. He had something evil in him, Natalie, something twisted. He got off on wielding power over anyone weaker, and that meant pretty much everyone his age and younger. The other kids at school were scared stiff of him. I was too, but he had me by the balls from the start.'

'You didn't tell anyone? Try to get away from him?'

'Once. Did my best to avoid him, hang out with the other boys. Didn't work. As for telling someone, who exactly? Most of the teachers at school were scared of him as well. As for my mother - well, you'll have gathered what a cold fish she is. You read my grandmother's letter, after all. My father was dead by then. I had nobody.'

'So he singled you out.'

'Yes. He carried a knife, too. Wasn't afraid to use it. Anyway, that day, I had no idea what he'd planned. I tried to stop him, honest to God I did, but he threatened to kill me.'

'I thought as much. Once I'd had a chance to calm down.'

'When the police questioned me, I was shit scared, Nat. I was only eleven, for Christ's sake. My mother wanted nothing to do with me. All I could think about was how I must be as guilty as Adam, because I stood by and let him do it.' He shakes his head. 'I was weak. Too frightened of Adam Campbell to save Abby Morgan. I swear to you, though, I had no part in her death, other than failing to prevent it.'

'I believe you.' She does, too. It's inconceivable anybody could fake the raw emotions etched in Mark's words, his tortured expression.

'I've always wanted to atone for my weakness.' His voice is a whisper. 'Find some way of making amends to the Morgans, crazy as it sounds, since nothing can ever bring Abby back.'

'I get that.'

'That was why I went to Moretonhampstead. Even though it's against all the rules. To get answers. Find out if a way existed for me to make things better.'

'When did you go?'

'I attended the annual vigil a couple of weeks ago.'

'But *why?* Doesn't it always get televised?' Natalie's stunned. An incredible risk to take, she thinks.

'Yeah, but I had to find out how Abby's murder affected the Morgans. I had some notion about how, if I knew that, then the way to set things right might become more obvious. Stupid, I know, but my brain wasn't working too clearly. Not after our break-up. You tore me up, Nat, when you walked out on me, with what you said. Not that I'm blaming you. I was a complete mess in my head, what with having the lid blown off my identity.'

'I'm sorry.' Her voice is a mere whisper.

'So I went to the vigil. Saw Adam Campbell there.'

'God.' Natalie's stunned. 'What the hell was he doing there?'

'No idea. Got his mobile number now. He's left messages and texted a couple of times. We eventually spoke last night.'

'He didn't explain why he went?'

'No, and I didn't ask, although I will. Listen, Nat, he's not important right now. Anyway, Michelle Morgan led the vigil, as she always does, with Rachel and Shaun, Abby's brother and sister.'

'Nobody recognised you?'

'Not after fourteen years. I simply merged in amongst the other bystanders. Afterwards, I hung around for a while. Watched Rachel Morgan head back towards Moretonhampstead. I followed, not on purpose, but because my car was parked there.'

Natalie's confused. Where's Mark going with this?

'When we were both in the town, I caught up with her. We started talking.'

Unease prickles down Natalie's spine. Jealousy uncurls inside her.

'But why? That's forbidden as well, isn't it?'

'Yes. I felt compelled to speak to her, Nat. She's so small, so fragile.'

The wrong thing to say. Unlike me, Natalie thinks. Not carrying at least twenty extra kilos in weight, worn as flab on the belly and thighs. Rachel's slim figure from the YouTube links slides into her brain. Too uptight to say anything, she's silent, her lips compressed into thin, mean lines.

'Once I'd managed to convince her I wasn't a reporter, we chatted. Turned out we share an interest in running.'

Another wrong thing to say. Finding out this woman is athletic to boot presses Natalie's buttons, and hard.

'I hoped I could get her to open up to me, tell me how it was for her and her family, find out if she had the answers to the burning questions I had inside. Like where her father was, for instance. Why she seemed so distant from her mother at the vigil.'

Natalie's silent, the fires of jealousy still licking at her.

'We made contact through Facebook, ended up arranging to meet for lunch one Saturday in Exeter.'

'*What?*' The flames flare higher, fierce and angry.

'Please, Nat, just bear with me. We met twice, once that weekend and again the following Sunday. She talked about her family, just as I'd hoped. It's bad, Nat. Terrible, in fact. They've all suffered some serious shit.'

Natalie finds her voice, pissed off though she is about Mark lunching with another woman. Twice, as well. 'Like what? I mean, besides the obvious, losing Abby.'

'Her mother threw her father out after it happened. He's now a raging alcoholic. Michelle Morgan, well, she's as bitter as they come. Turns out she holds Rachel responsible for Abby being taken, because she was supposed to be minding the child, but wasn't. Rachel blames herself as well. She cuts herself, Nat.'

Natalie's confused. What does he mean, cuts herself? Then an old memory surfaces, a Channel 4 documentary about people, women mostly, who self-harm. Who slice themselves with knives, pull out their hair, burn themselves. Shit. Serious stuff; Natalie doesn't feel as envious of the petite, sporty Rachel Morgan as she did a minute ago.

'Her arms are a mess. Her legs, too, apparently. Anyway, we were chatting and I let something slip, enough to make her realise I must be either Joshua Barker or Adam Campbell. She went ballistic, Nat, as you'd expect. She told me she intends to inform the police, get me arrested.'

Now Natalie understands. Why he thinks they can't be together; why he says he's been stupid.

'Mark, listen to me. She might not go to the cops. If she doesn't, then it's all OK, don't you see? We can be together after all.'

'No.' The word slaps her in the face. 'She'll tell them, I'm sure of it. She was so angry, and not just because she discovered I'm really Joshua Barker.' He glances away, seemingly reluctant to continue.

'Why?'

He sighs, still not looking at her. 'You'll get mad.'

'Tell me.'

'She'd got the idea in her head, you see, about something happening between us.'

'Why would she think that?' Natalie's suspicions flare up again, hotter and higher this time. 'Did you do something to encourage her?' *Please God, say no. Even if it's not true.*

'Yes. No. Maybe.' He clears his throat. Why won't he look at her? Tension pulls her stomach as tight as stretched canvas.

'What happened?' Her voice is high, shrill.

'It was nothing, honestly.'

'What did you do?

'She did it, not me. I didn't want -' He exhales noisily. 'Nat, you mustn't think -'

'Tell me. For fuck's sake, just spit it out.'

Mark sighs. 'The first time we met. I was about to leave. She kissed me.'

Natalie doesn't believe he just said those words. He kissed this woman? After saying he doesn't want anyone else? Bastard. Before she can give voice to her anger, he's speaking again.

'It was simply a kiss, Nat. Nothing more, I swear. She started it, not me. I felt sorry for her, and it just happened.'

'You kissed Rachel Morgan. Who you're expressly forbidden to contact in any way.' Fury washes over Natalie. In the space of one minute, Mark Slater has been transformed in her head from innocent victim to unfaithful boyfriend. This is a man, after all, who first tells her she's the only woman for him, and then admits kissing somebody else. Irrelevant that she'd already dumped him prior to him meeting this woman. Or that the bitch initiated what happened.

Besides, it's not just anybody he's kissed. No, he has to pick the sister of the child he's been convicted of killing. No wonder Rachel Morgan is so devastated, so angry. Natalie Richards is too. She's been a fool to hope for a future with such a man. Right now, she's no idea whether anything he's said so far has been true; she's struggling to untangle what's real and what's not. All she's certain of is Mark has admitted to kissing another woman, an admission pushing down hard on every insecure button she has.

He obviously registers the change in her tone from cool to frigid. 'It didn't mean anything -'

Pathetic. So weak. The kind of crap her father gave her mother whenever he fucked some new piece of skirt. The age-old excuse given by faithless partners everywhere, in the deluded belief that meaningless betrayal is preferable to deliberate intention. If it means so little, why do it?

'I can't deal with this crap.' She's amazed how steady her voice is, despite the turmoil she's struggling to contain. 'I can't trust a word you say anymore. There must have been some attraction between you and this Rachel, or else you'd have approached either her mother or her brother after the vigil.'

'That's not how it was. She seemed so vulnerable, I guess, not as strong as Michelle or Shaun. Besides, they were busy lighting a candle for Abby. It was pure chance she was parked close to me back in Moretonhampstead. Anyway, it seemed too good an opportunity to pass up. I never came on to her, honest, Nat.'

'Yeah, right. You're a total bastard, you know that?'

'Can't disagree with you there.' His voice is sad, resigned. 'You deserve better than a screw-up like me, Nat. That's what I'm here to tell you. It's why we can't be together, even if Rachel doesn't tell the police.'

'Too right we can't.' Her anger is beginning to assert itself now. The arsehole. He kissed his victim's sister, for fuck's sake. Sick, bloody sick. 'I hope this Rachel woman does get you sent back to jail. You deserve to spend the rest of your miserable life there. I bet you did kill that kid, you and that other bastard.'

'Wait, Nat. Please. There's something else I need to tell you. It's important. About how we met -'

'*What?*'

'That day when I first saw you. I've not been entirely truthful -'

The final straw. Natalie snaps. 'Get the hell out of here. You've not been honest about one single thing. Not ever. About you, about us, about anything. Fuck off, Mark. I never want to see you again. If this Rachel Morgan doesn't call the cops on you, I will.'

23

SEE YOU WEDNESDAY

Midday on Wednesday. Another cold, damp day in Moretonhampstead. Mark's waiting to meet Adam Campbell properly for the first time in fourteen years. Weird, as well as frightening, to talk to him on the phone Monday night. Mark replays the conversation in his head, desperate to avoid thinking about Natalie. In his mind, it's two days ago and he's sitting on the sofa in his flat, screwing up his courage to do what's necessary.

Adam answers straight away, as though he's been waiting for Mark's call. His voice still has the power to instil fear, command compliance, even after fourteen years.

'Been expecting you. Why'd you take so long to call?'

Mark's unsure how to respond. No way does he want to reveal what he's been up to with Rachel Morgan. He opts for deflection. 'Been busy. Stuff, life, that sort of thing. You know how it is.'

'Good to see you the other day. Often wondered where you are, what you're doing.' So far, so good, but Mark still intends treading carefully.

'I'm in Bristol these days. Assistant manager for a building supplies company. You?'

'Down in Taunton right now.'

Close by, then. 'Working?'

'On and off.'

'What's that mean?'

'Casual jobs, scaffolding, labouring, whatever's going. Sometimes round here; other times I've been sent to Southampton, Plymouth, wherever the work is.'

Mark cuts to the chase.

'Didn't get a chance to talk at the vigil. We should get together sometime, chat, catch up. Better than just talking on the phone.' His words are casual, masking his true intent, but he can hardly blurt out the questions he needs to ask without some preamble.

A throaty laugh sounds in his ear. 'Oh, yeah. That'll be good. Really good.'

'When are you available?'

'Not working right now. I'm free pretty much anytime. Can't do tomorrow, though.'

'Day after?' Mark holds his breath. Wednesday. He'll call in sick to work again. They need to meet as soon as possible. Before Tony Jackson comes for him. Mark's banking on Adam being equally curious about the two of them hooking up again.

'Meet you where it happened. Moretonhampstead. Twelve o'clock.'

Mark's instinct is to say no. Both of them there, where they're expressly banned from going - it's a bad idea, he thinks. Far better to find somewhere neutral, anonymous, discreet. Then he reconsiders. Adam, back where he killed Abby Morgan - if anything is going to reveal his true nature, it'll be standing on the spot where he battered and stabbed her. If he's the same cruel son of a bitch, he won't be able to help showing it. If - a big if - he's changed for the better, the significance of the place will flush it out in the open. Besides, meeting up on Wednesday is exactly what he had in mind anyway. Best not to risk pissing Adam off by quibbling about the venue. Even after fourteen years, he's still unable to defy him.

'OK.' Details arranged, he's keen to end the call. 'I'll see you Wednesday, Adam.'

'Carl.' Another laugh. 'New name, new identity and all that. Well, you know the drill. What name are you going by these days? Always thought Joshua sounded the sort of name a queer would have.'

'Mark. Mark Slater.' He chooses to ignore the homophobic comment. It doesn't surprise him, though.

'See you Wednesday, Mark Slater. Twelve o'clock. Don't be late.' The line goes dead. Typical of Adam, thinks Mark. Always needing to control, to be the one who sets the agenda. Some things don't change.

Two days later, Mark's back in Moretonhampstead. At the scene of Abby Morgan's death, where he's waiting for Adam Campbell. A hint of drizzle hangs in the air. Wind that bites through his clothing gusts across the field. He hugs his arms across his chest to keep out the cold, whilst glancing at his watch. Despite telling Mark to be on time, the other man's already ten minutes late. Of course, he's coming over from Taunton; there might be heavy traffic or something, but somehow Mark doubts it. It's all part of Adam's need for control again. Keep Mark waiting, put him on the defensive, get him off-balance.

When Mark remembers the anti-gay remarks of the night before, the scornful, mocking tone in which they were delivered, he's not hopeful anything's changed with Adam. If he's still the same arrogant, vicious individual he's always been, Mark thinks, he'll end their reunion early, head back to whatever awaits him in Bristol, and delete Adam's number from his phone. No way does he want to be under the other man's control ever again. He's here for answers, not to rekindle their unbalanced and dangerous connection.

Mark stamps his feet, blowing on his fingers to keep warm as he waits. He turns around, facing the lane leading from the town, and a jolt runs through him as he spots Adam walking towards him. At last, although he's now fifteen minutes late.

Adam strides up to him, a grin on his face.

'Hello, mate. Long time no see.' He hooks his thumbs into the belt threaded through his jeans, legs apart. The classic male intimidation posture, stating: *I'm higher up the ranks than you are, and don't you forget it.* So blatant that Mark almost laughs, before he remembers such tactics where Adam's concerned are unwise. Very. The effect of eyeballing the man properly, up close and personal, for the first time in fourteen years is electric. Adam's every bit as intimidating now as he's ever been, due to the sheer size of the man. Not just height-wise, although he's easily six feet four. Rather, it's the tree trunk neck, the beefy arms, the barrel chest. Coupled with the leader of the pack stance, it's a powerful combination that packs a punch of apprehension into Mark's gut.

He reminds himself the fact Adam's physically imposing doesn't mean he's still a killer at heart. He'll give the other man the benefit of the doubt, at least for now.

Mark finds his mouth has gone dry. 'Hi, Adam,' he manages.

'Good to catch up, Joshua.'

'Mark. New identity, remember. Fresh start and all that.'

Adam's mouth twitches into a sneer. 'Fuck that. You're Joshua Barker to me. Like I'm Adam to you, but Carl to everyone else.'

'Did you pick that name?'

'Carl Duffy. Yeah.' He reaches into his jacket pocket, pulling out a packet of Marlboros, and flips open the top. 'Want one?'

Mark shakes his head. 'Nah. Don't smoke.' He's

transported back fourteen years to the coughing, the spluttering, his futile attempts to impress Adam.

'You always were a wuss.' Adam lights a cigarette, drawing deeply on it. 'Anyway. My name. Got asked whether I wanted to choose it. Figured something like Ian Brady or John Christie wouldn't go down too well.'

Mark recognises the name Ian Brady but isn't sure about John Christie. He hopes to God that this is the other man's idea of a sick joke. Adam's always been twisted, sure, but wanting to name himself after famous killers? Sheesh. He picked Mark Slater because of its blandness, its ability to blend in. Nothing memorable, nothing unusual.

Adam's laugh is contemptuous. 'Jeez, look at your face. As if they'd release me with a name like either of those. Too well known. No, I had to play the good guy, act repentant, keep the parole board sweet.'

'So where did you get Carl Duffy from?'

Another long drag on the cigarette. 'Carl I borrowed from that character in the film *The Cell*. Carl Stargher, the one who liked to drown women. Fucking weird story, but what the hell. Duffy – British killer from way back. Common enough name, though. Told them I'd picked it at random from the phone book. The tossers didn't twig.' He grinds his cigarette butt into the ground, immediately lighting up a second one. 'You kept your nose out of trouble since you got out?'

'Pretty much. Apart from going to the vigil.' Mark seizes his chance. 'Been wanting to know something. Why did you go, Adam? What did you get out of being there?'

'I could ask you the same thing.'

'I asked first.' Christ Almighty. They've been talking all of two minutes and already they've reverted to childish behaviour. Not the way men of twenty-five should talk. Not that he feels a man, standing here beside Adam Campbell. They're both eleven again, and the old dread of the other boy has returned full force. This is someone who names himself after killers in some weird kind of tribute, after all. The odds are growing Adam's a leopard whose spots haven't changed, unless they've darkened, become even more menacing.

'Bet you anything I went for the same reason you did.' Adam steps right up to Mark, invading his personal space. He's so close Mark gets a full-on blast of his ashtray breath.

'Am I right?'

Mark's unsure what he's being asked here. He keeps quiet.

Adam takes silence as agreement. 'Yeah. Thought so. Deep down, you're not so very different to me, in spite of this act you put on, making out you're so moral. You went there for the same reason I did.'

'Which is?'

'Don't jerk me around. To get a kick out of it, of course.'

Mark's too sickened to respond. Chalk one up for his instincts, he thinks. This man hasn't changed; never will. Same leopard, same spots.

'Hearing that brat's mother whining on about how we should be behind bars, how she misses her precious kid, all that crap.' Adam's laugh is deep, genuine, coming straight from his heart. He's revelling in Michelle Morgan's pain, Mark realises. 'The daughter, too. Face like a slapped arse. Quite a looker, though. Given half the chance, I'd give her one.'

The insult to Rachel strikes Mark as particularly repulsive, not that he can claim to have acted well himself where she's concerned. Holy shit, can he endure much more of this? He's unsure how to extricate himself, though. Antagonising Adam Campbell isn't a smart move; he'd bet a truckload of money the man still carries a knife on him.

'Don't tell me it wasn't the same for you.' Adam moves even closer. Something warped and twisted still lies behind his dark eyes, Mark notes. He's intimidated beyond words, but daren't show it by inching backwards.

'Answer me. Tell me you got off on it too.'

As Mark gropes for a response, Adam moves swiftly behind him, sliding his hand into his pocket and Mark realises, in one sickening second of awareness, what's coming. The blade kisses the side of his neck at the same time as the other man's forearm pulls backwards on him, exposing his throat. Adam's cigarette is clamped between his lips, its heat close to Mark's cheek. Tobacco-laden breath slithers over his flesh, sending a shudder of repulsion right down to his toes.

Adam's laugh, deep and throaty, sounds against Mark's neck. The knife presses a little harder, although not enough to cut the skin. Mark realises Adam won't follow through. No, he's getting off on the power trip he's created; slicing his former sidekick's throat would spoil Adam's fun.

'Say it. You enjoyed being there, didn't you? Knowing the Morgan bitch had no idea the two boys who sliced up her precious daughter were there as men, laughing at her.'

Mark's struggling to breathe. Play the game, he reminds himself. A lie now and he'll save himself a boatload of trouble. 'Yes. Yes, I did.'

'Thought so.' Triumph dominates Adam's words. 'You got off on seeing me kill the brat, too, didn't you? Admit it. We had fun, right?'

Mark's incapable of speech. Images of the blood, the rake, the unbuckled shoe crowd into his brain; sounds of the screams, both from Abby Morgan and himself, accompany them.

He nods, but it seems enough. Adam flicks the knife shut, replaces it in his pocket and steps away from Mark. Power trip completed.

'Abby Morgan. My finest moment. The first cut is the sweetest.' Adam laughs. 'Nothing I've done since getting out of jail has even come close.'

Mark feels sick. 'What do you mean?'

'Mind your own fucking business. Yeah, the two of us sure had fun with our Pretty Princess, didn't we?'

Mark nods again, hating having to do so.

'Did it too quickly, though. Should have taken longer, spun the party out a lot more.' Adam stamps out his cigarette, his foot hitting the ground hard, and Mark thinks of how easily he snuffed out Abby Morgan's life. 'Shame I never got to keep the souvenir I took, either.'

The green hippopotamus. The bloodied soft toy that got them convicted. Mark pictures Abby's blood staining the plush fabric a muddy brown. For him, the toy represents everything abhorrent about her death. Whereas to Adam it's a keepsake, symbolising every blow, every scream, all he relishes about killing a small child. Adam's altered all right. The transition from boy to man has hardened his fledgling propensity for cruelty, honed it, set it in stone. This is a man born to hurt, to kill. Other people are talented at sport, art, music; Adam Campbell's abilities centre on pain, fear, death. What was it he came out with a minute or so ago? *Nothing I've done since getting out of jail has even come close.* Shit. Did Abby Morgan start a chain of killing that stretches through the years to the present day? Have there been other victims?

Mark finds his voice. 'You asked me whether I've played it straight since prison. The answer's yes. What about you?'

Adam laughs. 'Well, listen to the wuss. Keen to

get all the details, aren't you?'

'Have you?'

'Think I'll keep quiet about that for now. Would be easy enough, though, wouldn't it?'

Mark shrugs. 'I've no idea. You're the expert.'

'Too right. You always were too chicken to get your own hands dirty. You wanna hear how to have some fun?'

Mark wipes his sweaty palms against his jeans. He's talking to one sick bastard here. He nods.

'Best way? Go to a big city, doesn't matter which. Never the same one twice, though. Check out the red light areas. Target some drug-addled whore who nobody gives a shit about anyway. A new hunting ground each time, different way of doing it, enough of a gap in between - who's going to join the dots?' He's so close, and Mark stares at the man's dilated pupils, thinking: *he gets off on this, he really does, the sick bastard.*

'We can talk about this stuff, you and me, Joshua mate. Can't do that with anyone else. Not the sort of thing you can drop into conversations, know what I mean?'

Mark loathes the jocular tone, being called 'mate'. Is Adam so determined to rewrite history? Has he forgotten how, aged eleven, he had to coerce Joshua Barker into smoking, how he pinned him down by the throat that time in the park? They've never been mates, not in the true sense; it's always been a relationship based on power and pecking order. Does Adam really believe Mark shared whatever sick fun he himself got out of attending the vigil?

Perhaps not. Adam's no dimwit. Is his actual purpose here to bait Mark, get off on his old power games, force him into saying he enjoyed what happened? Does he relish the fact Mark's sickened to his core by what he's hearing?

No. Mark realises his first hypothesis is closer to the truth. Right now Adam needs Mark, and not simply to dominate him. He's supplied the clue himself. *We can talk about these things, you and me.* All these years, Adam's been itching to discuss murdering Abby Morgan, about wanting to kill again, because he can't, not in everyday life. Mark's plugging a hole for him simply by listening. To get parole, Adam will have had to play the remorse card, and since then he'll have been living under his new identity, concealing who and what he really is. He'll have found that hard going. No wonder he's been so keen to meet up again. It's not just about re-establishing control over his old sidekick. Adam needs to vent.

'We should meet up again sometime.' Mark nods in reply. It's the safest option. Right now, all he can think about is the sanctuary of his car, driving back to Bristol, ensuring Adam doesn't follow him. Even worse, find out where he lives. Unlikely, but then he's no real idea what this man is capable of doing.

Michelle Morgan is right, he thinks. Adam Campbell is a sick bastard who should never have been released.

24

NO MORE THE VICTIM

Natalie's fury burns fiercely, worse than almost anything she's suffered to date. Greater than her ongoing anger at her father for abandoning his family, sharper than the pain inflicted by her errant ex-boyfriends prior to Mark. Only two things top what she's now experiencing. One is the memory of rough fingers forcing themselves inside her fourteen years ago. *Him.* The second being her discovery that Mark's a convicted child killer.

Her fantasy mocks her now. The one where she's so understanding, so compassionate, about his past. So naïve, in hindsight. *Stupid*, she berates herself. *You bloody daft bitch.*

A weird memory comes back. What the hell was that other crap he spouted? *I've got something else to tell you. It's important. About how we met.* Natalie's mind veers back to her first sighting of Mark Slater.

It's a Sunday; she's just arrived at her mother's house. Natalie steps out of her car, her mind on Callie Richards's lamb roast, when a male voice stops her. All the man says is 'Excuse me?' but she freezes, her old irrational terror the catalyst.

'Frigging fat bitch.' The contemptuous phrase that always sounds in her head when she's startled by strange men. In an instant, Natalie's mind reverts to the copse in the park. She's pressed against the earth again, a dog turd inches from her nose, rough fingers inside her.

'Are you all right?' The voice sounds concerned. 'I didn't mean to startle you.'

Natalie turns. The man is sitting behind the wheel of a parked car, his window lowered. Mark Slater. A dark hunk of eye candy, with a sexy lilt to boot. He needs directions, apparently. She points him towards where he wants to go, but the conversation doesn't end there. They chat, the air turning flirtatious between them. She mentions how the television studio she works for is nearby. How she often treats herself to lunch from the deli opposite. The fact their Szechuan beef rolls are sublime.

The next time Natalie goes to grab a bite in between logging shots and organising scripts, Mark's sitting at one of the deli's tables. He asks her to join him. Things move quickly between them after that.

She's puzzled about what he said. *I've not been entirely truthful.*

Then she shrugs. The man's an inveterate liar. She'll never get to the bottom of what he meant. Best not to concern herself with it.

Her thoughts turn to Rachel Morgan. The real reason Natalie's so pissed off. Slim, athletic Rachel, with her copper hair and air of vulnerability, with whom Natalie can never compete due to her excess weight. She glances down at her generous belly, the curve of which even her new jeans can't disguise, at her lavish breasts, which now appear vulgar instead of sexy. Her hatred of her body surges up, thick and nauseating, along with her jealousy, and if Rachel Morgan were in the room right now, Natalie's unable to answer as to what she'd do.

Hang on a minute, though. She remembers Mark's words about Rachel cutting herself. She represses a shudder; to her, the idea is repulsive. What kind of person draws a knife through her own flesh? The girl has to be disturbed, seriously fucked up in fact, and it's with that realisation that Natalie's jealousy of Rachel melts away. This woman isn't so very different from herself. They've both been badly damaged by life; they simply express their hurt in different ways. For Rachel, it's cutting herself; for Natalie, it's the biscuit tin. Rachel's pain, along with her method of self-medication, seems far worse than Natalie's.

Something else they share is the fact they've both been duped, well and truly, by Mark Slater. What dark emotions must Rachel be experiencing after finding out she's been lunching with her sister's killer? Who then piles on more mockery by kissing her?

Only a truly sick bastard would behave in such a way. Natalie no longer believes Mark's excuses about Abby Morgan. A man who seeks out his victim's sister and kisses her must be so warped, so twisted, that he's definitely capable of brutally murdering a child. Natalie now agrees, heart and soul, with Michelle Morgan. A pair of child killers has been let off too lightly and both the fuckers belong back in jail.

Memories force themselves into Natalie's brain. Herself and her mother, watching a Channel 4 documentary about American women who contact serial killers on Death Row. How they imagine themselves in love with them, even marry them. At the time, both Natalie and Callie Richards are incredulous; how can anyone sane want to connect in a romantic way with such evil? The programme goes on to interview various psychologists as to the root cause.

'These women are driven by a misguided belief that the power of their love can transform these men. That they can reach in and nurture the wounded child inside these killers,' is the comment of one self-styled expert in the psychology of these matters. Natalie remembers her own disbelief at the time. The man's words are reinforced when a woman says she believes her husband, who she married after his conviction for butchering six prostitutes in South Carolina, is a loving and gentle soul who's desperate to prove how repentant he is.

'He's a changed man since he fell in love with me.' Her voice smacks of certainty as she addresses the camera. 'So kind and caring.'

'What a deluded woman,' Callie Richards comments. 'Probably doesn't think she can get any other man to love her. Not that he does, of course.'

At the time, Natalie's fascinated by these women's refusal to acknowledge how irredeemably warped their men's souls are. By their need to transform, like some weird form of alchemy, evil into good, oblivious to the futility of their mission. She's also embarrassed by the gender issue. By women being the ones who gravitate towards serial killers, who are predominantly male. OK, so female multiple murderers are rare, but Natalie's prepared to bet legions of lonely men aren't desperate to write to the ones that do exist. Have sex with them. Marry them. Certainly the documentary makes no mention of men who convince themselves love conquers evil when it comes to female killers. Men, Natalie decides bitterly, have more common sense to act in such a fucked up way. What that says about her gender, she's not sure, although she suspects it's nothing good. Maybe her sex is too prone to searching for everyone's wounded inner child, even when it's evil lurking within.

She compares herself to the women from the documentary. Hell, her own behaviour isn't so different. After all, some of the interviewees in the programme exhibit a stubborn refusal to believe in their men's guilt, despite overwhelming evidence. Natalie now understands she's been doing the same. Believing Mark innocent, because it suits her, when both the facts and his conviction scream otherwise.

She can always go to the police, of course, reveal Mark's parole violations, get his arse locked up in jail again, but Rachel Morgan will probably do that anyway. Something else is called for. Revenge, dark and satisfying, to quench the lust for payback lurking within her. If Mark were here right now, she'd pound her fists into him, fury at his betrayal in every blow.

With that thought, an idea thrusts itself into her brain.

Enough, thinks Natalie. She's done with playing the victim. She's spent enough time crying over the hurt caused by the men in her life. No more behaving like the women from the documentary, blindly believing that love triumphs over evil. No more persuading herself hope exists for a successful relationship with a child killer.

The memory of the Morgan family at the vigil comes back to her. Not Rachel or Michelle, but Shaun, the tall, stocky guy whose meaty arms suggest a familiarity with the gym. Her idea crystallises then, although she's unsure how to execute her plan. Of course, she can always try to get phone numbers for the Morgans, but she's no idea where they live. They're still local to the Exeter area, she thinks. The name's too common to search on, though, so she'll need to find some other route.

The answer clicks into her head almost immediately.

On Wednesday morning, Natalie calls in sick. She waits until she's sure Mark will have left for the day and drives over to his flat. For the second time in recent weeks, she retrieves the key from under the potted plant. A sense of self-righteousness guiding her steps, she enters her bastard ex-boyfriend's flat, dumping any guilt at the door. Devious she may be, but Natalie's a woman on a mission. Seek and destroy.

As usual, the place is pristine; to Natalie, the neatness that once struck her as amusing now seems symbolic of a twisted, obsessive personality. Patrick Bergin, a.k.a. Martin Burney in *Sleeping With The Enemy*. She shudders when she enters the bedroom where, not so long before, they last had sex. Natalie no longer considers what they did as making love. She avoids the bedside cabinet, where the letter from Linda Curtis lives. Mark Slater's laptop is what Natalie's after and there it sits, where it always does, on the tiny table he uses as a desk. She switches it on and prepares to try to crack his password.

No success with his name or date of birth in any combination. In the mood for some self-flagellation, she types in her own name, and sadness tugs at her as the laptop whizzes into action. *I must have meant something to him after all*, is her initial reaction.

Then the doubts kick in; she reminds herself she's dealing with a brutal child murderer, who probably uses her name out of some warped sense of gratification. Pleased with himself about how easily he's fooled her. Natalie's anger returns, elbowing out her wistfulness.

On his desktop, she sees the icon for his mobile; she's grateful for Mark being anal enough to back up his phone on his computer. She's relying on Rachel's number being in his contacts list; whilst she's in there she'll check how many other women he's been hoodwinking, because there'll be more, Natalie's jealous streak is certain of that.

She clicks the icon, navigating to his messages and contacts. The one at the top of the list leaps out at her, with the sole initial A. Nothing else, just A. Natalie's sure at first it's another of Mark's female conquests but then she reads the accompanying text. 'Got your message. Things a bit busy right now. Will be in contact.' The truth, foul and disgusting, hits her. A stands for Adam Campbell, his co-murderer. He's admitted they've been back in touch, after all. The thought strengthens her lust for revenge. The bastard's going to get what he deserves and she'll be the one to gift-wrap his retribution with the tatters of their relationship.

Underneath A is a number for A.J. The bitch he's been shagging on the side. Then Natalie remembers; A.J. is the police officer supervising his parole. Does she believe him, though? Who's to say it's not some other female?

Natalie taps the number into her mobile and places the call. A brusque male voice answers. 'Tony Jackson.'

She excuses herself, pleading a wrong number. Her bastard ex wasn't lying about A.J., then. Probably the only thing about which he's ever been truthful. She adds the number to her phone contacts. Might be handy to have if Rachel Morgan chickens out on shopping Mark for his parole violations. What she has in mind right now, though, is something best kept well away from police involvement.

Her stomach growls. Food is singing its usual siren song to Natalie. She breaks off, striding into the kitchenette to raid Mark's biscuit tin. Carbohydrate comfort beckons from within. She settles down on his sofa, cramming digestives into her mouth, taking pleasure in the crumbs falling between the cushions. Bloody neat freak, she thinks. He won't be around much longer to care what's festering down there anyway.

Her greed sated, Natalie seats herself back down at the laptop, Mark's contact list in front of her. Something strikes her, a weirdness that hasn't been noticeable before due to her preoccupation with the entries under A. The brevity of the list. If she ignores Mark's garage, doctor, dentist, etc., there are only five personal contacts. Surely far less than most people have. Hers is there, as well as Steve Taylor, Mark's boss at the building yard. For an instant, compassion hits her for this man who has no friends, whose contacts are so limited. Then her desire to punish Mark kicks in, elbowing out the empathy. Self-righteous judgement replaces sadness; here's a man who's obviously a loner, a word loaded with negative connotations. All those newspaper articles about rapists and murderers, they always describe such people as loners. Sad bastards who find it impossible to interact with their fellow humans. What she's previously viewed as Mark's social awkwardness is now transformed, like his neatness, into a dark personality flaw.

The other name is, of course, Rachel Morgan. Natalie checks the messages between her and Mark, but, perversely, finds nothing to fuel her jealousy. Simply confirmation of their lunch date in Exeter the previous weekend. Rachel's number also gets added to her phone contacts. Then the real self-flagellation comes. Natalie skims through her own recent texts with Mark. 'Missing you', she reads, her heart tight against her ribcage, before she reminds herself how the bastard's practised in the art of deception. She clamps down on her regrets. No more of that shit. She refuses to be like those gullible women from the Channel 4 programme. She's here for a reason, to ensure Mark Slater, child killer and sociopath, receives his comeuppance. What they shared is now long past – she squashes down a flicker of disappointment at the way things have turned out – because if it's not, she's no different from the deluded women in the documentary.

Easy enough for Natalie to desire revenge. It's proving a lot harder than she's imagined to carry out her plan, however. She stares at Rachel's number in her contacts list, summoning up her rage against the man who's betrayed her, but somehow it's insufficient to make her press the call option.

What she fears, she realises, is Rachel's condemnation. For not having realised Mark's identity as Joshua Barker before, for being so gullible as to believe his innocence. For Natalie being Rachel's rival as far as Mark's concerned. Ah, that last one rings true, deep in her gut. Jealousy, the real reason for her hesitation.

More time slips by. Finally, she manages to bolster her courage enough to call Rachel.

The other woman's mobile rings several times. Natalie's on the point of giving up, and then Rachel answers.

Her voice is girlish and breathy. Natalie conjures up the images she's seen of Rachel at the vigil, all frail and fragile-looking. A perfect match with the nervous timbre of her *hello*.

She identifies herself, dismayed at the dryness in her mouth.

'I'm Mark Slater's ex-girlfriend. My name is Natalie Richards.'

The stunned quality of the silence greeting her announcement weaves its way down the phone to Natalie.

Eventually Rachel speaks. 'Why are you calling me?'

In the background, Natalie hears a male voice, shouting. Loud, aggressive, angry.

'That's not him, is it? Is that sick bastard phoning you, Rachel? Tell me you're not talking to him.'

Natalie thinks: *Shaun Morgan.*

'Rachel,' she says. 'I need to talk to your brother.'

25

YOU LEAD, I FOLLOW

Wednesday evening. Mark's in his flat, sitting on his sofa, nursing a beer, raking Adam Campbell over in his mind. No police waiting for him when he gets back from Moretonhampstead, thank God. Rachel obviously hasn't informed them of his parole violations yet. She will, of course, but for now, Mark's simply grateful for the extra time.

His eyes are drawn to a crumb nestling between his sofa cushions. He pulls it out, holding it up so he can examine it. A fragment of biscuit. Must be from when Natalie raided his kitchen after finding the letter from Linda Curtis. Odd he never noticed it before, though. Mark shrugs. Biscuit crumbs are insignificant in comparison with Adam Campbell.

Adam's an itch he's unable to stop scratching. It's as though the man represents the final piece of the jigsaw concerning Abby Morgan's murder. He'd thought the Morgan family might be the answer, but now, with Rachel an open wound for him, he's uncertain as to whether that's the case. Sure, he's discovered more about the Morgans, but at what cost? All he's done is fuck with Rachel's mind and ensure himself a swift return to prison. Right now, the ends don't appear to justify the means, and with time running out for Mark, perhaps he'll do better concentrating on Adam Campbell.

Nothing I've done since getting out of jail has even come close. The words worry away at Mark, in the same way the little Italian girl used to. Along with the *first cut is the sweetest.* The need to find out what Adam Campbell's been up to since prison is an itch Mark's desperate to scratch. One thing's for sure. Adam's also suffering an itch. The urge to brag, and if Mark handles things right, the man won't be able to resist scraping his nails over it much longer.

Only one thing for it. He needs to contact Adam again if he's to get any answers. Whether he can handle two doses of the man in one day, even if one of them is over a phone connection, is another question. He breathes in deeply, starting a counting ritual in his head. *One, two, buckle my shoe.* It takes two rounds of the nursery rhyme before he's up to dealing with his old nemesis. When he's finally ready, he pulls out his mobile.

Adam answers almost immediately. 'You again?' He laughs. 'Can't get enough of me, can you?'

'Adam.' Mark wills himself to stay calm. 'Good to catch up earlier on, mate. Like you said, it's been far too long.'

'Yeah, well, I guess that's down to getting banged up for ten years. Not to mention our new identities.'

'Been mulling things over. What we were talking about before, I mean. How what we did was…' Mark's forced to pause before he can bring himself to say the word. Ordinary enough in itself, but grotesque in the context in which he intends to use it. 'Fun.' God, how he hates having to come out with such shit, but it's a means to an end.

'Yeah. Well, I certainly got off on it.' A pause. 'You, though - thought you were about to piss your pants at times.'

'Didn't expect what happened. Came as a shock.'

'Bullshit.' The word erupts down the phone. Mark's glad Adam's not there to witness the way he flinches, as though stung by a whip. 'Don't give me that crap. You knew what I had in mind, right from when I persuaded the kid to come with us. What the fuck did you think I was going to do with her? Play hide and seek? You stupid bastard.'

Mark's confusion at the time, born from his naïveté, as well as a total unawareness of how the psychopathic mind works, comes back to him. Adam's wrong. He didn't have a clue back then what was going on, so he needs to ensure this time is different. No more being weak, he tells himself. Adam's pissed off now, the last thing Mark wants or needs. Time to placate the bastard.

'You're right, I suppose. I mean, I kind of knew. Just wasn't sure what exactly you had in mind.'

'Stupid fucker, you are. Always have been.' The aggression's gone from Adam's tone, if not from his words, causing Mark to release the breath he's been holding.

'Yeah. I guess you're right. At the time, though, I'd not seen anything like that before. Got to me a bit, I agree. Almost did piss my pants, too.' True enough, besides which he needs to keep his place in the pecking order. 'Thing is, I had plenty of time to think things over, once they banged me up. Couldn't admit it to myself at first, not for a while.'

'What? Spit it out.'

'That I liked…' The words choke Mark with their vileness.

'What? That you enjoyed seeing the kid bleed?'

'Yeah.'

'I was right, then. You got off on it, same as I

did.'

'I guess.'

'Took you long enough to realise it.'

'I'm not like you, Adam. I couldn't do something like that, you see. But watching you - that's a different matter. Wish I had your guts, mate.' Mark injects a note of wistfulness into his voice. 'More of an observer, me. Not got the balls for it myself. Doesn't mean I wouldn't enjoy being an onlooker, though.'

'Well, listen to you.' The sound of a carton being opened, the hiss of a lighter. Adam drags on his cigarette. 'The wuss does have a dark side after all. Everyone does; it's just that most people never let it see daylight. Too busy playing life straight, keeping in line with all the other sad bastards.' Contempt fills Adam's voice.

Mark makes his tone reverential. An acolyte worshipping at the feet of his master. 'Not like you.'

Adam takes the bait. 'Nah. Those sad shits; such narrow lives they lead. Working nine to five each day, paying the mortgage, hatching out brats. No individuality; sheep, all of them. Always playing by the rules. Not like me.'

Mark's silent, unsure how to follow up, when Adam catches him unawares. 'You should watch me sometime. Be just like old times.'

Watch me sometime. Words implying more Abby Morgans, either already accomplished or planned for the future. The itch that's been bothering Mark ever since their earlier meeting flares up again. He scratches it.

'You said...' Mark licks his dry lips. 'You said nothing since has come close to her.'

'Too right, in spite of me doing it too quick. But you never forget your first, right?'

Your first. The itch prickles harder.

When Mark doesn't reply, Adam laughs. 'No idea how good it is to snuff out someone's life, have you? OK, so you watched whilst I killed the brat, but you're too much of a wuss to do anything like that yourself.'

'Horses for courses,' Mark forces out. 'Like I said, I'd rather be an onlooker. Do it by proxy.'

'Yeah. Too fucking gutless yourself.'

'But it works better that way, doesn't it?' Now Mark's found the way forward, he goes for it, his disgust temporarily shelved. 'Any partnership – someone always takes the lead.'

His ploy succeeds. Mark can almost hear Adam's ego inflating. 'Not many of us around. Like I say, too many sheep in the world.' He laughs. 'You're a prime example, mate. I remember when we were at school. Useless, you were, without me to show you the ropes.'

'We work well together,' Mark replies. 'You lead, I follow.'

'Reckon it was probably that way with, say, Leopold and Loeb.'

Mark's lost. 'Who?'

'American killing combo. Did some teenage kid with a chisel, way back when. Spent months planning it.' Adam's tone is reverential, before switching to disgust. 'Stupid prats got caught, though.'

Mark's chilled by Adam's study of the murder game. 'It's true, though. About one person out of a pair taking the lead.' He warms to his theme. 'Look at Fred and Rosemary West. Or Myra Hindley and Ian Brady. One of them the doer, the other the helper.'

'Don't get any ideas about taking a walk down Queer Street with me.' Adam's tone turns belligerent. 'Touch me and I'll cut your hand off. Followed by your dick. Got that?'

Even over a phone connection, the man intimidates Mark into forgetting where he is. He's no longer safe at home, with Adam miles away in Taunton. Instead, it's as if the other man's beside him, coercing him into submission. They're back in the park after school; Adam's pinning him down, his knife at his throat, and the eleven-year-old Joshua answers rather than Mark.

'I got it, Adam.'

'I lead, you follow.'

'Right.' Mark's breath is coming more easily now. 'The thing is - all those people we've mentioned. They got caught, same as we did. It doesn't bother you? The thought of going back inside?'

'I've learned from my mistakes. Not going back to jail, not ever.'

Mark tries again. 'You've kept your nose clean since you got released?'

'Wouldn't you like to know?' The voice of an eleven-year-old again, bragging, and Mark's suspicion that Adam's nose is pretty damn dirty gathers force.

'Nearly ran into trouble when I first got out. Stupid bitch I'd been fucking gave me some lip one night, so I knocked her around a bit, taught her a lesson. She knew better than to make waves about it, but her mate didn't. Ran into her the next day and she gave me a load of shit about her pal's busted nose. Banged on about going to the cops. Who gives a shit about some broad's nose? Not as though she was much of a looker in the first place.'

Mark's mouth is dry. 'What did you do?'

'Knew where the bitch's mate liked to hang out. Followed her one night. I let her live, but only because someone saw me approach her. She'll be keeping her mouth shut from now on.'

Thank God. At least he didn't kill her. Mark

wonders whether Adam Campbell's pupils, blackened with the lust for murder, have ever been some other woman's last sight before death, though.

'You ever think about…'

'What? Spit it out.'

'Well, you know. About…'

'Killing again?' Adam laughs. 'What makes you think I haven't?'

Shit. Draw him out gently, Mark tells himself. 'Have you?'

'Why, you want to help me? Be Bianchi to my Buono?'

Mark's stumped again. 'Who?'

'The Hillside Strangler duo over in the States, idiot. Although, as I recall, one of them testified against the other to get a lighter sentence.' Adam's voice grows tinged with menace. 'You ever snitch on me and I'll slice your balls off. That's assuming you have any.'

Mark's transported back through the years once more, to Adam's threat to kill him if he blabs about Abby. He does his best to tame the unleashed tiger.

'Not going to happen. Didn't snitch on you before, did I? Besides, you said it yourself. You've learned a thing or two. You won't get caught again.'

'Too damn right. Been honing my skills.'

'Care to elaborate?'

'Not right now. So, you up for doing it again?'

Mark stalls for time. 'Might be.' He needs to establish a rapport with Adam, gain his trust, make him think they're the same under the skin. How he's Rosemary to Adam's Fred West, the other half of a dynamic killing duo. The only way he'll ever get the better of the man.

Adam laughs. 'Think of the fun we can have. As well as giving our do-gooding parole officers the run around. God, those meetings every month, having to fake being all sweetness and reformation, especially after sticking it to some bitch who had it coming to her anyway. Doesn't it make you sick, having to pretend? Not that you do, what with you living the life of a regular Joe. Working at some shitty builder's yard. My parole guy, he's always on at me to find a steady job. Like they grow on trees.'

Mark's itch prickles back into life. 'You get work from time to time, though, don't you? What is it, labouring, scaffolding, you said?'

'Yeah. Here, there, everywhere.'

'You work away sometimes?'

'Occasionally. The odd contract job. Places like Plymouth or Southampton. Have myself some good times along the way. Cash in hand, as well.'

'How long do you normally go for?'

'As long as it takes. Sometimes a week, other times it drags on a while. Southampton, now, that was a big job. Groundworking; digging drains, foundations, all that stuff. Stayed best part of a month. Had me a blast down there. Went back for my parole meeting, of course. Gave the guy a load of crap about still being in Taunton, not being able to find work.'

'And Plymouth?'

'Didn't see so much of Plymouth. Last September, that was. Shorter gig down there; lasted about a week, as I recall.'

'I've heard it's an interesting place.' A non-committal reply, designed to distract Adam Campbell about what lies beneath Mark's seemingly random questions. Ones that need to be asked, because they're providing answers to Mark's itch.

He's heard enough. Time to wrap up the call.

'Got to go, Adam. I'll be in touch. Soon.'

He will, too. First, though, he has to consider what he's learned.

He feels soiled by his contact with Adam Campbell, contaminated by someone for whom murder is a recreational sport. Christ, the way he exults in roughing up a woman. His expression when they met earlier on, when he tells Mark killing Abby Morgan was fun.

A spot of research is needed. Time to hit the Internet. Once he's in his bedroom, something about the position of his laptop jars him. Almost as though somebody's moved it. Get a grip, he tells himself. What with all he's had on his mind, the neat freakism's obviously taken a back seat. Not as if Natalie will have been snooping around again, not after their showdown last night. He aligns the laptop flush with the edge of the table before switching it on. A few minutes of searching on Google, and he gets answers to more of his questions.

Shit. Adam Campbell is one sick bastard.

A man who needs his freedom taken away now, before he kills again. A man about whom Michelle Morgan has been right all along when she's said he should spend his life behind bars.

Especially chilling is the urge he expresses to murder again. More slowly. Take his time, enjoy the process. Mark's no longer so naïve as to assume Adam is simply bragging. Not after what he's learned from Google. No, this is a man who makes a study of serial killers and is on his way to becoming one. Time to ensure the bastard doesn't get to hang anyone else's life off his trophy belt. A coherent plan is paramount.

Fear, dark and paralysing, strikes Mark. Can he muster the strength to deal with a sadistic killer like Adam? If he doesn't act, though, the man will kill again, and soon. Weakness isn't an option any longer. He owes it to Abby, Michelle and Rachel. Not to mention Shaun and Matthew Morgan. As well as the little Italian girl of so long ago.

Not forgetting Mark. He's spent ten long years in detention, lost most of his family, suffered the wrenching break-up with Natalie. He owes it to himself, too.

He needs to fathom out, and fast, what to do with the knowledge he's gained from Google. There's the option, of course, of an anonymous tip-off to the police. About Southampton a few weeks ago, about Plymouth last September. To Mark, though, that's the coward's way out. One that neatly avoids the risk of squaring up to Adam Campbell in person, of facing down his fears of the man. One not compatible with his newfound resolve to ditch being weak.

No. He needs the satisfaction of taking the bastard down himself.

Christ, he's overlooking the obvious, though. Tick, tock, goes the clock. Will Rachel Morgan afford him the luxury of sufficient time to deal with Adam? It's seeming increasingly likely. In a way, Mark's strangely grateful Rachel's so emotionally screwed-up. Chances are she's hesitating over her threat to go to the police. Too ashamed, perhaps, or scared of her mother. Whatever the reason, Mark prays his reprieve will last until he's managed to nail Adam Campbell.

An idea is germinating in his mind. Two things are in his favour.

Firstly, Adam Campbell is cocky, overly sure of himself. Mark plans to use that to his advantage. Adam won't expect anything other than compliance from his former sidekick. Not after holding a knife to his throat earlier on. He'll assume he's still Buono to Mark's Bianchi. Time for the two of them to switch roles. Mark intends to become the leader, Adam his sidekick.

Secondly, and most importantly, the man's a psychopathic killer. He has needs Mark will never comprehend, urges he plans to tap into to prevent him killing again.

Adam Campbell's arse will definitely land up back in jail if Mark's successful. Permanently. He'll only get one chance, so he needs to get this right. Adam has the advantage of size, dominance and sheer brutality. This is, after all, a man who's drunk on his self-deluded fantasises of being a notorious serial killer.

Yes. His plan is percolating nicely.

A while later, it's brewed to perfection.

Mark eyes his mobile. He needs to be completely ready for this. The counting starts in his head. *One, two, buckle my shoe.*

Half an hour passes. It's now approaching midnight, but Mark's finally calm. Time to call the bastard again.

He picks up his mobile.

26

TROPHY TIME

'Mate.' Amusement in Adam's voice when he answers his mobile. 'I mean, come on. Two phone calls in one evening? Can't keep away, can you?'

Mark ignores the bait. 'The reason I'm calling you - ' He's sickened to his core by the role he's being forced to play. Here comes the hard part. How best to persuade Adam Campbell they've been cast from the same mould, even if Adam sees Mark as candyfloss to his steel. Adam's words come back again to him: *Can't talk about these things with anyone else.* Mark remembers his plan. Establish a sense of kinship in Adam's mind between the two of them, that's what he needs to do.

'When you mentioned taking the kid's toy, the green hippo, off her. As a souvenir.'

'Yeah? What about it? That nosey mother of mine, poking around in my room. Should have hidden it better, seeing how it was covered in the kid's blood.'

Mark would give a lot to have a parent like Adam's, snooping or not; at least both the Campbells stuck by the bastard. Now's not the time to drink a cup of bitterness, though. He has a trap to bait.

'Made me remember. Bagged myself a little souvenir of my own from the occasion.'

'What the fuck are you talking about?'

'See, when I got the chance to think, in Vinney

Green, that's what made me realise we're more similar than different.'

'Get to the point.'

'I took a little token to remember her by.' The lies come easily, now he's started. 'You didn't see me do it, because I was behind you; you were already heading out the door to clean the knife.'

'You serious? You'd better not be jerking me around.'

'Straight up.'

A pause. Then, 'Bit of a dark horse, ain't you?'

'You're surprised.'

'Yeah, well. You blame me? A wuss like you.'

'Told you. We're not so different, mate.'

'What did you take?'

Mark tells him.

'Fuck. Yeah, I remember that. Why'd you take it, though?'

'Same reason you bagged yourself the hippo.'

'How come you're telling me about this now? That'll have been found when you got arrested.'

'No. I've still got it.' Mark manages to inject a suitable amount of false pride in his voice.

'How the hell did you manage that? Once my mother discovered the kid's hippo and my dad went to the police, our house got searched pretty thoroughly.' The suspicion is back in Adam's voice. Good job Mark's on a roll with his story.

'It was tiny, remember. Easy to hide inside a broken Power Rangers toy I had from years before, in an old box in my wardrobe. The police searched the house, sure, but they'd already found the knife you tossed. They weren't looking for the murder weapon any longer so the whole thing was more or less a routine exercise.'

'Lucky bastard.' Adam still sounds pissed off. He won't, not when Mark dangles the bait in front of him. 'Having something to remember our Pretty Princess by, I mean.'

'Yeah, I was lucky. Mum never got rid of any of my stuff, kept my room exactly the same. Got her to pack everything up for me, right before I got my new identity, became Mark Slater. Mum took it bad, the idea of not seeing me ever again.' Adam won't know about Joanna Barker's rejection of her son, what with the two of them being sent to separate detention centres, so it's a lie Mark can easily get away without arousing Adam's suspicions.

'Been thinking.' Time to hook Adam on the line. 'I mean, you should have it, really, not me. Seeing as how you killed her. Doesn't seem fair me keeping it.'

Silence from Adam. He won't be able to resist, thinks Mark, now I've offered it to him so openly; he wants his trophy too badly. Hell, the bastard's probably getting hard just thinking about it. He adds some extra meat to the bait. Adam's getting the scent of the lure, nice and strong. 'It's yours, if you want it.'

'You serious?'

'Yep.' Reel him in, Mark tells himself. He'll believe it, simply because he wants to.

'You'll give it to me?' Lust oozes from Adam's voice.

'If you want it. Like I said, it's more yours than mine.'

'Yeah, I want it. Hell, that'll be good.'

Job done, Mark tells himself. Now all he has to do is follow through.

They make arrangements. Mark tells Adam he's free to meet any time. He'll call in sick to work again. What with the other man not currently working, he figures he'll want to hook up as quickly as possible to claim his trophy, and he's not wrong. Adam tells Mark he'll meet him tomorrow. Thursday. Which, as it's now well past midnight, is actually today. Same time, same place.

'Don't be late.' The line goes dead as Adam ends the call.

Mark needs to prepare. He goes into his bedroom to rummage around in his bedside cabinet. Does he still have what he's looking for? Yes, he does. Lodged at the back of one of the drawers is an old writing pad along with a packet of envelopes. Nobody writes letters anymore, not the outdated paper type, but the purist in Mark refuses to commit what he has to say to the impersonal tone of an email. Besides, the old-fashioned approach seems appropriate, given how Natalie's discovery of the letter from Linda Curtis sparked off the events of recent weeks. The important thing is to get both letters written, no matter how tough the words are to write. Mark has it all planned in his mind what he needs to say, but whether it'll translate onto paper is hard to judge.

The letters prove even more difficult than he's anticipated, taking him past two a.m., through several drafts, until he's satisfied. He seals them in their envelopes, ready for delivery tomorrow.

Exhausted, Mark drops into his bed, but his mind has never been so clear, so calm. He's being strong for the first time in his life, and it feels good. Very good. His sleep is deep, refreshing.

Thursday morning arrives. Shower, clothes, breakfast; his routine's as precise as ever, in spite of the fact the rest of the day will be far from normal.

Time to call his boss. He registers disbelief, coupled with annoyance, in Steve Taylor's voice as Mark pleads a continuing stomach bug, but what the hell. He's taken precious little sick leave in four years and the odds are good he'll soon be back behind bars anyway. Ensuring Adam Campbell enjoys the same outcome matters more than keeping Steve Taylor sweet.

First thing on Mark's agenda concerns the letters. He intends to deliver them by hand; their content is too important to entrust to the vagaries of the postal service. Thankfully, Natalie's an early bird where work's concerned, often at her desk by eight a.m. No risk of running into her. Same for Rachel, for the opposite reason. She's mentioned how she frequently sleeps in late, what with doing catering events several evenings a week. God knows the last thing he needs is an encounter with her. He drives over to Natalie's, hastily shoving her letter through her mailbox. Rachel's will be delivered to her flat in Exeter before his meeting with Adam in Moretonhampstead.

Next, it's time to go shopping. Thank God for the Tesco store at Eastville; Mark's pretty sure they'll have what he needs. If not, he'll drive into Cabot Circus. Whatever he buys won't be exactly right, of course, but that's not an issue. He's willing to bet Adam won't remember the precise details, not after so long.

Five minutes later, he's in Tesco. Mark can't locate anything suitable at first, and his chest starts its familiar dance with panic, before he reminds himself an approximation will suffice. Then he spots one of those displays that supermarkets tack on to the ends of aisles; what he's after is bang in front of him. Near enough in size and shape, and dead right with the colour. Job done.

Back in his flat, Mark pulls a small backpack from his wardrobe, slinging the letter to Rachel and his purchase from Tesco into it. His plan simply requires him to get in his car and drive the now familiar route down to Moretonhampstead, via Exeter. Twelve o'clock will be the last time he'll ever have to endure Adam Campbell's shit, if all goes to plan with nailing the bastard's arse to the wall. No need for any anonymous tip-off to the police as he'd originally considered doing;

he'll inform them later, and he won't be nameless when he does.

He pulls on his jacket and grabs his mobile phone. Keys, backpack. Breathe. In. Out. One. Two. Mark's apprehensive, despite his resolve to quit being weak. Adam Campbell makes a formidable opponent, one who still holds the power to instil terror. He's facing the prospect of a knife through his neck should Adam suspect his motives. He forces himself to remember Abby Morgan's bloodied body, Rachel's scarred arms. As well as the little Italian girl. He can do this. For them, the ones he's let down, he'll be as strong as he needs to. It'll only be for a short while anyway.

Several rounds of counting later, Mark's as ready as he'll ever be.

It's post-rush hour on a weekday morning. Traffic is light on the M5, despite the ever-present roadworks outside Bristol. Mark makes good time. First task is to drop off Rachel's letter at her flat in Exeter. No sign of her, thankfully, but he can't shove the letter into the box quickly enough. Time to get to Moretonhampstead. He arrives just after eleven thirty, parking up in the same car park as where he talked with Rachel after the vigil. A ten-minute walk through town takes him as far as Michelle Morgan's house. Mark forces himself to look this time. No more Mr Weak Guy, after all.

Everything's more or less the same. The place still wears an uncared-for air, the paint peeling, the gutters as sagging as ever. The garden is more unkempt than he remembers. He stares at the long grass, right where he first saw Abby Morgan. She was playing on that exact spot, he recalls, absorbed with her dolls' house, the plush green hippo beside her. He hears again the tinny voice singing *One, Two, Buckle My Shoe*.

A movement at one of the upstairs windows

jerks him out of the past. The drawing back of a curtain.

A woman is watching him.

Michelle Morgan. Has to be, although he only gets a glimpse of whoever it is. Doubtless wary he's some opportunistic journalist, sniffing out a story.

Mark doesn't believe in Fate, but eyeballing the woman for whom he's caused such pain flags itself up to him as an omen. Whether it's good or bad, he's not sure, but for now he'll take it as a sign he's doing the right thing at last. He turns his back on the house, anxious not to arouse her suspicions further. An actual face to face confrontation with her isn't part of his game plan. Doesn't stop his heart from attempting to thud its way out of his chest, however. Once he reaches the sanctuary of the lane leading to the murder site, Mark counts his way back to calm. *One, two, buckle my shoe*, he chants in his head.

A few minutes later, he's standing where Abby Morgan bled to death. Now the shed has been demolished, it's hard to tell. The day is cold but unusually sunny for the time of year, a sharp reminder of fourteen years ago. Adam's late again, of course, but Mark expects that. It gives him time to breathe, to centre himself, go over in his head what he's planned, before the other man arrives. Imperative that he doesn't allow Adam Campbell to intimidate him, whilst preserving the illusion of being an obedient sidekick. Chances are he'll only get one shot at this. Don't screw up again, he tells himself.

Ten past twelve. Ah, he's here at last. Adam Campbell is striding across the field, his bearing as cocky as ever. Despite his resolve, nerves clench Mark's stomach. He hugs his arms across his chest in mock protection, psyching himself up for what's to come.

'Mate.' Adam's standing in front of him now, dominance oozing from the man. 'Don't see you for fourteen years before the vigil, now it's twice in two days.' He glances around. 'Can't get enough of this place, even though it's all different now. Happy memories, eh?'

'Not the part where we both got banged up.'

Adam shrugs. 'I've learned from my mistakes. I'm more careful these days.'

Mark's banking on the fact Adam's arrogance has prevented him from learning as much as he thinks. 'You'd do it again?'

'We've had this conversation before. Don't you listen? I'll ask you once more. What makes you think I haven't already?'

Mark's mouth becomes desert dry. He manages to force words out of it, mindful of the need for Adam to believe he's on board with this shit. 'You serious?'

Adam moves up close, his fag-ash breath hitting Mark's nostrils full on. 'You don't reckon I've got the balls for it? Is that what you think?'

The man's so near to Mark it's unbearable, and what's worse is his expression. Vicious, feral, like he's itching for any excuse to lay hands on Mark, probably whilst holding a knife to his throat again.

Somehow, Mark manages to speak.

'Course not, mate. Never doubted you for a minute.' Breath held, his chest tight with terror, he watches as Adam's expression tones down a notch, the killer countenance morphing back into mere aggression.

'You'd better not. Or you'll end up with my knife blade in between your ribs.' He steps back, enabling Mark to expel the breath clamouring for release from his lungs. 'Course I'm serious.'

Get the bastard to brag, Mark tells himself. Best way to get him to spout out what he needs to hear.

'Who? Where?'

Adam shrugs. 'Couple of street girls. One in

Plymouth, the other in Southampton.' His self-satisfied ego sneaks a smirk onto his face. 'All over the news a while back. You can't have missed it.'

'I remember.' Mark does, too. Back in his flat after the break-up with Natalie, reading the report on the BBC website about the Southampton murder. Along with his Google searches of the night before, detailing the deaths of the two women. Sparked off by his suspicions, themselves fuelled by Adam's unsubtle boasts, along with the fact he works away from time to time. Plymouth and Southampton. Not exactly difficult for Mark to connect the dots.

Two women have died at Adam Campbell's hands. A stark lack of evidence in both cases, the Plymouth case already cold as far as the media are concerned. The Southampton one is also cooling rapidly. Nobody seems to be linking the two murders, at least not from what's been broadcast in the news.

The respite in Mark's chest is only temporary, apparently. He's struggling to breathe once more. He reminds himself of the end game: Adam Campbell's arse back behind bars.

'You killed them both.' Mark forces reverence into his tone. He needs to put on the performance of his life here; convince Adam the murders of the prostitutes turn him on. Seems the act's working, from Adam's next words.

'Yep. Did a snuff job on both of them. Strangled the first bitch. Stabbed the second one.' That ties in with what Mark's found out from Google.

Adam scrutinises him. 'You like that? Gets your nipples hard, does it?'

Mark nods.

'Because it sure tweaks mine. I tell you, hearing those tarts beg for mercy didn't half get me stiff. In all the right places.'

'You went for a different method with the second one? How come?'

'Two reasons. One – throw the police off their game. See, they think they're so clever, what with all their profiling shit. Figured they wouldn't connect the two whores, not if I did them in different cities, changed the method.'

'Makes sense.'

'Second reason – wanted to experiment. Discover what suits. Next time, I'll give something else a go.'

'A new place, as well?'

Smug pride etches itself on Adam's face. 'Told you, mate. That's the plan from now on. Like I said, I'll go for another street girl, some big city, doesn't matter where. Leeds, perhaps, or Glasgow. Some clapped-out junkie who nobody gives a rat's arse about. Find somewhere quiet to take her, so I can have myself some fun. Nice and slow, it'll be, same as with those hookers, not quick like when I killed the brat.'

'You made them suffer?'

'Hell, yeah. They didn't die easily, that's for sure.'

Mark recoils before he manages to catch himself. The last thing he needs is for the other man to sense he's not fully on board with what he's saying. Adam doesn't, though. Too wrapped up in reminiscing.

'Sweet, it was. You should have been there. Not that you'd have done anything. No, you'd have stood and watched, the way you did when I was having fun with our Pretty Princess. Screaming at me to stop. Leaving me to do all the dirty work. Not that I minded, as it happened. Horses for courses, eh, mate?'

'I guess. About those two women -'

'Took myself a little something from each one to remember them by.' Adam closes his eyes, relish oozing from his expression. Mark's hardly surprised, not after the pink diary, the green hippo. Adam's lust for trophies is why they're here today, after all. Nothing's been mentioned in the online news reports about missing items, but there wouldn't be. Not the kind of thing the police release to the media, and besides they might not even be aware something personal has been stolen.

'What did you take?'

Adam shrugs. 'Silver charm bracelet off one, a gold ankle chain from the other.'

A bracelet and an ankle chain. Items with edges and nooks, where skin cells can lodge, providing vital DNA. Adam should be easy to flag as the women's killer, assuming the police can locate the jewellery. They will, Mark thinks. Adam will keep them close by. For him, they're sacred relics, to be brought out often, caressed, savoured. Probably giving him a hard dick in the process.

'We make a good team, you and me, Joshua mate.' Adam swings out a meaty hand, slapping him on the shoulder. His expression turns feral. 'We should join forces again sometime. If you get my meaning.'

Mark does, dark and foul though it is, and it's an effort to force himself to nod, as well as plaster an expression of pleased surprise on his face. Make him think you're gratified, honoured even, that he's including you in his fucked up plans, he tells himself. Stroke the bastard's ego. The prick either intends Mark to be a fall guy if things go belly-up, or else he reckons the pleasure he gets from killing will be heightened with an audience watching. Probably both. This is one seriously screwed-up motherfucker, and he intends to relish every moment of taking the bastard off the streets.

Adam slaps him again on the shoulder. 'You got the goods, mate? Didn't come all this way for nothing.'

'Here.' Mark delves into his backpack, bringing

out the pink plastic child's bracelet he bought that morning from Tesco. Removed from its packaging, the elastic deliberately dirtied and the beads scuffed to conceal its newness, it looks more or less like the one Abby Morgan is wearing when Adam kills her. What with Adam intent at the time on cleaning the knife, he'll never know Mark didn't steal the bracelet or that this isn't the original one. Adam's desperate for his souvenir; Mark's baiting the trap with fresh, tempting meat.

Adam snatches the bracelet, turning it over in his fingers, his expression gratified, like a kid given cake. The bastard's probably halfway to a hard-on, thinks Mark. He can't stand much more of this crap; he needs to get away from the sick bastard in front of him, from the pretence he gets off on murder by proxy, before Adam clocks his bluff.

Too late. Adam shoves the bracelet in his pocket. 'Sweet. Now I've got trophies from all three.' He slaps Mark hard on the shoulder. 'Come on. Let's find a pub and get some beers down our necks.'

27

WHAT YOU DESERVE

By the time Mark's back at his flat in Bristol, Adam Campbell's warped personality clings to him like a bad stink. He strips off all his clothes and stands under the hottest shower he can bear, scrubbing off the bastard's vileness, swilling away the memory of having to pretend to be as twisted as the other man is. Being forced to sit with him in a pub, drinking alongside him, as though he's the mate Adam always refers to him as, makes Mark want to puke. He counts, working his way up through the numbers, and gradually the tightness in his chest eases. Once he's out of the shower and into clean jeans and T-shirt, he's back on track with his staying strong resolve. Besides, he reminds himself, with any luck he'll never see the fucker ever again, and all that remains is to execute the last part of his plan.

Mark heads back into his bedroom, opening his laptop. He's aware it's displacement activity, postponing the inevitable. What he should be doing is phoning Tony Jackson. As soon as he does, though, his freedom will end. Mark's clinging to his last moments of liberty, procrastinating on his laptop. Eventually he picks up his mobile.

The one recording Adam's confession to the murders of the two prostitutes. After all, Adam Campbell is a man convinced of Mark's – no, Joshua Barker's – unswerving loyalty to him. A killer so intent on bagging himself his trophy he never sniffs out his sidekick's betrayal. Duplicity that starts when Mark's fingers initiate the sound clip facility on his mobile, concealed in his pocket.

Shit. His call to Tony Jackson goes straight to voicemail. Mark leaves a message.

'Call me. It's urgent.'

Damn. So much for his hopes of ratting Adam out immediately. Tony Jackson is the only one Mark intends to speak to, at least at first, given his distrust of the police. The obsessive side of him chafes at the delay, but what the hell. They're due to meet tomorrow for their monthly meeting anyway.

Next on the agenda is Natalie. OK, so he's already written to her, but she's made it very clear she wants nothing more to do with him. His concern is she'll tear his letter up unread. He composes a text.

'Nat. Read my letter. Stuff you need to know. Sorry about everything. Hope you now understand.' Whether she ever will is another matter, and if he's to go back to prison perhaps it's a moot point, but Mark loathes the thought of her believing him an Adam Campbell clone. Moreover, as he's already informed her, she needs to know certain things. *I've got something else to tell you. It's important. About how we met.* Mission accomplished, via the letter.

Mark retreats to his sofa. He lies down, pillowing his head on his hands, mulling over the afternoon's events. Weird, sure; terrifying too, but definitely a success. With any luck, today is Adam Campbell's last day of freedom. His sorry arse will soon be back in custody, with a life sentence without parole for murder heading his way. Mark will take care of the details when he eventually speaks with Tony Jackson. Christ, the man has one hell of a shock about to land on his plate. More than one, actually. First, Mark's parole violations. Second, the information about the killing of the two prostitutes by Adam Campbell. If that doesn't shatter the man's sang-froid, nothing will.

It's not late, but Mark's exhausted, his emotions drained bone-dry. Time for some reading before bed, a chance to unwind. He's just grabbed the latest Stephen King novel when a knock hammers on his door, loud and insistent.

Mark has no friends, never gets visitors, unless he includes Natalie. Who the hell - ? For a moment, hope flares in Mark that it's her, before he rejects the idea; whoever's the other side of his door, they knock far more aggressively than Natalie does.

The cops. Come to arrest him. Can't be anyone else, despite the lack of 'Police! Open up!' he's so familiar with from TV dramas. Rachel's informed them at last of his transgressions. Here ends his freedom.

It's a Victorian building, with old-style features, no spy holes, so Mark's unable to check the identity of his caller before he pulls open the door.

When he does, Shaun Morgan is standing in front of him.

Rachel's brother enjoys an extra inch in height over Mark, as well as a good ten kilos or thereabouts of solid muscle, born out of frequent gym training. Before Mark's had a chance to assimilate his shock, Shaun's crashed through the door, slamming it behind him with his foot. His hands grasp Mark's throat, squeezing, as he uses his bulk to push Mark across the floor and pin him against the wall.

Mark's arms grab at Shaun's, but the grip on his neck is too tight; every millilitre of breath is being throttled out of him, and his fingers clutch uselessly at the air. The man's eyes bulge with his effort, as well as the rage erupting through him. Useless for Mark to kick out at Shaun's shins; he's wearing nothing but socks on his feet. The pressure in his chest is beyond bearable, and then Shaun drops his hold on him. Mark sags to the floor, sucking oxygen inside him as though he's a crack addict getting a fix, his lungs burning. He crouches over Shaun's boots, heaving, gasping, trying to get a grip on his breathing. Is Shaun intending to kill him? Fuck, he can't die, not like this, not when he's about to nail Adam Campbell for murder.

Before he manages to get his breath under control, however, Shaun's booted foot lifts and connects with Mark's crotch, slamming hard into his balls, and all thoughts drain from Mark's mind. He's reduced to the agony between his legs, sparking red-hot and shrinking him to ectoplasm, less than human, focused solely on the pain. His gasps alternate with half-formed, indistinguishable words, his brain desperate to find a way to stop Shaun administering the beating – or the killing – he's come here to deliver.

He doesn't stand much of a chance. Apart from the fights at Vinney Green, Mark's never been a brawler; as an adult, he's simply unused to playing macho with his fists. Besides, Shaun packs way more muscle than Mark and he seems very familiar with how to use it.

The other man's voice filters through Mark's haze of pain.

'You bastard.' Shaun ejects the words from his mouth as though they're maggots. 'Not enough for you to kill a two-year-old child and blow my family to pieces, was it?' His feet edge closer towards Mark's head. Mark, still fighting for breath on the floor, can't wrench his eyes from the black menace of the toecaps. 'You had to fuck around with Rachel.'

Mark manages a few strangled syllables. 'I never…didn't mean…' His attempts at placating the man end when Shaun's boot connects, hard, with his thigh. He's driven backwards by the kick, his head cracking against the wall. His hands move away from his burning genitals to clutch his leg instead.

'You deliberately sought her out.' Through his haze of pain, Mark's aware how calm Shaun's voice is. Cold, controlled, along with a measure of restraint Mark finds chilling. No crazed act of revenge, this. Rather, it's a steady, cool-headed resolve to even the score sheet with Mark. A desire that'll only end one way. To balance things up, Shaun needs to kill Mark, and he possesses the wherewithal to accomplish his mission.

A hand grabbing his shirt and hauling him off his knees cuts off all thought, as Shaun's fist slams into his nose. A crunching noise sounds as the bone breaks, with pain instantly exploding across his face and through the back of his skull. He's been punched back against the wall again, his head cracking hard against it. Mark's incapable of anything bar crumpling at Shaun's feet.

'You deliberately broke the terms of your parole.' Shaun grabs hold of an armchair and drags it closer to sit in front of Mark, who's huddled on the floor, clutching his nose. Fire flares throughout his face, a red wetness trickling through his fingers. It's a huge effort simply to drag each breath in through his mouth. He tastes the copper tang of his blood as he weighs up whether he can avoid dying this evening. Shaun will be immune to protestations of innocence; in fact, they'll only inflame his anger. Mark stands little chance of out-fighting the guy. Only one possibility comes to mind. Scream loud and long enough to attract help from one of the other tenants. They're all male and the bloke who lives upstairs is built like the Hoover Dam. In addition, the walls in the building, whilst thick, aren't particularly efficient at keeping out sound. Thank God it's his nose and not his jaw that's broken.

'She says you went to the vigil. Had to return to the scene of the crime, didn't you? You sad fucker.'

Again, no emotion from Shaun, simply calm detachment. More blood runs down the back of Mark's throat as he strains his ears for any sound from the flat above. He's rewarded with silence as the pain in his head increases; a solid throbbing from his nose coupled with a jagged hurt from where his skull slammed into the wall. His groin still feels as though it's tangoed with a sledgehammer. To make matters worse, Mark's chest is impossibly tight, but his breathing is limited to the air he can gulp past the blood in his mouth. Panic rises in him as he struggles for oxygen, all the while eyeing up Shaun's fists and feet, anticipating the next blow.

'How…' The constriction in his chest renders Mark incapable of completing his sentence, but Shaun gets what he means.

'How did I find where you live? That what you're trying to say?' Shaun reaches out a hand, producing instant recoil from Mark. This time his chin is grabbed, forcing his head up so their eyes meet. The movement sends pain shooting through his skull. Shaun's green irises blank Mark at the same time as they stab through him. He senses the rage coiled up in the man, a sleeping serpent about to awake, giving Mark the answer to one of his questions. He understands now how Abby Morgan's death has affected her older brother, the man who always appears so strong, so calm. Fourteen years of picking up the pieces for his sister lie behind Shaun's gaze. Throw an alcoholic father and a dysfunctional mother into the mix and the result is an explosive combination when thrust on the shoulders of a teenage boy. He's a bottler of his emotions, this man. Not for him his mother's tirades, his father's alcoholic oblivion or the knife's kiss like Rachel. Shaun's shouldered the trauma for his family for too long, forced when too young to be tough beyond his years, and the cork's about to burst free from his bottle.

Mark's realisation that he may soon die gathers force, although he's not convinced his life is worth fighting for anyway. Then the overwhelming urge to ensure Adam Campbell returns to prison floods through him, and his survival instinct resurfaces. He drags a huge lungful of air past the constriction in his chest, screaming out as much of the word *help* as he can manage before Shaun's fist connects with his face. Agony sears through his chin. His mouth drops open, bloodied saliva pouring out, and Mark knows he won't be doing any more shouting. His jaw is either broken or dislocated and the only sounds leaving his body are tortured ones.

'Your girlfriend told me,' Shaun continues. 'Ex-girlfriend, I should say. Seems like she's seen the light about you.'

Mark's consciousness has been reduced to a throbbing J-shape of pain; a line connecting his nose and jaw with his groin before curving round to his thigh. Shaun will take his time; Mark's in no doubt about that, and only two questions remain. *Will he kill me*, and *how much pain will I suffer?* The answers appear to be *yes* and *one hell of a lot.*

He doesn't blame Natalie. She's precious little reason to trust the male sex, after all. Mark's simply the end of a long line of his gender to hurt her. Must be hell to believe your boyfriend's a convicted killer who's lunched with his victim's sister. A lunch followed by a kiss, no less. The strings of Natalie's jealous streak will have been twisted, a falsetto note played on its chords, driving her to contact Shaun. How she got in touch with him, Mark has no idea, but it scarcely matters now.

He slumps further down the wall, prompting his aching groin to protest.

'See, prison's too good for a piece of crap like you,' Shaun says. 'Three meals a day. A bed to sleep in.

No worries about work or paying a mortgage. Plus you get to avoid all the things I don't. Like watching your mother turn sourer, year after year; realising neither you nor your sister matter to her because she's locked in the past. Dead the moment she discovered what you and your twisted accomplice did to her daughter.'

Shaun rises to his feet, his movements slow and controlled. He balls his right hand into a fist, slamming it hard into his left.

'Like witnessing your father slide into alcoholism.' Shaun pounds his fist against his cupped palm again.

'Like having a sister who can't wear anything except long sleeves because she's sliced her arms like they're joints of meat.'

Smack goes his fist for the third time.

Mark understands now he's going to die, battered, bloody and beaten to death, and he wonders how long it'll be before anyone – Tony Jackson? Steve Taylor? – misses him.

'The other bastard,' says Shaun. 'Adam Campbell. Can't do anything about him, but you – you're different. You – I can sort. When Rachel told me what you'd done, I was all for reporting you immediately for parole violation. Get your arse slammed back into prison. She wouldn't let me, though. Thought she was crazy, but I ended up promising her a few days' grace. Time to get her head together before we contacted the police. Glad I did now.'

Shaun raises one foot off the floor, inching it in the direction of Mark's groin.

'See, after your ex called, I did some thinking. Seemed like a gift from heaven, her on the phone, saying she'd give me your address. Better than the police. Jail for violating your parole? Sure, you'd spend some time inside, but not life. Not what you deserve. A few years with good behaviour, then you'd be back to preying on more vulnerable women.'

Shaun swings his foot back, then drives it forward, aiming for Mark's balls, catching his injured thigh instead as Mark twists his body away. Tidal waves of agony surge through him. A tortured groan rips from his wounded jaw as he collapses sideways across the floor, clutching the coffee table as he does so. His mobile slides off onto the carpet beside him.

'I'll be the one in jail, not you.' Shaun grabs Mark's collar, hauling him upright again. 'You – you'll be in the mortuary.' Shaun's gaze locks onto Mark's own. No emotion flickers in the other man's eyes. 'Got Rachel to agree to psychiatric help at long last. I can go to prison easier if I know she's getting the care she needs.'

He moves forward, crushing Mark's mobile underfoot as he does so, the casing smashing under the pressure. Shaun lifts his foot, kicking away the broken phone, its recording of Adam Campbell's confession to murder now destroyed.

Then he positions Mark against the wall and raises his fist, hammering it into ribs that crack under the force. He follows the blow with more to the stomach, chest, head. Mark's last memory before he loses consciousness is the blankness in Shaun Morgan's eyes.

28

PROJECTED GUILT

Rachel's been out all day and doesn't open the mailbox at her block of flats until early evening. Mark's letter greets her. At first, she's thrown by it. A letter? Who writes those these days? It's been hand delivered, too. Her name and address are on the envelope, penned in a tight, neat script. The writing's unfamiliar. Rachel opens it with curiosity, keen to discover the sender. She flips the pages over, catching her breath when she sees the signature.

Mark Slater. The bastard. The fucking bastard. Why has he written to her, for God's sake? Hasn't he heaped enough humiliation on her?

The last few days have been beyond hard for Rachel. The doctor's disapproval still stalks her. She frequently bangs her wounded arm against things. Her sense of having failed Shaun yet again piles extra guilt on her. Not to mention her shame over the kiss.

Yep, Rachel's been more than a little screwed-up in her head these past few days.

Now here she is, with a letter from Mark Slater, a.k.a. Joshua Barker, in her hands.

Impossible not to open it. Once she starts reading, she's hooked by the contents.

Dear Rachel,

First, I need to apologise for the distress I've caused. I've hurt you, and that was never my intention. I

*was drawn to you right from the start. For selfish
reasons, I'm afraid. My emotions about Abby's death
were eating me up inside, and I hoped you'd provide
some answers.*

*From the first, I sensed a bond between us, what
with neither of us having our fathers in our lives. As well
as being rejected by our mothers. I never told you this,
but mine cut off all contact with me when I was sent to
juvenile detention. She's always been cold and
unforgiving, not unlike your own mother.*

*As well as an apology, I owe you thanks. I needed
answers from you and I got them. You'll never know how
much guilt I've suffered over the years, wishing I could
have prevented your sister's death. Now the burden's
been lifted. By you, Rachel, when you told me how your
mother blames you for Abby's death. She's wrong to do
so. You were only a child at the time. Undeserving of the
guilt heaped on you. The thing is - my situation's not so
different. Once I heard how badly your mother has
behaved towards you, it helped me realise I've treated
myself far too harshly. Like you, I was only a kid at the
time.*

*I have two more things to say to you, Rachel.
Firstly, I've been back in touch with Adam Campbell.
We've met twice recently, and on both occasions, he's
convinced me he's still the monster he always was. He's
killed two women since his release. Admitted their
murders, boasting he'll do it again. He's evil, a
psychopath, but I should soon have evidence that'll lock
him away for good, so he never harms anyone ever
again. With any luck, I'll also get evidence proving I
didn't kill your sister. I wasn't lying to you, Rachel,
when I told you Abby's death was all down to Adam
Campbell. He killed her, not me. Once I get what I'm
after, I'll go to the police, admit breaking my parole and
accept whatever prison sentence comes my way. I'm at*

peace with going back inside if it means Adam Campbell gets life behind bars.

The second thing I need to tell you should explain why your mother's been so unfair in her treatment of you. Every minute of the day your sister died is imprinted on my brain, Rachel. I saw something before Adam abducted her that I've never mentioned to anyone. At the time, it didn't seem significant. As we walked towards your house that day, I spotted a silver Mondeo parked down a side street. One I'd seen before, because it belonged to Adam's father. Adam was striding on ahead, so he never noticed it. His father was standing by the driver's door, with a woman on the passenger side. From what Adam had previously told me, his dad was always having affairs. Jon Campbell's attention was on the woman; he never saw Adam or me. The two of them were kissing in the car before he drove off. I didn't think any more about it. Until the trial, when I saw your mother in court, and recognised her as the woman with Adam's father that day.

Adam told me he had cousins who lived near your house in Moretonhampstead. That's how he first discovered Abby, and presumably how his father first met your mother. Nobody ever found out about their affair; it never came out at the trial. Only three people knew, and none of us said anything. Your mother lied about her whereabouts at the time of Abby's death, as did Adam's father. Their relationship was too recent for anyone to suspect; when your mother claimed she'd been visiting a neighbour with dementia, nobody had reason to believe otherwise.

Anyway, your mother was most likely having sex with Adam Campbell's father whilst his son murdered Abby. Not doing the good neighbour bit or taking care of her kids. How hard must it be for her to accept she'd been having an affair with the father of her daughter's killer? A double blow, coming on top of Abby's death. That's why she says she blames you for what happened. But she doesn't. She blames herself. She's been projecting her guilt onto you ever since, Rachel, because you're a soft target. Far easier to hate you than it is to admit her own culpability.

I've no idea whether any of this will help you. Perhaps accepting your mother has far more reason than you to reproach herself, along with finding out Adam Campbell is heading back to prison for life – I'm hoping it might ease your burden of guilt a little. If I could wish anything for you, Rachel, it would be for you to let go of all the self-blame and be happy.

Yours
Mark Slater

Rachel's unable to take in what she's just read at first.

Her mother was having an affair at the time Abby was murdered.

With the father of her child's killer.

Not visiting a neighbour with dementia whose Swiss cheese brain provided the perfect cover for illicit sex.

Michelle Morgan has lied for the last fourteen years. Foisted her guilt onto her surviving daughter, neatly avoiding accepting any responsibility herself. This is a woman who fucks, albeit unknowingly, another man whilst her daughter dies. A hypocrite who pretends to be the Good Samaritan to cloak her own selfish agenda. One who must hate herself for fucking around with Campbell Senior that day.

Rachel recalls her ten-year-old self on the doorstep, Christina Aguilera pounding in her ears, her fingers caressing her kitten. She sees a child, too young to be entrusted with a toddler's care, one innocent of the blame heaped so readily on her by her mother. A tiny seed of anger unfurls deep within her and embryonic though it is, it starts to elbow out her guilt. Over time, she realises, it'll grow bigger, this sense of injustice at how her mother has been quick to condemn her daughter for being nothing worse than ten years old with a short attention span. Rachel savours her anger, the way it empowers her, infusing her with strength.

'You're not to blame for Abby's death.' Shaun's words, heard so often over the years, echo through her head. She believes him at last. The fact that she's in no way culpable for Abby's death slaps her in the face, astonishing her. Shit happens, she decides, and that day, fourteen years ago, the crap landed on the Morgan family doorstep. Not her fault, though. Rachel accepts, right down to her toes, that she was ten years old and too young to be saddled with her mother's responsibilities. Time to lay down the burden of guilt she's hauled around for so long. When she attempts to do so, she finds she's no longer carrying it anyway.

Rachel peels back the sleeves of her top, laying bare the self-hatred she's carved into her flesh, partly masked by the bandages on her latest additions. Her fingers stroke the livid slash marks as the tears come. She cries for her mutilated arms, sobs for her disfigured legs, weeps for her years of self-loathing. On one level, Rachel understands why Michelle Morgan has behaved so monstrously, but on another, she's angry. Desperately so.

She's my mother, she thinks. *She should damn well have acted like it. All these years I've worshipped her, endured all the shit she's heaped on me, only to find out she's a hypocrite.*

Rachel's well aware she has a long road to travel. The light bulb in her head may well be flashing brighter than the Blackpool Illuminations, but the crap wedged deep in her psyche will need time to flush it out completely. She can't guarantee she won't cut herself again, given how ingrained the habit is. Moreover, she doesn't yet have substitute behaviours for when things get rough. Shaun's there for her, sure, but she's a big girl now; running to her older brother whenever she faces some problem isn't the answer.

For the first time ever, she seriously considers the idea of psychiatric help, counselling, a shrink, whatever. Oh, sure, Shaun's finally badgered her into promising she'll seek professional advice. She's been hoping to sweet-talk him out of it, but a shrink now seems a definite possibility. A safe environment, one in which she can explore what it means to have a cold, self-serving bitch for a mother.

A strong urge to call her brother hits Rachel. He needs to know this shit. He doesn't answer his mobile, though, and it's then she thinks *oh God*. The phone call with Natalie Richards bursts into her mind. Shaun now has Mark Slater's address and although she's begged him not to, she can't be sure he won't pay him a visit.

The two of them are supposed to be informing the police tomorrow about Mark's parole violations. Ever since Natalie's phone call, though, Rachel's sensed Shaun's barely leashed fury. A lust for revenge, something that can't be satisfied by being a good citizen and going to the police. She suspects her brother wants Mark Slater's blood in retribution for Abby Morgan's.

She doesn't completely believe his promise not to use the information Natalie Richards has provided. The unanswered phone doesn't bode well. Normally, fearful she's about to cut herself, he answers her calls immediately.

He won't do anything stupid, she reassures herself. Too prone to playing by the rules, too self-controlled. Incapable of violence. Besides, what can she do? Call the police and tell them her brother may be about to assault someone, when he's already assured her he won't? She shoves aside the inner voice reminding her of the fury she's glimpsed in him, and prays he'll keep his word.

As for Mark, Rachel realises she no longer wears their kiss as a badge of shame. Why he responded the way he did when she kissed him isn't clear to her, but she accepts what he says in the letter. About needing answers. How he played no part in her sister's murder. Rachel's practical side warns her to wait for the proof he's promised, but her intuition's telling her what he says is true. Impossible to fake what he's told her.

Rachel's brain flips back to Mark's claim he'll get enough evidence to send Adam Campbell to prison for life. If he does, the whole Morgan family might be able to move on. Michelle will have no further need for her tirades, although what she'll replace them with Rachel has no idea. Right now, she doesn't care. She'll never have to attend the God-awful vigil again and endure her mother's rants. Adam Campbell, the murdering bastard truly guilty of her sister's death, will be behind bars. Justice satisfied, Abby avenged.

Right now, though, Rachel intends to deal with her mother. She grabs her mobile.

Michelle's about to experience a radical change in her daughter. Rachel's moving beyond being a stress-head who reacts to pressure by grabbing a knife. Instead, she's a woman in control of herself, for whom a dramatic metamorphosis is beginning. No more meekly accepting her mother's hostility. Oh no. Instead, she'll give her Mark's letter to read, the contents of which arm Rachel against any attempt on Michelle's part to deny the affair with Adam's father. It's her way of slamming her hand up close and personal in her mother's face, palm forward, saying: *No more saddling me with your guilt. Deal with Abby's death by yourself, because I'm done with the self-blame.*

Rachel grips Mark's letter, drawing strength from it. Then she calls her mother. Her voice is steady when Michelle Morgan answers.

'I'm coming over,' Rachel informs her mother. 'No buts. We need to talk.'

29

SHATTERED PRECONCEPTIONS

Natalie finally stops work after her second hour of overtime and heads for home. Tonight will be different, she promises herself. No more brooding about Mark Slater. She'll treat herself to fish and chips and wash it down with cheap white wine before vegging out in front of the telly. Whatever crime drama is on 5 USA should keep her mind off her ex-boyfriend very nicely.

Her mood is buoyant when she arrives back at her flat, her stomach already anticipating the crispiness of the fish in its batter, the greasy chips, the coldness of the wine. She tugs off her coat, slinging her handbag through the open bedroom door, before turning to pick up the mail lying on her mat. A credit card statement, a couple of circulars, a bill for the previous tenant. Then Natalie draws her breath in sharply as she gets to the final letter in her hand. Mark Slater is the sender, a fact forcing food far from Natalie's mind, so great is the ball of tension in her guts.

Mark's handwriting. She'd recognise it anywhere. So neat, so precise, like the man himself. No stamp. Hand delivered, then. Oh, God. He's been here, to her flat. She turns the envelope over, delaying the moment when she tears it open to discover what he has to say to her. Because she'll read it, of course. Natalie doesn't fool herself she'll do the sensible thing and tear it up, unread. Mark Slater: she's tried to burn, blast and bomb her feelings for him, reminding herself he's a convicted child killer, but it's not worked. Flickers of tenderness survive. Natalie tells herself breathing life into the embers isn't a good idea.

The faint sound of her mobile distracts her. She goes into her bedroom, rummaging in her handbag, pulling out her phone.

Shit. A text from Mark.

'Nat. Read my letter. Stuff you need to know. Sorry about everything. Hope you now understand.'

She returns to the living room, letter in hand, trying to fathom why he's written to her. If it's simply to repeat how sorry he is, how he never meant to hurt her, then she'll be disappointed. He's said all those things already. Likewise, if he's pleading for a reconciliation then the answer will be no. Besides, he's prison-bound anyway. Once he gets out of hospital following the visit Shaun Morgan will probably make to him. Natalie's unwilling to send her emotions on another rollercoaster ride. She remembers her hopes of a happy future, of marriage and children. Her devastation when Mark smashes them into more pieces than she can count. All she wants is a quiet life, with the right man, something Mark Slater can't deliver. She needs a partner who doesn't come with such heavy baggage. Give her some ordinary problems to be forgiving about, like the toilet seat being left up or dirty socks on the bedroom floor. Not child murder.

No, a way forward for her with Mark Slater doesn't exist.

Her eyes drift over the familiar handwriting again, following the slants and loops as they spell out her name. She urges herself to destroy the letter; either tear it to shreds or incinerate it in the flame from her gas hob. She doesn't, though, especially now she's received Mark's text. Her fingers shake as she takes hold of one corner, inserting her index finger under the flap, but she follows through, ripping it open with a jagged tear.

She pulls out the contents and begins to read.

Dear Natalie,

You're probably wondering why I've written this letter, as you've made it very clear you want nothing to do with me. Don't worry; I won't contact you again in any way. I'm writing because there are things I have to tell you. Before I do, let me say I'm sorry for the pain I've caused you. I've always cared so much for you, right from our first date, so it hurts me that I've not been what you deserve.

The first thing I want to say is this. Whether you believe me or not, I had no direct participation in the murder of Abby Morgan. My only crime that day was not stopping Adam Campbell when he lured the child away from her garden and later when he attacked her so brutally. I've been weak, Natalie; afraid to stand up for what's right. It's something people who prey on others' vulnerabilities, like my mother and Adam, can sense. They're bullies, tyrants who suss out we won't fight back, so we end up getting crap heaped on us. My father was much the same; it seems I've followed, unknowingly, in his footsteps.

The thing is, Natalie, I don't want to be weak anymore. Being a coward when I should have shown some balls instead has brought me nothing but grief in my life. I've made the decision to change, do the right thing in future, no matter how hard it is.

The irony is, I've managed at last to get over my guilt about Abby Morgan's death. It's taken me fourteen years, but I now accept I wasn't to blame. I was eleven years old, still grieving over my father's death, friendless, with a cold, emotionally abusive mother. A ripe target to be bullied by Adam Campbell. I stood up to him as best I could, though. Something for which I've never given myself credit before now. I screamed at him to stop hurting the child, but he had a knife. He threatened to kill me if I implicated him. When the police questioned me, I told them I'd helped kill Abby Morgan. Given how screwed-up I was back then, they were almost as terrifying as Adam Campbell. I ended up confessing to a crime I didn't commit. Like I said, it's ironic. I've finally forgiven myself for what happened, accepted I do have a right to love and be loved, right at the point I'm heading back to prison.

I mentioned I have two things to tell you, Nat. The second one will bring back painful memories for you, because it concerns the abuse you suffered when you were eleven.

Without you mentioning anything about your attacker's age, I already knew you'd been hurt by a boy rather than a man. How? Because Adam Campbell is the one who assaulted you that day, Nat. You told me how your attacker smelled bad. I'm guessing you meant cigarette smoke. Adam started on the fags when he was ten. Always reeked of his dad's Marlboros. He found you whilst on a trip to Bristol with his parents to visit one of his uncles. He got bored, went off exploring and that's when he attacked you. Nothing you could have done would have stopped him. He's too big, too strong. You have no reason to blame yourself.

You'll be wondering how I found all this out. A long time ago, I held your diary in my hands. The pink, flowery one, with your name and address written at the front. The bastard likes to take trophies from his victims, Nat. He bragged about what he'd done, although he didn't mention the details. You became an obsession with me throughout the years, all the time I served in detention. I promised myself I'd find you one day, reassure myself you were all right, that Adam Campbell hadn't hurt another child the way he did Abby Morgan.

That's what I meant before, when I tried to tell you I'd not been honest about how we met. Before that day, I already knew your original name, Natalia Abruzzo, written in the front of your diary. To me, it seemed so unusual, so pretty. One I always remembered, along with your address. When I was released from prison, I fully intended to look you up. Without revealing who I was, of course. I found it harder than I'd anticipated, though, to adjust to life on the outside and the years slipped by whilst I got a job and sorted myself out. The urge to find you never left me, though, and a few months ago, I decided to act on it at last.

I ended up going to your mother's house in Copthorne Close. I didn't dare ring the bell. I spoke with one of the neighbours, pretending I wasn't sure of the exact house where the Abruzzos lived. Found out your mother, an agoraphobic, was still at the same address. How she hadn't used her married name since the divorce. The woman told me the split had been bitter, how Callie Abruzzo wanted no reminders of her Italian husband. How she switched both of you back to her maiden name of Richards. Along with changing yours from Natalia to Natalie. How you'd moved out from home a few years before, but visited your mother every Sunday for lunch.

I needed more, Nat. However relieved I was that Adam Campbell hadn't killed you, I had to see you in person to reassure myself. All part of being an obsessive-compulsive, I suppose. I waited for you near your mother's house one Sunday, sitting in the car until you arrived. You thought I was some random stranger asking for directions, didn't you? We got chatting and my gut instincts told me we'd be good together. When you mentioned the deli you use for lunch, I went there every day, hoping to see you again.

*Then you told me about the abuse. Your fears
about your attacker finding you again one day, even
though you realise it's unlikely. The thing is, our deepest
emotions are never logical, Nat. I'm hoping what I tell
you next will reassure you Adam Campbell will never
hurt you or anyone else in the future. With any luck,
he'll soon be arrested for murder. He's killed two
women since his release. The prostitutes who were
murdered in Southampton and Plymouth. He's boasted
to me about wanting to kill more street girls. By the time
you read this, I'll have met him again, with the aim of
recording him on my mobile as he admits to the murders
of the prostitutes. He won't be able to resist bragging to
me about their deaths, seeing how I've convinced him he
can trust me. He's also taken trophies from his latest
victims, which the police should find. With all that, they
should have enough proof to put him away for good.*

*What I've said in this letter must come as a huge
shock to you. All I can say is - forgive me, Natalie. Try to
understand the reasons I've failed you so badly. I've
done what I can, though, to ensure Adam Campbell
never kills again.*

*Take care of yourself
Yours, Mark*

Natalie's mind is blank, unable to process what
she's read. Everything's a mess in her head as her
preconceptions shatter one by one. In her brain, Mark's
no longer a vicious child killer. Instead, he's transformed
once more into a helpless bystander in a toddler's death,
nearly as much a victim of Adam Campbell as Abby
Morgan is. A man who's finally facing up to his
nemesis.

She attempts to digest what she's read in the letter.
Adam Campbell, the notorious child killer, is the bastard
who lay on top of her that day in the copse. The
memories flood back. His fingers probing and tearing,

making her bleed. The stink of cigarette smoke hanging around him. The turd inches from her nose. The damp earth pressing against her body.

'Frigging fat bitch.' His taunt, spoken in a pubescent treble, making her aware her attacker's about the same age she is, although his size and strength belie his years. Something impossible to admit to Mark when she tells him about the assault; bad enough to be overpowered by an adult, but another pre-teen? Shameful. Now, however, her self-recrimination begins to fade, given her newfound awareness of who hurt her that day. No ordinary boy, but one hiding the makings of a vicious killer within him.

The attack pre-dates Callie and Stefano Abruzzo's divorce. At the time, she's still Natalia Abruzzo. Half Sicilian, brought up bilingual, her diary written solely in Italian. Forbidden by Callie Richards after her parents' divorce to speak, read or listen to the language. She recalls how, bloodied and shaking in her bedroom after the attack, she thinks she must have left her diary behind. A casualty of her desperate scramble to shove all her belongings back into her bag and get the hell out of the copse. Now she knows the diary became the trophy of a vile killer.

'Frigging fat bitch.' The memory slaps Natalie in the face as she recalls Adam Campbell's breath against her ear. She's possibly his first victim, the one with whom he began honing his craft, leading him from finger rape to the murder of Abby Morgan. Dear God. Not to mention the fact he's killed two women since his release. Boasted about killing more. The memory of biscuits and Crimewatch with Callie Richards floods back to Natalie. Her mother's caustic comments about men who use and kill prostitutes. The woman in the grainy CCTV footage of the Southampton red light district, walking to her death in her fake fur jacket.

Natalie's legs tremble beneath her, threatening collapse, forcing her to crumple on her sofa. Prior to opening his letter, she's wondered what other shocks Mark might be keeping in store for her. He's certainly hit her with more information than she can handle right now. Thing is, he's also given her the assurance she'll be safe from her abuser forever. Along with reiterating his innocence where Abby Morgan's murder is concerned.

Natalie no longer doubts Mark Slater. His letter rings true. This man's no twisted child killer, no Adam Campbell clone. Instead, in her brain he's morphed, for the final time, into a decent guy who's had a shit life so far. Undeserving of the crap she's shovelled his way.

Oh, fuck. Shaun Morgan may be at Mark's place right now, beating him up, hurting him, and it's all her fault. Natalie grabs her mobile, stabbing at the screen, desperate to call off the hellhound of vengeance she's unleashed.

'Pick up, for fuck's sake,' she hisses into the phone, but Shaun Morgan doesn't respond. Straight to voicemail. She leaves a message, the words almost incomprehensible in her desperation to head off whatever retaliation he's planning. Natalie tries Mark's number next. One opportunity is all she needs to warn him, make sure he's safe. Something's wrong, though. For some reason, the call's not being connected. Mark's mobile seems as dead as she fears he may be, and it's all her fault. She should have trusted him; instead, she's been a total bitch. Sobs of self-recrimination choke her throat.

The tears stop abruptly as she pulls herself together. *Think, Natalie, think.* Shaun's phone being off doesn't necessarily mean anything. People don't always keep their mobiles on. Mark, though – he's a different animal, preferring to leave his switched on all the time. Part of his obsessive nature, she guesses. The fact her call can't even be connected concerns Natalie. If his mobile's not working, chances are it's been a casualty of Shaun beating the shit, or even the life, out of Mark.

Natalie briefly contemplates calling 999, or Tony Jackson – she has his number, after all – but rejects both ideas. What the hell can she say? That she deliberately leaked Mark's address to someone keen to wreak vigilante action on him? How she's sorry, concerned she can't reach him, but all she has to go on is the fact his mobile's not working?

Yep, that's guaranteed to end badly. And result in a possibly fatal delay for Mark.

Only one thing for it. Natalie grabs her jacket and keys. If she drives fast, if not much traffic's clogging the roads, she'll be at Mark's flat in ten, maybe fifteen minutes. Her hands fumble with everything she touches. Her handbag, her keys, the door latch. Then, once in her car, the ignition, the gearstick. She stalls as she attempts to pull away from the curb. Furious, cursing, she restarts the engine. The voice in her head berates her. *Drive, for God's sake. Get to him before Shaun Morgan does.*

The traffic-free roads she's praying for don't materialise. Twenty minutes of slow drivers, red lights and roadworks grind against her nerves before she pulls up outside Mark's building.

The light is on in his flat, thank God. Natalie runs from her car, not bothering to switch off the engine. She punches the entry code into the security console, yanking open the door into the communal hallway. Once inside, noises, loud but indefinable ones, reach her from Mark's flat. Sounds like those of furniture being overturned.

Oh, dear God. Please let him be all right.

For the third time in recent weeks, she takes his key from under the potted plant.

Then she hears another sound, an unmistakable one this time. A fist hitting into flesh, pulverising muscle and bone. Her fingers still shaking, she pounds her hand against Mark's door, shouting his name, as she pushes his key into the lock.

30

NO PROMISES

Brightness stabs Mark's eyes as he peels them open, causing the ache in his face to flare into life. He slams his eyelids shut. He becomes aware he's lying down, in bed, covered by a thin blanket. He prises his eyes open again, slowly this time.

Fluorescent lights overhead. White walls. Thick swing doors with glass panels. A plastic bag, half-full of a clear liquid, attached to a pole, draining into his arm. Noise, bustle, sounds. A cough to his left. Mark turns his head towards the cougher, wincing as he does so. Another drip bag, another pole. A bed, identical to the one Mark's in, its occupant an elderly man hacking into his hands.

Hospital. How he got here, though, he's unable to fathom. Memories of the attack float back to him, despite the fog in his head. Shaun's knuckles and boots, exacting revenge. Fists and feet on a mission to kill. Mark's not dead, though, although his nose feels fairly moribund. Nasal breathing is certainly difficult. He remembers the crunching sound as Shaun Morgan's fist shatters the bone. His last recollection is of knuckles and feet slamming into him, searching out his vulnerable points, reducing him to a grovelling mass of sheer agony. Unable to scream for help. He recalls Shaun's boot cracking down on his mobile. No chance of him phoning 999, injured jaw or not. So how the fuck did he get here?

Right now, he's incapable of caring. He appears safe from Shaun Morgan's fists and feet, and as comfortable as it's possible to be given the beating he's received. Moreover, he's getting pain relief via the tube in his arm. Enough reassurance for now. Mark drifts towards a light doze, allowing his battered body to rest. A short while later, something far more urgent than discovering how he got here slams into his brain, jolting him fully awake.

The murders of the two prostitutes. Shit. He needs to talk to Tony Jackson, and fast. Adam Campbell might be stalking his next prey whilst Mark lies in bed, useless, and his plan for the bastard doesn't allow for such eventualities. He opens his mouth to yell for someone's attention and manages about a centimetre's gap before the ache in his face flares into something much worse. Instead of a shout, what emerges is a strangled gasp of pain. Shit. He'd forgotten his injured jaw. He slumps back, defeated. It's a hospital, he tells himself. A nurse, a doctor, someone, anyone, will come through those swing doors and he'll get them to contact Tony Jackson on his behalf. Soon, please God. No time to waste where Adam Campbell's concerned.

Five minutes later, a doctor is standing next to Mark's bed.

'Mr Slater,' he says, before Mark clutches at his white coat, cutting off whatever the man is about to say. Carefully, slowly, he eases his mouth open.

'Police,' he manages, amazed he can speak at all. Perhaps his jaw isn't broken, then. Still one hell of an effort to talk, however.

'They'll be back later,' the doctor says. 'One of them came by earlier. Got an officer stationed outside the door, too. Totally unnecessary, in my view. You won't be going anywhere for a while, not the state you're in.'

None of this makes sense to Mark; he's unsure how the police have become involved, unless one of his neighbours heard something and alerted them. Right now, he doesn't care; he simply wants Adam Campbell arrested for murder. He opens his mouth again to impress on the doctor the importance of getting the officer on the door in here, right now, when the man silences him with a gesture of his hand.

'Best not to talk too much,' he says. 'You've suffered a dislocated jaw. It's been reset, but your mouth will be sore for a while yet. As to the rest of you...'

The doctor takes Mark's notes from the foot of the bed. A recital of his other injuries follows. Severe bruising over most of his body, a broken nose, along with six cracked ribs. One testicle ruptured, now surgically repaired. Hairline fracture of the skull, mild concussion. He'll be in the Bristol Royal Infirmary for a good while yet, but it's all fixable by rest and time, helped by generous quantities of painkillers.

'Police,' he tries again. 'Need to speak to...' The effort is exhausting. 'Tony Jackson. Number in my phone.' Then he remembers Shaun's boot cracking down on his mobile, and slumps into his pillows, defeated.

'That was the name of the guy who was here earlier,' the doctor says.

Thank God. If he has to deal with the police, at least let it be A.J. But how did Jackson...?

The doctor replaces Mark's notes at the end of the bed. 'Like I said, he'll be back later.'

Mark sleeps.

When he awakes, Tony Jackson is sitting by his bedside.

'You look like shit,' he says.

Mark doesn't reply. Too wary of his sore jaw, but also because he's confused. Jackson's tone is relaxed, despite his words. Not the voice of someone who's intending to arrest him for parole violation. He's reminded of Adam Campbell and the need to tell Tony Jackson where the police will find the evidence that'll jail the bastard for life.

'Didn't think our monthly meeting would take place in a hospital.' Jackson leans back in his chair, folding his arms behind his head. As usual, sweat patches soak the armpits of his shirt. Mark remembers. Their regular session, scheduled for today. The one in which he'd intended to admit breaking parole, as well as informing Jackson who killed the two prostitutes.

'Adam...' he manages, before he's cut off.

'Probably better if I do the talking, seeing as how your jaw must be pretty sore right now,' Jackson says.

Mark nods. Sore's an understatement, despite the pain relief he's getting.

'Not here in an official capacity. Just wanted to give you the heads-up about a few things first. Adam Campbell's in custody. Been arrested for the murder of two prostitutes. The ones killed in Southampton and Plymouth.'

Thank fuck for that is the overriding response in Mark's brain. But how...?

'You'll be wondering how we nailed the bastard, since Shaun Morgan prevented you from telling us,' Jackson continues. 'You wrote a letter to Natalie Richards. Your girlfriend, or rather your ex-girlfriend, although you managed to forget her existence each month when we had our meetings.' His tone hardens.

Mark shifts uneasily under Jackson's scrutiny, causing pain to prickle in his ribs.

Seems like the man's prepared to let the issue slide, though. For now.

'She gave us the letter. Told us about the audio recording. Your phone, the one you used to trap Adam Campbell, was smashed to bits, though. Then she admitted how she got Rachel Morgan's mobile number. Said the police should check your computer. So we did. And found the copy of the sound clip.'

'I always back up my phone.' If Mark speaks slowly and doesn't open his jaws too wide, talking is bearable.

Jackson grins. 'If only everyone were as conscientious.'

'What I had on it was doubly, triply important to keep safe.' Yup, he can speak well enough, it seems. 'Listen, A.J. Rachel's number. How exactly did Natalie...?'

'She's a woman, Mark. Likes to snoop.'

'Yeah.' His grandmother's letter edges into Mark's mind. 'You're not wrong there.'

'Seems she broke into your computer, found your contacts list. Called Rachel Morgan, told her brother where you live.'

His misaligned laptop. The biscuit crumb between his sofa cushions. Both make sense now.

'Then she received your letter. Seems what you said caused her to have a change of heart.'

Hope flickers in Mark, before he quashes it down. Too much water has flowed under Natalie's bridge – and his as well – for them to have any kind of a future.

'Seems she came over all remorseful about setting Shaun Morgan on you. Went over to your place, interrupted him beating the crap out of you. Called an ambulance. She's in custody now, along with the Morgan bloke.'

Mark's confused and disturbed by this. His brain still isn't working too well; why the hell has Natalie been arrested?

Tony Jackson clocks his puzzled expression. 'Don't forget she conspired with Shaun Morgan to commit grievous bodily harm towards you.'

'I pissed her off. Told her I'd had lunch with Rachel Morgan. Twice. She didn't take it too well.'

'Understandably.'

'You shouldn't blame her.'

'She broke the law, Mark. Almost got you killed. Vigilante action's precisely the reason you were given a new identity.'

She called an ambulance, though, Mark thinks. Once she read his letter. His pleading text obviously worked. Natalie now believes his innocence in the murder of Abby Morgan. Along with knowing her sexual abuser will spend the rest of his life in jail. Mark's no longer in any doubt as to that. Adam's been arrested. The police will find his little hoard of trophies. They'll match his presence in both Southampton and Plymouth to the times of the murders, uncover forensic proof, backed up by the evidence Mark's gathered. At least we don't have the 'fruit of the poisonous tree' rule here in the U.K., he thinks, recalling the crime dramas he watches. In the U.S., trapping Adam the way he's done might well bar the evidence from being taken into consideration. Whereas over here the recording from his mobile phone should be admissible in court, no matter how he obtained it.

'She'd like to visit you. Once she's released on bail. Doesn't think she'll be welcome, though.'

Mark turns Jackson's words over in his head, savouring the effect they have on him. 'She's wrong about that,' he says. 'Do me a favour, would you, A.J.?'

'What?'

'Pull some strings. Make sure charges aren't pressed against her.'

'Doesn't work that way, mate. Like I said, she committed a serious offence in instigating the attack against you. Christ, she almost cost you your life! Don't tell me Shaun Morgan didn't intend to kill you.'

'He didn't.'

'Yeah, right.'

'It's the truth.' Mark harbours no qualms about lying about this. He'll gain nothing by Shaun Morgan going down for attempted murder, and Rachel will lose heavily. No matter what Shaun said about her getting professional help, she'll be far better off with her brother around to shore her up emotionally. A lesser charge will mean a lighter sentence for him. 'He never mentioned wanting to kill me. Hurt me, yes. Rough me up, definitely. But murder? No way.'

Tony Jackson's sceptical expression tells Mark his bullshit radar's not fooled, but what the hell. 'If you say so. We'll let the courts decide. Natalie Richards will definitely be charged, though, Mark. Odds are, given it's her first offence, together with the particular circumstances, she won't be dealt with harshly.'

Mark's relieved, although not totally. The idea of Natalie going to court, being sentenced, doesn't sit well with him, but there's fuck all he can do about it. Seems he's fixed the main thing, which is getting a murdering bastard sent back to prison.

'Let's talk about Adam Campbell.' Jackson rests his elbows on the bed, leaning in towards Mark. 'We'll be able to match the voice on the audio recording to him. In it he says you weren't involved in Abby Morgan's murder.'

'I wasn't. I had no choice. He made me go along with it.' Even now, true as they are, the words sound childish, as though he's making excuses. Tony Jackson nods his understanding, though.

'Never could picture you as a child killer. Didn't fit somehow.' A question edges into Jackson's expression. 'Can I ask you something? Why confess to Abby Morgan's murder when you weren't guilty? OK, so I've read what you wrote in your letter to Natalie Richards. I'd prefer to hear it from you, though.'

'Two reasons.'

'Shoot.'

'First one. Scared stiff of the cops. I was eleven years old, remember.'

'The police shouldn't have been rough on you. I get what you're saying about how young you were, though.'

'They were sweetness and light in comparison with Adam Campbell. Second reason? He said he'd kill me if I ever blabbed. He'd already demonstrated he'd use his knife on me if I didn't do what he wanted. I assumed – wrongly – we'd end up being sentenced to the same detention unit. He scared the hell out of me. Still does.'

'Yeah. That bit in the recording when he threatens to stick a blade in between your ribs. He's one fucking violent bastard.'

'You're not wrong there. Anyway, I always mistrusted the police after I got put inside. Yeah, I know it's partly down to me being unable to stand up for myself as an eleven-year-old. When all this kicked off, though, I couldn't come clean to you, A.J. Didn't feel able to admit the parole violations and put the cops on to Adam Campbell for the murders of those two women.'

'Fair enough.'

'Had to do it myself.'

Jackson nods, 'More to it than that, though, wasn't there? You wanted to get the fucker to admit, whilst you were recording him, your innocence in Abby Morgan's murder.'

'Yeah.'

'How exactly did you trap the bastard?'

'With a bracelet,' Mark says.

'What the hell are you talking about?'

'He likes to take trophies from his victims. You'll find ones from those women he killed. He refers to them in the sound clip. A silver charm bracelet and a gold ankle chain. Anyway, remember the green stuffed hippo he took from Abby Morgan? Well, it's always pissed him off how he didn't get to keep it. So I pretended to be as sick as he is.'

Jackson nods again. 'I'm guessing you lied to him. Told him you took something of Abby's.'

'Yeah. Reeled him in like the proverbial fish. Bought a pink plastic child's bracelet from Tesco, dirtied it up a bit, handed it over to him. Gave me the perfect excuse to meet with him again.'

'Smart.'

'So I could get him to admit to the murders. And to confirm I played no part in Abby Morgan's. You'll find the receipt from Tesco for the bracelet in my flat. Proof it was never hers.'

'Won't find any of her DNA on it either. Skin cells, for example.'

'No.'

'Something I'm curious about, though.'

'What?'

'Given Adam Campbell's fully aware you had nothing to do with killing Abby Morgan, why did he believe you'd be sick enough to swipe her bracelet?'

'Again, I played him. Told him I couldn't kill anyone myself, but I'd come to realise I got off on seeing him hurt Abby Morgan. That I was the same as him, in wanting a trophy.' Shame forces his eyes away from Jackson's. 'He always loved having me as a sidekick, the lesser half of himself. Fancied us as some great partnership, mentioned murdering twosomes I'd never heard of. Sick bastard compared us to Brady and Hindley.'

'Fucking prick.'

'He had delusions of us killing more women together.'

'He reckoned you'd get off on watching him hurt other victims?'

Mark nods. 'Told him I was too chicken to murder anyone myself. Made out I admired him for having more guts than me. He fell for it.'

'People believe what they want to believe. Must have taken some balls on your part.'

'You've no idea. The adult version of Adam Campbell makes the eleven-year-old one seem like Peter Pan.'

'I'm guessing it's no coincidence none of what you've just told me is in the audio evidence?'

Mark shakes his head. 'Pressed stop as soon as I got what I needed. Not going to record myself agreeing to such twisted shit. What with the trophies and the audio, I'm hoping you'll have enough proof to nail the bastard. I'm betting once he's back inside, he won't be coming out again. Ever.'

'Amen to that.'

'What happens next? With me, I mean?'

'You'll be receiving a formal police visit, probably tomorrow, so you can make a statement. We'll need to interview you about the attack by Shaun Morgan, but also about your involvement with Adam Campbell. Not to mention contacting Rachel Morgan.' Tony Jackson shakes his head. 'You won't be getting a free and easy ride, Mark. No matter what that recording says.'

Mark nods. He didn't expect any of this to go smoothly; hell, his life's been a bed of thorns ever since he laid eyes on Adam Campbell, and believing it'll be silk and satin from now on would be naïve.

'I get that. Straight back to prison once I'm discharged from here.'

Jackson shakes his head. 'No.'

Mark's stunned. 'How come? I broke parole. Not once but several times.'

'Don't forget you also recorded Adam Campbell confirming you weren't involved in Abby Morgan's murder. Suggesting your original conviction was unsound.'

'Won't I go back inside in the short term, though? For the parole violations?'

Jackson shakes his head. 'Most likely scenario is you'll be released on bail pending the new evidence being lodged with the Court of Appeal. If you were wrongly convicted, the powers that be won't want to compound the problem with extra jail time.'

No prison, at least for now. Mark's chest starts to tighten, but for once, it's with relief.

'What about my sentence? For Abby Morgan's murder?'

Jackson draws in a deep breath before slowly exhaling. 'You'll be wanting to get it overturned.'

'I presume that's possible. From what you've just said.'

Tony Jackson's clearly considering his answer carefully. 'You can apply for it to be quashed. No guarantees, though. There has to be compelling new evidence.'

'The audio recording.'

'I'd say that probably qualifies.'

'Got to at least try.'

'If I were a betting man, I'd risk a quid on you getting it overturned. Eventually.'

'I'll take my chances.'

'You'll need another new identity, though.'

'Why?'

'Yours has been breached, and if you end up in court battling your original conviction, more people will get hold of the name of Mark Slater. Even if you win, I can guarantee some vigilante nutter somewhere will reckon there's no smoke without fire.'

'I guess.' Shit, another identity. Perhaps it's no bad thing. A new name for a fresh start. Might be a good thing to shed the skin of Mark Slater and move on.

'Like I said, none of this will be easy, Mark. But then you'll be aware of that.'

'Knew the risks involved.' Mark shrugs, wincing as one of his cracked ribs overrides the painkillers. 'Worth it to me. If it gets Adam Campbell back behind bars.'

'Can't disagree with that.' Jackson stands up. 'Listen, mate, I need to get going. You should rest. Like I said, no free and easy ride is heading your way.'

Something occurs to Mark. 'Hang on a minute.'

'What?'

'You.' Mark forces himself to meet Jackson's eyes. 'Will you get into trouble? Because I broke my parole on your watch?'

Jackson shrugs. 'Bound to be an enquiry.'

'They shouldn't blame you.'

'Someone will doubtless point the finger.'

'You can't be expected to track me twenty-four hours a day.'

'No. Thing is, people break parole all the time. You had a steady job, never gave any trouble. Nothing to indicate you screwing up in any way.'

'If I'm asked, I'll tell them you did everything by the book.'

'Which I did. Don't sweat this, Mark.' Tony Jackson grabs his jacket. 'Get some rest. Like I said, someone will be in to talk to you at some point.'

Alone again, Mark settles himself against his pillow. Shit. He's got one hell of a lot of stuff to process in his head.

He doesn't waste much time on Adam Campbell. The man's stolen enough of Mark's life already. He'll have to give evidence against him, of course, but he intends to detach himself emotionally from the bastard. Doesn't matter whether he's still scared of Adam – he is, and always will be – but fear won't dictate his actions any longer. He's bigger than Adam Campbell is mentally, and he'll remember that, however things pan out. What's certain is that Adam will go down for the rest of his life. Mark strikes him off his mental worry list.

Life doesn't present any guarantees, he decides. Perhaps his conviction will get overturned, perhaps it won't. If his sentence isn't quashed, he'll cope. If life provided certainties, people would never test themselves. Grow, adapt and change, and Mark has. He'll never again be the terrified eleven-year-old who allowed everyone to use him as a doormat. Nothing's definite in his future, but right now things are looking the best they've done for a long time.

Which brings him to Natalie. A saying comes back to him. *The heart wants what the heart wants.* Well, his wants Natalie. She's flawed, sure, as insecure and imperfect as all humans, but they're two of a kind when it comes to being damaged goods. What's more, she possesses a certain something that calls to him.

Don't go there, Mark warns himself. Hell, he has to let Natalie go. Until his conviction is quashed, by no means a certainty, he's still a convicted killer who's broken parole. Besides, getting his sentence overturned won't happen quickly. Once lawyers get involved and the appeal process is launched, Mark faces months of waiting, possibly longer.

Not to mention the fact that she herself faces jail time.

No, being with Natalie isn't an option.

Forget her, he tells himself.

Mark sleeps on and off for the rest of the day, his battered body grateful for the chance to recuperate. His jaw's a lot less painful the next day, thankfully. Still sore, but definitely improving. Eating isn't too much of a problem. Neither is talking. Mark flicks through the channels on the TV, listens to the radio, chats with the old man in the next bed. He doesn't take much notice of the time. Two o'clock comes, the start of visiting hours, and a stream of friends and relatives walk through the heavy double doors. Mark watches as they disperse between the beds in the ward, dragging chairs alongside them, delivering gifts, kissing whomever they've come to visit. His attention is drawn by a particular family down the far end of the ward, when a voice to his left causes it to jump back to his own bed.

The heart wants what the heart wants.

Mark turns his head as rapidly as he dares.

Natalie is standing beside him.

'Mark?' She chews her lower lip. 'Oh, my God. Your face.'

Mark remembers the splint on his broken nose. The smashed-up visage staring back at him from the hospital bathroom mirror this morning.

Tears are in Natalie's eyes as she inches closer to the bed. Her face is tired, pale, puffy, as though she's not slept. 'Mark...I'm so sorry...I never meant...' She swallows, takes a deep breath. 'You tried to tell me. I should have believed you.'

'Doesn't matter. No, really,' as Natalie shakes her head. 'None of that's important now. You got bail, obviously.'

She nods. Silence for a while, broken by Mark. 'Why are you here, Nat?'

She swallows again. Her eyes stray over the bed, the ward, anywhere but him. 'To tell you I'm sorry. About everything. Not trusting you. Getting Shaun Morgan to do -' Her hand waves towards Mark. 'This.'

'Grab a chair. Sit down.'

'You're sure?' Natalie doesn't wait for Mark's answer, but pulls one alongside the bed.

'Nat. It's OK, really it is.'

'I thought -' Natalie grabs a tissue from the box beside Mark's bed and blows her nose. 'Rachel Morgan. You and her.'

'Never was a me and her.'

'I got jealous. Didn't think straight.'

'You were angry. I understand.'

Natalie pulls her chair closer. 'I want to tell you something. Mum and I watched a documentary a while back. About murderers in jail.'

Mark's thrown by the sudden twist in the conversation.

'Not so much about them,' Natalie continues. 'More about women who write to them, visit them, form relationships with them.'

Mark's still unsure where she's going with this. 'What are you on about?'

'They all say the guys concerned aren't guilty,' Natalie says. 'At the time, Mum and I agreed they were all deluded, or worse. Most of them are, of course. Not all, though. I get it now. Sometimes people really are innocent. Even though everyone reckons they're not. Like you.'

Mark's silent, undecided how to respond.

'Here's the deal,' says Natalie. 'You didn't kill Abby Morgan. I know that now.' She glances away, resumes chewing on her lower lip. 'We can be together. If that's what you want. You said in your letter -'

Important not to give her any false hope. 'Natalie, everything's up in the air right now. I might end up back in prison.'

'But why? If you're innocent, and it gets proved, then -'

'Not guaranteed, Nat.'

'But you're going to appeal your conviction, aren't you?'

'Yes. In the meantime, though, I'm still a convicted murderer, and one who's broken parole. If my sentence doesn't get overturned, then I'll be back in jail. Long-term.'

Natalie chokes back a sob. 'Doesn't seem fair. Not when you got evidence about...' She breathes out heavily. 'About *him*.'

'He'll never hurt you again, Nat. Or anyone else.'

'You always knew it was Adam Campbell.'

'Yes. Your diary.'

'You came looking for me.'

'You became one of my obsessions. Probably the first one.'

'Can we...' She's clearly groping for words. He fathoms her meaning anyway.

'You and me. Can't happen.' Mark sighs. How to make her accept this? 'I've no idea what's heading my way or how long it'll take. Don't waste your life waiting for me. I'm not worth it.'

Natalie's mouth tightens. 'Listen up, Mark Slater. For years, I've been looking over my shoulder, afraid that bastard might find me again. He's the main reason my eating's so out of control. He's fucked me over in more ways than one. Then I got your letter. Thanks to you, he'll spend the rest of his life behind bars.' Her fingers jab angrily towards Mark. 'You're worth it all right.'

'Natalie -'

'Another thing. What I can and can't do. That's my decision. Not yours.'

'I don't want you to -'

'Like I say. Not your choice.'

'Why me?'

Natalie's mouth relaxes into a smile. 'Because when I'm in bed with you I'm not size eighteen and covered in stretch marks anymore.'

'*What?*'

'Straight answer? I've no idea. Who knows what draws one person to another? You said it in your letter. We clicked, that first time we met. You and me, we're alike in so many ways. Both of us damaged goods.'

Mark sighs. 'It's not just me who's facing jail time, remember.'

Her shoulders slump.

'Everything's too uncertain, Nat. For both of us.'

'Doesn't stop me wanting you.'

The flicker of hope he's tried to extinguish where Natalie's concerned ignites again. 'You're serious.'

'Get used to it.'

One last attempt to convince her. Mark pulls himself up in the bed, as much as his cracked ribs will allow. 'Nat, remember what I said. If I don't get my conviction overturned, then I'll be in jail for God knows how many years.'

'Mark, listen -'

'You might be in prison too. If that's the case, we can't be together. Simple as that.'

'If we both end up free, though? Would you -'

The heart wants what the heart wants. The flicker inside him inches higher. 'Yes.'

'Then surely - '

Mark shakes his head. 'Don't get your hopes up, Nat. If – and it's a big if – I get my sentence quashed, then maybe.'

'You mean it?'

'Yes. We'll also need to sort out whatever happens with you, too.'

'We. You said we.'

'In the meantime – no promises.'

'But -'

'That's the deal, Nat.'

Natalie smiles. She reaches over to grasp Mark's hand. 'OK.'

Nineteen, twenty, my plate's empty. Not anymore, he decides.

POSTSCRIPT

If you liked Guilty Innocence, I'd be very grateful if you would write a review on Amazon for me.

Why not check out some of my other novels? The first chapter of both His Kidnapper's Shoes and Sister, Psychopath have been included after this postscript for you. Both can be purchased in both Kindle and paperback formats from Amazon.

The official website for Maggie James is www.maggiejamesfiction.com, or you can connect with me on Facebook (Maggie James Fiction) or via Twitter (@mjamesfiction).

One, Two, Buckle My Shoe

One, two, buckle my shoe
Three, four, knock at the door
Five, six, pick up sticks
Seven, eight, lay them straight
Nine, ten, a big, fat hen
Eleven, twelve, dig and delve
Thirteen, fourteen, maids a'courting
Fifteen, sixteen, maids in the kitchen
Seventeen, eighteen, maids a'waiting
Nineteen, twenty, my plate's empty.

'One, Two, Buckle My Shoe' is a popular English language nursery rhyme, used to help children

with counting. While there is no accurate historical evidence for when it originated, it is generally thought to be about lace making and other working class roles in the 16th, 17th or 18th centuries.

One, two, buckle my shoe refers to the lace maker getting ready in the morning for work.

Three, four, knock at the door: the lace maker receives a customer.

Five, six, pick up sticks: the sticks are wooden pins used on a lace making machine.

Seven, eight, lay them straight: the pins are placed on the machine to go straight across the fabric from side to side.

Nine, ten, a big fat hen: a type of pillow that supports and holds the lacework.

Eleven, twelve, dig and delve refers to the gardeners employed at a large house or estate.

Thirteen, fourteen, maids a'courting refers to the maids at the house, probably in connection with the gardeners.

Fifteen, sixteen, maids in the kitchen: a meal is being prepared for the gentry of the house.

Seventeen, eighteen, maids a'waiting: dinner is served with the maids in attendance.

Nineteen, twenty, my plate's empty: the meal is over.

His Kidnapper's Shoes

Sample chapter

Maggie James

1

JUDGEMENT DAY

My body aches. The wall against my back grinds into my bones, as does the bench under my bottom; however much I fidget, I can't get comfortable. I guess they don't build police cells with such considerations in mind. There's no clock and I've lost track of how much time I've spent in this place. Two, maybe three hours? I wonder - why, I don't know - how much longer they'll keep me here. I remind myself it doesn't matter. I feel strangely disconnected from such things. All I can think about is my son.

The door swings open. I don't bother to look up, not at first. A pair of black shoes steps in front of me; slim legs encased in pale tights lead up from them. The police officer who arrested me. I register her voice telling me to stand. I glance up, observing the harsh judgement staring back from her eyes. She's young, probably mid-twenties. No ring on her left hand and I'd bet she doesn't have children. Her body doesn't look like it's ever split itself open forcing out a child. This isn't a woman who spends her nights attempting to soothe a bawling copy of herself to sleep, whilst trying not to scream with frustration and sheer bloody exhaustion. She's not a mother. Had she found herself in my place, would she have done what I did? Perhaps not. However, she's not yet walked a mile in my shoes; if she's lucky she never will, so what gives her the right to judge me?

It seems she's taking me somewhere. They must be going to question me. Looks as if the doctor who examined me has decided I'm fit to be interviewed.

It's not going to do them any good. I won't be giving out any answers. Even if I talked for a week, a year, forever, I'd never make them understand. They're police officers; rules and their enforcement are everything to them, all black and white and rigid. According to them, I've committed a crime. I believe what I did was right and the only thing possible in the circumstances.

What's that saying, about the law being an ass? I reckon it's true. On the one hand, it states we're supposed to protect children from danger. Love them. Keep them safe. Punish those who hurt them. Yet I'm the one they'll put on trial. Even though I protected my son, took him away from harm. To my mind, it makes no sense for them to judge me with contempt in their eyes. They're firing accusations at me that would only apply to somebody who doesn't love her son in the way I love Daniel. It's a crazy world we live in.

I hear your voice in my head, Gran, reassuring me, telling me not to worry.

The police officer orders me again to stand up. This time her tone is sharper, and I get to my feet, thankful not to be sitting any longer on that unforgiving bench. It makes no difference where they take me anyway. Here or in a police interview room, I'll still need strong tea and time alone with my son. Doesn't seem like I'll be getting either one anytime soon.

I follow the police officer along the passageway to another room. I take in my surroundings. This room's not built for comfort either. Magnolia walls, beige carpet. A table and chairs and some sort of recording device. Nothing else.

The police officer yanks out a chair and orders me to sit down. She thrusts a paper cup of water in front of me and I gulp it down in one go. My eyes focus on a chip in the wall. I let them wander over the blemish and idly wonder whether, if I stare at the mark long enough, it counts as meditation. Another part of my brain registers somebody pulling out the chair next to me and sitting down. From my peripheral vision, I see it's a man, suited in dark grey; I guess this must be some sort of legal representation provided for me. Somebody else is in the room too, a mental health social worker, from the words filtering into my brain, although I'm not paying much attention to what's being said. Two police officers pull out the chairs opposite me and sit down. One is the young woman. The other is male, considerably older. I continue to stare at the wall. I won't say anything. They can't make me.

My thoughts drift away. Your voice, gentle and soothing, is in my head again, Gran, telling me Daniel didn't mean to be so cruel towards me. I draw comfort from your words. I was always able to talk to you, something that was never possible with Mum, not with her being the way she was. You have to reassure me that everything will be all right with Daniel, Gran. He's the only one whose opinion I care about; I don't give a toss what any of the others think.

Ian is included in my indifference. My husband has never truly mattered to me. It sounds cruel to admit it, Gran, but I only married Ian for what he could do for Daniel. To provide my boy with the father figure he desperately needed. I wasn't interested in myself; finding a man to love was never on the agenda. I had my son for that, and he was all I had ever wanted or needed. Ian – I've grown fond of him, even if I can't love him, but it's always seemed to be enough. For me, anyway.

I think it's worked out well, despite my lack of feelings. Who says marriage has to be about love and living happily ever after? I've done my best to give Ian what he needs, even if I've always been out of reach for him emotionally. He's never been able to touch the true Laura, the essence within; I suspect it's been a disappointment to him. You see, Ian really does love me, and there's no denying he's been a good husband. He's given my son and me a home and security, as well as his name. He's provided me with the family life I craved, even though I never considered having a child with him. I'm not prepared to walk down that road again.

You and Ian would have hated each other if the two of you had ever met, Gran; chalk and cheese doesn't come close to describing it. He's Mr Conventional, with the career in financial planning and the golf club membership. The man who can't see any other way through life except doing what people expect of him. You know, Rotary Club dinners, drinks with business associates, that sort of stuff. All the things you, with your batik skirts from Bali and your silver earrings from India, would have scrambled to get away from as fast as possible.

Anyway, I know you understand. You always did. I'm certain you don't condemn me, not like the police officer who brought me here.

Not like Daniel, either. Right now, he's judging me. I'll change that, though. I have to.

To lose my son for a second time would be unbearable. I won't lose him. I can't. I yearn to make things right between us. Since the day – when was it? Probably a few days ago, perhaps as long as a week, I'm not sure. The day when Daniel burst through the door, shouting, thrusting those papers in my face, the ones saying ugly things, making him turn against me. Ever since then, I've felt as if a fog has invaded my brain. I can't think straight and all I want is for Daniel to tell me it's all right. That he didn't mean those awful things he screamed at me.

It doesn't matter if they lock me away, if only Daniel will look at me and tell me he understands. Until he comes to me and tells me the words I crave to hear, I won't speak. I can't talk to him when he has such fury towards me in his eyes; his forgiveness will be the trigger that releases my frozen tongue. Given the chance to be with him, instead of this place, I'd find the words to explain and everything will be all right. He won't stare at me as if I'm something vile found stuck to the sole of his shoe. There'll be no more yelling or accusations; he won't tear me apart with words loaded with blame and anger. He'll be my son again, my beautiful Daniel, and the world will be as it should be once more. I don't care if they lock me up in jail. That won't matter at all, so long as he doesn't hate me.

He's angry with me now, but I'll change that. He'll remember how I always loved him, even though, as a young child, he'd push me away when I tried to cuddle him. His rejections always pierced me deep inside, every time. I'd remind myself that being a mother is more than hugging your child. It's being there for them in the night when they wake shouting and desperate from some dreamtime terror. It's nursing them when they're feverish and sponging them down when they're soaking the sheets with sweat. It's listening to stories of their day at school, plastering skinned knees, pinning their paintings of wobbly houses on the fridge door. I did all those things. I was always a mother to Daniel where it really counted. He'll realise that eventually.

He'll tell me he understands. Then everything in my world will be all right again.

I vaguely register words coming at me.

'…Laura Bateman, you knowingly and wilfully broke into the Cordwells' flat…'

'…quite deliberately… without thought for the distress and hurt you would cause…'

'…for reasons unknown at this stage …'

I don't deny the breaking and entering part. In that respect, I admit I'm guilty. My mind spins back through the years and I remember my fear as I stood outside that flat, summoning up the courage to carry out what I'd decided to do.

I planned it very carefully. I thought of nothing else since I found they were going to take Daniel away from me. The only question was when to act, and sooner was better than later. My son's wellbeing was at stake.

More words filter through the fog in my brain.

'…psychiatric evaluation…'

'…best in his field…find out why she did it…'

They're so stupid. I did it to get my son back. What other reason could there be?

Except they say Daniel's not my son.

They say he has another mother.

There's that ugly word they keep throwing at me.

Kidnap.

They say I kidnapped Daniel.

Sister, Psychopath

Sample chapter

Maggie James

1

VENUS FLYTRAP (MEGAN)

My sister Chloe. Half-sister, I should say, to be accurate. A cold twisted bitch, in my opinion. Possibly worse. How did one define a psychopath? Would it be too harsh of me to slap such a label on her?

Unable to help myself speculating, I gazed at her bored, petulant expression as she sat opposite my mother. Few people would ever call my sister a nice person, although the men she suckered would probably declare her a sex-soaked gift from heaven. Initially, anyway. As for Mum, she'd blinded herself over the years to her younger daughter's less desirable traits. Chloe certainly exhibited all the cunning manipulative skills associated with psychopaths. Used them to their full extent, too, to get whatever - or whoever- she'd set her mind on.

My half-sister. My opposite in so many ways. The way we looked, for example. Over the years, I'd grown accustomed to fading into the background once people spotted Chloe. Something about her hooked people's attention, hoodwinking them into seeing her as an exotic orchid rather than the Venus flytrap she really was. Beside her, I rated as a daisy at best.

Because Chloe was a looker. Petite, a mere five foot two, curved like an archer's bow. She came across as all soft chocolaty-brown, what with her long dark hair and cocoa-rich eyes shooting out I'm-so-vulnerable

i

vibes. Not to mention the pale cappuccino hue of her skin, handed to her by her Spanish father. We were half-sisters only; same mother, different fathers.

Ah, yes. My father. I had no idea who had given me my height, all five feet ten of it, along with my pale skin, blue eyes and brown hair, such a contrast to Chloe. Father unknown, my birth certificate said. Our mother had never enlightened me about him. One thing was for sure; Mum hadn't given me the tall gene. Her height was somewhere in between Chloe's and mine. Same thing with her skin tone. As for her hair, she'd been a dark blonde before it had faded to grey.

Father unknown. It hurt. Rankled, even.

I forced my thoughts away from the ancient thorn of my parentage to glance around. Toby was late, as usual. Places like Grapes wine bar made me uncomfortable right to the tips of my toes. Such a wannabe trendy place, set on Bristol's Harbourside, full of business types, suited and booted and gabbling management-speak into their iPhones. I returned my gaze to Mum and my sister, neither of whom took any notice of me, although they'd seen me arrive. Chloe never paid me much attention anyway, unless to goad me. My mother's gaze was fixed on the tall man at the bar getting her drink. Eight ten, said my watch, although I'd arranged to meet Toby at eight. Not late at all by his standards.

A voice sounded behind me. 'Megan! How long has it been?'

Toby Turner grinned at me as I spun around, and damn me if he wasn't the same six feet two of sex appeal he'd always been. I melted into his trademark rib-cracking hug, savouring the essence of the man. He smelt of Hugo Boss aftershave and I inhaled his scent deeply, returning his hug before pulling away to poke him in the stomach.

'Too long, that's for sure. You going to enlighten me about this?' I swept my arm in the direction of Chloe and my mother. 'How come I seem to have gate-crashed an evening out for my mother's workplace -' My swinging arm encompassed the tall man from the bar heading towards her table. 'When you said on the phone your new love interest would be here tonight?'

'The two events aren't mutually exclusive, Megan.'

I stiffened. Chloe was my first thought, even though she didn't work at Mum's firm. Jeez. Hadn't Toby been burned enough the last time they got it on together? My sister had the ability to reel men in like a lizard catching flies on its tongue. A few years back Toby Turner had been no exception.

'Don't look so sour, Megan. I'm not planning a walk down Memory Lane with Chloe. Been there, done that. No repeat performance planned.'

I didn't share the same conviction. Despite my sister tossing him aside like a soiled nappy once she'd finished with him, I'd never heard Toby say a bad word about her. The excuses got trotted out when her name was mentioned: she'd been too young, he'd rushed her, she hadn't meant to be cruel.

'So what the hell are you doing here? How do you know the people at Mum's office?'

'James invited me.'

'James Matthews? Her boss?' I glanced over towards the tall man from the bar placing a lemonade and lime before my mother. A man with whom I was already familiar, although not overly so. I noticed how both Mum and my sister fixated their gazes on him. Not surprising. Not my type, but definitely attractive, well preserved for a man who'd recently come smack up against the Big Five-0. A gym body, hard and muscular, demonstrated by his tight polo shirt and well-fitting jeans. The glow from the candles on the tables highlighted the grey creeping into his brown hair. His grin was as lopsided as Toby's, but on the opposite side. His eyes struck me every time I met him. Pale blue, they made an unusual combination with his dark hair. A looker all right.

'So which one of them do you reckon is my new love interest?'

I looked around at the women from James's firm. A couple of twenty-somethings, all spiky heels and fishnet stockings, talking too loudly in an effort to impress. Two older women, clearly ill at ease, staring into their wine glasses. My mother and my sister, the latter with her hand on James Matthews's arm, smiling, aiming her honeyed darts at him.

'Hell, Tobes, I've no idea. You say it's not Chloe - thank God - and my mother's obviously off limits. One of them, I suppose.' My hand waved in the direction of the giggling fish-netted pair. Toby laughed.

'Give me a break, Megan. As if.'

'You've changed. Thought you'd shag anything female and breathing.' Including me. Once. Such a long time ago.

'Yep. OK, so my new love interest isn't my usual type, but my tastes have altered since we last ran into each other.' He winked at me.

'You going for tall, dark and intellectual these days?' The words, 'so do I stand a chance with you after all?' never made it out of my mouth. I'd fancied Toby like crazy at school, for one mad summer, knowing I was way out of his league. All the girls were wild about him. He could take his pick, and he did. One night, during the final week of school, he chose me. Why, I was never sure. On my down days, I told myself he'd been working his way through the girls in our year and me naked in the back of his car, jubilant at losing my virginity at last, was necessary to complete the set. We never spoke of it. To my surprise, he remembered me when we bumped into each other five years later.

'I've left London. Back in Bristol now,' he'd said. 'Working here.'

We went for a drink that night to catch up and had stayed friends ever since, sharing a curry or a bottle of wine on a regular basis. Before tonight, though, we'd not run into each other for a good six months or so.

He laughed. 'Yeah, I suppose. Definitely tall and intellectual. As for the dark – mostly, but there's a bit of grey creeping in.' What the hell was he talking about? Toby had never gone for cougars, preferring to be the predator, not the prey. I looked back at the two older women on the table beside Mum. Both of them had pewter-toned hair sculpted into middle-aged waves. I didn't attempt to picture Toby getting down and dirty with either of them; the idea was absurd.

He saw my puzzled look and laughed again. 'You haven't a clue what I'm talking about, have you?'

'No. Enlighten me. You found yourself a sugar mummy? Am I treading on your toes by being here? If so, why ask me along tonight?'

'Two reasons. Not seen you for ages; I reckoned we should catch up. As well as having someone to talk to, if things get a bit weird here. It's all been flirting and innuendo so far. Nothing's happened with -' He shrugged. 'Not even got to first base yet.'

'Not like you to be slow off the mark. Is she married, Toby?'

'Yep.'

Surprise hit me. Toby had never gone for married women before. Too many complications, he'd always said. As well as all the single females needing his attention.

Messy, I thought.

Toby wasn't looking at me anymore. His gaze rested over my shoulder. I turned and saw James Matthews making conversation with Chloe. I glanced back at Toby, confused.

Then I twigged.

It seemed Toby's tastes were rather broader than he'd been letting on.

I decided to play it cool. Despite the fact that what I'd discovered bothered me. Badly.

'Get you, Toby Turner! Never would have pegged you as swinging both ways.' He laughed.

'It's an age thing,' he said. 'Quite common, apparently, for people to believe they're straighter than the proverbial arrow, then in their late twenties they start fancying a walk on the wild side. Been strolling that way for a while now, testing the waters. The odd man here and there. Let's say my arrow isn't as straight as it used to be.'

'The fact he's married doesn't bother you?'

He shrugged.

'It gets worse, Toby. His wife's a friend of mine.'

'Seriously?'

'Yeah, although I've not seen Charlotte for ages. We did art classes together. Right up until the time when she lost the use of her legs.'

Toby drew in a breath. 'She's crippled? I didn't realise.'

'Been in a wheelchair for the last five years. Car accident.'

Silence from Toby. I decided to steer the conversation away from Charlotte Matthews. 'How did you meet James, anyway?'

'Through work. He owns his own financial consultancy - well, you'd know that anyway, what with your mother working for him. My firm booked James to give us sales guys a presentation on pensions.'

'What did your boss have to do? Threaten to make pretzels out of the testicles of anyone who didn't show up?'

'More or less. Anyway, there I was, prepared to be bored witless and then James walked in. He had something about him, Megan.'

'Yeah, he's easy on the eye, all right. Not my type, before you go all jealous on me. Never gone for older men. Since when have you targeted mature and sophisticated, though? Whether it's male or female.'

Toby grinned. 'Maybe the rules change when you switch teams. The other men have been older too. Yeah, go on. Tell me I've got a father fixation.'

'Armchair psychology's not my style, Tobes.' Ironic, considering my earlier musings about Chloe.

He shook his head. 'Who gives a fuck, anyway? Does anyone know what attracts one person to another? I'm telling you, Megan, he got to me, right from the start. I've seen him a few times since, always for professional reasons. That is, until now. He invited me, out of the blue, to come along tonight. Some leaving do for one of the secretaries, he said. Probably the one over there in the skirt doubling as a belt.' He grinned again. 'I've flirted with him. Subtly, of course.'

I laughed; subtlety had never figured large in Toby's game plans for getting laid.

'Although I'm not sure whether I'm getting anywhere. He has all the hallmarks of being ramrod straight: wedding ring on the finger, mentions of his wife. Despite all the warning signs, though, I reckon he's interested. Call it a gut feeling. And then he asked me here tonight.'

'Doesn't have to mean he's set his sights on you. Perhaps he's being friendly, nothing more.' I hoped so, for Charlotte's sake.

Mine, too.

I squashed that particular thought.

'He's interested all right. No idea what the set-up is, what with him being married, but it sure as hell isn't a one-sided thing.'

'So let's say you've caught his eye. Doesn't mean he'll want to take it further.'

Toby shrugged. 'You might be right. Time will tell. Let's go join them.'

Shit. That meant risking Chloe's sour tongue. My mother - well, I'd long ago resigned myself to her lack of interest in me. Acceptance of Chloe and her barbed comments didn't come so easily.

Her eyes scratched over me as we approached, her hand dropping from James Matthews's arm. I braced myself. Whatever she said, it wouldn't be pretty.

My mother spoke first, though. 'Didn't expect you to be here tonight, Megan. Oh, I get it; you're with Toby. Nice to see you again, young man.'

'You too.' Toby returned Mum's smile, but his gaze stayed fixed on her boss.

James smiled briefly at me, but it didn't reach his eyes.

'It's good to see you again, Megan.' His tone was polite, but his expression seemed wary. My trusty intuition waved a white flag at me; although I wasn't in any sense competition, this man viewed me as such. Definitely not as straight as he made out, then.

'You're one of Toby's friends?'

'We were at school together,' I said, unsure what else to say. Fortunately, Toby did, obviously keen to dispel any suggestion I might be his girlfriend. I should be so lucky, I thought.

'Megan and I go way back. She's a good mate.' The emphasis increased ever so slightly on the word mate. The smile I got from James then seemed more genuine.

'Thought I'd ask her along as I don't know anyone else here,' Toby said. 'Call her backup. Or my wingman.'

'Always thought you'd make a good man, Megan.' Chloe's voice, laced with equal amounts of cruelty and amusement, warned me what was coming. 'That flat chest of yours could double as an ironing board.'

I'd heard that particular jibe from my half-sister so often it barely registered. Toby laughed; the word 'traitor' danced through my brain, my feelings wounded by his careless endorsement of her cruelty.

Apparently, I wasn't worth any more of Chloe's attention. My sister turned her gaze to James, replacing her hand on his arm, her smile all sweetness and sugar. 'So James, tell me more about your dog. What did you say his name was - Sienna?' The smile grew wider, the interest more faked and pronounced. 'I've always adored dogs. Especially German Shepherds.'

Liar, I thought. You wouldn't know a German Shepherd from a Chihuahua and if you've ever mentioned dogs, it's to comment on how disgusting and smelly they are. Chloe clearly wanted to impress James Matthews, not that he appeared game for her machinations.

Amusement stirred in me. Score a first for him, I thought; at last, a man who was unimpressed by Chloe's charms. James Matthews was probably too old to fall for her crap. Turning fifty might well render him immune to a woman half his age coming on to him.

'Senna, not Sienna. Famous racing driver.' Irritation laced its way through James's tone. His eyes had already slithered away from Chloe back onto Toby. Chloe's hand fell off his arm as James turned towards him. 'Glad you made it, Toby. Can I get you a drink?'

'Pint of Doom Bar'll do me. I'll come with you.'

I followed my mother's gaze as James headed for the bar. She has a thing for him, I thought. Such a clichéd situation, fancying her boss, although she didn't stand a chance. Too old, too grey in both hair and character, beaten down by years of pills and psychiatric wards. As for him, he was too married, too out of her league, to notice her as anything other than an employee, if he noticed her at all.

Too bisexual as well, it now seemed.

Shit. What a frigging mess.

And Chloe also wanted to sink her carefully manicured nails into Mum's boss. Not hard to guess the reason, not with my half-sister. She'd know about his financial consultancy business from my mother, as well as the BMW Z4 he drove, a car over which I'd often drooled.

No doubt she also knew he had a wife who'd never walk again.

Not that Chloe would care about Charlotte Matthews. My half-sister was targeting James Matthews's money, figuring she'd bat her eyelashes and jiggle her tits into getting her hands on it. His marriage wouldn't mean anything to her. Neither would our mother's feelings for him. Odds were Chloe had clocked my mother having a middle-aged crush on her boss and she didn't give a damn. Knowing my sister, it would make landing James Matthews and his wealth even sweeter.

Money. Chloe's driving force. She'd never been worried about working for it either. Why should she, when she lived with our mother, always the willing cash cow?

The only thing she'd like better, I thought, would be if I fancied him too. Yeah. She'd love it if she could shaft me as well.

I shrugged. Toby seemed to stand more chance with James Matthews than Chloe or Mum did.

The rest of the evening passed quickly. Toby, as always, proved good company, and I was curious about this new thing he had about men. I kept tabs on him and James, noticing the way he frequently touched the other man's arm, making it seem oh so casual. Along with the fact that James didn't pull away.

I wondered how things would pan out. Mum's boss was hotter than a backyard barbecue, but married. Although with many men having a wife didn't make much difference. He probably wanted a little casual fun, and with Toby's reputation as a player, I couldn't see that being a problem. They'd have a brief fling and then go their separate ways. None of my business. Apart from Charlotte getting hurt, but she'd almost certainly never find out anyway.

'Definitely got the vibe from him tonight.'

Toby's voice cut across my thoughts towards the end of the evening. James had just left, brushing Chloe aside as she tried to engage him in conversation, my mother's eyes stapled to his back as he moved through the bar.

'Just a vibe? Nothing more concrete?'

'Not sure what his game is, to be honest, Megan. You might be right. Perhaps he doesn't want to take things further.'

Chloe's voice sounded behind me. With James gone, Grapes held nothing of interest for her. 'Let's go, for God's sake, Mum. Isn't it bad enough you dragged me here in the first place? If you drove like every other normal person does, I wouldn't need to chauffeur you everywhere.'

About all you do to earn the money she slips your way, I thought. My sister seemed incapable of holding down a job for more than a couple of months. Either she ended up sacked or else she walked out, claiming she deserved something more suited to her talents. Prostitution came to mind whenever I heard her trot out that line.

I was glad to leave. Much as I'd loved catching up with Toby, I needed space to sort out my head. The man I'd always had a thing for wanted to get it on with my mother's boss, who also had my mother and half-sister competing for him.

Nobody, to my knowledge, had ever competed for me.

ABOUT THE AUTHOR

Maggie James is a British author who lives in Bristol. She writes psychological suspense novels.

Before turning her hand to writing, Maggie worked mainly as an accountant, with a diversion into practising as a nutritional therapist. Diet and health remain high on her list of interests, along with travel. Accountancy does not, but then it never did. The urge to pack a bag and go off travelling is always lurking in the background! When not writing, going to the gym, practising yoga or travelling, Maggie can be found seeking new four-legged friends to pet; animals are a lifelong love!

Join Maggie's mailing list and receive a free copy of The Second Captive, along with freebies from other authors and the latest news and discounts. Find out how to get your copy of The Second Captive as well as her free novella Blackwater Lake, at www.maggiejamesfiction.com.

Facebook: Maggie James Fiction
Twitter: @mjamesfiction

39870403R00222

Made in the USA
San Bernardino, CA
05 October 2016